"Lady Genevieve." Lord Prydeen greeted her, coldly, but not correctly.

"The proper title is 'Your Grace', messir."

And if she told herself that a few more times, perhaps she could dare to face him.

A wintry smile passed over the sorcerer's lips – gone as quickly as snow in the Summer. "No longer, I fear. My former master stripped you of your titles for your treasonous activities."

"My Lord Prydeen! What passes here?" The mild voice interrupted from the direction of the stairs, but was no one Genevieve recognized.

Lord Prydeen's voice was a curious mix of ingratiating and dismissive. "Nothing you need trouble yourself over, Your Majesty. Some rabble found her way up here, clearly to cause some trouble to you. It is my task and my privilege to safeguard Your Highness. We'll be away momentarily."

Gentle hands cleared away the thongs that had begun to lash her wrists. "Surely you are mistaken, my Lord Prydeen. This is no rabble, but Her Grace, the Duchess Genevieve Stellarine of Elaarwen."

"Yes, my Lord, the so-called 'Rebel Duchess'," Lord Prydeen's voice was growing impatient. "I am taking her to the castle dungeons to have out of her what she knows."

The Rebel Duchess

Book One of the Chronicles of Ilseador

Kerridwen Mangala McNamara

Also available in eBook and hardcover editions.
McNamara, Kerridwen Mangala
The Rebel Duchess / by Kerridwen Mangala McNamara Indiana:
Rising Dragon Books, 2023
316 p.; 2 maps
(McNamara, Kerridwen Mangala. Chronicles of Ilseador; bk. 1)
Summary: Duchess Genevieve has been leading a rebellion against the evil sorcerer king but now needs to make peace with his successor, help him fight off an attempted coup, and - just possibly - fall in love with him.
ISBN 978-1-960160-05-8 (pbk)
1. Kings and rulers - Fiction. 2. Rebels and Romance - Fiction
ISBN 978-1-960160-06-5 (hc); ISBN 978-1-960160-04-1 (eBook)

For further information, email RisingDragonBooks@gmail.com

ISBN: 978-1-960160-05-8
First Print Edition: February 2023
10 9 8 7 6 5 4 3 2 1

A note to sensitive souls:
Ilseador is a land that has been misruled for eighty-three years by a tyrant who was also an evil sorcerer in every sense of the word. Up to four generations cannot remember a time before the old king assumed the throne... and the morals (or lack thereof) of a country often develop - intentionally or not - from the example at the top. This is particualrly true of the upper echelons of society, which this story focuses on. The result is that it's basically an entire nation of traumatized people who have seen that greed and cruelty and o'erweening ambition are rewarded. The old king's Apprentice is still around to cause trouble as well...

Proceed with caution...

For my husband... we may not be “soul-bonded”, but he's always willing to support me in whatever insanity I come up with. (Even discussing becoming a vigilante “Robin Hood” type superhero like Erawan the Kind Robber... though I'm not sure either of us really want to test that one out in real life.)

CONTENTS

Chapter ONE

Caught!

GENEVIEVE HAD NOT FORGOTTEN THE old king's pet sorcerer. She *had*, however, assumed he would not be a problem. This was clearly not the case.

She ducked into a rubbish-strewn alley and prayed that one of the doors leading off of it would open to somewhere that was not a dead-end. Unlike the alleyway itself. Genevieve really wasn't familiar enough with the layout of the capitol to be doing this sort of thing. As her advisors had repeatedly told her. Her chagrined memory replayed the scene of her tossing her head as she assured them that "the Rebel Duchess" could handle anything.

Not that she had *planned* to have to handle anything at all. She was just going to come in as part of the crowds hoping to get a glimpse of the new young king, on this last day of the coronation festivities. Just another gawker from the countryside. She still had no idea how Lord Prydeen had identified her.

The second door on the right opened at her frantic tug, and Genevieve hurried into darkness, pulling the door tightly shut behind her. She could hear people talking somewhere off to her right and the darkness seemed a little less dark in that direction. Perhaps there was a way through the building and back to the main street she had veered off of so abruptly. She needed to get back to the streets to complete her mission. The inhabitants of the room ahead would be startled, but if she could get past them quickly – before they decided to hold her for a thief – she might make it.

Just as the young woman started towards the sounds, the door behind her crashed open and the sorcerer stepped through.

Lord Prydeen was a master of dramatic effect, some odd corner of her mind noted absently. He stood framed in the doorway, too deeply cowled to see his face, his ankle-length black cloak flapping and curling about him in the sudden cross-currents of air between building and outside. The alley was brighter than the room – so perhaps he merely paused to let his eyes adjust – but in that moment he was more silhouette than shape, more demon than man.

Genevieve could not – *could not* – lead him towards those unsuspecting innocents in the room beyond. Perhaps the completely unexpected would gain her – well, *some*thing.

She took a deep breath, but carefully did not think too hard about what she was doing – though whether it was because Lord Prydeen was rumored to be able to pull one's thoughts from the air itself or because she wouldn't have the nerve if she did–

She spun on her heel and charged directly at the sorcerer, startling him sufficiently that she shoved past him and back out into the dead-end alley. Then to her left and back out to the main street – perhaps she could lose him in the crowd. She had to try.

In her haste, however, Genevieve's own hood was pushed back, exposing her signature red-gold hair – and confirming what had surely only been Lord Prydeen's guess about the identity of his quarry.

Fool that she was for not having dyed it.

Thrice a fool for deciding to skulk about the coronation festivities – like any small child playing "Erawan the Kind Robber" – instead of listening to the reports of her spies as the mature, careful, strategic leader of the rebellion should do. That stupid, romantic title – "Rebel Duchess" – really *had* gone to her head, as Rosa had accused her. She would do the Cause no good by being taken by the king's sorcerer. Even if the new young King Damien lived up to his month-old reputation for fairness, Lord Prydeen would never give her a chance to find out.

No time for this.

Genevieve jerked her hood back up and tried to blend into the crowded market square, trying to outguess Lord Prydeen. Which direction would the sorcerer be unlikely to go? – or which way would he be unlikely to follow? Surely the feared and hated Royal Sorcerer could not make his way through the crowd without causing an uproar that would let her dodge away... though he had before, when she first caught him following her. Could there be *any* safety for her here in the capitol, just six days after Damien's crowning? Surely the old guard was still in place and *no one* (not even the young king?) would dare to gainsay Lord Prydeen.

Abruptly, and entirely on instinct, not daring to look back to measure her pursuit, Genevieve swerved and tore for the royal viewing stand. Damien, if the stories were right – the stories that she had not believed and had come in person to verify – would merely have her executed for a traitor. Lord Prydeen – as she had reason to know – would sell her soul to demons and wring every last memory and secret from her shrieking heart.

The fine bright day taunted her travails, small poofy clouds ambling across a sky as blue as her own eyes. The market square – packed with a crowd of pleasantly frolicking merchants and peasants – impeded her swift progress. The swarms of children playing games of tag nearly tripped her up. The very *joy* of it all nearly derailed her thoughts, for such gaiety could never have been shown in the old king's rule, and part of her could not leave off trying to determine if there was still the undercurrent of desperation that she expected from her previous, and more successfully clandestine, visits to the capitol city.

But the Rebel Duchess knew exactly where the royal platform stood, both due to having marked it well when first she arrived and for the fact that it stood as tall any of the half-timbered two-story buildings surrounding the square. She had hoped to catch a glimpse of the young king from afar when first she arrived, and the royal platform had seemed like the right place to start. She had perhaps stayed still too long, staring too intently at the brilliantly bunting- and flower-clad structure, trying to discern which, if any, of the milling nobles on its three ornately decorated levels was the young king. Then, as now, the top level was empty, save for a matched pair of guards.

Part of her – the part that had insisted on this mad mission against all rational thought and advice – was certain that, if she could but look into his eyes, she would know if Damien was all that the reports claimed... or if he had been corrupted by his grandfather and Lord Prydeen.

Part of her – if she dared admit it – wanted to believe, even if it seemed beyond belief, that he could have been untouched. That the Cause was won, the need for a Rebel Duchess was done. That the Rebellion could quietly fold itself up and her folk could slip back to their homes, to their lives... though perhaps not the Rebel Duchess herself, recognizable as she was as a symbol...

Yet – how could those two old, evil men *not* have insured that the crown prince was a "fit successor" to the king who had controlled a creature such as Lord Prydeen?

Genevieve had met the prince once, when they were both children. He had barely been of an age for his first pony, and she – a few years older – had just graduated to a mild-mannered horse... and her father's half-tamed, firebreathing mare that Duke Aldred had no idea she would even attempt to ride. Her father had brought her to Court to make her curtsy to the old king and see her named his Heir. Damien had been but one of a pack of the old king's grandchildren – a nondescript royal child, good-looking as they all had been, but special in no particular way. They had spent perhaps minutes in each other's presence, on separate ends of the audience hall that had seemed miles-long to her then.

Now those other siblings and cousins, aunts and uncles, were all gone and Damien – unremarked offspring of an unremarkable parent – had been named Crown Prince, and now King. For him to have inherited would seem to signal that he had done something to earn the old king's approval – perhaps by being ruthless enough to have ensured no other contenders were available. Certainly, he had made no mark by protesting his grandfather's policies while the old king lived, no mark of any kind, in fact. Despite all the time Genevieve had spent at Court, she did not recall ever noticing him again.

Yet she could still remember a certain clear-eyed gaze from that long-ago child. A gaze that seemed to recognize and promise to right all the wrongs that existed in the world. A gaze that had haunted her dreams since she had heard he had been crowned, and had kept her skepticism from becoming outright denial when rumors of the new king's beneficence came to her. And so, she had come to see for herself...

She had reached the royal platform at last, and hunted for a spot to clamber up. Not an easy endeavor, as it was so heavily be-ribboned – in every color, not merely royal gold and turquoise – with bright buntings stretched between triple rosettes made of actual rose petals. An elegantly illuminated sign noted that these were the coronation gifts of the Weavers' and Florists' Guilds – but the small barrel that the sign rested upon was of more interest to her, as it gave her a leg up to the first level, which was filled with younger noblemen. These young men were here to satisfy fathers and mothers who wanted them close to the source of power. They eyed her with interest – her cloak had of necessity been pushed aside to climb and she was dressed in hunting leathers fit tight to her athletic frame – and she in turn ignored them, using the spigoted ale kegs at which they were amusing themselves to give her a step up to the recessed second level.

The older noblemen and -women – and their maiden daughters – on this level looked at her quite askance. Genevieve hoped her hood shadowed her face enough to keep any of them from recognizing her, for she knew no few of them, though she did not recognize the barely-grown girls, nor more than a handful of the hardly-older lads below. These nobles had toadied up to the old king while Genevieve – and her father before her – had sought to protect their people. She knew all too well that they would as soon sell her out to Lord Prydeen as look at her. Even now they were trying to toady up to King Damien, bringing their marriageable daughters to parade before him – an array of maidens scarcely past puberty, for their elder ones had been taken to serve the old king and Lord Prydeen in years gone by, many never to be seen again. They, too, must surely be hoping for better from Damien, yet she saw nothing but avarice in the faces of even the children.

A good-looking young man – unusual only for being the only *young* man on this level of the platform, did someone think the new king's taste ran to boys? – with very dark hair and clear grey eyes offered her a hand onto the level. Genevieve was not too proud to accept help, even from a scion of one of *these* families. They exchanged a startled look and nearly let go of each other as an electric spark seemed to jump between their hands. Surely it wasn't dry enough today for such things, and so close to the harbor besides.

Putting such irrelevant details aside, Genevieve brushed off her hands on her breeches as she looked up towards the highest level of the reviewing stand, but saw only the pair of Royal Guards – two blondely handsome men so perfectly matched as almost to be twins – decorating that august space. Knights chosen for their beauty, just as were the horses that pulled the royal carriage. She wondered who they were – might they have enough real skill at arms to have faced her in the Battle of Siovale seven years earlier? She'd caught no more than a glimpse of either of them so far, as they turned, watchfully, eyes raking the crowds. Perhaps they were more than merely decorative.

Hopefully the king himself was sitting down and merely out of view. Genevieve needed for him to be there, before Lord Prydeen caught up with her. It was a wild gambit – praise all the Gods at once that Rosa really could handle the Rebellion, since it looked like she was going to have to. Rosa – would never forgive her for getting herself captured and killed. The Rebel Countess – surely that sounded just as impressive. They had known it couldn't last – this would free Rosa to wed and produce the Heir that she needed. Genevieve's own proper title – Lady Stellarine, Duchess of Elaarwen (she dared not think "Princess of the Realm", though her bloodlines were as good as the king's) – would pass to a collateral line...

No matter. The issue at hand was to get up there to the top level and there was no obvious stair or ladder.

Genevieve dropped her useless disguise of a cloak before it could hinder her further in climbing higher, ignoring the massed gasp from the gathered nobles, and looked for a convenient way to boost herself to the king's level. The balustrade of the king's level – still festooned with those slippery buntings and banners – was more than head-high to her. It was higher than she could hoist herself on arm-strength alone.

That young man was still watching her – looking slightly amused, damn him. Or maybe that was *be*mused. Surely, he had little idea what to make of her and her sudden arrival. But he seemed to come to a decision and wrenched a ring with a large grey pearl on it off his finger, thrusting it towards her. It was the sort of thing a nobleman might offer a noblewoman to indicate interest – a sort of "let's get to know each other" offer, not quite a tryst, but more than an offer of acquaintance. The ring would have a house sigil on it, perhaps even a personal seal – enough information for her to find him again later on. A crazy thing to hand to the highly recognizable Rebel Duchess as she attempted to single-handedly besiege the new king's festival viewing platform. The young man must be completely daft.

And then he bent and cupped his hands as a stablehand might do to help someone into the saddle. The sparkle in his eyes suggested he was prepared to toss her high enough to pull herself up over that balustrade.

Again, the gathered nobles gasped, but this time there were also mutters and a fearful eagerness... and she guessed someone had spotted Lord Prydeen approaching.

There was no time for this. Genevieve stuffed the ring onto her finger – her beltpouch would take too long to open – put her foot in his hands and leapt up in concert with his toss.

And got the – third? fourth? – shock of the day as her reaching hands were grasped from above and an all too familiar voice gruffly said "Young miss, this is the king's place, you can't be climbing... up... her–" The voice cut off as and the hands fumbled and nearly dropped her back down, as their owner peered over the edge and then grabbed her more securely and helped her over the balustrade.

The Royal Guard was looking at her in exasperation and some of the same confusion Genevieve was feeling. It was the strangest and least appropriate timing on anything ever – but the touch of his hands had inflamed her with desire. *Not now, not now!* The Rebel Duchess thought frantically. She'd heard of this, but thought it a fairytale... Rosa, *Rosa* was her love...

"Jason Solway?" she managed to gasp out.

"Genny?" He was as flabbergasted as he was, and if the blush rising in those perfect cheeks was anything to judge, he was suffering from the same reaction. Suffering...

"Here now," said the other Royal Guard, coming forward from his ceremonial position. "Jase, what's this all about?"

She looked almost gratefully at the other man, just as gratefully *not* recognizing him as yet another childhood friend. But his familiar behavior towards Jason – were they lovers? Why did that thought make her heart – or something lower than her heart – do flips? And why, oh, why, *was this all happening at once?*

"Stand back, gentlemen," growled a low, cultured voice.

Lord Prydeen.

Apparently, she wouldn't have to sort any of this out after all.

The two Guards obediently stepped aside, though she rather thought that Jason only reluctantly let go of her hands, and she could see that the sorcerer had come up a set of stairs at the back of the reviewing stand. A brief surge of wind whipped the cowled hood from off Lord Prydeen's spotty, balding head, and tossed his long, drooping mustaches. He had not aged well since the old king's death; his hair had been thinning, but was still full when last she had gotten a good look at him, some months earlier, and the lines around his mouth were graven deeply, where once they had been entirely masked by his whiskers. Genevieve had heard tell that evil sorcerers cast vile spells to keep themselves young – by sacrificing true youths and maidens to demons, some said. She had scoffed, even as she wondered. The old king had lived long past his age, and Lord Prydeen, some said, had not aged at all, even as those noble daughters came to serve them both and were rarely seen again.

"Lady Genevieve." Lord Prydeen greeted her, coldly, but not correctly. He needed nothing besides himself to emphasize his authority, but he had brought a squad of his personal guards up with him. They fanned out behind him, blocking the path, even to headstrong young women who might push past a sorcerer.

She tilted her chin up – her nose was too snub to properly glare down it, but she was tall enough to try... and the arrogance might mask the tremble that the tumult in her stomach had settled into. "The proper title is *'Your Grace'*, messir." She was actually in line for the throne herself, with all of Damien's family gone, and 'Lord' Prydeen was, after all, a sorcerer of no particular breeding.

And if she told herself that a few more times, perhaps she could dare to face him.

A wintry smile passed over Lord Prydeen's lips – gone as quickly as snow in the Summer. "No longer, I fear. My former master stripped you of your titles for your treasonous activities."

Genevieve inclined her head. "So, I have heard. But even a Royal Decree does not make a thing reality. Even His – belated – Majesty never put it to the test in *Elaarwen.*"

Something sparked in the sorcerer's eyes. Anger, perhaps? Could such a one as he even feel something as tender as grief? He gestured to his men. "Bind her and bring her."

Jason bestirred himself to protest, "My lord–!" but the other Guard pulled him back and Genevieve found herself being roughly seized and turned around by hands that made no pretense of not enjoying their task. Even the king's own Royal Guards, it seemed, dared not speak against the sorcerer. Not yet anyways. If only she had waited to see if the young king could consolidate his power; if, indeed, he would continue in the way he had begun!

"My Lord Prydeen! What passes here?" The mild voice interrupted from the direction of the stairs, but was no one Genevieve recognized. She had been turned to face outwards towards the square whilst they bound her, and could not see the speaker.

Lord Prydeen's voice was a curious mix of ingratiating and dismissive. "Nothing you need trouble yourself over, my lord. Some rabble found her way up here, clearly to cause some trouble to you. It is my task and my privilege to safeguard Your Highness. We'll be away momentarily."

Gentle hands cleared away the thongs that had begun to lash her wrists. "Surely you are mistaken, my Lord Prydeen. This is no rabble, but Her Grace, the Duchess Genevieve Stellarine of Elaarwen."

"Yes, my Lord, the so-called 'Rebel Duchess'," Lord Prydeen's voice was growing impatient. "I am taking her to the castle dungeons to have out of her what she knows. You can make an example of her later on – you must not detract from your coronation festivities."

"Nonsense, Lord Prydeen," the mild voice replied. "That isn't how we treat visiting royalty... not to mention that the people would rise in protest and not even you could put them *all* down at once."

He came around to Genevieve's right side, and before she could register that this was the same young man who had cupped his hands for her boot like any stableboy, he gave her that same enigmatic smile, and faced the crowd – who had begun to turn as they saw their king. Damien lifted Genevieve's right hand in his left, holding them high above their heads and called out, "I give you Genevieve Stellarine, the Rebel Duchess!"

It was the sort of moment a Duke's Heir is trained for and – bemused as she was at the turn of events – Genevieve flattened her palm against the king's and stood tall before the crowds, the errant breeze tossing her red-gold curls like a mane. She smiled fiercely, trying to think if this would be taken as some sort of inadvertent admission of surrender.

Even as the people roared their approval – and Lord Prydeen fumed behind them – a sudden, strange crackling noise erupted and ribbons of white fire fountained up between their pressed fingers. It wreathed down to wrap their hands and curl around their arms.

For all that she was the reigning duchess of a province, the leader of a rebellion against an unjust king and an evil sorcerer, and had spent most of her life in that struggle... Genevieve was tempted to faint right then and there. This was absolutely the *last* thing she had expected. If she hadn't seen this happen before, she would have thought it was some new and clever attack by Lord Prydeen.

But she *had* seen this before. And, likely, so had every member of the crowd below.

At least young King Damien looked nearly as befuddled as she felt.

He, however, recovered more quickly than she.

"And your future Queen!" he announced in what sounded like a calm voice.

He pulled her in and kissed her.

And the crowds went absolutely wild.

Chapter TWO

Bound!

GENEVIEVE WENT ABSOLUTELY STILL. ANOTHER spark had seared her lips as Damien's touched hers, and, with the white fire still wreathing their hands and the internal turmoil that had only barely subsided since she touched Jason's hands, it was all simply too *much*.

Damien released her a bit – though their still inextricably fire-wreathed hands stayed together, of course – smiled and waved to the crowd...

... and they turned to face Lord Prydeen.

Seething and fuming did not *begin* to describe the sorcerer's mien. Towering fury *might* be a start.

"What did you think you were doing, you young fool?" he hissed. Below, the crowds were celebrating as if it were the first feast day instead of the last – as indeed it might be, for a royal wedding. Even Lord Prydeen – as Damien had so cavalierly reminded him – needed some care for such masses of people. "Now you are *bound* to this traitorous wench!"

Damien put a naïve and helplessly innocent smile on that Genevieve had small doubt was entirely contrived. "Why, Lord Prydeen, I had no *idea* Her Grace was my soulmate. Though I will admit that when I saw her climbing up the platform, I thought I saw a way to end the rebellion bloodlessly..."

He reached out with his right hand and lifted her left one – where his grey pearl ring glistened on her finger still. Surely, he hadn't...

He had.

The ring wasn't some token of a noble house carrying with it a suggestion of possible romantic interest or alliance. It was the *Ring of the Heir.* Her only excuse for not recognizing the bloody thing was her haste and the absolute insanity that a random young man would hand her the Ring of the Heir to the Throne as she scrambled the wrong way to the top of the royal reviewing stand.

Lord Prydeen snarled soundlessly, turned on his heel and stormed towards the stairs. His men followed him silently, casting incredulous looks back at the king. Said king maintained his guileless expression until the last of them was out of sight before turning to his Royal Guards.

"Jason, thank you for catching my signal to bring Her Grace up here."

Ah, so that explained why he'd nearly dropped her before helping Genevieve over the balustrade. Or at least *one* reason. And the less said – or thought – about any other possibilities, the better.

Jason bowed with perfect precision and carefully avoided her eyes. "Your wish is my command, Your Majesty." But then his perfect-soldier demeanor fell away. "Damien, you've made him a worse enemy faster than we'd planned."

"Aye," the other one agreed grimly. "I hope it was worth it." He gave Genevieve a dark look. "Fool king. Whatever possessed you to give her the Heir's Ring? And don't give me that cockeyed tale you gave Prydeen. I'll grant you recognized her – that hair is like a battleflag – but you couldn't possibly have known she'd support you."

Damien gave them that maddening, enigmatic smile again. "It was obvious she was fleeing Prydeen. The Ring was all the protection I could give her, Adam. You know what it *does.*" The second Guard nodded slowly, still looking grim.

Genevieve had had about enough of this. "What *does* it do? And why should you care about protecting me? I *am* leading a rebellion against your throne." They had let their arms come down, but the white fire still bound their hands tightly and it was a slightly awkward position. The physical discomfort coupled with all the internal dislocations of the day made her tone perhaps a trifle sharp. She did not *want* to be soul-bonded to this irritating, manipulative man... and it was doubly annoying to realize that her body was flaring with desire again, this time for *him*.

No one knew why or how soul-bonding happened. It was always fiery, dramatic, and the cause for much rejoicing. The common lore held that it was a deeper version of "love at first sight" – a sort of "love at first touch." It could happen between people who had been wedded for decades, or – obviously – between complete strangers. The two people so linked were bound inextricably, first by the fire that announced the binding, and then by a sense that caused actual physical pain if they were too long separated. And if one partner died, the other was sure to follow.

Genevieve had always thought it sounded more like a trap than a romantic plot twist.

Damien gave her a graceful nod – considering that their hands were magickally linked and likely to remain so for some time, it was better than a courtly bow. "Your Grace, I am desperately short of friends. From what I have heard of you, I hoped you would become one.

"And at any rate," he added with a touch of irony, "the Ring is yours by right. You *are* next in line for the throne, and I would far rather see it come to you than to my 'lord' Prydeen."

She had not realized she was that close in the succession... surely... or perhaps not. Not that that explained the rest of her question.

Her multitude of questions – and disagreements with his attempt at logic – must have shown on her face because Damien shook his head even before she had decided which one to start with. "Later. Suffice it to say that we are both safer now than we were this morning. Adam," he addressed his Guard again. "Please go bring up a squad of *our* boys. No one will be surprised if Her Grace and I retire now – in fact," he gave Genevieve another slightly ironic smile, "they may be surprised if we don't."

Indeed. The intense physical desire for the partner was a well-known piece of a soul-bonding – the merchants and peasants were probably laying odds how long it would be before they left. And how long a wedding could wait before the bride would be too obviously pregnant for discretion – soul-bondings between complementary-gendered couples were invariably fruitful. Yet another thing Genevieve did not look forward to, for all that she needed an Heir as much as did the young king.

Adam grunted and headed down the stairs.

"Jason," Damien continued, "you know Her Grace of old. And you know me. Brother-mine, would you vouch for me?" It was definitely an appeal. And Damien could have no idea how impossible his request was.

Genevieve and Jason had known each other since they were children. His mother's townhouse was sited next to the Stellarine mansion in the capitol city and the two of them had met when he caught her as she was sneaking out to explore on her first – and only *official* – trip to Emeralsee. Jason, though only a year older than her own age of twelve, had felt honor-bound to accompany her, and had perforce been dragged into a series of adventures that resulted in both of them being confined to their rooms on bread and water. The penitent Genevieve had snuck out of that as well to bring him purloined sweets, since none of it was his fault. When they were officially released by their parents they became friends in a less surreptitious manner, finding that they both enjoyed riding and strategy games. They had kept in casual contact for years, breaking it off only as the Rebellion consumed first Genevieve's father and then her as well... and as Jason's mother became one of the staunchest supporters of the old king. They hadn't spoken – or even written – since Genevieve became the Duchess of Elaarwen, and she had not even thought about him in several years, being busy with her work and with... *Rosa...*

They had been friends that Summer of childhood... Good friends, but only friends. Genevieve hadn't waited upon his letters... or conceded to an arranged marriage for the Rebellion's benefit only after she realized Jason wasn't coming to join the Rebellion – and her. The marriage had been a disaster...

And now... now they had this other thing between them, as confusing as anything else that had happened today.

He could not meet her eyes, but gamely offered an encomium for the king... who was also clearly his friend. "You can trust Damien,

Genny." He seemed to be trying to say more, but she decided to spare him the effort.

"One thing about a soul-bonding is that I know *that,*" she said, rolling her eyes and addressing Damien directly. "You, I can trust with my very life. Indeed, neither of us have a choice about that. But I know nothing else about you. How you think, what you believe, your morals, your desires–"

She had not meant to phrase it that way, quite... but her own body responded as Damien pulled her close with almost a groan. "What I *desire* is *you,*" he said, his voice low. Jason gave her an agonized look and stepped away to look down the stairs, giving them privacy.

I don't want this, Genevieve thought fiercely, even as another part of her made it clear that she did, indeed. *This* kiss was not polite and intended for public viewing. They definitely needed to get out of here before this crazy thing overwhelmed them both.

Rosa... she thought despairingly, then gave herself up to the bonding... and the kiss.

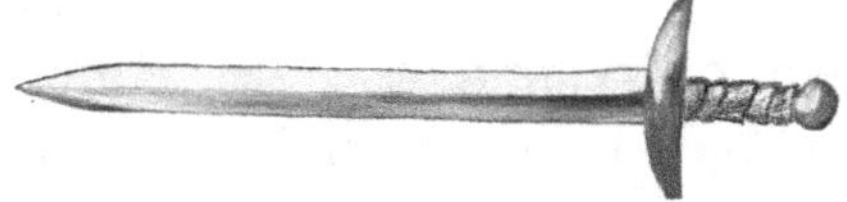

Many – *many* – hours later, Damien looked up at the Rebel Duchess with a feeling of deep content. Genevieve had her head propped on her left hand, her eyes half-lidded and a small smile on her face. In the dim lantern light, her eyes were an impossibly dark blue and her hair seemed an almost sunset red. He could almost dare to believe that she felt as he did.

They had made it to his bedchamber, but it had been a near thing. Damien's extensive reading about soul-bonding had led him to believe that a major purpose of the magic was to conceive children with some special mix of qualities, and very little, if any, of it had to do with romantic love. A shiver of delight ran through him at the thought of *their* children, his and Genevieve's.

She noticed the shiver – how could she not, when they lay length to length, with not a shred of fabric to separate them – and raised a golden eyebrow ironically. "Ready again so soon? No complaints," the beautiful woman added quickly, leaning in to give him a quick kiss. Feather-light, and it was almost too much.

"I think we should eat something first, though," Genevieve added judiciously, looking away.

"Agreed," Damien said immediately, and only a little reluctantly. She was everything he could ever have dreamed of... everything he *had* dreamed of, since he had been eight years old and had seen her make her curtsy to his grandfather. However, almost certainly *she* had not spent the last sixteen years with that same dream; so now he needed to make sure she never regretted this turn of events, in small things or in large...

Getting out of bed necessitated some negotiation. Their hands were still magickally bound, though the white fire was now almost invisible to the eye. At least there was some slip in the connection; they had discovered that while their palms would not come apart, they could rotate to find a more comfortable position. Genevieve had to roll onto him slightly in order to get up, and that almost undid him right then. From the look in her eye, he might not be alone, and he wished they knew each other beyond reputation and the soul-bond. This awkward moment of trying to rise... the entire awkwardness of having their hands unable to separate and of the soul-bond itself... It could all be less awkward with kisses and giggles.

However, that wasn't where they were, and they had now had quite a bit of practice in managing with their Bound hands – though their clothes would never be the same. When Damien and Genevieve had finally gotten around to removing their remaining clothing, they had discovered the impossibility of sleeves and hands that would not separate. Genevieve's hunting leathers were mostly laced tight, and would need but new thongs and a bit of reworking at the shoulder, but were, after all, hunting leathers and not fashion accessories. Damien's silk shirt was an entirely lost cause.

They re-arranged themselves with the rumpled sheets drawn up strategically before Damien reached for the bell-pull to summon a servant. It was not a servant who entered, however, carrying a tray of covered dishes and a pitcher; it was Sir Adam Loveress, the Captain of Damien's Royal Guard, and he had a very self-satisfied expression.

"We're taking it upon ourselves to make sure you're not disturbed," Adam replied in answer to Damien's look of question.

"Jason and I – all the Royal Guards. We had the food prepared – and we watched the cooks, yes," he finished.

"There's planning to be done–" Damien began at the same moment that Genevieve said "I need to send a message–" They looked at each other and smiled, because they couldn't help it.

Adam rolled his eyes. "Lady Theresa has begun planning the wedding and second coronation." He bowed slightly to Genevieve, not seeming to notice her unclad state. "And I believe she has also dispatched a rider to Elaarwen, though whether he'll arrive before your own spies bring back the news, I cannot say." He leered a little at Damien, teasing but appreciative. "Now eat. You'll neither of you do anyone any good for awhile. We have things under control out here."

Damien grinned at this man who was one of his oldest and most trusted friends. "As if you and Jason were any different when you finally sorted yourselves out."

Adam snorted as he headed for the door. "A little different, my liege. We weren't responding to a soul-bond so we had normal physical limitatio–" He ducked out, laughing, as Damien launched a piece of fruit at him.

The young king turned back to his soulmate, still smiling, to find her regarding him thoughtfully.

"You seem to know more about soul-bonding than I do. How long are we likely to continue enjoying this unusual level of – hmmm – energy? And how long are we likely to be so tightly bound?" She picked out a small meat roll with her left hand – Adam had brought all finger foods, nothing that would be awkward to eat one-handed. She was right-handed, Damien knew and clearly somewhat uncomfortable using the other one.

Damien found himself blushing and picked out his own treat, a shrimp canape. "My reading – which is all from legends and fairystories, you'll understand – suggests that we go back to normal when you conceive." He studied the canape with rather more attention than it deserved, completely unable to meet her eyes.

"Oh, dear..."

The young king looked up to see her caught between horror and amusement.

"That could present a problem. I'm at the absolute wrong end of my cycle. Are there stories of this lasting for *weeks?*" Genevieve lost her battle and began to laugh. It was just too ridiculous to contemplate. Damien had a kingdom to gain control over and she had a Rebellion to run... or win... or, he hoped, bring to an end and support him. Just to spend weeks with their hands and arms in this ridiculous position...

"I hope you miscounted!" He found himself choking back laughter as well.

"How do you know all this anyways?" Genevieve asked, wiping her eyes. Laughing together had made them both easier with each other. She held out a goblet. "Here. You pour."

Damien guessed that she felt awkward pouring with her left hand – *she* had not spent years studying *him* and assumed he was also right-handed. He took some pains to make the small operation seem effortless. He shrugged, poured them each a cup of what turned out to be well-watered wine, and took a long, cooling drink.

"I like to read. And spending time in the castle library was safe. My lord grandfather and Lord Prydeen had eyes everywhere. My sister was just a hair too well-liked by the army. My cousin Salleen was too good at negotiating with the merchants – when he was given that task by the king. My parents –" He shrugged again, swallowing what he might have said. "A boy without much arms skill who spent all his time reading fairystories was no threat. Too unworldly to do any harm. Too awkward to engender any dedicated supporters."

Damien kept his eyes down. What a coward she must think him, to have stood by while all those he cared about were done away with.

"Jason Solway follows you." The quiet comment made him glance up to see what might be sympathy in her eyes. "I knew Jason when we were children. He's an intelligent man."

"Jason... Adam... my other Royal Guards... My lord grandfather gifted me a cadre of younger sons when he gave me the Heir's Ring." Damien looked down again. "I was the last legitimate heir, so I suppose he felt he had no choice–"

"The last legitimate heir?" she interrupted. "There are none left at all? Weren't there twenty sons and daughters? And several score grandchildren?"

He shook his head. "None," he confirmed. "I had *thirty* aunts and uncles and nearly a *hundred* cousins. And of course, my grandfather's *bastards* have never all been counted..." There had already been one open challenge for his throne, and several assassination attempts. Adam's care in preparation of the food was not unwarranted – though they still could not be sure whether it was Damien's bastard cousins or Lord Prydeen behind the attacks. The old king had lived well past a normal human lifespan – seven queens had provided his legitimate heirs, some of them simultaneously (who would have dared to naysay him?), and he had taken full advantage of any woman, maiden or wife, who caught his eye.

And any one of the offspring that showed any promise in any way at all was made an example of – or simply disappeared.

Damien felt smaller and more cowardly every time he thought of it. The only thing he could do to try to make up for all those losses, those bright futures ended, was to – somehow – get rid of Lord Prydeen and rebuild the kingdom in their honor. To give bright futures back to those who still lived and protect them from the depredations of the lesser nobility that had been not merely sanctioned, but encouraged by his grandfather.

He *had* to do it.

He still didn't know how to win Genevieve to his cause willingly, and he could not do it without her. They were *soul*-bound, but her *heart* and her *will* were what he needed.

"Adam took pity on me," he dragged his way back to the story. "He and Jason somehow managed to winnow through my Guards and... *discouraged* anyone who didn't meet their standards." It hadn't been safe to openly replace any of the dissolute or perverse young men with their more stalwart sisters or female cousins – but Adam had arranged for a quiet cadre of female Guards to surround the young prince in disguise as his lady companions.

"They taught me – everything. Everything I needed to know about real people. I'm *not* just a figurehead!" Damien added hotly, responding again to what he saw in her eyes. "I owe them everything, but they ask for nothing. Just that I be a better king and a leader of my people. They taught me – but now they follow. And *I'm* the one who knew the secret of the Heir's Ring that made it all possible," he finished, knowing that would be enough to make her ask and finally having brought the conversation around so that he could tell her.

Both golden brows arched high. " 'The Secret of the Heir's Ring'," she said, clearly capitalizing each word. "Sounds impressive." She held her left hand up to examine the ring with some skepticism. "It *sounds* like a fairystory."

Damien caught her hand and – because he couldn't resist, the tension of desire beginning to build again – he kissed her palm. Genevieve shivered delicately, but let him hold her hand so they could both look at the large, grey pearl, shimmering softly in the lamp light. The setting was silver, tiny traceries enwrapping the stone in patterns that seemed to suggest meaning but were not quite meaningful.

"Reading all the old stories had some benefits. The Heir is protected from magick to read thoughts and overhear spoken words so long as he – or she – wears the Ring. That may be why my grandfather never named an Heir until he was forced to by circumstance. Once I had the Ring, Lord Prydeen lost most of his power over me. And since I had been too insignificant to bother with – or even to remember..." Nothing like stories of miserable old men and past humiliations to quench the inner fires...

She still seemed skeptical. "Why bother with the Ring at all then? In fact, why not get rid of it entirely? Did you ever test this so-called power?"

"I don't think they *could* get rid of it," Damien answered. "I suspect they tried. They'd have been fools not to, and fools they are – *were* – not. It's one of those magickal objects that keeps re-appearing. It's said to appear from thin air and fall onto the king's plate before he has been served if it hasn't been worn for more than a year. I actually saw that happen once," he added with a ghost of a grin. "It made my royal grandfather's golden plate ring like a bell and the tone lasted for a full day. Supposedly it rang for longer each time, and the only cure was to name an Heir and bestow the Ring."

Damien did not explain that the tone had only ended *that* time when his grandfather had irritably called him into the royal presence and thrust the Ring at him. 'Put it on and keep it out of my sight you ineffectual puling wretch,' the old man had ordered as he gulped down headache powders and wine.

"So. It's enchanted. How do you know it acts to protect?" Genevieve asked, reasonably. "And why didn't it protect the previous wearers – your aunts and uncles and cousins?"

"My grandfather had them put it on only briefly for the ceremony, then had it stored away in a vault to be taken out once a year. I'm not sure why he let me keep it." He did, though. The old man hadn't wanted to admit he'd made a mistake – Damien had overheard him arguing with Lord Prydeen. His telling argument had been that a feckless boy like Damien posed no threat to him no matter what magickal bauble he might hold – whether it was the Heir's Ring or the Monarch's Sword. And, indeed, Damien hadn't...

"You know the rumors that Lord Prydeen can hear the thoughts of others?" he asked. At her nod, he continued. "That's not quite the case. He can hear whatever is spoken – no matter where or by whom – should he care to be listening. He's also enchanted numerous mice and birds to listen on his behalf when he's otherwise occupied and then to reveal to him what they've heard, at his convenience."

She whistled, low, like a man. And sneaked a look around to the darkened corners of the room. "Not quite as bad as hearing our very thoughts. But quite nearly. How do you know all this? And so precisely?"

"Because he told me so." Damien did not try to conceal his grimace of distaste – and the remembered humiliation. *'My lord king wishes you to know the extent of my powers so that you will know not to bother with some foolheaded rebellion,'* Lord Prydeen had stated as the king himself watched with his sunken, burning eyes. *'I think he overestimates you, boy. But a day will come when it is wise that you recall who is the master and who is the servant – no matter what robes you wear, nor what coronet sits upon your head.'* Damien suppressed a shudder at the memory of those cold words – and his knowledge that it had not been the king who thought him likely to rebel. The king was gone, but the threat remained.

"...And because so long as I was touching someone, Lord Prydeen never heard what was said. Yes, we tested it," he assured her. "And, yes, we had to live with the consequences of our testing. It works quite well." He had endured jeers from the courtiers currying favor when Lord Prydeen informed them all of Damien's (entirely fake) confession of how he'd lost his virginity – but at least he had been able to shield Jason and Adam's relationship from the sorcerer's ken, though it had meant he was privy to more of their intimate life than any of them would have preferred. Fortunately, the magicked animals could only relay what they *heard*, not what they *saw*...

"Which is why you can tell me all this, now. And why you wouldn't discuss it before we left the reviewing stand in the marketplace." Genevieve nodded, then made the leap that he had done as they stood, hands aloft and wreathed with fire, in the marketplace. "And how does that work with a soul-bond? Will the magick of the Heir's Ring protect *you* even when we can actually be apart?"

He remembered dodging her questions – and Adam's – regarding this issue, immediately following their discovery of this amazing, unexpected gift. But along with that thought came the very physical memory of the first surge of soul-bonding-induced desire...

"I hope so," he said, and it came out a bit more huskily than he had intended. "Since I was crowned, it was clear that the Ring has no longer had any use for me." Surely the crown itself, or the royal signet ring, should have been similarly enchanted. But they weren't, and it had been clear that Lord Prydeen was enjoying his new vulnerability. Only the careful vigilance of his Royal Guards had kept him alive these six days.

"So why *did* you give me the Ring? There was no way to guess we'd discover a soul-bond."

Her question was not unexpected... but how could he answer? What he had told her before was true enough – she really was next in line for the throne. Genevieve's grandmother had been his grandfather's first cousin, her title of Grand Duchess coming not from her husband as Duke of Elaarwen but was her own from birth as a granddaughter of the former Queen. There were no others with as close a kinship, and none at all but Genevieve and her father who had shown the leadership to speak up against the atrocities perpetrated by his grandfather and Lord Prydeen and, indeed, to lead a rebellion.

Damien was well aware that leading a rebellion against the crown was not usually grounds for being named Heir – or Queen-Consort. But it was equally true, and he could tell her so, that he had hoped that his action might prove his willingness to let the past go and work with her and her (hopefully former) rebels to rebuild the kingdom.

That giving her the Ring was not only to name her Heir, but to show trust by protecting the leader of the Rebellion.

But he could not, dared not, tell her that his truest motivation was to protect *her*, Genevieve, from whatever Lord Prydeen might throw at her, for the sake of a memory and a dream. *His* memory, *his* dream. She'd think him thrice a fool alongside being a coward.

He had waited too long to reply. Genevieve thoughtfully pushed her long mane of wild curls back from her face. "You are a clever man, Damien, and I'll need to be careful not to underestimate you. I doubt you ever do anything for just one reason. Your grandfather and Prydeen had no idea who you are and what you are capable of." A slow smile curved her mouth. "But your impromptu attempt to co-opt me to your side has worked. Even without your scheming I had been hoping to find that you were someone I could work with. The reports I was getting said you might be, but I had to see for myself to believe them. Rosa –" Her glowing eyes lost some of their luster, and she faltered slightly as if suddenly remembering who she was, and where... and why. "Rosa told me I was a fool..."

"The Rebel Countess." Damien knew who she was, of course. He knew by heart every detail of Genevieve's life that he had been able to discover – the ill-conceived marriage, planned to try to bring more supporters to the Rebellion and ending with the death of both her father and her husband, though exactly how he had never heard. The determination with which the grieving wife and daughter had taken the reins of the Rebellion and brushed aside all further offers. Until Rosa, newly-made Countess of Zialest had come over to her side.

He swallowed hard. Genevieve must never again know regret or loss if he could help it. Damien was bound to her soul and would be the father of her children – he could survive, somehow, if she wanted no more of him than a political partnering.

"You can bring her here," he made himself say. "Once it is safe for her. I – have some idea of how much she means to you. You need not give her up."

His unwilling soulmate looked away. "We always knew it was not forever. She has a duty to provide her line with an heir of her body. As do I."

Genevieve looked back at him, and quite deliberately let the sadness go. For now.

"Speaking of which..." his beautiful Rebel Duchess purred. Their hands – his left, her right – were still bonded, palm to palm, but that was no hindrance at all when she pushed him back down on the bed.

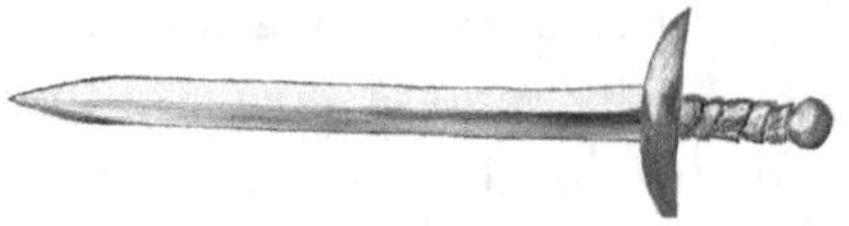

"You – are amazing." Damien whispered. She could hear the smile in his voice – and was that *awe*? For her? "I would ask you to marry me," he added, "but –"

"But you already did. Sort of." She was still more than a little put out by the way she had been manipulated... but she could no longer deny that they were indeed a good match. Better, did she dare admit it, than she and Rosa had ever been. She was still stunned at what Damien had been through; stunned that he was (as she knew through the soul-bonding) heart-whole and not broken. How he had, as a child, come through losing everyone and everything that had ever mattered to him and still have not only the strength and determination to make right all that he had had no part in making wrong, but also the depth of character and charisma and soul to still be able to love...

Genevieve guessed that his parents had loved him and each other. With such a place to begin from, it was possible to weather many things, as she well knew.

Damien's eyes were drifting closed, his breathing slowing and deepening. He lay on his back and she on her right side, snugged close. Their bound arms, his left, her right, were tucked upwards in a somewhat awkward angle – every position was awkward right now. Her left hand rested gently on his abdomen.

How different he was from her husband. Her *first* husband, she supposed she must think of him as now. Genevieve, together with her father, had studied the possible marriages she could make to strengthen their political position. They had still hoped to avoid outright rebellion at that point, thinking that they could pressure the old king into changing his ways, perhaps even to putting aside Lord Prydeen and naming one of his children or grandchildren as Heir.

Harald had been the younger brother of Duke Tomas Elsevier of Siovale, good-natured it had seemed, but a tad dull in both spirit and intellect. He would be completely unlikely to challenge her as the ruling Duchess of Elaarwen, when her father passed the title to her, they had surmised, and the marriage would bind their two duchies together without alarming his brother that a rival heir to his own children would be generated. Genevieve had thought it wouldn't matter – she had been eighteen years old, confident as only such a young adult can be. Her heart was given to her people, after all, so she hardly needed a spouse except to conceive an heir.

Her father, she recalled, had been dubious, having loved her mother to distraction and never having looked at another woman in the ten years since she had died. He'd offered to let her drop the plan, even the night before the wedding. What Duke Aldred had seen at that late date to encourage him to make such an offer... Whatever it was, he'd turned a blind eye to what followed for as long as he could, presumably to respect the choices she'd made and her own determination to live up to her vows.

Genevieve could not suppress a sigh, though she kept it to just a breath to avoid disturbing the sleeping Damien. Her father had known better than she. Perhaps if she had become pregnant quickly – or at all – it would have been bearable. But a year had passed, then two, then five. Then *eight*. Harald had begun to feel like a fifth wheel on a cart – there was no need for him in Elaarwen, and he had conceived the idea that the people were laughing at him because there was no child. At last, he had begun to rail at her that she must be barren, for *he* had done *his* duty by her – and claimed that he had half a dozen illegitimate children by as many women.

She had known that Harald visited the local brothels – her work kept her busy and he was... vigorous, if nothing else. She had been somewhat grateful, for he would return to her bed with much more imagination than was ever his to own – since all that was between them was duty, it had reduced the boredom somewhat. The courtesans in Elaarwen were healthy, well-paid, and well-treated – and very careful not to conceive a child with a patron.

These bastards he claimed were from liaisons with *other* women – maidservants and clothiers' apprentices. Apparently, his fondness for elaborate costuming was not the innocent indulgence she had assumed.

Harald had the paranoid poor taste to fling his accusations over dinner. With her father. To his credit, he had realized himself, paled, and then stormed from the room. Genevieve had sat frozen in shock. Her father, the lord Duke, had excused himself quietly.

A few days of awkward avoidances went by. Genevieve had investigated Harald's claims, and found them true. She made sure the children were provided for – something Harald had not bothered to do – and noted that none of the mothers was particularly surprised to see her. They had nothing terrible to say about him, but nothing particularly good either. He had found no greater love with them, than with Genevieve. But none of the children was older than two years old.

Genevieve had missed a conference with their spies, and her father had found her sitting in the bay window of the room which had been hers as a child, knees pulled up to her chest, staring blindly out at the late Fall day. Grey clouds, a fine drizzle, the bright colors of leaves all turned to dull browns, a thin, chill wind from the east. It matched her insides – what was wrong with her that she could neither love nor conceive a child with her husband of eight long years? The Duke had not needed to ask what was wrong. He told her that there would be someone for her to love some day and that her role was not to be a broodmare for the duchy but rather to lead it in the struggle against the king's cruelty – to independence if that was the only choice.

And then he had kissed her hair, patted her shoulder and gone away. To let her think, she had believed at the time. It was the last time she ever saw him.

The Rebel Duchess pulled her mind away from the ache that always came from those memories. Her father would be happy for her now, she thought, and forced away the fearful thought that perhaps she *was* barren. What had been a legal inconvenience – to find and name an Heir – could become a physical one if the soul-bonding would not release her hand from Damien's... ever. Not to mention that, as king, Damien required an Heir of his body. And if *she* was truly the next in line for the throne... there were likely no other options for him to adopt an Heir. They were third cousins through Queen Marian, their great-great-grandmother.

But he was so very different from Harald. Deep and spirited, where Harald had been dull and shallow.

And inventive... a smile curved her lips, all unknowing, and her free left hand caressed her king and soul-bonded's silken skin. Harald had cared only to do his duty in their bed, save for when he wanted to use one of the techniques learned from his whores. He had taken his pleasure and that was all. She had not even known there could be more than a modicum of pleasure for *her* until Rosa.

But Damien... despite the awkwardness of their bound hands and the urgency of their magick-induced desire, he had looked for ways to let her know she was special, to ensure she was just as enraptured with delight as he. The magick had forced them to have sex – *he* had transformed it into making love.

Her hand wandered lower, enjoying the fuzzy, curly feel of hair contrasted with the silken smooth skin just above it, the thin trail of fur leading down from his navel...

Damien groaned and mumbled something about needing sleep. It sounded like, but surely could not have been, for he was more than three-quarters asleep, "Woman, I love you more than life, but my head is aching for sleep..." Surely, she must have misheard... it was enough to chase any of *her* remaining sleepiness away.

Genevieve's hand moved lower...

He somehow flipped them around so that she was now curled up behind him and on her left side, her free hand trapped between them and their bound hands more comfortably wrapped around him. She snuggled closer. The back of his neck was perfectly placed and too tempting not to kiss. His skin had a different texture there. She kissed him again, this time tasting as well. And his earlobe was right there, too... Would he say it again?

"Genevieve, my body is willing – more than willing! But I simply can't stay awake any longer."

"Then sleep," she teased, sucking on his earlobe.

Another impressive flip, and he was curled up behind *her*, on their right sides now, with their bound arms wrapped around her as well. He kissed the back of her neck, and she shivered down to her toes. "Sleep, beloved," he murmured, and this she had no doubt she had heard correctly.

She lay very still for what seemed a long, long while.

The soul-bonding had assured her that he was a good person. Their talk earlier had told her that they would make excellent partners in doing what was needed to rebuild the kingdom.

But *this*... this was not about *magick*. Or intellect. He had spoken in the haze of sleep, when truths will out because there is no Will alert to mask them. Harald had mumbled things she had learned to ignore. Damien's words had sounded comfortable, relaxed.

Could this truly be? Or did he say that to every woman who shared his bed? He clearly was no stranger to sharing sheets.

Thanks to Rosa, she believed in love. But it had always seemed like something fleeting. It simply wasn't wise to make long-term plans while debating how best to overthrow one's king. And in fact, she and Rosa had spent half their waking hours negotiating with Rosa's fiancé to bring his territory into the Rebellion's camp – and to accept Rosa as his bride. That, too, was a political marriage, though Rosa had seemed content enough with it in her quiet, intense way. She knew the young Count of Dalizell well – but he had shied away from Rosa when the old king's youngest son, Damien's uncle, had decided to exercise *droit d'signeur* with the Count of Zialest's daughter the night before the wedding and ended up murdering the Count and Countess and their son before raping Rosa after all... and gentle Rosa had stabbed him in the gut with a fire-poker.

Rosa had fled her home, crossing into neighboring Elaarwen in the middle of the night. After leaving a letter claiming responsibility for the prince's death as her blood-price pinned to his naked body. And yes, *pinned*.

She had turned to Genevieve for sanctuary, not daring to trust her not-yet husband to stand against the vengeance of the king. For that and for joining county Zialest to the Rebellion – and for becoming Genevieve's lover – Dalizell had required much and many assurances. But the marriage was still a good one for both sides – merged together, Zialest and Dalizell might be able to claim the title of a duchy – and Rosa had pressed to keep her betrothal from unraveling.

'Do I love ***him****?'* Genevieve asked herself. And she could find no sure answer.

But her body told her what it wanted, what the magick wanted, and she could find no disagreement in her heart. Somehow... she wanted to let Damien know that it was not *just* the magick for her either...

He... wasn't as soundly asleep as all that...

Chapter THREE

Released...

"THAT WAS SUPPOSED TO BE for you and for me, and *not* the bedamned *magick!*" Genevieve declared, half-complaining... She'd tried to offer herself to Damien – out of love – in the way that Harald had demanded of her for his own selfish pleasure. Definitely it hadn't been for hers – though she rather supposed *Damien* might have found a way to change that for her. Not that there had been a chance to find out, since the soul-bond had taken over again and turned it into another attempt to conceive a child.

Of course, she mused, without the help of the soul-bonding magick they would have been worn out long before. Right now, she was neither tired nor sore – anywhere. She was sleepy, at long last, and gratefully so. Hungry, vaguely, but not enough to move and disturb either of them to nibble on food gone cold and stale long since.

Damien reached up to caress her hair, and she could feel him smiling, the bristles of his no-longer-so-shorn face moving against the skin of her shoulders. "I cannot damn magick that brought you to me..." He paused. "Genevieve... I'm using my left hand."

They both rolled into a sitting position.

Which was entirely possible to do, because their hands were no longer joined.

Damien's eyes were round. "Could it be already–?"

She shrugged, feeling uncomfortable with the question. "I don't see how," she answered unhappily. "I told you I'm at the wrong end of my cycle." She had hoped that perhaps this would prove Harald wrong at last... not that she *wanted* to grow large and ungainly...

"Then how–?" he marveled.

Genevieve stayed silent. She had a feeling that his hypothesis about what factors caused the release was off. He was a man – and by his own admission had been a fairly sheltered one. He might not know how much variation there was in the length of gestation – a month or more was fairly common – and given that his information came from fairystories she guessed that the descriptions were couched in lyrical language about moons and seasons to begin with.

Her own suspicion was that it wasn't about conception. It was about acceptance. When both partners had accepted the bond, the physical binding was no longer necessary.

Accepted the bond – or perhaps something more – but she wasn't ready to acknowledge that out loud. Not even out loud in her head.

Instead, she shrugged. "Regardless, it should make it more comfortable to sleep."

The young king – her affianced husband – eyed her with minor disbelief. "And *now* you want to sleep."

"Mmm-hmm." She lay back down and snuggled into the very nice, soft blankets on his – on *their* – bed. "Join me."

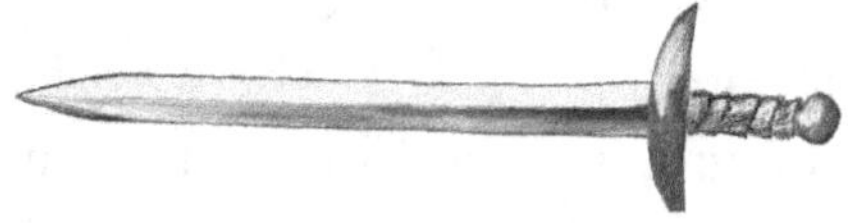

The world came back in shades of grey. And with an insistent hand gently shaking his shoulder. It stopped as its owner realized his eyes were fluttering open, even though everything was still a blur. He wanted to lay there in perfect comfort with his beloved sprawled possessively half across him as she slept...

Damien was suddenly aware that Genevieve was no longer asleep, although she had not so much as moved a muscle. That brought him fully awake as well, although he had to blink several times to bring everything back into focus.

The person who had been shaking him waited impatiently beside the bed. She was a delicate-looking woman – closer in age to Genevieve than to himself. Dark-haired, round-bosomed... Ciriis Celavell had never been long on patience, which was probably why she had been the first to make a lover of the awkward young prince. She was also far more deadly than her fussily fashionable appearance suggested, and had the sharpest head for Court intrigue among the secret female cadre of his Royal Guards.

"Ciriis?" he inquired. His throat, too, was stuffy with sleep.

The woman sighed. "Adam and Jason told me we had to wait for you to emerge on your own, but there is simply no time. You know how precarious things are; we need you out there. And we need Her Grace out there as well." Ciiris' lips quirked. "Even if we have to drape blankets around the both of you because no clothing will fit over two!"

"No need." Damien began gently extracting himself from under Genevieve. She made it easier by moving herself aside. It was easy to see that their hands were no longer bound... but as he got out of bed – Ciiris had seen him naked before, after all – he was pleased to realize he could still feel Genevieve. Not her thoughts; it was somewhere between emotions and physical sensations. It was enough to know that she was uncertain of how to proceed but that hell would freeze over before his beautiful, fierce duchess would let that show.

Ciiris raised an eyebrow. "Well and so. That was faster than any of us expected. Seems the lad has grown up." *That* made him blush.

"Cirii..." he said in a voice that he tried to make sound like a warning, but came out rather more like pleading.

"Hush, Damien. I've drawn you a bath and laid out clothing. Go make yourself decent. Your Grace," she addressed Genevieve and the two women regarded each other coolly. "I've laid out several outfits for you to choose from as well. We had to guess at your measurements – though Jason has an eye for such things – but there's laces for fit. You'll be quite presentable as a visiting dignitary and future Queen."

"How kind of you, Lady Celavell." Genevieve's face was closed, her tone icy. Damien knew that just as he had sensed *her* emotions, Genevieve had sensed his and knew – *knew* – that Ciriis had been his lover. That he still was fond of her.

Supposedly soul-bondeds were unable to bear the view or thought of someone else touching their partner, although there were other tales that suggested that some pairs were hardly inconvenienced by the entire event and certainly had no sense of each other's emotions. Clearly they were somewhere in the middle of that spectrum. Surely this reaction of Genevieve's was only the result of the magick that had so altered their path forwards. Damien didn't dare hope yet that she might harbor some finer feelings for him.

In this moment, however, the cause hardly mattered.

The young king looked at the two women looking at each other and fled to the bathing room.

When he came back, the tension had eased only slightly. Genevieve rose languidly to take her turn in the bathing room – not bothering to wrap a sheet around herself as she went. While part of his mind was well aware that she was making some kind of a point, he could not take her eyes off of her until she had vanished behind the door, and the sight of her left him slightly dazed and unsure to whom she had been making her point.

It was only when he realized that Ciriis was lighting lamps around the bedroom that he realized she was still there. It must be well past noon – of which day? – if the grey light had faded already from the high, narrow, clerestory windows in the peak of the tower. The ones on the northwestern side of the tower were blocked from sunlight by the castle's outer defensive fortifications.

Adam and Jason – and Ciriis – had examined every suite of rooms available to the Crown Prince when he was Named Heir and had chosen these as the least likely for assassins to get into. The bedchamber had exits only to the bathing chamber and an outer office and sitting room; the bathing chamber had no other exit at all. His men kept Guard on the door even when he was not in the rooms and escorted cleaning staff in and out. For that matter, as much of the cleaning as possible was done by the Royal Guards – both the obvious men and the secret cadre of women – themselves, despite their noble births, one and all. They were up in the top of a steep-pointed tower – part of the defensive battlements of the original, smaller castle – and only the side that faced the original inner bailey had a few windows besides the ones in the cap of the tower itself. It was a careful arrangement, but it was chilly in Winter and it did necessitate lamps, even in the daytime.

"Well," Ciriis said dryly as he finally looked at her. "At least your mouth isn't hanging open and drooling." She set the lamplighter down on a table and approached him. "I hope your wits will be better placed when you confront Lord Prydeen."

As was the habit with all of his Royal Guards, she placed a hand on his arm before mentioning the sorcerer's name. Not that it had helped since the crown had become Damien's and the Heir's Ring had refused to so much as stay on his finger. He'd taken to carrying it about in an inner pocket of his doublet in hopes that it would still lend him *some* protection, which was why he'd had it handy to give to Genevieve when she appeared so unexpectedly.

Confront Prydeen? Feeling as tongue-tied as ever in her presence, Damien could only give her a look of alarm and hope she was joking. But Ciriis' grim expression told him otherwise.

"Go out into your office," she shoved him towards the other door. "Adam and Jason have a report for you. I'll help your 'blushing bride' with her laces and stays."

"Ciriis...?" He wasn't sure what he should say, but he was positive that saying nothing was the wrong thing. There was no unfinished business between them, he had thought. He'd had other lovers – always from his Royal Guards, for whom else could he trust? – since their affair. Ones chosen by *her*, if it came to that.

And they had always all known that his marriage would be a political one. Some foreign princess, or the daughter – or ruling lady – of one of the Lost Provinces they were hoping to win back to Ilseador's ensign. Surely Ciriis had not thought he would choose *her* to be Queen-Consort...she was too tough and practical for such romantic notions.

The elegant woman shook her head, her careful and perfect chignon shining in the gentle lamplight – he knew that two of the long pins in it were actually poniards, but he could not guess what else she might have about her. Even if Ciriis were stark naked, she would be the least unarmed person in the room. Should he warn Genevieve?

"*Go*, Damien. Her Grace and I must come to our own understanding. You *did* draw her a fresh bath, I hope? Good boy, I taught you well – and running water to even such remote places as this is *one* thing we have to thank your grandfather for."

And he found himself in the outer office with the door shut firmly behind him.

Adam and Jason were waiting, as she had said. The former lounging against the wall, his usual look of irony more firmly in place than usual, the latter sitting in one of the comfortable leather chairs but leaning forward with an earnest expression on his face. Had they just been arguing?

"You're alone!" Jason Solway exclaimed, leaping to his feet. But his face fell as quickly as it had brightened. "Is everything all right?"

Damien did not even need to breathe a dreamy "Yes..." before Adam had strolled over and clapped Jason on the back. Apparently, his face gave it all away. "See, Jase, no need to worry. We expect an Heir before Summer then?" Adam grinned. "That was your theory, right?"

"I don't know, she said not, but then we were no longer handsfasted, but she's still with me..." Damien realized he wasn't making a lot of sense, but his friend just laughed.

"You'll be fine after some food," Adam opined and gestured to a tray.

Damien's stomach began gnawing on his ribcage as soon as he saw the piles of fresh sliced bread, butter, cold fried eggs, bacon, and porridge baked with apples. Still, out of responsibility, he doggedly began saying "Adam–"

"Eat," Adam insisted, pressing the young king to sit in another smooth leather chair, its ancient stuffing compacted to conform to the sitter. "We can't sort it all out without Her Grace's presence anyways, and you need to get your head on straight. And Ciriis would kill us if we either left *her* out or didn't feed you," he finished dryly as Jason laid a fried egg on a slice of buttered toast and handed it to Damien when he still hesitated. He was hungry enough to be nearly as single-minded about eating as he had been about *not*-eating when it was just him and Genevieve...

Simply the thought of her, drew him out of his food-focus, but the ladies had not yet appeared, so he continued eating, though a bit less singlemindedly.

"You know," Adam said idly, as Damien stuffed himself. "I wasn't too well-pleased with the spectacle you two made of this whole thing at the first, but I've come to see how it can be made to work. Certainly no one can deny the bond, nor that the Duchess of Elaarwen will be Queen-Consort." He selected a fresh apple and began peeling it the hard way, in one long spiral.

Jason stood back up and began to pace. Usually Adam was the more cynical, the more cagey of the two and Jason almost phlegmatic, though with the curiosity of a cat. Damien could not understand why Jason seemed to be the one filled with nervous energy today. "It's not *our* people, it's *hers*. She came here in secret, then vanished. Will they believe rumors? Lady Theresa sent a messenger, but when was the last time they had reason to believe a message from the Crown–"

"Surely they had other spies," Adam put in mildly, his words sounding like they were re-hashing an argument they had already had several times. "Even *had* she insisted on coming alone – and I know you say she well might have–" Adam waved off this consideration, "–even if she *had*, and I should hope she's grown in her savviness since you were children together, it having been nearly twenty years. But even if she had insisted on coming here alone, surely her people would have followed. *We* would have if this young idiot tried such a thing." He winked at Damien.

Jason had known Genevieve as a child? Well, they were of an age, and Damien vaguely recalled that Jason had been there at Court that same year he had seen Genevieve. Though he had been barely eight years old himself, and his memories of most of the rest of that time were, perhaps not surprisingly, incomplete. Or at least... uncomfortably inaccessible compared to his usual ability to recall. Not that improving his recall of those following days would be more comfortable.

He'd asked Jason to vouch for him on the viewing stand out of some instinct that had noticed a connection between his old friend and... his soul-bonded bride-to-be. Jason had mentioned a few times, in their deliberations on how to treat with the Rebellion, that he knew the Rebel Duchess, never quite suggesting that he should be the messenger but stating that he felt she could be trusted to negotiate in good faith. But Damien hadn't realized they might have been *close*.

Jason was going to wear a track in the rug. "She can be damned convincing and strong-willed when she wants to be. You don't know her. It's been so long *I* don't know her."

'I know her,' Damien wanted to say, but his mouth was full of porridge. He knew that she was confident in her people, and that she would give up her life and – yes – *his*, before she let them down. It didn't bother him – he felt the same way. Or... mostly. The young king wasn't certain that he could give up *Genevieve's* life for... anything. Or any*one*.

"She has to be willing to bring the Rebellion to an end or it's all for naught," Jason fretted.

"*She* might very well be willing to do that," commented the voice that made every bit of Damien perk up and pay attention. Genevieve's hand brushed his hair as she seated herself in the chair adjacent to his and something he hadn't even realized was tense in her absence relaxed. "What you have to understand, all of you," his beautiful soul-bonded continued as she proceeded to serve herself the porridge and pile it high with crunchy, fresh apple pieces and soft, brown sugar and crushed nuts and salted butter, exactly the way he liked it himself, "is that I am not the whole of the Rebellion, but merely its chief tactician. Rosa is the diplomat."

Having followed the duchess in, Ciriis seated herself elegantly across the table and accepted a cup of tea from Jason with a polite nod before raising a delicately sketched eyebrow. "Indeed. The Countess of Zialest, who turned the old king's youngest son into a poked pig is your diplomat. I begin to see why your rebellion has not improved its state over its long existence."

"Prince Oskar was a pig long before he ever encountered the young Countess," Adam stated grimly, and Jason winced and came over to squeeze his lover's shoulder in reassurance.

Ciriis tilted her head to grant Adam the point, though she clearly *conceded* nothing. "Our concern now is how to unify the rebels with the Crown – in a more than symbolic sense."

Her light, ironic way of speaking had never left Damien feeling frustrated before. How could she not understand that the soul-bonding changed everything? Was she really such a cynic – or was she jealous? Yet, down the bond itself, he sensed that Genevieve grudgingly agreed with Ciriis' assessment.

"We speak too plainly," Adam said abruptly.

Ciriis nodded and reached out one graceful, be-ringed hand to Damien. He caught it, marveling as always at how her skin was so perfectly smooth and silken – no calluses despite the skill he knew she wielded with long blade and knife.

Adam dropped into the chair to Genevieve's left and took her hand, startling Damien with how he didn't really want Adam to touch her. Which was entirely silly, since Adam – and Jason – were the last people whom he should ever have to worry about sharing Genevieve with, bound up with each other as they were, not to mention being his oldest friends and mentors. Jason leaned forward in his chair and accepted both Ciriis and Adam's other hands. They nodded to Genevieve and Damien to complete the circle.

Genevieve quirked an eyebrow at him, then with a half-smile and a shrug held out her hand. Sword- and bow-calluses matched his own, once more, and Damien could feel the tendrils of the bond reaching out to wrap their hands again... all he could notice was Genevieve's incredible eyes...

"This... may not have been a good idea..." Ciriis' ironic voice. She was here?

"But necessary. We have to talk." Adam.

Genevieve gently wrested her fingers out of his with a feeling of apology down the soul-bond. She wrested her beautiful blue eyes with that magickal hint of green gently from his as well, and turned to the rest. "Both a good idea, my lords and lady, and not."

She picked up the half-eaten bowl of porridge one-handed and balanced it on her knees. "We definitely need to talk. But Damien and I don't need to be in physical contact for this. Indeed," and why was *her* irony so much more palatable to him than Ciriis'? "I doubt we could make that work just yet – talking and physical contact."

"Damien?" Adam queried. "*She's* the one wearing the damned Ring."

Damien nodded. "I can feel it, though," he answered. "Pretty much as I did when I wore it myself as Heir."

Ciriis pursed her perfectly painted lips. "I hope 'pretty much' is enough, then."

"I suspect," Genevieve drawled, "that we don't even need to be in physical contact with the rest of you to make this work. But we can keep it up for now – since it makes you feel better." Damien picked up the distinct sense that she liked Ciriis' hand in his as little as he liked hers in Adam's.

The other woman's eyes sparked, but Adam cut in sharply. "We'll test the limits later – it would be handy to have more flexibility in these meetings. For now, though, we need to establish what the plan is, going forward. Jason?"

Jason ducked his head a bit. "The army is solidly with Damien. We've finally made contact with the last of the generals and there seems to be nothing but relief. Their overall response has been that a civil war benefits no one and that there are better things for their forces to be doing." He hesitated. "They want to put a stop to the territorial encroachments that became so common over these last few years, of course, but they also want to reclaim the Lost Provinces and pursue what they refer to as 'suitable chastisements'."

The army had been diverted in greater numbers over the past many years to deal with the Rebellion. It had hurt recruiting even when they tried to bring in soldiers from distant provinces so they weren't fighting their own kin, and had resulted in mass impressments. But the loss of five provinces that had rebelled earlier in the old king's reign and joined the neighboring Realms – and the fact that the old king had never seemed to care – was what really irked his generals.

"No surprise," Ciriis commented. "We've always planned to move the army to reclaim the Lost Provinces."

Damien nodded. "Agreed. So... what's the problem?" Jason's manner had suggested something was awry.

"Well..." Jason looked at Adam, plainly not willing to be the one to break the bad news. Jason was an excellent diplomat and messenger, but he tended to hate confrontation unless it involved a sword. Luckily – or not – his life-partner made up for this lack. In spades. And with a dry wit that cut as sharply as his sword.

Damien looked to Adam as well, but it was Genevieve who explained.

"Our dear Lord Wizard is the problem," she surmised. "He needs to demonstrate that he is the true power now... and he does that by opposing even your most rational and obvious policies." She turned to look at Adam directly. "He's insisting that the Rebellion must be crushed before anything else can move forward."

Damien swallowed hard. Surely even Lord Prydeen could see that wasn't necessary now that Genevieve was on their side.

But Adam was tilting his head in ironic acknowledgment. "Exactly so, Your Grace."

"He's putting about the word," Ciriis commented from the other side of the table, "that it is for Damien's benefit. That it must be clear that the young king is not your puppet."

"Indeed. I am sure he will approve of the wedding if I am come before the throne in chains." Genevieve did not sound surprised at all. And Damien had thought *he* had no unwarranted idealism left to lose...

Adam's eyes twinkled in appreciation. "I think he might be satisfied with bowed head and bended knee. Perhaps gilded ropes as a symbol of submission."

"Mine or Damien's?" she retorted. Clearly, they had a similar sense of dark humor. Surely it was a good thing that they should get along?

"There won't be any chains or ropes – or *submission,*" he declared. "Nor am I backing down on moving the army."

"All the same," Ciriis broke in smoothly, pulling his attention back to her. "Perhaps it would be better to do it quietly. Have General Celavell begin re-ordering the troops on the frontlines, shifting them without bringing them through the capitol."

"Not General Direlien?" Genevieve asked curiously. "Isn't he the Commander of the Army? Is he not within Damien's camp?"

Ciriis smiled coolly. "Indeed, he is. But General Celavell is his second, and as he is my uncle, I can get word to him without sending it through official channels." Genevieve frowned slightly. She momentarily seemed to want to say something else, but instead turned her attention back to her cooling bowl of porridge.

"All right," Damien moved things on after a brief pause. "What else? Have we heard back from Countess Zialest or anyone else from the Rebellion? Any sign that they are standing down?"

"No to both," Jason answered. "Lady Theresa sent off messages immediately, but there has hardly been time for the messages to be received, let alone get a reply. It's most likely that they simply don't yet know about yesterday's events." So, it had been only one day that he had been permitted with his newly soul-bonded bride-to-be. It seemed... unfair. Soul-bondings were known to take a week or longer before they settled. But he was a king, and she was the Rebel Duchess, and neither politics nor Lord Prydeen would await them it seemed.

It was seven days to Genevieve's ducal seat in Elaarwen on a good horse. Perhaps five if the rider pushed hard. Nearly two weeks before they would hear back at the earliest. Unless Countess Zialest had followed on the heels of her vanished lover to steal her back from whatever danger she might have fallen into...

Or at least to support her at slightly closer range; the Rebel Countess had a somewhat more cautious reputation than Genevieve... the impaling of his unlamented late uncle with a fire-poker notwithstanding. Not that Rosa Teraseel had had a great many options then either in the wake of her parents' and younger brother's murder and to save herself and her people. Prince Oskar had been known to cause 'general calamities' to occur to cover up his more egregious 'errors of judgment'.

They'd had no earlier word from their spies, but one woman alone could travel fast and light; likely all their secret eyes were still playing catch-up.

"Lord Prydeen is putting about the impression that Her Grace will now be considered a traitor to the Rebel Cause," Ciriis put in. "He has been saying that she would surely not have been in the city – would not have been atop the *royal reviewing stand* – if she were not actually fleeing the Rebellion to make common cause with you," she told Damien directly.

He could feel Genevieve rolling her eyes. "Well, at least he's not telling everyone I was there to murder Damien. Though I suppose that would only make a more dashing story – with the soul-bonding being so very obvious to everyone."

Adam laughed aloud, though with his usual wry twist. "Perhaps we *should* be worried about you, Your Grace. You seem to see into Lord Prydeen all too well. That is *also* exactly what he is suggesting."

"How does that work if she was supposedly fleeing for my protection?" Damien demanded. "Or... controlling me?"

"I'm sure it depends on whose ears he's pouring this stuff into," Genevieve noted. "Call me 'Genevieve,' Sir Loveress.' We can stand on ceremony in public, but we're used to much less formality out in the hills... and since you are Jason's love, and Damien's friend, I can safely say you are my friend as well." She fixed him with a stern look. "But *not* 'Genny,' no matter what Jason has told you."

Adam gave her a smile that had much less irony in it than usual. "I would be pleased if you would call me 'Adam'."

"Very nice," Ciriis interrupted the moment. "But the part about Her Grace controlling you is serious, Damien. You daren't let the Court see anything that might lend credence to that idea. You need to be seen as strong and not under anyone's control."

"Which means..." Jason put in reluctantly, "...that you cannot touch each other in public."

Damien met Genevieve's gaze. They both knew it was true. They had lost track of time shortly ago with several people talking directly to them and holding their hands. The Court, whether or not Lord Prydeen was present, would be too dangerous a place for such a lapse. It would be better for all the gathered nobles to see each of them as a powerful leader in their own right and not to remind them of just how strongly – and potentially fatally – the soul-binding connected them.

"Perhaps you shouldn't even look at each other," Ciriis' voice cut in so dryly that Damien almost reached for a cup of water.

He wrenched his attention back to Ciriis. "Why not?"

"How long was it this time, Jason?" she asked.

"Only about thirty seconds," Jason replied.

"That's not so bad..." Damien protested.

"Do you know what we were talking about in that time?" Ciriis challenged him. "Adam asked you two questions and you mumbled something affirmative each time."

"Oh."

Genevieve gave him a sympathetic look. "It might be easier when we aren't sitting so close... or linked in this circle through the others... or when we're more used to it. But until then... they're right, I'm afraid."

Adam pulled his hand free from hers. "We should be heading out. There is a Royal Council meeting, and then Damien has Audiences. It would be the obvious opportunities to introduce Her Gr– Genevieve – to the Council and the Court." He stood up and stretched, Jason following suit.

"I will escort Damien, as usual," Ciriis announced. "Jason must escort Her Grace. The Solways are only Counts, of course, but that will do." To Damien's surprise, both Genevieve and Jason seemed discommoded by that.

A further minor power struggle ensued when Genevieve returned to the bedroom for footwear (he had noticed her naked toes with a secret delight while they ate) and came back wearing her riding boots instead of the delicate slippers Ciriis had provided. As Mistress of Protocol, Ciriis was dutifully scandalized. But his beautiful soul-bonded pointed out, quite reasonably Damien felt, that the slippers did not fit her very well.

The riding boots also added a couple inches of height, he realized, as Ciriis lined them all up with some disgruntlement. Genevieve was almost exactly his height while wearing them... he resolutely turned his thoughts away from how that could be... *useful*... and focused on the inevitable confrontation with Lord Prydeen.

Chapter FOUR

Betrayed...

GENEVIEVE VERY CAREFULLY PLACED HER hand in the curve of Jason Solway's proffered elbow. The fabric of his shirt covered all of his skin, of course. It was safe. Not that it could be anything but safe – she was soul-bonded to the king, after all, a more permanent and inextricable connection than any other besides the Binding of a ruler to her lands. Nonetheless, the woman knew her old friend was just as discomfited by what had happened between them on the reviewing stand as she was... and just as relieved not to have to touch her bare skin.

They exchanged a quick look laden with irony, and she tilted her chin up in a tiny gesture somewhere between acknowledgment and defiance. His smile twisted ever so slightly.

She hoped Damien hadn't noticed the exchange at all, but he was standing at the door with Lady Celavell, ready to step out, and she had been engaging him in conversation about something or other. He seemed oblivious. Lady Celavell, however, had eyes even sharper than her tongue and Genevieve was not at all sure *she* hadn't seen the odd exchange.

Adam Loveress had slipped out the door ahead, presumably to prepare the escort of Royal Guards to accompany them. Genevieve was startled to realize that she trusted him implicitly – and his sharpness and dark irony reassured her in a way that Lady Celavell's remarkably similar approach did not.

Of course, it didn't help that the woman – clearly a former lover of her soul-bonded husband-to-be – had appeared in their bedchamber whilst they slept and then tried to get her to wear those slithery slippers. No heel at all; barely even a sole. They would hardly stand up to walking and had slopped around her feet, making 'slippers' rather too descriptive a term. Her boots also took her from being a woman of slightly above average height to being a tall one. Genevieve's father had taught her that one needed every tool in dealing with courtiers, and the couple extra inches of height that those boots gave her kept taller men – like Lord Prydeen – from being able to look down at her as if she were a child.

She rather thought that the savvy Lady Celavell knew that trick, too. And that not all her outrage was merely at the impropriety of wearing riding boots with a court gown.

The woman was one of Damien's most trusted advisors, Genevieve reminded herself, as she was introduced to the trusted young men guarding the door and mentally filing away their names. It made no sense that Lady Celavell would try to undermine or sabotage Damien's intended co-ruler and consort. She would have greater opportunities and greater safety under his rule than under any alternative and had actively worked, despite the terrible danger, to ensure he reached his throne. Perhaps she had not yet come to realize that Genevieve and Damien were so tightly bound that to undermine one would be to damage the other.

And yet... and yet she was pushing for Damien not to openly exert his powers and issue new orders to the army, even when the generals apparently agreed with those new orders. How did that help him solidify his position, if he was not to be seen exerting his authority? Perhaps it was merely that the four of them had been working covertly for so long. Old habits were hard to break...

Genevieve wished she truly felt that it was that simple.

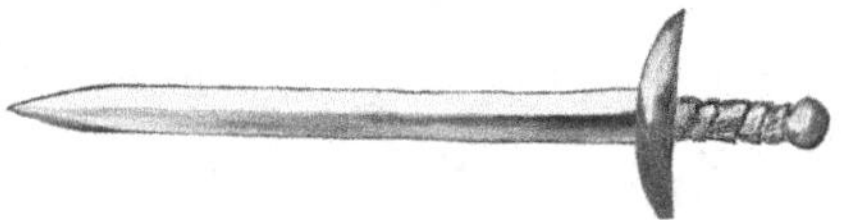

The Council meeting was brief, to Damien's mingled concern and relief.

He introduced Genevieve to everyone. She knew them all, of course, some even familiarly (was it disturbing that his Lord Exchequer was on grandfatherly terms with her already?). They knew of her at minimum by reputation, and seemed willing to give her the benefit of the doubt.

These were all redoubtable men and women, lords and ladies of the Realm, who had weathered the old king's whims by being both very unremarkable and very, *very* good at their jobs. It was a mixed blessing. Because they had kept the kingdom functioning, his grandfather and Lord Prydeen had been freer to wreak their evil plans, but on the other hand it was to their credit that Damien had a kingdom at all. His studies of history – well-hidden amongst the legends and fairytales – had made it very clear to him that, without a working bureaucracy to levy taxes and dispense funds, a ruler was essentially powerless because he had to do everything himself. Beyond the rule of a hamlet, it was simply impossible to handle all of the details alone.

Thusfar, Damien had seen no need to replace any of them, though he was keeping a close eye on the Minister of Trade and the Minister of Public Works. They both seemed to have prospered a bit too much during his grandfather's reign to be truly honest. He had wondered about the Lord Exchequer, not seeing how the others could have succeeded without his collusion, but Genevieve seemed genuinely fond of the old fellow, and he trusted her judgment.

There was only one woman currently on the council: the redoubtable Lady Theresa Anvliyar, Dowager Baroness of Cedarwen, whom he had appointed as his Secretary and Chatelaine. His grandfather had not retained anyone for those positions in some decades. Damien was not yet sure how that could possibly have worked, since her job was to organize his papers, his castle, and large events such as his coronation, and in just this short month he had seen how overwhelming that task was. What the ministers were to the kingdom, Lady Theresa was to the king himself. He had known the baroness for some years, for she had served as Royal Librarian since the death of her husband. Ciriis, in her official capacity as Mistress of Protocol, reported to Lady Theresa.

Lord Prydeen did not deign to attend.

Genevieve was brilliant, but reticent. She answered the Council's anxious questions about the likelihood of a *détente*, or even a treaty to end the Rebellion, but she volunteered nothing and deferred to Damien where possible. He knew from his studies of her that his beautiful soul-bonded studied and assessed a situation before taking action. She was unlikely to defer to him for long.

The questions wound down and Damien dismissed the Council.

Royal Audiences were next; Ciriis reclaimed his arm and Jason escorted Genevieve. Adam played rearguard and four other male Royal Guards were conspicuous to the fore and sides as they passed through the halls. Damien fretted a bit, wishing that it could be Genevieve on his arm instead, but Ciriis' arguments were all valid.

She delivered him to the throne with her usual flair, curtsying deeply and backing away to end standing behind his right shoulder as usual. Was she just a shade farther forwards than normal? She seemed to block his view a bit more than he was used to, though that didn't bother him since Ciriis' presence was as much secret bodyguard as to see to any of his needs and carry out his orders while he sat in audience. She must have her eye on some particular situation developing among his nobles, he decided. Knowing that she would tell him of it when there was something he needed to know was a great relief. Damien was a practiced people-watcher, but it had become far more difficult to do that as king than it had been as the disregarded grandson or even the "laughably innocent" Heir. Ciriis, Jason, and Adam had become his surrogates in that respect and he was grateful that he had people he could trust.

Damien introduced Genevieve formally to the gathered nobles before sitting down on the throne, inviting them to "Give welcome to Her Grace, Duchess Genevieve Stellarine of Elaarwen, newly named Heir to the Throne and soon to be your Queen-Consort!"

The nobles applauded politely enough, but made no move to approach her, even after Genevieve had been seated on a regal-looking chair of carved wood. It was placed to Damien's left, off the rather narrow stepped dais on which the throne sat, and turned so that she could easily face both the nobles and the king. Adam stood at attention at her left shoulder, a Knight of the Realm and a perfect bodyguard. Damien's grandfather had likely introduced all of his queens just so, but the attractive center of power had never shifted away from the king and Lord Prydeen. Genevieve came with her own measure of power, but how she might retain it was yet to be seen, as far as the nobles were concerned.

Jason had bowed her quite properly into the chair and then drifted off to mingle. His major function at these audiences was to gauge the mood of the nobles, pick up gossip, and be an informal ear for the king. His role was well-known if unremarked upon, his honest, open countenance a mirror of his depths such that he rarely was privy to anything particularly dark or urgent. It was the ladies of the Royal Guard who were Damien's true spies among the nobles.

Golden Lena, pale Arillys, Felena who never wore anything but teal, and nearly a dozen others. All of them had been his lovers after Ciriis. They were all discreet, but also highly trained in the many arts and weapons that a noblewoman might wield even under his grandfather's repressive regime. His rank as Heir had been able to shield them somewhat from both his grandfather and Lord Prydeen, for neither had been willing to take them after Damien and both had been content that the young Heir had appeared to be indulging himself in thoughtless pleasure. (Truth to tell, most of them had come to his service after having "served" the old king. Ciriis had approved their addition to the secret cadre of his bodyguards with a certain grimness. Damien had asked no questions, but had made it his mission to never let these young women suffer such things again... and to show them as best he could that they were wonderful and lovable.) The young ladies were at least as dedicated to his success as king as were their brothers and cousins. In some cases, they had been recruited – by Jason, Adam, or Ciriis in most cases – to *replace* a brother or a cousin who had been assigned to Damien's guards and who was either corrupt or dissolute.

He watched them now, glittering jewels moving about his Court. It would make sense, Damien mused, for at least some of them to be assigned as ladies-in-waiting to Genevieve. It would provide her with a cadre of unexpected but highly trained guardswomen as well as a source of information. He beckoned to Ciriis, who stood at his shoulder for just such things, and asked her to see to it. She still seemed to be standing a little closer than normal, but that merely made it easier for him to pass on the instruction.

The Royal Audience was as dull as ever, leaving Damien much time for his own thoughts. His grandfather had held Court in recent years only for his own amusement – usually to announce some punishment or to survey the younger children remaining to the noble families – and never for the purposes of dispensing justice. The nobles gathered to bask in the presence of royalty, hoping to gain some shine of their own by proximity, but not to rouse his interest and be invited so close as to be burnt. In the month since his passing, Damien had held Royal Audiences daily, extending the offer for any noble to air their grievances and seek the King's Justice. Surely there must be many unresolved difficulties that his grandfather had not addressed; nobles could not seek redress from the commoners' courts.

In that long month, not one had yet sought to do so.

He had thought about hunting out the problems that they were dealing with out of the reports Lady Theresa brought him. Bring out a couple of cases that could be resolved to everyone's satisfaction just to create a sense that his nobles could trust him... even if *he* didn't really trust the ones who actually attended the court. Lady Theresa had advised against it, suggesting that he should simply be patient once more. Damien was very tired of patience.

Perhaps Genevieve would have some advice on the subject. She had been ruling her duchy for the last two years.

It was completely natural for Damien to turn his gaze towards his soul-bonded... his *betrothed*. One of the other women – Lena?

– was talking to Ciriis on his right, so she wouldn't notice that Damien wasn't obeying her injunction not to look at Genevieve. She had actually stepped forwards slightly, but she would still be on her guard on his right, so he was free to turn to his left...

His eyes caressed Genevieve, noting that she was carefully watching all the interactions of the glittering crowd. He could hardly wait to hear her evaluations...

Because he was watching the red-haired duchess so closely, and because he was so very attuned to her just now, he could not help noting when her eyes took on a slightly glassy look, her ears flushed just a bit, and her hands trembled on the arms of her elegant chair. It was a look that made all those same things happen to him. He remembered it well from their time alone together.

Perhaps it was time to end this farce of an Audience and take her back to the bedchamber... Was she thinking the same? She seemed to have her gaze fixed in one particular direction...

Damien's eyes followed the direction of Genevieve's gaze...

...she was looking at Jason Solway. Who was standing half-frozen staring back at her with the same glassy look and slight flush.

Surely, *surely* Jason must be looking at his lover, Adam, standing at Genevieve's left shoulder. Damien had seen them exchange lovesick gazes often enough, though rarely in public. Though perhaps things were different enough now that he was on the throne...

But no. Adam was scanning the room for dangers as a good bodyguard should.

Jason's expression was unhappy, even desperate.

Genevieve's was... Damien suddenly realized he had known her for less than two days and had no idea how to interpret her expression. Or no idea beyond the fact that her interest in Jason Solway clearly went beyond that of a childhood playmate.

Something inside of Damien felt like it was crumbling. Or freezing. Or both.

"Your Majesty," Ciriis murmured. "The herald."

Damien looked across the room to the broad archway that marked the distinction between the antechamber and the throne room. The herald stationed there was just filling his lungs to announce the arrival of Lord Prydeen.

The sorcerer was flanked by his picked guards, but they stayed on the other side of the arch, as per protocol. This Audience was for those of noblebirth alone; Damien had others open to commoners, where the goal was justice dispensed rather than to detect dissatisfaction and collusion amongst the so-called peers of the Realm.

The cloak Lord Prydeen wore today was of somewhat finer stuff than the more serviceable one he had worn in the marketplace, but it was still deeply cowled and his face still shrouded in shadows.

"My Lord Prydeen, the Royal Sorcerer!"

Lord Prydeen strode forward as if he owned the room and the gathered nobles shrank back as if in agreement that he did. Damien still had to force himself to stay seated, even sprawled, lounging on his throne as if the thought that he belonged anywhere else had never crossed his mind.

Oh, would that he had some magick to match the evil old man.

It was said that the Monarch's Blade defended its owner against all spells, even as the Heir's Ring defended one's thoughts and words. The Blade was supposed to be somewhere in the Royal Treasury, but he had not yet found a way to hunt for it without arousing Lord Prydeen's suspicions. Should the man know Damien was looking for it, but had not yet found the Blade, it would be a disaster. And that was assuming that the Blade was still about somewhere to be found and not hidden away in Lord Prydeen's possession already. Damien could not imagine why the sorcerer would not have claimed it, but since he felt sure that, too, would have been flaunted in his face, it gave hope to his own eventual search.

Lord Prydeen stopped his advance at the very foot of the dais, not slowing until he actually halted, and giving the impression that he intended to stride right to the top and perhaps take the throne himself, Damien or no. He certainly did not kneel or bow as he had done with the old king, but stared haughtily at the young one now lounging on the throne.

Haughtily, but with his head tilted slightly upwards, tall though the sorcerer was. This smaller Audience room – along with every other official space within the palace – had been redesigned some fifty years earlier by the old king and Lord Prydeen himself to use every trick to intimidate. Damien knew it irritated the sorcerer to have those tricks working against him now and always made certain to act the innocent about all the small touches that made it work.

"My Lord Prydeen," he stated. It always felt like he was somehow losing some sort of contest by speaking first, but protocol required that no one else could speak before the king acknowledged them.

"Your Majesty," Lord Prydeen ground out. Damien supposed it was some sort of courtesy that prevented him from simply stating his demands rather than following Court protocol.

"Is there aught that you are seeking today, my lord?" Damien inquired carelessly. "We had noted your absence in Council, and so had not thought to see you this day." While he always took care to sound both innocent and slightly disengaged when speaking to Prydeen, usually it left his innards in a knot. A series of knots. Simply knowing that the man in front of him had the Power to do whatever he wished and Damien still had no idea why he constrained himself from simply taking the throne was terrifying, and it was all the young man could do to hide his reaction.

Today, however, Damien's thoughts and emotions were elsewhere and the evil old sorcerer seemed somehow less terrifying. Or at least he was less aware of the terror.

"I am come to see how true are the rumors about this woman." Lord Prydeen did not turn to look at Genevieve, who was slightly behind him, but directed a sneer in her direction nonetheless. Damien could feel – unwillingly – how intense was her scrutiny of the exchange. "And to arrange for private converse with you. Your *Maj*esty."

Lady Theresa had recommended moving his Royal Audiences from the cavernous and cold throne room of grey stone that was central to Castle Alsterling to this one. The floor here was warm tiles of brown and yellow marble, the walls covered with muted tapestries of historical events instead of the garish war banners that fluttered in high recrimination in the old hall. But best of all, the ceiling here was barely twice Damien's own height. Lord Prydeen simply could not *loom* and spread a feeling of chill fear in this space. Sometimes Damien wondered if his grandfather had designed the room to intentionally cancel out some of his pet sorcerer's minor powers; certainly, most of the arguments he had overheard between them had been here... *after* the courtiers had been dismissed.

The young king smiled, feeling as reckless as his heart felt frozen. "And what could rumor possibly say that you would not have seen for yourself, my Lord? You were there beside Us when We found Ourselves soul-bound. One might assume that the binding occurred under your blessing – if not more."

He heard Ciriis' sharp in-breath though it was all but soundless. He felt eyes all over the room fastening upon him with avid interest. It was as close to a challenge as Damien had yet dared make for the confrontation that everyone knew was coming.

"I had discovered her in the city, Your *Maj*esty, and sought to prevent her from damaging your royal Presence or the solemnity of your coronation festivities. It is not meet for a king to receive rebellious vassals without proper precautions."

Take me *to task for carelessness? In front of the full Court?* Damien seethed internally.

"Indeed," he said aloud, allowing a small smirk to play about his lips. "How fortunate that the Gods had Their own plans and deigned to protect Us Themselves."

Touché? The sorcerer had implied he was there to protect Damien, and the young king had implied he hadn't been very good at it. Indeed, that the soul-binding suggested the very Gods were watching over him in the sorcerer's place. Perhaps time for a retreat, no matter how much Damien felt like letting this play out. Discretion was surely the better part of valor in dealing with a man whose Power he couldn't – yet – hope to match.

He stood and stretched and spoke the words that Lord Prydeen would have expected.

"It pleases Us to grant the more private audience you have requested." More private, yet not alone, for Damien would never be such a fool as to be left alone with Lord Prydeen. It had occurred to him that Prydeen had never pressed for perfect privacy – perhaps *he* did not wish to be seen to be turning Damien into a puppet-king.

Or perhaps he merely disregarded Damien's thusfar minor efforts to exert his kingly status, and the young king himself, as inconsequential.

What *was* the long game that the sorcerer was playing, now that the old king was gone?

"My lords and ladies," Damien spoke to the room, "I bid you good day. Do accompany Us, my lord," he said politely enough to Lord Prydeen, descending the dais in Genevieve's general direction, but only because that was the same direction as the door he intended to leave by.

She had risen as well, of course, since it was against protocol for anyone else to remain seated when the king stood. Jason was at the Duchess' side, and he felt Ciriis come up behind him, both of them ready to take the arms of their respective charges and properly escort them away. There was no way he was going to allow Jason to touch Genevieve again in his presence. Damien's skin prickled at the very thought.

Though somehow, he didn't want Ciriis by his own side just now either.

"Lord Solway, you shall ready the practice courts. I fear I have not had leisure to hone my bladework under your tutelage during the coronation events and it is surely time to remedy that lack. Lady Celavell, please settle her Grace of Elaarwen in a suitable apartment and with suitable personnel that she may exert her best efforts on behalf of the Realm." Damien noted that both Jason and Genevieve seemed somewhat startled. Good. Now to keep Adam also out of Genevieve's orbit. "Sir Loveress, Lord Prydeen and I shall be conversing in the Amber Room. Send ahead to be sure it is prepared with food and drink."

With not one look at the Duchess of Elaarwen, and with the still fragile bond locked down tight between them, Damien swept out of the audience chamber, his hated sorcerer at his heels.

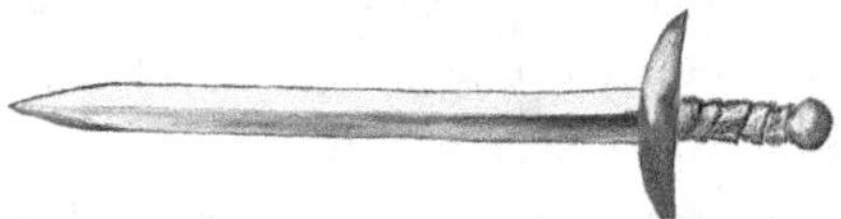

The rooms were nearly as secure as Damien's, and only a floor below his in the same tower. The arrangement was similar. There were no windows at all here, however, not even the nearly useless clerestory ones that lit Damien's suite. Perhaps this was *more* secure. It was certainly more *depressing*.

Genevieve raised her eyebrows at the sparse lamps Lady Celavell had sent ahead to have lit. Two maids were still changing out the linens for fresh, but the air was unbearably still. It was not dank, since they were still several stories above ground-level, but the air was stale. She found herself hoping it would be cool enough, in the opinions of these lowlanders, to light a fire, since that would draw fresher air into the room.

The maids left, bobbing curtsies as they did so, laden with linens as they were.

"Is this *your* plan, Lady Celavell?" Genevieve decided to be blunt.

Damien's behavior in the audience chamber made no sense.

This *room* made no sense.

It *might* have been all a farce put on for the benefit of Lord Prydeen and those vulpine nobles who remained from his grandfather's court. But something told her it had not been.

Ciriis Celavell did not pretend to not know what she was talking about and gave her a smile with too many teeth in it. "Damien makes his own choices, Your Grace, no matter what you may think."

A sharp knock and young Sir Timothy Ancellius poked his head in. Genevieve had been introduced to him on the walk back here – the energetic and humorous man was apparently Captain Loveress' Second and therefore in charge of her own security for the time being.

"Lena and Aryllis are here, Ciriis, Your Grace." Two beautiful women entered following this statement, and Sir Ancellius closed the door behind them.

"Your Grace of Elaarwen, may I present Miss Lena Devergnon and Lady Aryllis Ieldore," Lady Celavell introduced them very properly.

Miss Devergnon was a merry golden-brown blonde with warm brown eyes, and a pleasantly rounded figure. Lady Ieldore was blonde as well, but a shade so pale it was almost white, serious grey eyes, and was on the willowy side. They were close to Genevieve and Ciriis' own age, in their mid- or late-twenties, and carried themselves with the confidence of people who knew how to defend themselves by force of arms. Their brocade gowns were highest court fashion, but the Duchess suspected they had been designed to let the women move freely. Genevieve did not need to be told that they were members of Damien's secret Royal Guards.

"Lena and Aryllis will be your first Ladies-in-Waiting," Lady Celavell went on. "You may rely upon them to see to whatever you need. Starting with a visit from a dressmaker, I should think." She gave them a sharp nod, and they nodded back. "There will be two Royal Guardsmen outside your door at all times, and we will take the same precautions with your safety as we do with Damien's. He asked me to be sure you had some of our ladies with you."

"Excellent," Genevieve forced herself to drawl it. It would not do to show any weakness before these women. She understood that the pair of blondes were Damien's spies on the Court and that they reported to Lady Celavell. They were here to honor her, yes, but also to protect her. And, doubtless, to report on her to Lady Celavell, if not to Damien himself. Genevieve's heart constricted. "Will not all this duplication of effort strain your resources, Lady Celavell?"

The small, dark-haired woman shrugged as if she honestly did not know why they were doing all this. "We all serve at His Majesty's pleasure. I'm sure Damien has good reasons. I hope you will wait to ask him yourself and not rely upon – old acquaintances." Dammit, she *had* seen the awkward moment with Jason earlier. "If you will permit me to make my farewell, Your Grace, I have other duties to attend to."

Genevieve made a gesture of acquiescence, and Lady Celavell departed. She was left regarding the two newcomers. Not quite knowing what to do next, she seated herself at the well-appointed small desk, noting in passing that the ebony wood of the writing surface had been polished to a high sheen. Ebony was precious stuff, having to be shipped from as far away as Zigazwe. Nothing but the best for the – Queen-Consort-to-be? The Rebel Duchess-imprisoned? She wondered how hard it would be for her leave these quarters.

Apparently, the women were not long on ceremony. Miss Devergnon flung herself onto the couch in the central seating area and twisted around to lay her arm along it's back and face Genevieve. Lady Ieldore collapsed rather more gracefully into a chair, shaking her head. "This place needs far more lighting. It's easy to secure, and it's close to Damien's rooms, but there's absolutely nothing else to recommend it. I don't suppose you're fond of embroidery, Your Grace? There's a lovely solarium not far from here that the fifth and seventh queens used to use. It would get us out of this gloom and would be nearly as safe."

Genevieve quirked a half-smile. "I'm afraid I'm not much of a hand with a needle, but I suppose I could develop a sudden passion for learning."

Miss Devergnon laughed. "Oh, Aryllis didn't tell you the best part. The solar has lovely long mirrors, thick rugs, and enough space to practice hand-to-hand sparring and even some bladework if we set the place up properly. We hear," she added enthusiastically, "that you are excellent with a sword."

That brought a real grin to Genevieve's face. "That *is* a sharp object I do have some skill with," she admitted.

"It's one I'd like to learn better," Lady Ieldore told her. "Our opportunities to learn were severely limited under the old king. My best skills are with the garotte and hunting hawks," she said frankly. "I'm a bit shy of knifework – all that blood close up – but I have some of the Old Skills and I can sometimes see through the eyes of a hawk."

"I'm the royal poisoner," Miss Devergnon put in. "No one ever guesses, because I am an absolutely hopeless cook. It's mostly about watching for attempts to poison Damien rather than anything offensive. You, too, now. And Jason and Adam insisted I become adept at some sort of weapon, so–"

With pride she pulled a short but sturdy chain out of her skirt pocket. As Genevieve looked baffled, she demonstrated the clasps at either end. "I can use it on its own or attach it to any number of common objects about the castle. My favorite is to use a candlestick and a metal pomander ball to turn it into a chain-mace. Candlesticks are everywhere, of course, but it's hard to find a reason to carry a pomander around, so frequently I use two candlesticks like this..."

Miss Devergnon demonstrated how two silver candlesticks connected to the short chain could be swung around to devastating effect. The curvaceous, merry blonde laughed again. "Another blunt instrument. I'm not much for blood either."

Genevieve regarded them both with some bemusement. Their skills were creative and subtle. She herself had been trained in the use of the sword and the bow from childhood, and trained to lead troops in battle, as was a noble's place. She had been the Rebellion's chief strategist for the Battle of Siovale, as well as the on-the-ground general for the Elaarwen troops and fought at the side of her new husband,

Harald. His brother, Duke Tomas, had served as field marshal for their forces. That had been the Rebellion's first real declaration of its intent to refuse the authority of the old king…

It had become harder for noblewomen to follow that tradition of becoming warriors as the old king's reign had ground on, given his irrational distaste for women who bore arms. Yet these women had found their own options. And in the close confines of the castle, their approaches might be more effective. Genevieve had been masquerading as a commoner in the marketplace and had borne no weapons besides a few knives – her sword and bow were stored for now with a sympathetic farmer out beyond the limits of the capitol city. Could these 'ladies-in-waiting' use their multifarious talents to somehow have them retrieved? Or find her new weapons? Could she learn to use theirs?

"You're both being very open about all of this," she suggested. "Doesn't Lord Prydeen have ears everywhere?"

"Oh, milady," Miss Devergnon laughed. "Jason told us that you said you can shield others without even touching them, now that you wear the Heir's ring."

"*Such* a relief," Lady Ieldore sighed. "Conferences with everyone trying to put a hand on Damien or on someone touching Damien... that was the extent of his range."

"Not that touching Damien was a chore," Miss Devergnon giggled, then rolled her eyes at Lady Ieldore's sharp look. "Unnecessary secrets only cause trouble, Aryllis. Better she know straight off than have one of those horrid Court vultures throw it in her face unexpectedly." She turned to Genevieve with a serious, but kind expression. "All of the women in the secret Royal Guards – including Aryllis and myself – have been Damien's lovers."

"Including Lady Celavell." Genevieve didn't ask, so much as state it as a fact.

"Lena..." Lady Ieldore moaned.

Miss Devergnon nodded briskly. "She was his first."

Genevieve smiled over another brief constriction of her heart. "Then it seems I have a debt of gratitude to all of you, but perhaps most of all to her." And she did. These women had done more than introduce her soul-bonded to the ways of loving. They had directed his youthful passions in safe directions... Harald had proved to Genevieve just how important that was. She paused. "Let's dispense with the 'Graces' here at least. We're much less formal in Elaarwen."

Lena Devergnon beamed at her. "Jason told us you'd say that. He said you threatened Adam with dire consequences if he called you by a short-name, though! Did you really know Jason Solway when you were children? I can't recall seeing you at Court."

Genevieve relaxed. Even if these women were planning to spy on her for Lady Celavell, they could still be friendly. There was nothing she had to hide from Damien, after all, and little she would wish to conceal from Lady Celavell. Her heart twinged slightly at the almost-truth. That she hadn't yet decided how to handle her reactions to Jason Solway meant there was nothing to conceal, didn't it?

"I wasn't at Court for long. Just one Summer. Though it was *all* Summer. The sixty-seventh year of the Old Reign, I think it was. I was twelve and Jason was thirteen. I decided to explore the city after my nurse thought I was tucked in bed. The Solway's home abutted ours, and Jason's window overlooked the wall I was climbing over. He decided not to let me get into too much trouble. We exchanged a few letters – mostly about my continued hijinks – for the next few years, but then we drifted out of touch as we both... grew up." What a euphemism.

Aryllis nodded. "Jason was twenty when I came to Court. All the girls were swooning over him."

Lena grinned. "They were doing that when I arrived when he was fifteen. How did you escape his 'glamourie', Your Gra– Genevieve?"

Genevieve shrugged a little self-consciously. "He was just Jason."

And *he* hadn't been interested in *her,* even knowing that it was 'safe' to do so given that her father and his mother were playing with the idea of betrothing the two of them. People married early in the mountains of Elaarwen, so she knew what that meant; Genevieve had used that Summer to see what sort of person the serious young man might be. It hardly mattered – then *or* now, though she'd spent years daydreaming over the idea.

Now, of course, it was obvious that he 'leaned the other way' and his pairing with Adam was clearly a good one. She'd rather have had Jason Solway as a friend at any point anyways.

Lena nodded wisely. "You were twelve – not interested yet."

"Not that it would have done her any good," Aryllis noted, as she looked over her perfectly manicured nails. "And later it might have been dangerous to come between Prince Oskar and his favorite toy."

This was history Genevieve had not heard. "What?"

Aryllis refused to meet her eyes. "It's his story to tell. Or not. But I daresay Jason is looking forward to meeting your Countess of Zialest."

Chapter FIVE

Broken...

TWO WEEKS LATER, GENEVIEVE WAS looking forward to seeing the Countess of Zialest far more than Jason Solway could possibly be.

When Rosa swept into the room, the Rebel Duchess practically collapsed into tears in her arms. Lena and Aryllis were torn between discreetly leaving the two of them together and staying to translate, since Genevieve couldn't seem to put words together.

Genevieve had arranged to have Rosa come to her in the sitting room of her prison-like suite. She didn't want anyone – least of all Lady Celavell – to see her in this state. She wasn't worried about Lena and Aryllis anymore. They had watched her decline helplessly and they seemed to have been won over to her side in sympathy. Genevieve had watched her grandmother, the Grand Duchess, wither away when she herself was a child and knew how disconcerting the loss of strength of a powerful person was for everyone around them. To watch a decline happen in days rather than over months and years... must only be the moreso.

"My dear!" Rosa held her at arms' length after the first storm of weeping. "Gen, what has happened? Surely *this* can't be the result of a true soul-bonding! What has that boy done to you?" She pulled Genevieve close again as the weeping renewed.

Lena sighed from Genevieve's other side, and patted the long, red hair. It hung lank, and lusterless, just as the beautiful new gowns made since her arrival hung loose on her gaunt frame. "It's the result of a soul-bonding *denied,* milady Countess."

Rosa looked at the ladies-in-waiting, her eyes full of questions.

Aryllis shrugged. She hid her concern behind her usual cool manner, but loose strands of her straight, pale hair crept out of her neat coiffure where she tugged at it in distress. "We don't know what is wrong. The first day, in the Royal Audience, Damien couldn't keep his eyes off her. She was studying the room, but sneaking glances at him whenever she could. It went on for two hours like that – she tells us that Lady Celavell had told them not to look at each other because when they did at breakfast, they lost all sense of time. But by the time Lord Prydeen walked in, Damien wouldn't look at her at all."

"Milady has been attending the king for the morning strategy session," Lena added in. "With Lady Celavell, Lord Solway, and Sir Loveress. And the Council sessions. And she sits in on the Royal Audiences. But Damien won't acknowledge her presence else."

Kindly, Lena did not mention that Genevieve had taken to watching Damien practice at arms from a hidden window. She knew by now that the Rebel Duchess was as strong a person as the rumors had painted her and that even in this state, and even to someone as dear to her as the Rebel Countess, she would hate to appear so... dependent. Even when she'd just greeted Rosa by collapsing in tears.

The three women had taken to practicing their own weapons-work in the solarium for much of the rest of the day, since Genevieve had so much nervous energy to use up. She was teaching them the use of the sword, and they were sharing their own, more subtle, techniques with her. Some of the other women of the Royal Guard had come in to participate in the lessons. They were not precisely excluding their male counterparts, but there was a certain understanding that it might be inappropriate for the king's betrothed and soul-bonded bride to be practicing hand-to-hand combat against men in such circumstances.

Unfortunately, the intense sessions only made the overall problem worse. Genevieve had been eating less and less. She hadn't been able to keep anything down for the last three days and hadn't even tried eating today.

"Ciriis might know." Aryllis had turned away to lean casually on the mantelpiece, and did not turn back to make the comment. Her face was paler than her hair, and her lips were compressed tightly. She clearly didn't want to say anything, but felt compelled.

Rosa pursed her lips and bundled the limp Genevieve back into Lena's arms.

"I'll be back shortly."

It was a shorter trip than the Rebel Countess had anticipated. As she stepped out the door to demand that one of the door guards take her to Lady Celavell, she practically tripped over the woman.

Ciriis looked like a woman whose plans had gone vastly awry... but only to someone who was as good at reading people as Rosa. Or who had known her as long as Rosa.

"My office," Ciriis said, and led the way.

Ciriis' office was larger than Rosa would have expected. It was attached to the Royal Archives and included space for several large tables. Maps pinned to the tables showed complex seating arrangements and orders of precedence for some sort of parade. Books were left open showing family trees and traditional heraldry banners.

"The Royal Wedding," Ciriis waved at the papers in answer to Rosa's raised eyebrow at the mess. "Have a seat... somewhere." All the chairs and stools were covered in scrolls and books.

"I thought the Dowager Baroness Anvliyar was in charge of planning the Royal Wedding." Rosa said mildly.

Ciriis put both her hands on her face and rubbed them up and down. Her shoulder sagged. "I'm the Mistress of Protocol. It's my job. Lady Theresa said this might keep me out of trouble," she muttered the last almost inaudibly.

Rosa, Countess of Zialest, Rebel Countess, and soon-to-be (possibly and by His Majesty's leave) Duchess of Zialest-Dalizell, put her arms around her cousin. "Cirii... what have you done?"

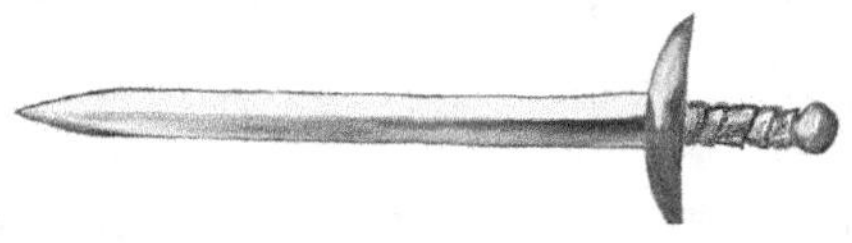

An hour later, a somewhat chastened Lady Celavell sat with the Countess of Zialest and the Duchess of Elaarwen.

Lena and Aryllis had quietly departed when the other two arrived.

Genevieve paced. Her face was clean of tears and she had put on a fresh gown. She had never liked gowns much before meeting Lena and Aryllis, finding them too constricting. She had accepted wearing gowns as one of the things a Duchess must do on formal occasions, but hunting leathers had been her preferred mode of dress. These new gowns, however, were made to the specifications of the Royal Guardswomen and, despite being as stylish as anything else worn at Court, Genevieve knew without question that she could fight, ride, or run in them.

It didn't hurt that she looked beautiful in the gowns. When she found herself near and next to neat, perfect Ciriis Celavell it did not hurt at *all*.

Lady Celavell had just admitted that Damien was suffering as much as Genevieve. And that she had had something to do with it.

"*Why?*" Genevieve demanded, after pacing a bit more. Was he really wandering the halls to catch glimpses of her, and ducking away if he thought she might see him? She knew he must also be feeling the strain on their bond – the Gods, it seemed, did not take well to mere mortals disrupting their plans – but she had thought that the work he was doing would keep him too preoccupied to fret. She, on the other hand, had so little to do that her hands practically *itched* for a task.

And if Damien was wandering around like a lost soul, instead of using every minute consolidating his power, what use was Lord Prydeen making use of this time? The Rebel Duchess had needed to spike the plans of would-be usurpers of her position in the Rebellion in the past... she much misdoubted that the sorcerer had been sitting quietly on his hands. The slight, sarcastic smile the sour old man sported every time Damien answered her without looking at her during a Council session seemed confirmation of that hypothesis.

"Does it matter?" Rosa cut in. "Isn't the question really about what we should do *now* to mend this breach?" Genevieve had not known she was Ciriis Celavell's cousin. Should have, perhaps, for there was a similar set of behaviors, a similar way of turning the head, a similar tendency towards neatness. They were similar in coloring and height, but their features were very different. And Rosa seemed so warm, while Lady Celavell was... not exactly cold, but certainly not open and welcoming.

"It *does* matter." Genevieve felt implacable. This wasn't a girlish broken heart – this was interference with a magickal bond to a degree that would eventually have killed her and Damien both. It still *could* do that. It verged on treason. "I need to know if I can trust her in the future. If *Damien* and I can trust her," she added, and saw the otherwise imperturbable brunette flinch from her words.

She decided to push harder. "If she is in league with Lord Prydeen, *or* merely his unwitting tool, I need to know."

Lady Celavell's face became absolutely wooden.

Rosa subsided, having no ready answer to that and seeing that her former lover was speaking from a place of considered calm.

The silence stretched on, and then...

"Jason Solway."

"What?" Genevieve wasn't exactly surprised, but she wanted clarification.

Lady Celavell looked at her steadily. "You were given this amazing opportunity and instead you were panting after Jason Solway. *I* didn't need to *do* anything. Merely let him notice you *looking* at Jason."

She jumped when Genevieve gave a little bark of laughter. "All of this over a *look?* He's nearly killing us both. Over a *look?* And you encouraged him? I half think you *are* Prydeen's creature–"

"No!" Genevieve had not known that Ciriis Celavell could look so outraged. "I would never – I *could* never–"

"Really?" Genevieve drawled over her splutter. "Seems like you have. This isn't about Jason. This is about you. And Damien. Isn't it."

Lady Celavell looked away.

"Isn't it."

Genevieve waited, but there was no response. "You were planning to marry him yourself, weren't you. After all, it was completely natural that he should turn to you, the first woman he ever bedded. The woman who already tells *poor, naïve Damien* how to run his kingdom–"

"No!" she cried again, and this time she met Genevieve's eyes. "I knew he'd have to make a marriage of state. That was fine, but you're right, I assumed I would still be there, because a marriage of state would be a marriage of convenience. I wasn't planning around a *soul*-bonding–"

Genevieve snorted and muttered "You weren't the only one!" but Rosa gave her a *look* herself and she quieted.

"It was when I saw you lusting after Jason – that was the end." Lady Celavell glared up at Genevieve. "You weren't here all these years. You don't know what Jason went through. How hard he and Adam have had to work to keep their relationship going. You just come blazing in here like a falling star, ripping apart everything... Adam and Jason, and poor Damien caught in the middle..." She turned to Rosa. "The poor boy has had this fantasy built up around her all these years. He thought he hid it, but I'm his spymaster and I saw how he devoured every word about her and asked for more. And then for it to turn into a *soul-bonding*... and for her to *throw it all away...*"

Genevieve threw up her hands. "The Gods bonded my soul to Damien's, but they gave me a different connection to Jason. I don't know why and I don't want it. I simply hadn't, haven't, figured out what to *do* about it yet." She collapsed onto the opposite end of the couch from where Lady Celavell sat so straight and perfect.

"You were going to break that poor boy's heart and destroy his best friends all in one fell swoop." Lady Celavell somehow made it less an accusation and more a statement of an undeniable truth.

"He's not a *boy,*" Genevieve snarled. "He's a man grown and your *king*, and you need to stop treating him like he isn't capable or by all the Gods at once, eventually he'll realize it and give up and *become* the incompetent, naïve child you're treating him as!"

Both Lady Celavell and Rosa seemed slightly taken aback by her vehemence.

"You may not realize you're doing it," Genevieve relented grudgingly. "But you and Adam in particular are doing it... and most of that Council. Not to mention Lord Prydeen, who is striding around as if he owns the place." Whether the Council was following Prydeen's lead – or Adam and Ciriis' – wasn't easy to tell.

"And you would know this how?" Lady Celavell challenged. "While you sit on your hands and don't speak up to support Damien or offer any information about your wonderful Rebellion? Or while you skulk around, sniffing after him like a bitch in heat? Or *is* it Jason you're sniffing after?"

It wasn't hard to see how the woman might have come to such a conclusion since Jason was almost always in attendance on the king, including serving as the royal armsmaster... Seeing the two of them together as she discreetly observed Damien's arms-practices had been quite nearly as much of a challenge for the Rebel Duchess herself after all.

But it was hardly the place of a minor noblewoman to call Genevieve out on her behavior. No matter the place she held for her loyalty and efforts in seating Damien on his throne.

Genevieve glowered at her, but it was Rosa who replied first.

"What did you expect Genevieve to volunteer about the Rebellion, Cirii? Military secrets? Positions? Plans?"

"Why *not?*" Lady Celavell returned Genevieve glower for glower.

"Because it wasn't Genevieve's place to do so." Lady Celavell wrenched her gaze away to land incredulously on Rosa at the gentle words.

"It's true," Rosa continued. "She was here on her own recognizance, against the wishes of the Rebel Council. Her responsibility was not to be captured–" she favored her former lover with an ironic half-smile, "–which she arguably failed at. She has no authority to speak for the rest of us.

"That's why *I* came."

Lady Celavell seemed to be digesting this. "I thought you came at her behest. And that she should ask *you* to return *here...*"

Rosa shook her head. "No. I came because the Rebel Council decided that the change in circumstances justified making some overtures to King Damien. We trust Genevieve, but she was coming here entirely on instinct. We weren't ready to risk the Rebellion on that, but when the soul-bonding happened, it seemed to be a sign from the Gods validating her instincts. It still took a fair long while to come to agreement," she added wryly. "There were a number of reasons I was the one chosen to come, but if we intend to return to being part of this Realm, I'd be returning to this Court eventually. Prince Oskar is long gone," Rosa finished quietly. "I need to let myself move forwards, Cirii, or he wins."

Lady Celavell seemed floored. "Your great rebellion is ruled by a *committee?*"

"It is."

She began to laugh, though with a slight edge of hysteria. "Our great Lord Prydeen was defeated by a *committee!*"

Genevieve snorted. "Hardly 'defeated,' and weren't you, Jason, Adam, and Damien another committee? But we're not likely to finish the job if we're fighting against each other. What has he been up to while Damien and I have been involved in this badly written romance, Lady Celavell?"

The brunette looked away, which was an answer of sorts in itself.

Genevieve sighed. "This situation isn't by my choice, milady." She put aside childhood memories of Damien's serious grey eyes – the memories that had sent her to the capitol in the first place. She had come to assess a possible ally or enemy. Nothing more.

"Cirii... do you love him?"

Rosa's question dropped into the waiting silence.

At last, truculently, Lady Celavell replied with her own question. "Does *she?*"

Genevieve drew in a sharp breath. It felt like knives of air cutting through her heart. How could she answer such a question? She barely knew him. A memory of a child's grey eyes. One ridiculously amazing night and a handful of confidences. Two weeks of watching, watching, watching... trying to focus on evaluating him as a ruler, not on the shape of his lips and the strands of dark hair that were always falling over his right eyebrow.

She should have had every confidence that she could trust him with anything – there was the soul-bonding, after all. But the last two weeks had damaged her faith. She could trust him to do the best he could for her country, her Rebellion... but for her?

Two weeks ago, she had been on the verge of believing it was possible... but if this was a test given by the same Gods who had placed the soul-bonding upon them, they were failing it miserably. Both of them.

Rosa trusted Ciriis Celavell. Genevieve trusted Rosa.

Ciriis Celavell needed to be able to trust Genevieve.

She blew out the breath slowly.

"I don't know. I think it's... possible. Likely even. The soul-bonding won't give us the opportunity to *not* be together, but... I'm not unhappy that it happened." Lady Celavell was meeting her eyes now. "I need time to find out." She paused. "Are *you?*"

The intense, dark-haired woman gave a long, deep sigh. "No. I'm not *in* love with him, though I care for him very much. There was always a piece of him that I never seemed able to touch. He was always so sweet... but it was as if any attempt to go beyond that sweetness just... slipped off."

Rosa patted her shoulder gently. "I know what you mean." She smiled a little sadly at Genevieve, who looked back at her in some shock. She had thought Rosa's long-term plans were completely invested in her future marriage... had she misread her beloved friend? Was it because there was some piece of herself that she hadn't let Rosa into? Rosa, who had taught her that romantic, sexual love was real? Surely not!

Lady Celavell sighed again. "The other girls had the same experience. I was hoping he'd find a love-match with one of us – so he wouldn't be so alone, trapped in that eventual marriage of state. Eventually I decided *I* would keep him from being lonely, even if there wasn't anything more. For either of us." She laughed a little, bitterly. "My duty to king and country, I suppose."

"And to your friend." Rosa added.

Lady Celavell nodded sadly. "He would be so easy to fall in love with. But I couldn't. Watching Jason and Adam made me so jealous sometimes. They're so fragile in some ways and so solid in others... but they're always there for each other."

"What..." Genevieve couldn't stop herself from asking. "...what happened to Jason?" She'd seen shadows in his eyes these last two weeks that had nothing to do with his reactions to her. She'd seen how Adam made an effort to always be within sight of his love, and how Damien rarely ever separated them, sending someone else for tasks that would have made for sense for one of them.

Lady Celavell gave her a measuring look. "Normally, I would tell you it's his story and not mine to share. But–" She looked at Rosa, back at Genevieve, then lifted her chin slightly. "Perhaps you do need to know. Both of you."

Prince Oskar, she told them had, from early on, bid fair to turn out like his unlamented father. His approach was more... multifarious... however. The old king – and Lord Prydeen – had only been interested in young *women* for their darker purposes. Prince Oskar found entertainment in both genders and had small interest in pursuing dark magicks, using them merely for his own dark *entertainments*. The old men had not exactly seemed to encourage him, but they had given their tacit approval by not reining in his excesses. So long as he confined his more 'intimate' interests in females to the serving maids, it seemed there were no limits on what he could do with the nobles' sons. He was favored to be named as the next Heir to the Throne, though the king himself had said nothing.

The prince had been quite handsome – all the old king's descendants were – so the maidens of the Court threw themselves at him anyways. Lady Celavell hinted, with a grim set to her lips that Genevieve did not question, that there had been a hope that *his* interest might protect them from the king and his pet sorcerer. He enjoyed their attentions, presumably with a weather eye to the throne, entertaining himself with destroying their illusions before they were claimed by the king and then hustled into hasty marriages... if they survived.

When some of that feminine attention began to be diverted towards Jason Solway, not long after the Summer that Genevieve had spent at Court, Prince Oskar had been at first offended. Jason was merely the younger son of the Countess of Brindlewell, in training to become a knight. He had no promise of future power about him, no way to protect those girls from the king and Lord Prydeen's attentions unless he should actually deflower them – which might well mean something... unfortunate... would happen to him as well. It had happened before.

But Jason was incredibly handsome, even at age fourteen. Irresistibly handsome to a number of those noblemaidens and serving maids. And too kind to do much to discourage them. He was also excelling in his training, clearly on his way to becoming one of the foremost bladesmen in the country. It had left the prince seething.

"And then Adam sprouted up to nearly match Jason in height," Lady Celavell added. "They're a matched set, of course, with those perfect blonde good looks."

The two squires were paired up for any ceremonial tasks, since they presented an attractive picture. Adam apparently already knew where his interests lay and his cynical demeanor and obvious lack of interest discouraged female interest; a subtle discouragement that carried over to shield Jason from all those maidenly attentions when he was in Adam's presence. It was a strong incentive for Jason to spend time with Adam. Jason's inherent kindness to the younger boy, from a family of countrified nobility, all adrift in the lethal brew of the Court but determined to present a tough exterior, was an incentive for *Adam* to spend time with *Jason*.

Jason had been awarded his shield, with Adam just a year behind, and the friendship was growing slowly towards something more... when Prince Oskar decided to intervene.

He had Jason assigned as his personal bodyguard, given quarters adjoining his own suite – and it quickly became obvious that what the prince meant by 'personal' went far beyond the duties normally required of a guard. Jason acquired the look of quiet desperation that still shadowed his eyes to this day.

It got worse the following year when Adam earned his shield. Adam had been watching as his best friend – the man he was falling in love with – was methodically destroyed by the prince. He had planned to challenge the prince as soon as he could legally do so. It would mean his death, for though by that time the only swordsman who could take him with any regularity was Jason, he had small hope of killing the prince and not feeling royal reprisal.

But the Rebellion had made a larger push that year – the same year that Genevieve had married Harald and the resources of Duchy Siovale had been added to those of Duchy Elaarwen. Adam was in his saddle and on the way to the battlefront before the paint had dried on his shield. Jason and Prince Oskar were already there since the prince was nominally in command of the royal forces. But the prince stayed far back among the command tents... drinking and wenching, apparently.

Adam had distinguished himself in the Battle of Siovale – Lady Celavell did not provide any details, but she didn't have to. That had been Genevieve's first battle. She had fought beside her new husband; no one had ever claimed that Harald was not a most excellent warrior, though – for obvious reasons – neither she nor he had sought the knighthood that by law only the king himself could grant. She remembered Adam's shield: puce with a rose, argent, crossed by a black sword. Harald had struggled against the knight who bore it, finally resorting to the dishonorable solution of saving his own life by slaying the other man's horse. Genevieve had put it down to an accident of battle for years until Harald had actually boasted of it in his cups – naming it as the reason he had beaten the redoubtable, and by then much renown, Sir Loveress. To his credit, Adam had rolled free of his horse and continued the attack, though he had little hope of success afoot against a mounted warrior. Harald had laughed and spurred his horse on to a more worthy opponent, and Genevieve had followed him and thought no more of the encounter at the time.

Since Prince Oskar had nominally been in charge of the battle and the battle had been declared a victory – Genevieve suppressed a snort of indignation, for the Rebellion had won territory in that encounter – he was rewarded with the Ring of the Heir.

Which meant that any challenges he was offered would be met not by him, but by his chosen Champion. There was no question that would be Jason.

Lady Celavell paused in her narration. She didn't need to say anything to make it clear that the next several years had been a living hell for her friends.

Eventually Oskar had become secure in his position as Heir – and that of course, was when the old king had taken back the Ring. By that time, Oskar had tired of making Jason miserable and had chosen a new bodyguard, one who caroused beside him instead of beneath him – Lady Celavell and Genevieve both sneaked a look at Rosa, whose face was closed in a way Genevieve had not seen for over a year.

"Adam still wanted to challenge the prince," Lady Celavell concluded. "But first there was the matter of helping Jason recover... and by then we had realized that the king had only one remaining legitimate descendant besides Oskar. Damien had spent all of his time hiding in the Royal Library since his parents – well. He was quiet and bookish, no preparation to command anyone, and years too late to begin training as a knight."

"No threat to the king," Genevieve interpreted.

Lady Celavell nodded. "Exactly. We knew the old king could never abide Oskar for long, so it was only a matter of time before he named Damien as Heir. And even *Oskar–*" her lip curled in disgust, "–would eventually realize that his only competition was a hapless child. So, we... took it upon ourselves to... protect and prepare him."

Genevieve leaned back, a smile playing across her lips. "You did far more than that, didn't you. You somehow made sure that Prince Oskar was nowhere near the capitol when the Heir's Ring began to make it impossible for the old king to avoid naming an Heir." The smile disappeared from her lips. "Oh, no..." She looked at Rosa in horror. "You didn't. You did. You were part of this... Oh, Rosa!"

There was one thing that had drawn the prince away from the capitol at about that time... One very *specific* event which he had attended as his royal father's representative...

Her friend, her former lover, her forever love, looked back at her with eyes bright with pain. "I knew what I was getting into, yes. And before you ask, so did Zachary. And my parents, though they didn't agree with the plan.

"If I had known that my wonderful, stupid little brother would decide he would try to avenge my honor..." Her voice broke and Genevieve drew her into her arms, looking daggers at Lady Celavell again.

The idea that Count Zachary Miramar had been on board with exposing his bride to Prince Oskar's attentions was anathema alone. Genevieve knew Rosa's intended fairly well by now... and how many of those 'negotiations' had been merely to mask his involvement in the first place? Or merely to clarify Dalizell's part and perquisites as a member of the Rebellion? The young count's adoring eyes when looking at Rosa across the negotiating table had always made Genevieve uncomfortable, given that Rosa had fled to *her* and not *him* that evil night... and given that Rosa was sharing *her* bed...

How much of what had been between herself and Rosa was real? If her friend had been willing to prostitute herself *on her wedding night* for what she considered the betterment of the Realm, had she done the same to ensure that Zialest was given a secure place in the Rebellion, even though she and her people had showed up hat in hand and desperate?

No. Perhaps that had been Rosa's early motivation – to tie Genevieve, and thereby the Rebellion, to her personal interests as Countess of Zialest – but surely that had fallen away when she discovered that the Rebellion was run by committee. And that had been nearly two years ago…

And, regardless of the beginnings, Genevieve had loved Rosa without reservation. And to some extent she always would.

"You set her up for this." The Rebel Duchess' tone was accusing.

The dark-haired woman bowed her head, but then lifted it defiantly. "I asked nothing of her that the rest of us had not already sacrificed. Gavin... should have followed the plan." As if there was anyone in that part of Ilseador who didn't know that Gavin Teraseel was impulsive and hotheaded and was as likely to stick to a plan as he was to catch the greased pig at the Harvest Fair.

Genevieve started to reply, but Rosa whispered, "Gavin and Ciriis were to be wed next, Gen," before pulling herself upright again.

Genevieve shook her head, her anger at the machinations blunted in one sense, but a sense of distrust beginning to build. "I don't understand. Why didn't you all just come over to our side? We would have *welcomed* you in the Rebellion! Rosa – I thought we had been honest with each other, but you never told me *any* of this. And you argued against seeing if Damien could be reasoned with! When you knew all along that he could."

It was Lady Celavell's turn to rise and pace. There was a nice open space for pacing now, Aryllis and Lena having had the heavy furniture pushed back to accommodate Genevieve's long stride.

But it was Rosa who spoke first. "I didn't argue against talking to King Damien, my dear. I argued against *you* coming in playing at Erawan the Kind Robber." As Genevieve blushed in memory, Rosa added, "And sometimes it's more effective to oppose something in our Rebel Council than to support it."

"Rosa has never met Damien," Lady Celavell put in. "She was trusting *me*. As for why we didn't 'just come over' to the Rebellion..." her dark eyes were full of pain and arrogance as she turned to fully face the Rebel Duchess, "...until Damien had the Heir's Ring, we could hardly make any real plans. Once he did, we debated seriously whether that would be the course of wisdom. Time will tell us true, but we didn't know whether *we* could trust *you* – your *people,"* she corrected herself, with an eye-roll that seemed more like her usual ironic self. "Damien was adamant that we could trust *you* from the beginning."

"The Rebellion does not harbor spies," Genevieve said a bit stiffly, trying to ignore the small thrill that the thought of Damien's unasked-for trust shivered up her spine.

Lady Celavell snorted at this naïvete.

"Genevieve," Rosa said gently, "Ciriis says the king explained to you how Lord Prydeen overhears others. There are mice and birds everywhere."

Damien *had* told her about this that first wonderful day. Presumably Rosa had gotten the word from Lady Celavell. Genevieve would have to assume that Rosa hadn't shared that knowledge with the Rebel Council – or even with *her* simply because it sounded so incredible. It had been believable from Damien only because she could *feel* the truth of his words across their soul-bond. What haughty and mighty sorcerer would ever bother himself about enchanting *mice?*

Still... Rosa should at least have *tried* to tell her.

Or... had she? And had Genevieve brushed off the idea like the hundred other useless suggestions people had thrown at her every day about how to actually overthrow the old king and his pet sorcerer?

They'd tried sending assassins – and discovered that even those who weren't found out before they made their attempts were stymied by some spell that prevented any weapon from touching either king or sorcerer. The same with poison. The Rebellion had been forced to resort to nibbling away at the men and women who supported the old king – who were not so carefully protected. Genevieve's own preference had been to persuade them to turn their coats, but some of her allies had been less... patient.

Jason's mother, Countess Alexa Solway, had only survived that *impatience* because Genevieve had insisted that she had the situation in hand and it mustn't be disturbed lest the old king take more of an interest. County Brindlewell was a potential bottleneck in getting supplies and information to Elaarwen; Genevieve was fairly sure neither Jason, nor his mother, nor even his elder sister, the Heir, had a clue as to what half the trade that passed through their ancestral seat included. And nevermind that the hidden half of Genevieve's reasoning had been to honor the memory of her father's friendship with the terrible old woman.

Mice. Even if her people could be trusted, could they be trusted not to say anything vital in front of a mouse? Yet how could a mouse make it back to Lord Prydeen to report? If he could read their thoughts from hundreds of leagues away, they would have been destroyed long since... But how many of their councils might have been held with windows open and small birds flying in and out? Had there been a correlation between plans being leaked and more pleasant weather?

Genevieve's face grew thoughtful as she tried to make the correlations from memory.

Unless... unless Lord Prydeen simply didn't *care* what the Rebellion did or didn't do.

That the man was evil, Genevieve had no doubt. She had heard enough stories and felt the man's presence for herself. But what was his long game? He had made no effort to unseat Damien at all, as far as she had been able to tell... though perhaps she had simply been too distracted. Did he have less magick than they all assumed? Had he merely been a tool of–

"–what was the old king's name?" she asked, abruptly.

The other two looked at her oddly.

Lady Celavell began to answer sharply, then stopped, looking confused.

The three of them looked at each other with growing alarm.

"I had hoped," Genevieve said softly, "that it was merely another effect of the disrupted soul-bond that I could not remember. Some things are very sharp, and others that should not be are... vague."

"Hunger?" Rosa suggested uncertainly.

"Perhaps," Genevieve conceded, but her eyes remained on Lady Celavell. "Is Damien eating?"

The other woman looked away first. "Not much. You saw him slip during arms-practice yesterday, I'm sure," she noted snidely, before adding in a more defensive tone, "His *wits* are as sharp as ever!"

Genevieve lifted an eyebrow. "Are they? *I* feel like my head has been wrapped in a blanket, like part of my body has fallen asleep. I'm nauseous and exhausted and it has been taking more and more effort for me to focus on anything. Anything other than *Damien,*" she clarified with some irritation. "It began as worst during the Council sessions, but now the only times my head feels even slightly clear is during our morning meetings and while Damien is practicing at arms. And at night."

She carefully did not think about the fantasies she built around seeing him, touching him, lest she blush. Genevieve suspected that it wasn't herself alone – that it was Damien's emotions reaching across the soul-bond despite his best efforts, yearning towards her though his pride kept him from surrendering to the yearning.

Lady Celavell looked like she was feeling guilty, and said stiffly, "Your Grace–"

"Oh, bother!" Genevieve interrupted. "We're on the same side, I think we've established. Just call me Genevieve. Stop and think about it. Other than our morning meetings and his arms-practice sessions, Lord Prydeen is with him all the rest of the time, isn't he?"

Lady Celavell's hand flew to her face in the first completely unscripted look of surprise Genevieve had caught her in. "Not all the time... but the last few days, yes. And he's suggested that Damien should quit his arms-practice. Several times."

"He can't keep close there," Genevieve commented grimly. "I didn't think Damien was shallow enough to give up on nearly twenty years of dreams and a soul-bonding that confirmed them over one questionable look. Lady Celavell–"

"Ciriis... please..." The woman had a stricken look on her face.

Genevieve nodded. "Ciriis. You may have created an opening for this – situation – but, as a true soul-bonding, we should have been able to work through this quickly. If it had been me alone, no matter how angry I was at him, I would have caved within a few days. A week at most. Keeping apart is making both of us ill, but from what I've heard we shouldn't be *able* to stay apart. I suppose that could be an exaggeration..."

"It's not," Rosa broke in. "Our chatelaine in Zialest and the head groom were soul-bonded. Their jobs put them in different parts of the castle, and they are both incredibly dedicated to their work. You have to look for it, but they are always in sight of each other, even if it is just through a window. My father said that, when Marc was first appointed to the position, the chatelaine's office overlooked the dairy pastures. Stella was only an assistant in the stables at the time, in charge of maintaining the tack. But somehow, she kept getting called out to help get the horses out of the dairy pasture. She was never anywhere near the horses – they seemed to get in from an adjacent pasture – but she was good with them so they called her out to help catch them. Papa moved Marc's office to overlook the courtyard, and Stella began to work at the stable entrance, and the horses stopped ending up with the cows."

She smiled. "It looks like the Gods will rearrange things for you even if you don't do much about it yourselves."

Genevieve smiled back a little weakly. "Seeing him *does* help..."

Ciriis Celavell nodded reluctantly. "Damien *is* sharper at the morning meetings and during the Council sessions. It's hard to tell in the Audiences, since no one interacts with him very much." She shook her head. "How could I not have noticed that Lord Prydeen is with him so much?"

"You've been busy on protocol for the wedding?" Rosa suggested.

"Oh, so there's still to be a wedding?" Genevieve barked a laugh. "That's reassuring."

Ciriis gave her a slightly irritated, but still somewhat guilty, look. "Of course, there is. Lady Theresa is your complete adherent and has been keeping me 'too busy to make trouble.' It's a problem with only being Damien's advisor unofficially. I have to report to that officious old lady when I've more important things to do."

She frowned. "Adam and Jason should have noticed something. *They* are with Damien from breakfast to bed." She began pacing again... the other two could see that she was thinking hard and kept silent.

"Tim – Sir Ancellius, Adam's Second who's in charge of your guards – teased Damien last week about how he could bear to have you so far out of sight." Ciriis favored Genevieve with her usual sardonic expression. "Apparently you have your adherents among the Royal Guards as well. I've never heard Damien respond to anyone that sharply. He said he could expect to see quite enough of you in the future."

During fencing practice, Genevieve had caught many touches on her thick, quilted jacket that bent the thin, blunted blade nearly double right over her heart. During longsword practice she *had* actually been impaled through her left thigh when her partner had unexpectedly stabbed instead of slicing, blunted practice blade or not. Lady Celavell's words felt like a combination of those two – a stab wound through her heart.

But the woman was continuing, "That exchange happened in the halls on the way back to his rooms. When they stepped inside a few minutes later, and it was just Jason and myself in attendance, Jason took him to task for it. Damien was contrite and said something about having said everything wrong... then excused himself and went to bed."

"Was Lord Prydeen in the corridor during the first exchange?" Rosa asked.

Ciriis nodded. "He was."

Genevieve still felt she was having trouble breathing.

Rosa looked alarmed and put an arm around her. "Gen, love, even Lord Prydeen can't keep you two apart much longer and still keep Damien on the throne. And it looks like he wants that."

"He prefers being the power *behind* the throne," Ciriis put in.

"And once the two of you are together, what chance do all his machinations have?" Rosa finished.

Genevieve took a long, shuddering breath. That would have been much more reassuring two weeks ago. Right now, she wasn't so sure.

"That's all well and good, if it's true," she said. "But since I can't get Damien to acknowledge my presence, even in a discussion of strategy, it's hardly likely that we'll spend any time alone together to find out."

Ciriis Celavell's face took on a crafty look.

"I think I have an idea..." she said.

Chapter SIX

Trapped...

DAMIEN STUMBLED SLIGHTLY AS HE entered his quarters, and Jason caught his arm to steady him. Adam waved away the concerned expressions of the Royal Guardsmen standing guard at the door to the tower suite, saying something about a few too many glasses of wine, and closed the heavy door behind the three of them.

It was true. Damien was slightly tipsy, though he hadn't had all that much wine.

He sat down somewhat morosely in his favorite overstuffed chair, letting the worn spots on the old leather guide him into a comfortable position. He did *not* look at the chair where Genevieve sat during the morning meetings.

The reception for the Rebel Countess had gone on for far too long. Ciriis and Lady Theresa had insisted on turning it into a real occasion, last minute preparations notwithstanding. There had been music – and his head still throbbed with it. There had been dancing – and he had been obliged to dance with both the countess and Genevieve. He throbbed with that, too, though in an entirely different way.

Not because of the countess, though she reminded him of Ciriis enough to stir some old and pleasant memories.

"You," Adam declared pleasantly, from his usual post of holding up one of the central pillars, "are drunk."

"It was only two glasses–"

"On an empty stomach," Jason said more sympathetically as he settled into the spot on the couch where Ciriis usually sat.

"I ate."

"Not enough."

Adam's eyes sparkled challengingly. "It's not *food* he's hungry for, Jase. It's Genevieve."

Jason sighed as Damien glowered at Adam. They had both tried to reason with him about this before. One did not deny a soul-bonding without consequences. And they had no idea why he was doing it, though he fancied that Jason's arguments were tinged with guilt.

Reminded, Damien glowered at Jason, then dropped his gaze. Jason had suffered too much and Damien owed him too much for the young king to task him with any of his own concerns - ever. Uncomfortably, that forced the younger man to remember when Jason had... distracted... Prince Oskar from his vulnerable young nephew. It had been brief compared to what the knight had previously suffered for the former Heir's amusement, but he had known what he was going into and had done it anyways, to keep Damien safe and whole.

Damien wondered how many people in that room had gone up to the Rebel Countess and thanked her for ending Prince Oskar. He wondered if Jason had done so when he had danced with her.

Damien himself had not said any such thing, no matter his personal feelings. He wished to deal honestly and fairly with the woman who had come – as Genevieve had not – to officially represent the interests of the Rebel Provinces to his Court. But if he was to pardon her for killing his last remaining uncle, a charge of treason in and of itself, he should use the pardon to enhance his negotiating position.

The young king was well aware that his military might looked better on paper than in reality.

"*No.*" He said it truculently. He was not up to verbal fencing with Adam just now. Though, ironically, he was feeling better than he had been on the long walk from the ballroom to the top of his tower.

He *was* hungry – for *food*, thank you very much – but the vague feeling of nausea that had been hounding him had coalesced this morning into a violent rejection of the food he had been able to eat. Lately the only times he felt like himself were when he was in his rooms or in the practice ring.

He refused to think about how he felt when he was skulking the halls for a peek of Genevieve. He couldn't shake Adam and Jason, so they knew all about his clandestine visits to the tower opposite the solarium where his betrothed and his Royal Guardswomen did *not* spend the day doing embroidery.

The throbbing in his head was subsiding now that he was away from the music and the heat and the press of people.

The throbbing in his loins was not.

He wondered if she had also left the party and was now in the rooms below... beneath him...

Adam snorted derisively. "Right. Well, if not for her, then for *someone* in your bed."

There was something to that. A lot, actually. Before... his coronation... he and Felena had been enjoying company again. She spent a lot of time with Gen– the Rebel Duchess now, though. In fact, *all* of his Royal Guardswomen were doing that, and they were the only women he would trust enough to share a bed with. The only women that the male Royal Guards would *allow* into his room.

And he couldn't 'summon' one of them. Their arrangements had always been mutual, and he had been careful never, ever, to treat one of them as a subordinate in this sense. Too many of them had been... damaged... by his grandfather, Lord Prydeen, or his uncle Oskar. Not all of it had been about sex. Mind-games were as damaging as bed-games, or moreso. If his friends chose to favor him for a time, he accepted it with joy, but it was always about their choice.

Ciriis hadn't been spending time with... the Rebel Duchess. Perhaps... but no. *That* was long gone.

Adam snorted again and reached out to ruffle Jason's long, blonde hair. "Come on, dearheart. It looks like Damien won't go to bed until we're gone, and he definitely needs some beauty sleep."

Jason laughed. "He's not that bad."

"No, but *you* look that *good*. Come to bed, love." Adam held out a hand, and Jason used it to pull himself up from the couch.

The smile they gave each other melted Damien's heart and he knew that – no matter who Jason had looked at – he would do anything he could to protect what these two had. Even if he might never have it for himself. The throbbing between his legs warred with the feeling of broken glass in his chest, but he had grown familiar with the latter sensation.

"Get a room, you two." The old joke.

"That's the plan," Adam retorted as they exited. The old answer.

Damien sat for awhile longer, brooding but unfocused. He was tired, that was all. It wasn't like he couldn't focus when he was well-rested. And that had nothing to do with *her* being here for the morning meetings and Council sessions. Nothing at all.

At last, he pried himself up from his chair and made his way into the bedchamber. One lit lamp, close to the bathing chamber so he wouldn't stumble there in the dark. Somehow, he felt a little less foggy, a little more alert, even in the darker space.

Carelessly he shed his soft, indoor boots and his other clothes, dropping them where they fell on his way to the bathing chamber. He'd pick them up in the morning, he knew, but it felt delightfully rebe– *defiant* to make a mess right now. He'd never caught the habit that so many of his nobles seemed to have of making a mess purely for the joy of giving the servants more to do – perhaps it was because Damien had first been so little regarded that he'd had no servants and then later his quarters were maintained by his Royal Guards... whose talents were better used for something other than chasing after scattered apparel.

Back to the bedchamber. The moon was full enough to cast some light through the clerestory windows. Enough to see his way to bed. He turned out the lamp.

So tired, and he could feel the effects of the wine and lack of food more clearly now. It seemed ridiculous to court a hangover over two glasses of wine. He didn't feel nauseous anymore, but he also didn't have the energy to put on a robe and hunt for the snacks he used to store in his desk.

And yet his now naked body was making it clear to him that sleep would be long in coming. Damn Ciriis for insisting on dancing, and for insisting he follow protocol and dance with the highest-ranking women there. He could still smell *her* faint perfume, and his skin tingled with the memory of *her* in his arms. He was alone, wasn't he? He could indulge the fantasy he'd built in his youth and completed in this very bed.

Damien began to climb into bed and realized the bed wasn't empty.

He didn't recognize who it was, but he trusted his Royal Guards, so it would be someone safe. One of the Royal Guardswomen must have taken pity on him after all. That was fine. Right now, he would take pity and be grateful for it.

The form in the bed was too tall; it wasn't Ciriis. Maybe Felena? Too quiet. Aryllis? His pulse pounded a little at his memories of the cool platinum blonde. But wasn't Aryllis engaged to the irrepressible Tim now? And she surely wasn't this curvy?

Nevermind. Whoever she was, she was here, and by her own choice. She was safe, or she'd never have been let in; that was the whole point of having a pair of guards on his doors even when he wasn't within. His wine-fuddled mind decided not to worry about it until morning. There were better things to do right now. And here he stood, with the glimmers of moonlight giving her a good view of him...

He threw back the coverlet and let the moon glimmer on her smooth skin. She lay on her side, head propped up on one elbow. Awake, aware... her breathing had changed, caught, when he came to the side of the bed.

With a suppressed moan, Damien joined her on the sheets. They reached for each other in unison and were engaged in a deep kiss before he realized he knew *exactly* – had *always* known, though he hadn't wanted to admit it – who it was in his bed.

His mind wanted to reject her, but his body wanted Genevieve. His heart was torn.

While he wrestled with himself, he realized that *Genevieve* had no such qualms. The fingers of her own hand twined tightly in his hair while the others... also were in his hair, but not on his head. He had no interest left in resisting when she rolled him onto his back and mounted his hips with her own.

He closed his eyes and lived into the waves of sensation. It seemed like the moonlight brightened around them, and he opened his eyes to find the two of them surrounded by the magickal white fire that had marked their soul-bonding. Except this time, it completely encapsulated them, and was so bright it nearly blinded him if he looked anywhere but at Genevieve. She was smiling down at him, her eyes looking more green than blue in this fey light.

It was a repeat of the day – and night – of their soul-bonding.

It was nothing like it.

They weren't bound in some awkward position, palm-to-palm or otherwise, and the bubble of magick did not subside when they had finished making love. They slept, both worn from two long weeks of denying this, then made love again. And *again.*

By now they were both starvingly hungry – any trace of nausea had faded long since – and the magick bubble showed no signs of releasing them. It had zapped them every time they weren't touching in some manner... and those zaps had been followed by surges of blinding desire that enveloped them both.

They still hadn't spoken to each other.

There was no way to tell how much time had passed. He couldn't see anything beyond the edges of the bed, the canopy and curtains that would be drawn for warmth in the colder seasons. Warmth was not something they needed more of right now.

"I would just about kill for a drink of water," Genevieve rasped at last.

Damien glowered at her. They were holding hands lightly to maintain the physical contact that their magickal shield seemed to demand of them. "So would I. This is all your fault, you know."

Genevieve raised an eyebrow at him.

"Well, yours and my guards," he corrected himself. "They were under orders not to let yo– anyone in who didn't need to be here."

She gave him the quirky smile that made – that *used to make* his heart flip. "I guess they decided that I needed to be here."

"I don't need you." He insisted on it, ignoring the fact that he felt better than he had in two weeks, except for being hungry and thirsty. His head felt clearer, too, despite the wine he had drunk, and he was having trouble remembering why he had been so adamant about not seeing her, being with her, holding her, touching...

Genevieve actually laughed, though it was a little raspy. "We both know that's not true."

She sat up, putting one hand on his chest to maintain the light contact, but also keeping him from sitting up as well. "Look, Damien, it's bad enough that we're living a fairytale with this soul-bonding–"

Bad? The parts of him that had begun to hope again in spite of all his reasons constricted again.

"–it's bad enough that we nearly starved to death for want of each other. It's bad enough that I've been haunted all my life by the memory of a pair of grey eyes I saw *once*–"

What? Haunted? Grey eyes?

"–and, oh dear Gods, you were all of eight years old and how weird is that?"

His eyes? She remembered seeing him when they were children? It hadn't been all just him?

"It's bad enough that this is our only chance because neither of us will ever be able to fall in love with anyone else – and that no one *else* can manage to fall in love with either of us–"

What? What was *that* about?

"–but I absolutely refuse to turn this fairytale into one of those badly-written romances where the whole plot revolves around otherwise sensible people refusing to talk to each other!"

"I hate those, too," he offered somewhat meekly in the face of all that beautiful... adamant earnestness. He struggled to get up, but the tips of her widespread fingers held him down. He could see the muscles under her smooth, tanned skin. Genevieve had been training as a warrior, he reminded himself, since she was a child, whereas *he* had been reading fairystories.

"I am *not* in love with Jason Solway, you nitwit," she stated firmly. "I *might* be in love with you. I *want* to be in love with you. I *think* I'm falling in love with you. But we kind of bypassed the love-at-first-sight thing and I hardly know who you *are* to *be* in love with you." She gave him a stern look. *"I* have not been having people spy out everything about *you."*

"Research on the enemy commander?" he suggested weakly, well aware that the details about her that he had demanded be provided went far beyond that.

"Hunh." Another elegantly raised golden eyebrow. "I made Ciriis give me the file you had on me."

"Oh," Damien could feel himself blushing. And in this light, she could see just how far down that blush went. She made it worse, by tracing the path with a look of amused interest.

"You... remember meeting me when we were children?" he asked, hoping to distract her attention, but also desperate to know.

Genevieve threw him a look that said she knew exactly what he was trying, then casually leaned across his abdomen, propping her elbow on his other side, and trapping him at least as effectively as before.

"I do," she said, seriously. "I'd put you out of my head for a long, long time," she added thoughtfully, and his heart constricted again. "I was married, after all." Oh. Her husband. Well, those were memories that were no threat at all. "And my memory of you was of an eight-year-old. And mostly of your eyes. I didn't have an image of the man you'd grown to be to match that. I didn't pay a lot of attention to when you were Named Heir–"

"No one did," he muttered. "Probably a good thing."

She wopped him lightly on the head. "Stop that. Maybe it was good *then* for you to be retiring and ignored, but you have to break those habits now that you're king. Where was I? Oh, yes. When I heard that the old king had died and you were to be crowned, I saw your eyes every time I fell asleep. And some of those dreams... let's just say I wanted an adult image to go with those eyes." Now *she* blushed, and it was his turn to chuckle.

"I want to hear about those dreams."

Her blush went in interesting places, too... "Maybe later. I'm telling you something important now. That's why I came to the capitol. I wanted to open negotiations with you, but the other leaders of the Rebellion felt that we needed to see more of what you would do, first. I... couldn't wait."

Damien felt his mind was filled with molasses. Mmmn. Molasses. And Genevieve... And this bed... No, wait, he'd been thinking something...

"You were sharing your bed with Countess Rosa while you were dreaming about me?"

Genevieve glowered at him a bit. "I've had two lovers in my life, and one of them I was married to. Who all were you playing bedgames with while dreaming about *me?* Oh, you do flush nicely, don't you! I haven't the slightest complaint. I suspect I've met most of them, and they are all much nicer than my – than what else you might have found yourself in, here. They taught you things that I get to have all the benefits of, and now you are all *mine.*"

That last was said so fiercely that it mended the last cracks in his heart. Yes, he was all hers, and would never look elsewhere again.

But he still needed to ask. "Then what about Jason? The look you gave him..."

She sighed, and rolled onto her back. Her head was now centered on his stomach, and Damien was able to prop himself up a bit to see Genevieve's face as she stared blankly up at the bed canopy surrounded by magickal light.

"I don't know. I don't want this. And I'm sure he doesn't either. But I can't completely control my physical reaction if I'm too close to him. Touching him. These last two weeks – horrible as they have been without *you,*" she glanced over and flickered a smile, "I've been able to see that I don't have a reaction to him if there's no physical contact.

"That's not true about *you,*" she added. "Just thinking about *you* is enough to make it hard to think about anything else. And *seeing* you..." She blushed again and he realized in delighted fascination that it made her freckles stand out brighter. "I've been watching you when you practice swordplay. From a window, so you couldn't see me. It helped me get through the last two weeks... and made it harder all at the same time."

Damien laid back down. He hesitated on telling her he'd been doing the same thing. He'd been exercising in a public area after all, although his Guards discouraged anyone from frequenting the surrounding rooms where they might have a clear shot at him... which suggested they had been assisting Genevieve in *her* clandestine surveillance... *She*, however, had been exercising in a private solar... he opted for a safer truth.

"I've loved you since I was eight. I told myself that I could stand to share you with your Countess Rosa–" She snorted with amusement and disbelief and he shrugged with embarrassment. "Well, I told myself that. And maybe... maybe if it was the only way you would take me... But Jason... Jason *knew* you. Remembered you fondly. And *every* woman has always wanted Jason. Even though he's never wanted any of *them*. And... after everything he's been through, after he gave himself *back* to Prince Oskar to protect me... if he *did* somehow want you..."

Genevieve had sucked in her breath sharply when he mentioned how Jason had protected him. She exhaled slowly. "Ciriis told me some of his story, but she didn't mention... that he'd gone back to Oskar..."

Damien closed his eyes to keep the tears in. It had been seven years and he still felt as guilty about it as if it were yesterday.

"I didn't even know about it until later. Adam took me to visit his family. I hadn't been out of this castle since my parents... For about six or seven years. I was so excited. And so relieved to be away from Court, from... Oskar. He'd begun to... to *notice* me. Ciriis came with us..." He stumbled to a stop. He had hoped to visit his other grandparents, whom his family had lived with until he was eight years old, had written to them from Adam's parents' home, in fact.

They had responded – but only to tell him not to contact them again. His hopes of not having to go back to the castle had crumbled with that letter, and Ciriis had found him crying... She had stayed with him until he cried himself out... And then given him something to find joy in instead.

A mixed blessing, for he'd been toying with the idea of running away to the Rebellion. Where he knew Genevieve was. Surely, she – *they* – would have kept him. He'd heard that Genevieve was married, but at least he would be near her... Would the soul-bonding have happened the first time they touched hands in greeting? A soul-bonding dissolved all conflicting oaths and contracts. Would it have saved her from years of her miserable marriage? Would the country have rallied around the pair of them as he hoped it would do now?

Or would it have broken the Rebellion's alliance with the Duke of Siovale and led to the eventual defeat of the Rebellion itself?

Or... worse yet... would nothing at all have happened, and they would had to watch each other for years and years... Soul-bonding sometimes took people who knew each well. It seemed that there was some aspect of timing.

Genevieve sighed. "We have refugees. I've heard their stories. I heard Rosa's. Most of Rosa's. I knew things were bad here. I don't think I ever knew *how* bad."

"I'm glad you didn't know." He said it fiercely. The idea that the corruption of this place could have reached out to touch *her*... he stroked her hair.

"How long were you gone?"

"Two months." He swallowed. "Oskar was done with him by then. Apparently, it was only the novelty of someone coming to *him* that had distracted him anyways. But it had worked. He'd forgotten about *me.*" He could not hide the tone of self-loathing. "They – Adam and Ciriis – wouldn't let me see Jason at first. So, I snuck in. He wasn't conscious. Bruised. Bandaged. She found me there and told me what had happened. And why." Later, Jason had asked him to come in. Had smiled and told Damien it had been his own idea and he knew what he was doing. That Damien was worth it.

None of them had needed to tell him that it was up to him be worthy of that sacrifice. And so many others that he had learned of in later years.

"I'm glad you were safe." Genevieve's words echoed his own of a moment ago.

"No one should have to make that sort of a sacrifice." He said it with conviction. "No one should have the power to hurt someone like that. Your Rebel Council – we all thought you were the leader, made all the decisions. But you do things by – a vote? By consensus? Maybe we could make something like that work for the whole Realm. Dispense with a king altogether."

He could hear Genevieve whistle.

"You don't have small dreams ever, do you?"

Damien smiled wryly at the – *his* – Rebel Duchess. "Do you?"

"Sometimes."

"You? How small is *small* for you?" The distinction between taking the throne for the Rebellion or declaring Elaarwen and its allies a new nation?

But then he felt her wicked humor down the bond that now seemed as wide as an open door.

"Oh, *very* small."

She turned her head and blew softly, and he didn't think about much at all for some time thereafter.

They woke a while later to realize they could see the room beyond the bubble of white fire. It looked more like a cage around them now, instead of a solid wall, and the streaks of brightness that made up the 'bars' left after-images when they looked elsewhere.

They looked at each other with one shared thought. "Water."

It turned out the bubble would move with them and pass through furniture. They made it into the bathing chamber and enjoyed drinks of water. By mutual agreement, they ran a bath in the deep, sunken tub and settled in to soak in hot water with an ewer of cold water and cups in easy reach. They had plenty of light from the bubble.

"Aaaahhhh. Now if we can only get some food..." Genevieve said, as she leaned back, rolling her shoulders. Damien admired what that motion did to her breasts and ended up slipping under the water. She laughed and rescued him.

"So, no king at all, hmmm?" she asked after they had settled in a more stable fashion.

He took a sip of his cold water. "Your Rebellion is proving that such a system can work."

Genevieve looked deep into her own cup. "Ye-e-es. I suppose it is. I'm not sure if what works under such extreme circumstances is ideal for a more normal life, though. And normal is what we *are* aiming for, I assume."

"Normal and boring," he agreed with a shudder. "We've all had more than enough excitement for several lifetimes."

She offered her cup to tap his. "To a normal and boring future. That wouldn't be the near future, though. I don't doubt Lord Prydeen has been taking advantage of this little lapse."

Damien tilted his head slightly. "I know this is going to sound crazy, but I've spent a lot of time with him these last two weeks. I think it was my grandfather that was the source of the true evil."

That earned him *two* arched eyebrows. "And Lord Prydeen was merely his unwilling tool? You're right, that does sound crazy."

The last two weeks the old man had shown Damien a different side. He had been helpful and neither condescending nor dismissive. Genevieve hadn't spent much time here – to her, his grandfather and Lord Prydeen were basically one.

"Have you noticed," she said thoughtfully, swirling the water in her cup. "That no one can remember your grandfather's name? He ruled for eighty-three years, it must be on proclamations all over the land. And yet... not one person refers to him as anything but 'the old king.' Excepting you," she added. "But calling him 'grandfather' is still avoiding use of his name."

Damien searched his memory and he couldn't find the name of the old king either.

"Isn't there some sort of magick that uses names?" Genevieve continued. "Isn't it odd that such a powerful sorcerer as your grandfather should lose his?"

"*He* wasn't the sorcerer, it was Lord Prydeen."

She gave him a *look*. "Please. You know better than that. He lived beyond any normal lifespan, was still fathering children into his eighties, and, somehow, he controlled Lord Prydeen. Usually, it takes a stronger sorcerer to control a sorcerer."

Damien blinked. He had never heard anyone call his grandfather a sorcerer before. He had feared the old man for his cruelty and his temporal power, but everyone knew that it was *Lord Prydeen* that was the evil sorcerer... but now Lord Prydeen didn't seem so evil and Genevieve's words made sense... except that Genevieve was still insisting Lord Prydeen was evil.

Genevieve looked at him with sympathy. "It's been well over a week since I had a good meal. I'm guessing about the same for you?"

He nodded, reluctant to admit that things were not making sense.

"Then let's see if we can do something about that." She rose, dripping in all sorts of interesting ways and food nearly receded from his list of most immediate needs again. But she was stepping out of the tub, and since she was holding his hand, he went with her perforce.

"Damien?" she asked over her shoulder, as she reached for a towel. He was trying to focus on moving and getting distracted by... pretty much everything about her.

"Your hair," he managed, trying for a neutral topic. "It's much longer than I'd realized." Indeed, dripping wet, all the curl was gone and it reached nearly to her knees.

He stepped up out of the warm water and stumbled, lightheaded. She caught him, bracing so they wouldn't both tumble back into the bath, and helped him find his balance and a towel. She was slightly shorter than him, barefoot as they both were. Bare... as they both were... He bent to catch her mouth in a kiss, felt her kiss him back, and then...

"No. We need food. Come with me." Food? What was that? He would follow her anywhere, and back into the bedchamber was a definite plus...

"Oh, thank the Gods. Or at least your friends."

"Genevieve..." How he loved saying her name... but she was putting something in his mouth and his body reacted to the taste of a rich, meaty broth. His brain took a little longer.

After a few swallows – broth alternating with sweetened tea – Damien realized that his vision had narrowed as if he was looking down a long, dark corridor. It was coming back now, and he felt light-headed, but he could see the room around him.

"Ah, back in the land of the living," Genevieve said lightly, but the look of concern in her eyes belied her tone. She was perched on the arm of his favorite overstuffed chair. Where, apparently, he was also sitting. The cage of magickal white fire flickered around them – dimmer? He wasn't sure. Her bare foot was hooked under his knee in wary acknowledgment. That freed her hands to manage the food items that she had been feeding him – and herself, he noted with relief.

"Yes," he agreed. "Thank you."

She shrugged nonchalantly. "We're bonded. It's not like I had a choice." Damien searched her face anxiously, but she was smiling and the concern was fading from her eyes. She noticed his worry and added. "That came out wrong. I've found I enjoy taking care of you... I just don't like that we're being forced. Or that when *you* feel ill, it makes *me* weak as well. We should be able to share strength, not weakness."

He wondered how hard it had been for her – trained warrior's muscles and all – to get him to the outer room of the suite. He remembered that his last coherent thought had been that, without those riding boots of hers, she was actually slightly shorter than him, and kissing her...

"Whoops! Settle down there, lover! That's how you got into this state in the first place." Genevieve hopped off the chair arm and sat on the couch – in the spot Ciriis usually took, he noted absently. The maneuver necessitated letting go of him and they both warily eyed the cage of white fire that had traveled with them, but nothing happened. After a moment they both relaxed.

"Did I do something wrong?" Damien asked, in some bewilderment.

Genevieve smiled back. "Not *wrong*, but I think your head needs blood more than other parts just now." She smirked towards his groin and he felt himself blushing again. "I thought *I* was in bad shape after these last two weeks, but *you*..." She laughed and scooped up a cup of something from the table. "Feed yourself, my love."

He picked up his own cup and was halfway through another swallow of the broth when he realized what she had called him and nearly drowned himself by forgetting how to swallow. She was at his side again, instantly, thumping his back.

"*You* are a mess," Genevieve said as she curled back up on the leather couch with her own cup. "At first, I thought it was just hunger, like me. And the dehydration obviously has more of an effect on you..." She gave him a quick, wicked smile, then the look of concern was back in her eyes. "But there's something else. Something subtle..." she added thoughtfully.

Damien decided he was too hungry to think quite yet, and tried manfully to focus his attention on the food. The low table that was often covered with plans was now liberally scattered with dishes, mostly covered. A deep tray on the far end had water with chips of ice floating in it to cool the dishes placed there, and he wondered what was in those dishes. It was coming up on mid-Autumn and the icehouses were running very low indeed. Even for a feast that was literally for a king, the ice would be quite dear.

"Where did all this come from?" he asked, searching for something a bit more substantial than broth and tea.

"Rosa and your dear Lady Celavell." Damien looked at her in surprise, for he had been under the impression that she and Ciriis were somehow at odds. Genevieve smiled. "Ciriis said you'd been eating as little as I had, so broth and sweetened tea would be easiest on our stomachs. Strategy, my dear, *is* my forte."

Now he smiled, too. "I know. You're probably the most brilliant strategist this kingdom has seen in generations. How you handled my grandfather's forces in Siovale nine years ago... Harald of Siovale was a complete fool." Damien stopped, aware that he might have trespassed upon things she didn't want to share.

It was the Rebel Duchess and strategist frowning at him now. "Now *that* is a problem. You know far more about me than I do about you. And clearly there are spies within the Rebellion..."

"That won't matter, soon, though," he said a little desperately. "Once we can find a way to end the hostilities entirely."

"Hmmmn," she replied noncommittally, taking a long sip from her cup.

"And I can tell you anything about me you want to know. Or you can have Ciriis and the others tell you. Wait..." Damien caught the wicked glimmer from under those long, golden lashes. "You've spent the last two weeks with Lena and Aryllis and the other women..." All his former lovers...

"I may have to keep finding ways to make you blush," Genevieve chuckled. "All that oh-so-fair skin colors up so nicely. You really need to get out in the sun more often, love."

"Not fair!" he retorted, though his heart was turning flip-flops with her second, casual, use of the word. "I can hardly quiz *your* former lovers."

Genevieve arched an eyebrow. "Well, Rosa *is* in the castle..." and she whooped with laughter as he felt his blush darken. It would be the perfect moment to throw one of those small, decorative pillows at her. Except the only ones available were on the couch where she sat – Ciriis had placed them there, though he and the other men scorned them. As a result, Genevieve had control over the only non-dangerous ammunition within reach, and a flick of her gaze told him she knew it. He made a mental note to have decorative pillows added to the rest of the seating.

There was one pillow at the other end of the couch. Perhaps he could get to it... through some subterfuge.

Damien stood up and wandered around the far side of the table to the tray of chilled dishes and began lifting lids. His light-headedness seemed well gone.

"You're blushing again," Genevieve informed him. "But you're also smiling. Amusing food?" She had stretched out like an elegant cat on the couch and captured the remaining potential missil – pillow, but she looked so beautiful that he had no complaints. Well, between that and the desserts.

"Does your Rosa have an – mmm – *particular* sense of humor?" he asked.

Genevieve frowned. "What do you mean?"

"Pranks? Jokes?" He was pursing his lips so as not to laugh.

Genevieve propped herself up on her elbows to see what he was looking at. "Oh. Oh my. I don't think I've ever seen peaches served with carrots... No, that doesn't seem like Rosa. Ciriis?" she said uncertainly. She was blushing rather nicely herself.

"Lena and Adam." Damien said definitively. Obviously, they thought he needed some inspiration. Annoying of them... "Apparently they think we need suggestions."

Genevieve smiled. "Hardly."

"Mmmmn, but *this* one seems... delicious..." Damien picked up a bowl of cream whipped thick and stiff, with two strawberries poking out of the cream. He came the rest of the way around the table and knelt beside the couch.

She rolled onto her side to look at him "What – oh!" and melted into his kiss while he stealthily moved her onto her back. A few hours earlier, he thought, the bowl of berries and cream would have been forgotten in that instant... but their presentation in the bowl had been such a *good* idea... He would take his time with this...

" 'For us, not the magick'," he quoted her when, eventually her lashes fluttered open and she looked at him, her eyes deep and dark blue.

She reached out and gently scooped a dab of cream off his cheek, and he grinned. She licked it off her finger, slowly... and he groaned.

"My turn," she said huskily, reaching to pick up the bowl of cream from where she lay. "Come up here." She didn't bother with the spoon, but she used up every last bit of cream...

“We... should go back to the bedchamber.” Genevieve murmured in Damien’s ear.

“Hmmn?” He nuzzled her neck again. The cage of white fire still flickered around them, though it seemed to have thinned and dimmed. They were clearly doing something right... but rebuilding their physical bodies after the stresses of the last two weeks had to be a part of it.

She sighed happily. “Damien. I asked them to bring us fresh food at regular intervals. But they won’t come in as long as we’re in here.”

That brought his head up abruptly, his beautiful grey eyes looking into hers at close range. “How would they know? They haven’t come in already, have they? While we...” He was too close for her to see it, but she could feel the flush starting. Mischievously she decided to help it along.

“You don’t think that door is perfectly soundproof, do you...?” She was laughing as he pulled her up and bolted for the next room.

Chapter SEVEN

Tricked!

DAMIEN LAY AS STILL AS he could, feeling Genevieve breathe, her heart beat. Her body twitched a little as she dreamed, and he was preternaturally aware of every smallest movement. The cage of white fire was barely a tracery now – how long had they been in here this time? Surely longer than that first day and night. Long enough for the bonding to be complete? Long enough for Genevieve to be bearing a child?

Their child... the idea warmed him thoroughly... then chilled him utterly.

His older sister, Kandra. Kandy had been a brilliant warrior, like Genevieve. Their grandfather had refused to knight women for some reason, but her talents had been too obvious. She had risen quickly through the ranks – having secretly enlisted as a commoner and somehow hiding her heritage until she earned her way to a commissioned rank. She, too had had a brilliant, strategic mind. And she had been loved by all for having been gutsy enough to start at the bottom.

She had been wild and strong and *meticulous*... no matter how worn that saddle girth had appeared, it couldn't have looked that way when she mounted up. Kandy would have checked. She had been paranoid, knowing full well how many of her cousins and aunts and uncles had met unexpected ends. But no amount of paranoia could answer for magick that could rot leather in an instant.

Nor would Cousin Salleen ever have drunk from a bottle of wine that his trading partner had not tasted first, but he had died of it, and the merchant hung for treason. Uncle Robert had been killed by bandits on his way back from successfully negotiating a treaty... along with his entire party. Cousin Alric, a too-clever poet, had slipped down the stairs and broken his neck. Aunt Selda had died of a toenail that became infected, despite a Healer's spells and even the amputation of her leg. His parents...

And then the long list of aunts, uncles, and cousins – like Oskar – who should never have had a chance so near the throne. A longer list, did he dare admit it, than of those who might have done well for the kingdom. Was that because of his grandfather's influence, or was there a strain of cruelty inborn to the lineage itself?

A Council to determine the fate of a land.

It was brilliant.

No one person could ever again wreak such devastation as his grandfather and Lord Prydeen had... done...

Somehow it was no longer impossible for Damien to believe that Lord Prydeen was at fault. What had changed his mind? He had lived in fear of the sorcerer for as long as he could remember.

Some part of his mind still whispered that the evil had come from his – nameless? – grandfather, that Lord Prydeen had struggled to find some way of mitigating it. Failed, but it would all be different with Damien as king. He would be a great king, and Lord Prydeen would be at his side, ensuring that he could do whatever was necessary to rebuild the Realm. It was more than a feeling, not quite a voice.

He wanted to shake his head to be rid of it, but didn't want to wake Genevieve, her head pillowed on his shoulder, her body wrapped around his in perfect trust. His previous lovers had been wonderful women, but they had never let themselves fall into such a deep sleep beside him, never trusted their comrades and him, to guard them and him while they slept. And the Heir... the King, must always be guarded.

A Council could solve all of these things. His children – *their* children – would not be subject to the fears that he had grown up under, the threats. Genevieve would never be at risk. He could abdicate...

NO, came the not-quite voice. It was his duty to rule.

His duty. His responsibility to repay Ciriis and Adam... and Jason... and so many others who had sacrificed themselves – or been sacrificed – to see him onto his throne. How could he step aside when they had given so much?

But how could he risk Genevieve – and any child they might have together?

"You're chilled all of a sudden," his beautiful soul-bonded murmured. "What's wrong?"

"I'm thinking..." he admitted. "Your Rebel Council. How does it work?"

She stretched and sat up. "You're really enamored of this idea, aren't you?"

"No more kings like my grandfather. What's not to like?"

Genevieve pulled her knees up to her chest, and wrapped her arms around them. Her golden-red hair was dry again and it hung in long curls like a cloak. "Well, there are some downsides. It takes forever to get anything done, and sometimes one doesn't have forever to wait. Some opportunities are gone before the Council can decide."

Damien sat up as well. He collected some of the scattered pillows and made himself a comfortable backrest against the headboard. "I heard about some of those 'opportunities'," he offered. "Some of them were traps."

She freed a hand to wave it dismissively. "I knew that. But a trap that you walk into while knowing it's a trap turns the advantage around. There were other things. Not military ones."

"The flooding in the Cedarwen valley last year," he recalled, and was pleased to see her surprise. "My grandfather was reluctant to send help and supplies." It had been one of the few times he had stood up to the old man. But Lady Theresa had begged Damien to do it, for her family's lands and people.

"We could have been there first," Genevieve said. "And won Cedarwen to our side. But the Council felt it was stretching us too thin. Rosa finally talked them into it, but by that time your grandfather's army was there with food and supplies and assistance rebuilding." She gave him a sudden sharp look. "That wasn't your grandfather's doing, was it? I've never heard of him sending Healers before. Or helping commoners to rebuild. That was you."

Damien nodded. His instinct was to duck his head and refuse credit. Maybe it *was* time to change those reactions. "You wouldn't have been able to switch the allegiance of Baron Rafael, though. Not with his mother, Lady Theresa, here in the castle as a hostage to their behavior."

"Hmmmn," she replied noncommittally, and he realized she knew every one of his grandfather's public executions... and what it had taken for the people they had been held hostage for to give them up. What she had probably said and done to convince them they had to give up their loved ones. A chill went down his spine. If he had lost Lady Theresa on top of everyone else...

"How are the Council members chosen?" he asked, to distract himself as much as because he wanted to know.

"That's the other weakness of the system," Genevieve answered. "We've brought on every lord and lady who has come to join us. And every senior military official and senior merchant. And some not so-senior ones, whom I asked to join because of their good sense. But they all defer to each other by rank. My father began building the Rebellion, but I'm the nominal leader because of my rank as duchess, not my training or any assumed wisdom or supposed military brilliance."

"But they didn't blindly follow you when you decided to come here," Damien pointed out.

"No..." she agreed slowly. "But I didn't ask them to, either. Or command them. Actually," Genevieve gave him an abashed look that seemed totally out of character. "I gave up arguing with the Council. I snuck out in the middle of the night when the watches changed. That's why I didn't arrive until the final day of your coronation festivities."

Damien laughed. "Somehow, I don't think Jason would be surprised."

She gave him a tentative smile. "Are we going to be able to make this okay? Between you and me... and Jason?"

"I don't want him to touch you again." It slipped out before Damien could even think about it. "Or any other man," he added a bit lamely. "Or woman." His efforts to imagine sharing her with Rosa had been nearly as devastating as the rest. *Too imaginative,* more than one of his tutors had called him in the early days before his parents...

"All right," she agreed readily, to his surprise... "But I want the same of you. No more Ciriis holding your arm or your hand or... or *whatever*. And no one else either." That *whatever* suggested that she had been indulging in as uncomfortable flights of fancy as he had.

She held out her hand, and they shook on it, but somehow forgot to let go.

Genevieve tipped her head to the side. "What about dancing? We're going to face protocol situations where we are expected to dance with visiting ambassadors, high-ranking nobles – Damien, you're hurting me." She said it so calmly that he had to almost shake himself to realize she was talking about how tightly he was grasping her hand. And *then* he had to slowly, consciously, release his grip, muscle by muscle.

But the image of her in the arms of another man – he carefully did not let himself imagine Jason – holding close together while dancing... It made his breath catch and his stomach tighten. The edges of his vision started darkening again....

Her body, soft, and smooth, and hard with muscles, was suddenly across him, her lips were on his. He relaxed.

"Ok, so dancing is out." She pulled out of the kiss and laughed up at him, framing his face with her hands. "I can't say I mind if it keeps me from having to dance with Lord Prydeen again. I'm sure Ciriis can find – or manufacture – some point of protocol that requires us to dance only with each other. I'm not giving *that* up!" That was a different image... and one that made his stomach tighten in an entirely different way. Aryllis had been the one to teach him to dance, but it had been giggly Lena who had chimed in with the idea that dancing was like making love standing up... and in public. He had been all of eighteen at the time, still barely past being a virgin.

Lena had nearly wet herself, laughing, as he turned as red as a beet and fled the room.

She was absolutely right, though.

"Line dances?" he suggested reluctantly. There were doubtless going to be times they couldn't get out of dancing with other people. "Quartets?"

"So long as your lovely Guardswomen aren't part of the quartet." Genevieve told him severely, then laughed. "That's probably silly of me. You're safer with them than with some foreign dignitary." Her laugh sounded a bit strained, so he kissed her again and stroked her hair.

"If you yield on this one, I have to yield, too, and I refuse to do that." His Royal Guards *would* be safer as her dance partners... no. "We'll make it work somehow." He paused. "We could set up the Royal Council to run things without me – they more or less ran things without my grandfather anyways. And I could abdicate."

Genevieve sighed, and played with his hair. "We might be able to work *towards* such an end, my love, but right *now* we have to rebuild an entire Realm. Those nobles who did not join the Rebel Cause – and even some of those who have – have had generations to learn that there is no redress for the commoner against them. If not you – and me – and our rank to outweigh the other nobles, who will stand up for the commoners and the lesser nobles – like Rosa's family?" Although the Teraseels were 'lesser' only by comparison to dukes and royals.

He dropped his head. "I know. And I owe... everything... to those who sacrificed themselves to bring me to the throne. They thought I could serve the kingdom better than my grandfather. I have to justify that faith."

"And without us to do it, who will stand up to Lord Prydeen?" she asked, but the look in her blue-green eyes was apprehensive.

He remembered his defense of the sorcerer and shook his head. "What was I thinking?"

Genevieve smiled in relief. "I don't think you were. He's been casting some sort of subtle spells on you these last two weeks. The Ring has been trying to warn me," she held up her hand with the huge grey pearl on it... the only thing either of them wore, "but I don't think it could do more than protect *me* when you were intentionally blocking yourself off. My impression is that these spells are hard to cast when the victim is alert..." She trailed off, hesitant.

"...but I was too angry that first day," Damien sighed. "He must have laid just enough groundwork then to ensure that I wouldn't turn a deaf ear the next time he sought to speak to me." He snorted. "My Lord Prydeen has been encouraging me to let him speak to you on my behalf and mend the breach between us. Do you think it will please him that we've done it ourselves?"

Genevieve chuckled. "Probably not. I suppose he knew that he needed to get control of both sides of the bond."

Damien felt cold all over again. "Then we're at a greater risk when he realizes he's lost his grip on me. On *both* of us." He buried his face in Genevieve's neck. "I've put us – *you* – in danger."

She caressed his hair. "Then we'll have to see if we can persuade him it's gone the other way. That instead of losing his grip on you, he's gained one on me."

"Genevieve..."

She shivered. "I love the way you say my name. Harald... called me 'Genny' and kind of ruined it for me." Damien could not help thinking with a sneaky, triumphant feeling that *Jason* called her 'Genny.'

Still... He lifted his head to face her. "Do you really think we can do that? Are you that good of an actress? I had years here... if Lord Prydeen doesn't still think I'm an ineffectual, useless seat-warmer, I'd be surprised." ***And** everyone else,* he thought and was surprised at how bitter the thought was. He was still alive, he was crowned. He had succeeded. Right?

She gave him a wry smile. "I was married to Harald for eight years. He... demanded... a certain performance in the bedchamber. And my own pride would not let me show that there were any problems between us outside of it. I think I can handle this." She saw Damien's stricken look and kissed the tip of his nose. "Long ago and far away."

Damien still had the irrational desire to do something horrible to the long-vanished Harald. "Long ago and far away," he granted her. "But he was still a selfish fool."

Genevieve grinned. "No argument here." Her face grew sober. "But eventually we *will* have to deal with Lord Prydeen directly. Is there any way we can do that? It will take magick – serious, powerful magick – to defeat him."

The young king sighed and leaned back against the pillows again. He ran a hand through his hair. "I was hoping you – the Rebellion – might have some ideas. I've heard that there are *good* wizards elsewhere in the world, but I haven't had the resources to send out to look for one."

"We've been looking," Genevieve admitted. "But we've had no luck yet."

"Then we have only the scraps of legend to help us." Damien closed his eyes. He didn't want to see her expression. That all their hopes should come down to fairystories...

When the silence had stretched on long enough, he opened his eyes. Was that wonder in hers?

"The Monarch's Blade," she whispered. "That's it, isn't it?"

He squeezed his eyes shut. "It's just an old legend. But yes. It's supposed to make the Monarch invincible. Including against magick." And now she'd ridicule him and his faith – no, his *hope* – in old stories. Not that he had anything else to maintain hope with. Jason knew the story and had been skeptical but quiet about it, but he hadn't even dared hint at this to cynical Adam or Ciriis.

"It's not just a legend."

His eyes flew open. Genevieve's incredible blue-green eyes seemed to glow.

"It's not. My Nana – the Grand Duchess Alicia, my grandmother. She told me that her mother actually *held* the Sword."

Damien visualized the family trees that had become needlessly broad and complex during his grandfather's eighty-three-year reign. "Her mother – that would have been the Princess Alexandria? Queen Marian's 'Autumn child'?"

Genevieve nodded. "No one could believe she not only survived the birth, but that she ruled for another seventeen years. Supposedly Queen Marian decided to conceive her because the Sword had rejected every one of her other descendants." She looked down, then up at Damien through her lashes. "That would have included your grandfather."

"Smart Sword," he commented. "It saw what no one else apparently did. Did the sword 'speak' for Princess Alexandria?"

Genevieve shrugged. "Nana wasn't clear on that part. It drove me crazy, but she died before I was six years old and her mind was a bit soft towards the end... she had been fond of jousting as a young woman and had suffered a few too many blows to the head, my father told me. Nana did say that *her* grandmother – Queen Marian – had said that she had caused the Sword to be placed where none of her unworthy descendants would be able to find it and thereby claim that they were the anointed ruler. But Nana was born some five years after her grandmother died... I don't know... maybe she meant it was her mother who had told her."

It was more than Damien had been able to glean from searching the records of the time. Hope sparked.

"'Unworthy descendants'," he murmured.

"It does suggest that her *worthy* descendants should be able to find it," Genevieve said with some excitement.

"That could be you," he offered somewhat diffidently.

Genevieve snagged one of the pillows from behind him and wopped him with it... rather hard. "*Or* you. And we're basing this on the childhood memories of a softheaded old lady. Who was remembering what was told to her by another very old lady."

"It's still *some*thing. Which is more than we had before," Damien pointed out. "And no one ever accused Queen *Marian* of being softheaded, I believe." This was a riddle, and solving riddles was one of his strengths.

"No. Her reputation was as hardheaded as mine," Genevieve grinned.

"But was she as wild and careless?" Damien asked, feeling a sense of mischief overcome him now that a glimmer of hope had occurred.

"What do you mean wild and careless?" she demanded.

"Well, you came into the city to find me all on your own, let yourself be noticed by Lord Prydeen, climbed to the top of the one place in the city he was sure to follow you, found yourself soul-bonded... and left your toes out where they could be tickled?" He grinned, feeling very confident of himself.

Genevieve had begun to blush as he listed the trail of events. It didn't paint her much-vaunted strategic mind in the best of lights. But at the last 'accusation', she cried "ha!" and proceeded to demonstrate that Damien was far more ticklish than she was.

A short time later, they were seated again against the headboard, this time with Genevieve leaning back against Damien's chest. He held her wrists cross-wise, her right in his left hand, her left in his right, having finally found a way to use his slightly longer arms to immobilize her. And he still had the nagging feeling she had *let* him...

They were both giggling and out of breath. The silly interlude had somehow broken the tension, not just of their recent situations, but of the overall one. The rest of life might have to be in deadly earnest, but they could have this.

She relaxed suddenly against him, and he tensed at first, expecting a trick that would end – again – with him gasping for air and crying her mercy. As she continued to lounge, however, Damien let his own muscles relax, though not releasing her wrists.

Genevieve heaved a long, contented sigh. "Damien Alsterling, I *do* love you."

Time seemed to stop.

She could have pulled free and returned to tickling him mercilessly and he would not have tried to resist.

After a long, long moment, he found his voice. "I've loved you since I was eight years old."

Her voice had a smile in it as she replied. "I know."

And in that moment the cage of white fires flared again into a complete, opaque bubble... and with an almost audible pop! it collapsed, seeming to be sucked into the Heir's Ring that Genevieve still wore on her left hand.

"Hunh. I guess that means we're free to do other things?" Genevieve said.

Damien sighed and let go of her wrists to pull her closer, burying his face against her hair. "Do we have to?"

She laughed. "No, and we probably shouldn't." She twisted her head up to look at him over her shoulder. "Damien, my love, when was the last time you went outside this castle – *other* than your coronation festivities?"

"Er–" He honestly couldn't remember. The trip to Adam's family had been seven years ago, when he was seventeen. He had wanted to go to Cedarwen last year, to help with the flood recovery, but Ciriis had reminded him that it wasn't wise for the Heir to be absent from the seat of power.

"The king is – or should be – the servant of the people, yes," Genevieve was continuing. "But that doesn't mean that you shouldn't take care of your own needs. Look what happened when you tried to put your own needs aside two weeks ago. Honestly, there was nothing happening that day that needed your personal attention. Adam and Ciriis could have handled everything that was going on."

He couldn't disagree her assessment... but he had spent his entire life watching his grandfather and other royals and nobles abuse their power. It was his job to mend that history, wasn't it? How could he do that, if not by making himself available to them?

Her hands slid up to caress his head, but her words distracted him from the interesting things that did to the feel of her torso under his hands. "Damien, I've been ruling my duchy and leading the Rebellion for nearly three years now. Do you think I've done a good job?"

He felt his mouth quirk into a wry grin. "The numbers speak for themselves. Your forces have defeated the Royal Army every time we were foolish enough to engage you. And our people have been fleeing *to* you, not the other way around."

"I take time to do things for me. I go hunting – sometimes that's the only way to get everyone to stop coming to me with things. I go on diplomatic missions. My people know that I'm not to be disturbed for anything less than a calamity when I'm in my personal suite." She looked up at him again. "If you are *too* available, eventually two things happen. One," she brought her arms back down to count on her fingers. "Other people will forget how much they can do without you, which is bad for *them;* and two, they will come to take you for granted and stop listening to you. Which is bad for *everyone.*"

"But–" Damien didn't really have an objection, but he felt he needed to say something. This ran counter to everything he had been doing. And thinking.

"New rulers usually have one of two problems," Genevieve went on. "The first is not knowing how to delegate. You have that one in hand, perhaps because Adam and Ciriis have taken so much of the job upon themselves. Hush," she said before he could even start to object to that. "If any of you are honest with yourselves, you'll see that that's what's happened. I doubt it was intentional, but they can't help seeing you as the hapless boy they had to protect and manage for his own good." Damien had read about someone's jaw dropping open with surprise... he had always thought it was a literary exaggeration, but Genevieve's strong, slender fingers had reached up to gently push his chin back into place. How she had even known...? "The second problem is to learn how to command such that one is listened to and obeyed. Without engendering fear, without being petulant. Simply to command."

"And that's *my* problem, you're saying."

She nodded. "That's your problem."

"Which was yours, might I ask?"

Genevieve snorted. "What do you think? My father had trained me to command properly since I was born by teaching me that there was no task too low for me to do. I mucked out chicken coops and scrubbed pots in the scullery and – oh, every unpleasant task you might imagine. And he, or my mother, were right there beside me until I was old enough to work without their supervision. They taught me to respect the work of every person and never to ask from others what I would not do myself."

Damien nodded. "So, you felt you had to do everything."

"Most things," she admitted. "And my father mostly taught me to delegate before he died, by gradually giving me more and more power... and helping me sort out the problems when I floundered."

"Whereas my grandfather permitted me no power at all..." Damien sighed. "And now I've been crowned and have it all..."

"You aren't floundering too badly," she hastened to reassure him. Though from her tone, he suspected she felt that it was *Adam* and *Ciriis* who weren't floundering too badly in managing him. What about Jason? She never included him in her lists, though he was always there with the other two. Was that because of a lingering fondness for her childhood friend (*or more?* He tried to tamp down the thought as unworthy) or was it a difference that she saw in how they treated him?

"My head hurts," he muttered, burying his face in her wonderful hair and then coughing as he inadvertently inhaled a curl.

Genevieve laughed. "Then how about we get some food? What you and I need right now is to rebuild our strength. And I did ask Rosa and Ciriis to put out fresh food at regular intervals."

Damien snorted. "More suggestive desserts? What could they possibly come up with this time?"

Genevieve shrugged, and this time he wasn't distracted by her words. "They may be more imaginative than we are – though of course they have a whole committee putting that tray together. Peaches and carrots," she chuckled, then arched back against him as his hands moved up to cup her breasts.

"Are you *very* hungry?" he asked, his words wistful but his hands moving with more confidence than his tone. He parted her hair to expose her neck for a line of kisses.

"Yes... but I think I could wait a bit to eat," she breathed.

Chapter EIGHT

Worries...

SOMEWHAT LATER, THEY MOVED INTO the outer suite, this time swathed in lounging robes that Damien had to admit he had never found occasion to wear before. Watching Genevieve's body move under the smooth silk, he decided then and there that he would make the time to see her wear it often.

A different array of dishes had been left for them on the table. They began with the hot dishes by mutual consent, removing lids and tasting samples until Genevieve uncovered the largest one and burst into... he could only call them giggles. He had heard her giggle a bit during their tickle fight, but otherwise she tended towards much more dignified chuckles.

It was his turn to give her an arched eyebrow. She gestured towards the dish, still trying to muffle her laughter, so he peered in and saw nothing but a large piece of meat. Baffled, he looked at her again.

"Oh," she gasped, "You really *don't* hunt, do you? You've never hunted a stag and had to dress out the carcass?"

"I've never been hunting," he answered, still confused. Then he took another look at the meat and blanched. "That isn't...?"

"It is." She choked back her laughter and wiped her eyes. "You might take it as a compliment. The king-stag of a forest can have a harem of forty or fifty does... and they all fawn about the same time, so..." She couldn't hold it back any longer as Damien hastily re-covered the dish and looked determinedly at some of the other offerings.

More than broth and light foods, this time, thank the Gods. Or rather Ciriis and Countess Rosa. Or... Adam and Lena, who were doubtless doubled over with amusement over their pranks. Damien settled down beside his betrothed on the couch this time and set to on a perfectly normal meal of stew and trencher bread and decided he would leave the cold dishes alone this time.

At least he thought it was a perfectly normal stew until he saw Genevieve fishing something round out of her stew and dissolve in snorts of laughter again. She clearly swallowed something the wrong way in her efforts and suddenly he was frantically pounding on her back and offering her a drink of water... while she... yes, she was *still* laughing.

Damien eyed his plate of stew with trepidations and resolutely set it aside, resolving not to ask. Bread would do. What else was there? Noodles baked in a cheese sauce was one of his favorites, and they knew that. Surely that was safe, too. On a fresh plate. To be certain, he carefully stirred through the noodles before beginning to eat.

"You've really never been hunting?" Genevieve asked, continuing to calmly eat her stew. "I thought it was something every noble did, at least on occasion."

Damien shrugged self-consciously. He was all too aware of the gaps in his upbringing compared to other nobles. "I spent almost all my time in the Royal Library after... after I was about ten. I didn't even have tutors. Most of the time I suspect no one remembered I existed." Except Lady Theresa, who as Royal Librarian had been all too aware of the royal waif in her stacks.

He forced a smile for Genevieve. He didn't want her to pity him. "It was probably for the best. I was safe there, and I really don't like hurting things. I fed crumbs to the mice to make pets of them." He grinned for real then. "It upset Lady Theresa to no end. I think she thought the mice would begin to chew on her books and scrolls."

Or it might have been that she knew Damien wasn't getting all that much to eat himself, since he was too terrified to actually eat on the occasions when he was summoned to dinners with the rest of the royal family. He'd managed the rest of the time snagging scraps as the servants cleared away... food that the servants saved for their own meals and families, so he had to be quick about it, and lucky.

She'd started bringing a basket of food with her to the library and leaving it out where he could get to it without having to go past her... taming him as surely as he had tamed the mice...

Genevieve gave him a wicked look. "Imagine what she'd think of this feast?"

Damien groaned and covered his face. "Please!"

But Genevieve wasn't done. "Which would be worse? That she'd be horrified – or that she'd laugh?" He could feel his face flaming, and could think of only one way to get her to stop... fortunately Genevieve was more than willing to trade taunts for kisses... and caresses... food be damned...

"Still hungry!" she said at last, surfacing after several minutes. Damien looked down into her glorious eyes, her beautiful face framed by that golden-red hair, and wondered how he could have gone a lifetime without her... not to mention have been angry enough to have denied himself these moments for two weeks when she was right *there*...

"I love you."

She immediately stopped wriggling to sit up and put her hands around his face. Gentle fingers made distinctive with her sword- and bow-calluses. "And I love you." She reached up and kissed the tip of his nose. "But I *am* still hungry. I'm not going away anywhere, you know."

Reluctantly, he let her sit up and return to eating. After a few prods from Genevieve, he went back to eating also. In between watching her, anyways.

At length, Genevieve was done. She sighed happily, set down her bowl, and leaned against Damien's shoulder. He hastily set his remaining food down and put an arm around her. His other hand met hers, and he rested his head against hers. They stayed snuggled like that for awhile.

"I suppose we should see what they sent as desserts this time," Genevieve said at last.

"Must we?" Damien asked, eyeing the large covered dish of... deer meat.

"We-e-ell, after all the trouble they seem to be going to, we should at least look."

She heaved herself up, grinned wickedly at him, and knelt beside the low table.

Damien sighed and sat up to look over her shoulder.

"Fresh fruit from warmer kingdoms," Genevieve noted as she lifted the wicker lid of a large dish. "Now I know I'm feasting at the king's table!" Damien had not thought about it that way before. He leaned farther to see what she had uncovered. Oranges and bananas. An entire pineapple, halved, cored, and refilled with chunks of its own golden innards.

She opened a small bowl, but her enthusiasm seemed dimmed. "Caviar." One of his favorites. He looked over to the hot dishes to see if there were any of the tiny slices of crusty bread... yes, there was some.

Genevieve was opening another bowl. This time she simply stared into it. He could see her jawline working as if she were trying not to say something, and down the bond he could feel her emotions in turmoil. Damien leaned closer, but the bowl seemed almost to be filled with shimmering red jewels sprinkled over a whipped cream. Some kind of fruit? It wasn't one that he was familiar with, but the whipped cream reminded him of their previous meal very pleasantly.

"What's wrong?" He asked.

"It's pomegranate," Genevieve replied as if that should explain everything. His bafflement must have communicated itself, because after a moment she went on. "It's supposed to promote fertility. So is the rest of this." Her wave included the covered dish of deer... meat. "I'll bet the rest is the same." She began opening up the other cold dishes. Apples mixed with figs. Hardboiled eggs of different sizes – quails, ducks and such. "Very... direct of them."

"Oh." The idea of creating a child made his loins tighten again eagerly, although this spread of foods seemed a bit over the top. Lena and Adam funning at their expense again, no doubt. But... "Last time you laughed it off. This is upsetting you."

"It's – just one was a clever joke, but when it's all of them..." Her whole body sagged as if in defeat. Her shoulders bowed, and her beautiful, curly hair fell forwards to hide her face. "I spent *years* eating these things. And more. I needed an Heir. And now... *you* need an Heir."

"It's not that urgent..."

She looked up at him, and he could see tears silently rolling down her cheeks. "I never even miscarried, Damien. I didn't conceive so that I *could* miscarry. It wasn't Harald – he proved that, clearly enough. As you know from those reports. So, it must have been me. I told you that I was at the wrong end of my cycle to conceive. But the truth is I've never had a regular cycle." She paused and swallowed hard. "A king can't afford to marry a barren woman."

"Come up here." Damien tugged gently until Genevieve came back up onto the couch and was curled up on his lap, leaning into his shoulder. "Perhaps the Gods simply were waiting until we could be together. I've heard of marriages disrupted when one of the partners soul-bonded to someone else, but never one where children were involved."

He'd meant it to be soothing, but she heaved a sound that was a half a sob, half a sigh. "That almost makes it worse. This – not having children – destroyed my marriage. If I'd only been able to conceive, then maybe he wouldn't have felt driven to prove he could sire them. To... And then maybe he, and my *father*..." Damien could feel her chest constricting with the grief, the... guilt? How could she blame herself? Genevieve had done everything she could, and more.

And how many days and nights had he spent blaming himself – his ten-year-old self – for not having found some way to save his parents. His sister. Grief was unreasonable.

He held her close, tucked her head under his chin, rocked her gently for several long moments.

"I can't say I would wish our soul-bonding couldn't have taken place," he said into her hair at last. "Or... if the stories are wrong, that it might have harmed your family. But... if having a child with Harald could have saved your father's life... it would be worth it.

"There is almost nothing I wouldn't give up if it would bring back my parents. Or my sister... or any of the dozen aunts, uncles, and cousins who would be a better ruler for this country than me." Although Genevieve *was* that 'almost'.

Genevieve stirred in his arms, turning to look up at him, reaching up to his face to wipe away the tears he hadn't realized he was crying. She must have felt them in her hair. "You do yourself too little credit, my love," she told him. "Your parents would be very proud to see how you are managing as king."

Damien smiled a little weakly. "You'd make a better one. You have the training. And the experience." He winced. "I'm sorry, I didn't mean–"

"I didn't think you did." She rested her head on his shoulder again. It felt more peaceful, but the young king could feel the tears still silently trickling down onto his chest. He had been mourning his family for fourteen years and it still hurt. Her loss was less than three years gone. No one had ever talked to him about the deaths of his parents and sister – it had been too dangerous to mention those that his grandfather and Lord Prydeen had done away with. He hated that their names were all but forgotten. Perhaps... perhaps talking about things... *helped*.

"What exactly happened?" he asked tentatively. "The reports I heard were that it was a hunting accident, but there were no details. My, er, sources were usually able to tell me more than that."

"Your spies," she corrected, but he could feel her smile briefly against him.

"Mmmn." He couldn't fairly object.

"Well, they didn't fail you. There weren't many more details. My father took Harald out hunting. I presume it was to take him to task for what he had said to me about his bastard children at dinner a few nights before. It was foggy, as it often is up in the mountains around Elaarwen in the Fall. We... we found the tracks of their horses. They ended at the top of a precipice." Genevieve drew a ragged breath. "It's at the top of a chasm so deep that even in good weather you can't see the bottom. Trees, bushes, rocks, that's all. Even the mountain-people who live in that area have never climbed to the bottom. Not and returned."

"That..." Damien hunted for the right words. "That would feel... unresolved. To me."

She nodded. "I couldn't help hoping, for the first year. I sent anyone who would dare to see if they could climb down, to explore to find the ends of the chasm. We don't even know if there's a river at the bottom. The cliffs are so sheer – it might simply be a place where the mountains split apart, though we don't even have legends of the kind of earthquake it would take to create that place."

"So... what did you do then?"

A long, shuddering sigh, but she relaxed a bit. "I went on. There's nothing else. I was Duchess. I couldn't just... stop. My people needed me."

"I stopped," he admitted to her hair. "As much as I could. I tried not to eat... or breathe. Anything, so I didn't have to think."

She didn't say 'you were ten', as if it was some childish thing. "Having other people needing you and trying to do too much works, too. Most of the time I was just too damned *tired* to think by the time I had a moment to myself." She paused. "And he had always told me that my life belonged to others. I didn't have the right to... to *stop."*

He. Her father. Who had been preparing her to face his own death for her whole life. As Damien would have to do with his own child. What a morbid approach to parenting a title necessitated.

"I didn't really start to *feel* again until Rosa arrived," Genevieve added.

"I imagine that was a dramatic entrance."

"It was, indeed." Was that a hint of a chuckle? His heart warmed in hope. "She blew in on a dark and stormy night – she and her retainers had ridden straight from Zialest, taking no more breaks than they needed to rest their horses. Straight over the mountains. No one travels those mountain passes – *no one* – and they made it in *three days.* I'd never heard of it being done in less than a week. And never with horses and children. I still don't know how they managed.

"She'd stripped her estates of every able-bodied person and sent the rest to beg refuge in Dalizell. Crown Prince Oskar had arrived ahead of the groom's wedding party, so Zachary wasn't even on the grounds when..." Her voice faltered.

She had known the Count of Zialest and his family well, Damien knew. They had been secret supporters of the Rebellion, just far enough from Reyensweir that their county had always claimed a level of autonomy from the Duke who would otherwise have been their liege-lord before the king. "The doors of my main hall blew in when Rosa brought her people in – informing me that they were here to stay, and that she intended to return to Zialest with the Rebellion's army as soon as we could plan it out."

Now Genevieve did chuckle. "She was still wearing the gown stained with Prince Oskar's blood. We hadn't yet heard what was going on, so I had no idea what this was all about. I'd been invited to the wedding, but since we knew there would be a representative of the Crown, I'd declined. The last time I had seen her in person had been maybe nine years earlier – she had just combed out her pigtails. And now she arrived on my doorstep with the storm behind her as an avenging goddess."

Damien smiled to himself as he imagined the scene. The Countess of Zialest was one of the most self-composed people he had ever seen. In those circumstances she would have been... formidable. And... enchanting. A *goddess,* Genevieve had called her.

"Once we got everyone settled and fed, the Council and I got the whole story out of her. She – she had just seen her whole family slaughtered before her, been raped, just slain her first human, and she never broke down." Genevieve's voice held something like awe. She moved her head as if she was about to add something more, then subsided.

"Shock?" The young king suggested.

"I suppose so. She did, eventually, when it was just us. But not until we had liberated Zialest and re-installed her people. If you need an ambassador to – well, anywhere – Rosa is your woman."

"When–" he cleared his throat, "when did you become lovers?"

His red-headed beloved tilted her head up at him. A faintly mischievous smile played around her mouth, though he could still see the tracks of dried tears; he longed to kiss them away. If only that would also take away the pain that had generated them.

"You know, I've had only two lovers before you, and you know a great deal about both of them. How many have you had?" She demanded to know. "Ciriis, Lena, Aryllis...?"

"Um..." Damien felt himself going red.

"What, surely not *all* the members of your Royal Women's Auxiliary?' she teased. Then, as he blushed even harder and tried to avoid her eye, she laughed. "You can't be serious! How many of them are there? Twenty?"

"Twelve," he said, somewhat desperately. "And it wasn't my idea at all. I'd go to my bedroom and someone would be waiting. They managed it all among themselves."

"I'm sure you hated every moment of it," Genevieve teased. Then looked at him more seriously. "You almost *did*, didn't you?" she marveled.

"Almost," he said in a small voice. He had known that the dreams he'd had of Genevieve Stellarine were probably going to stay just that... but he still felt he should have waited. Ciriis had known exactly how to ensure his body disagreed. And that he enjoyed every minute of it. If it had only been her, that might have been one thing, but eventually she had put Lena into his bed. Then Terellie, then... "I don't know what Ciriis was thinking," he muttered.

To his surprise, the Rebel Duchess had an answer. "I think she was trying to make sure your natural urges didn't lead you into dangerous situations. And hoping that one of those girls would capture more than your fleeting fancy – they're all nobly born enough for you to marry, or to keep as an acknowledged mistress if you did end up making a marriage of state." Genevieve favored him with a gentle smile. "She cares a great deal about you."

"I suppose."

"Did you know she was to have wed Rosa's brother?"

Damien sucked in his lips. "Gavin of Zialest was *her* Gavin? I knew she stopped talking about him, but honestly, it's been so busy since I was named Heir, I didn't pay attention." He paused. "I wouldn't have thought my levelheaded Ciriis would fall for such a hothead."

"Your?"

"Well, she *was,*" he said defensively. "Sort of. My friend and advisor, anyways." Damien was floundering and he knew it.

"Your pimp and procurer," Genevieve suggested, and he thought her tone was teasing, but...

"It wasn't like that," he objected, somewhat lamely, since he had to admit that was exactly what it was like. He'd never felt he had a choice in the matter, though, so was he the customer or... the prostitute? What had been in it for the ladies of his Royal Guard? A hope of a future with him? A sense of possession of him? He knew that some of them had been rescued by Ciriis after they had had the misfortune to come to the attentions of his grandfather or Lord Prydeen, but still they had come to his bed. And taught him about loving.

Perhaps... perhaps he had been *safe*. A naïve young prince being *managed* by his older, wiser friends. Perhaps... his honest, innocent appreciation and caring had been something they needed – at least some of them – to heal from what had been done to them. He knew it had always been by their own choice. He could hope he had given them something as beautiful as what they had given him.

Genevieve reached up to flick his nose. "Silly. I told you before, I have no qualms about this. They kept you safe and taught you all sorts of wonderful things. And," she added, hoisting herself up to sit on his lap facing him, her knees to either side and her robe distractingly pushed out of the way. "It puts us in the interesting position of me being older, but you being rather more... experienced."

It should have brought him to the blush again, but he was noticing that dressing gowns had the delightful attribute of being entirely open in the front...

Her eyes, much later, when she moved her head far enough away so that he could see her properly, were that dark, rich blue that somehow he knew no one else had ever seen. "I think they may have heard us this time..." she said teasingly.

"I don't care," Damien replied, and was surprised to find it was true.

Genevieve smiled and nuzzled into his neck again. "This is the best couch ever."

He was inclined to agree... although he was beginning to assess the other furniture as well...

Chapter NINE

Escape...

THEY HAD MADE IT BACK to his – to *their* bed – for some more sleep, and this time when Genevieve awoke, she had a plan. The clerestory windows high above suggested that dawn would be soon – of what day, she could not begin to guess. The magick had turned her time sense round about.

She slid out of bed carefully, without disturbing Damien – marveling that he was so exhausted that it was even possible to do that. By the time she had had a bath, however, he was stretching and looking around for her. The bond had told him that she was close by, as it had told her that he was waking up.

"We're going out today," she informed him as he contemplated her damp, nude form with interest.

"I thought you said–"

"Not out with people," she said, turning and contemplating the soiled clothes she had removed before surprising him in bed. However long ago that had been. "We're going to go hunting."

"You'll need clothes, then," he said, coming up behind her and sliding his hands around her waist. Nibbling at her neck. "Or we could go back to bed..." he murmured.

Genevieve let her head roll back and the shivers of delight work their way down her spine. Then, resolutely, she stepped away. "You need some fresh air and sunshine, my young king. As your loyal liegewoman it's my bounden duty to provide what you need. Not," she added warningly, "necessarily what you *want.*"

Damien sighed. As she had suspected, suggesting he might put wants before needs was a motivator for him, although he wasn't used to it being in terms of *his* needs.

"Can we get out of the castle without anyone knowing?" she asked.

"You don't ask for much, do you?" He eyed her a bit regretfully. "I think so. We'll need to go down to your apartment, but since you'll need more appropriate clothes anyways..."

She grinned. "I *had* been thinking of just wearing some of yours, if need be." That had the expected salutary effect on him. What was it about men that made them feel a woman wearing one of their shirts marked her as theirs?

"You could anyways..." he offered wistfully, opening a drawer to offer her one.

She pulled it on. They were almost of a height, so it barely reached past the top of her thighs. She measured his hips with her eyes as he seemed mesmerized by the hem of his shirt on her. "I think my own pants will be a better fit, though."

"Let me get a quick wash–" he began.

"Take your time," she advised, heading towards the sitting room, but making sure to let the hem of the shirt swish side to side as she did so. "I have a couple things to do."

He sprinted for the bathing chamber.

As the Rebel Duchess had suspected, a fresh set of food awaited, though the hot dishes were just warm and there were no longer ice chips floating amongst the chilled ones. The bread basket conveniently had a handle this time and she had no qualms in re-packing it with sliced meats and cheese, and those bedamned hardboiled eggs, and other foods that would travel well.

A bit of hunting around the desk in the corner found her paper and ink. She munched on some fruit while she wrote a short note, then took the basket back into the bedchamber with her. Damien had all but stated that there was another way out of this room.

He returned just moments later, his hair still dripping, but looking considerably more alert, to find Genevieve seated cross-legged on the bed. The young king smiled, and quickly dressed in the clothes she had chosen for him: the closest things he had to hunting clothes, the stuff he wore when practicing swordplay. And his sword.

"So... not even Ciriis knows about this," Damien said, as she had expected. "I have trouble finding it myself, now that I'm not wearing the Ring. But you should be able to see it clearly since you *are* wearing the Ring." He gestured, and she looked where he pointed, hopping off the bed to see better.

There was a shadow along the outer wall. The longer she looked at it, the more clearly she could see that it was a set of stairs winding along the inside of the wall up towards the roof. "Those stairs? They seem to go the wrong way."

Damien smiled wistfully. "They go up to the top of the tower, and there's a door to access the outside. It only gets you into the cupola of crenelations around the cone, and anyone looking through the windows from down here can probably see you–"

"Unless the magick takes care of that, too."

He nodded. "I've never had a way to find out." It was interesting to Genevieve that he had never told his protectors about this. She was about to comment on it, but he said, "look again," and she followed his directive instead.

"Does it go down into the floor?" Genevieve picked up her boots – the only clothing item she had brought with her that she would need after a trip back to her own rooms, since she had continued to scorn dancing slippers in exchange for the extra height of bootheels – and walked over to look more closely. She poked her toe tentatively at the place where she seemed to be able to see *through* the floor to stairs leading downwards along the curve of the outer wall, then looked quizzically at Damien when she met no resistance. "I can understand how no one else has noticed this, if it takes wearing the Ring, as you say. But how is it that no one has fallen down these stairs?"

Th young king grinned at her. "Once you can see it, it's there for you. Until then, you can walk right over it and the floor is perfectly solid. Adam was the first person I saw do that, when we were checking this space out. He wanted to know why I tried to pull him back from that wall... they were all a bit paranoid." Fairly so, he didn't need to add.

She raised an eyebrow. "What did you tell him?"

Damien snorted. "It didn't go well, let's say. I couldn't believe he couldn't see the stairs, and he was sure I must have somehow gotten concussed. How that could have happened without him knowing, when the three of them never let me out of their sight, it wasn't clear. He and Ciriis snarled at each other a lot that day, until I finally gave up and said there weren't any invisible, intangible stairs – I just hadn't wanted to admit I'd startled over seeing a mouse."

Genevieve gave him a sympathetic look. She could imagine how that had hurt his pride, and how the other two had been *ever* so slightly condescending for a time after.

But Damien just shrugged. "They stopped fussing at each other and over me. And once they were convinced that this was a safe place, they actually left me *alone* once in a while, and I could explore where the stairs went."

"Down to my apartment." Genevieve cocked her head at him. "So, this whole time, you could have come down to me any night."

He ducked his head. "I could have."

She thought about that. It still hurt, the two long weeks. But it was over. "I suppose I could have been more observant... I assume the stairs are visible from the room below as well?"

He looked a little relieved. "They are." He hesitated, then stepped forward and slid an arm around her waist. "Knowing you were there, literally *underneath* me..." he whispered. "The only way I could sleep at night and *not* come down was by exhausting myself before coming to bed. And even then, it took *hours* to fall asleep."

Genevieve smiled, and leaned her head against him momentarily. "Let's go down, I want to see what I missed! Bring the basket of food," she added, as she took her first step onto the barely-visible stairs.

Damien smiled back in relief. "Be careful and stay close to the wall. The stairs are as steep and narrow as they look, and that drop-off to the side is real – for us anyways."

It seemed very strange to Genevieve to be walking down into the floor. She could still see the flagstones, like fog that she was descending into. Damien followed her down, keeping one hand lightly on her shoulder. The floor proved to be as thick as she was tall, perhaps even slightly more. She was grateful to feel his touch as the 'stone' closed over her head and before she could see her bare toes emerging into dim light in the room below.

When her head was fully in clear space, even though she was still several feet above the floor of her own bedchamber, she breathed more freely. Touching the solid floor, more deeply still. But she noticed her first completely easy breath was when she saw Damien's head emerge from the foggy ceiling stone.

"The stairs continue down," she noted, having stepped adroitly to the side of the cavernous space she saw opening ahead and onto the thick carpet.

"Yes," Damien agreed, as he finished coming down the stairs to join her. "That's how we're going to leave the castle undetected."

"Hmmmn," Genevieve commented, eyeing the dark, 'foggy' stones with distaste.

"Or," he suggested, sliding an arm around her again, "we could stay here... in *your* bed..."

She could not resist a glance at the clean sheets. "And how would we explain being down here when someone comes in to trim the lamps?"

"We don't have to explain anything," the young king murmured, breathing into her ear. "Royal privilege."

Genevieve had to fight her instinctive desire to melt into him and go along with this idea. "I don't think Ciriis and Adam would accept that," she said dryly. "And it's one thing entirely for them to spend every single moment with you when it was just you, but hardly the same if they insist on staying in the room with us both. All night," she added pointedly, stepping reluctantly out of his embrace, but keeping her movements brisk and confident.

Damien conceded defeat, flopping down to sit on the bed while she sought appropriate clothing. "We're vanishing from the castle entirely. You don't think that they'll be fine with *that*, do you?"

She gave him a mischievous look over her shoulder. "If we're careful, they'll never know. I left a note thanking them for the *most* excellent and well-thought-out food items and letting them know that we'd be awhile longer."

"Thanking them–" he spluttered, and she looked over in concern, but he was laughing.

She grinned. "I may have said something about all the effort they put into it not going to waste. It's a shame I can't see how far that blush goes when while you're dressed."

"We can fix that," he offered, still red-faced. He lay back in the bed and raised an eyebrow.

Genevieve fixed him with a stern look. "You are not getting out of a simple outing that easily. Now turn around while I get dressed."

Damien gamely did as she asked, crossing his ankles and mussing the clean sheets, turning his head to look at the far wall. But he objected, "I've already seen you naked–"

"Yes, and if you see me naked right now, we probably aren't leaving this room."

"Would that be such a tragedy?"

"You need some exercise – *outdoor* exercise," she corrected herself quickly, before he could turn that into another suggestion that she would find all too tempting. "And no, sword-practice in indoor courtyards of the castle does not count as outdoors. I don't think I've been indoors this long since..." She paused. "Actually, ever."

She didn't have to remove Damien's shirt to get dressed – her leather hunting vest was a bodice almost as tight as a corset, though nowhere near as constricting. Underthings, pants, jacket, belt, sword and bow – Rosa had brought her own favored weapons, having somehow known which crofter she had secreted them with outside the city. A pause for thought and she added the almost-plain skirt she'd had made along with the fancier gowns.

"Really?" Damien asked. "Even in the middle of Winter?"

Genevieve sat down on the bed to pull on her stockings and boots. "There are a ton of things I have to take care of out of doors in the Winter." Yes, delegation was still something she struggled with.

"Can I look at you now?" He somehow made it plaintive without being whiny.

"Yes..." She turned to look at him. The light was dim – she had at first been surprised there were any lights on, since no one was supposed to be in this room, but it was likely that, with no windows, there had to be some light for when the servants came in. Or the Royal Guard, if they were giving her the same degree of protection that they afforded Damien.

His beautiful grey eyes gleamed in the low light, and she realized again how very handsome he was. And how goodhearted. His liaisons with the women of his Royal Guard had surely been no mere duty for them.

It would be so easy to lean in and kiss him... as he lay there in the bed where she had longed for him for those two long weeks...

Damien propped himself up, coming closer... and kissed her nose and rolled to his feet, offering her his hand. She accepted it, standing up into his arms for another peck on the nose before he stepped back and released her.

Feeling almost rebuffed, she turned away to pick up her bow, but he grasped her arm and pulled her back close.

"You look just like that moment when I first saw you in the city." His voice was low, his heart was in his eyes, and she knew he was simply accepting her determination on the outing. A note of bafflement entered his voice. "Except – you've braided up your hair? And – a skirt? I like the look of your legs in pants."

Genevieve smiled at him – the heels of her riding boots were higher than the low heels of his practical walking boots, putting them eye to eye. "I *should* have braided it up before sneaking into the city," she admitted. "It was a bit of vanity to leave it loose. Or dyed it, better yet."

"I knew it was you, because of your hair," Damien murmured. "Even before you turned, and I saw your face. All I could think about was that I might finally get a chance to put my hands in your hair." He fitted words to action, and she sighed and leaned in to the kiss, putting her arms around his waist.

They were both breathing hard a moment later when they broke apart.

"Are you *sure* this kind of exercise isn't enough?" Damien said, wistfully.

Genevieve rolled her eyes, though it took some effort to do it convincingly. "I didn't want to spoil the surprise, but if it will motivate you... There's this little glade, a couple miles out of the city. It's just far enough off the road that almost no one seems to know about it – I... found it during that Summer I was at Court." She took her own turn to kiss *his* nose. "I wasn't admitting to myself why I checked on it on my way in. It's still there. And it's *very* private..."

She laughed, as his eyes lit, and he began to tug her towards the all-but-invisible stairs.

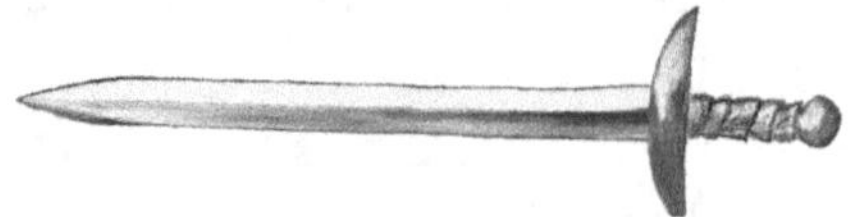

Getting out of the city was, of course, rather less difficult than getting out of the castle, but it took a great deal more time. The secret passage took them beneath the moat and back up to exit in an ordinary alleyway. Damien had wondered if this had been open countryside when whomever had made the secret exit had put it in.

In the present day, however, this was just to the north of the busiest market square in the city, and they had to make their way through the crowded streets: something Damien had never dared to do on his own. But he quickly saw the genius of how Genevieve had had them dress. Even her sword and bow over her leather vest and her relatively plain skirt wasn't incongruous in streets packed with people from a half-dozen countries and nearly every province in his own Realm. He had worried that they should have drawn the cowls of their cloaks up, but it was quickly clear how that *would* have stood out from the crowd. Despite his having been in front of their eyes for most of the week of his coronation, not one person seemed to recognize the young king.

"I guess it's a good thing we haven't had time to strike new coin yet?" he suggested as they wended their way, arm in arm, the basket of bread and meat on his elbow.

Genevieve laughed. "Oh, they would never notice even if you had. No crown, no royal robes, no scepter. Who would even imagine you'd come out here like this? How long has it been since anyone of the royal family deigned to move among the common folk?" She stopped – for the fifth time – to look over some of the goods for sale. Flowers it was, this time.

Damien was slightly offended by that. "My sister–"

She looked at him with sympathy in her eyes. "But she was the only one in a very long time. She was special. No one expects a repeat, even from her brother." Genevieve leaned in to kiss his cheek and whispered, "Because they don't know you yet, love."

The flower seller smiled at them and waved a bouquet at Damien. "Flowers for your lassie, young man? I've love-in-a-mist, bleeding heart, roses, and – best of all – jasmine from the north, right here in this bunch! Here, have a sniff!" This time she directed the flowers towards Genevieve, who smiled almost as sensuously as... earlier.

"What's so special about jasmine?" Damien asked, entranced by the look on his beloved's face.

The flower seller leaned in as if confiding. "They say the smell of it does make a lassie very *friendly*, if you take my meaning. I've seen it true with my own dear wife, so it's no fairystory."

It gave him a start to hear the old woman refer to her wife. Same-gendered spouses were not exactly approved in Ilseadoran legal precepts... but not forbidden either. The old king had discouraged them amongst the nobility for so very long that Damien had been sure there was a general disapproval of them amongst the commonfolk as well. It had made hiding Adam and Jason's relationship even more of an imperative – it was a more powerful lever for his grandfather to use on them than if one of them had been a woman.

Damien was suddenly very happy Genevieve had insisted on including a small purse of coins in his accoutrements. The flower seller handed the bouquet to Genevieve as she accepted the coins, with a broad wink to Damien. "The flowers are only available here in late Summer, but I sell the scent as a perfume and an incense as well, if you want some later," she told him in a quiet voice. "Oh, my, those roses have nothing on your cheeks, young man!"

Genevieve's peal of laughter sang like a perfect bell in Damien's – rather pink – ears, but it didn't seem to attract the slightest bit of attention from the rest of the crowd of bustling, busy people. "I tell him the same thing all the time, good dame!"

The older woman leaned close to Genevieve's ear this time and murmured something that ended with the exchange of a few coins and some smiles and sidelong glances that made Damien both extremely curious and slightly nervous.

She tucked the bouquet in the basket with their lunch, and they moved on, Genevieve stopping here and there, but the excitement of being out in the city – and, to be perfectly honest, doing something which Ciriis, Adam, and Jason would be horrified over – began to pall for Damien. The young king had, as he had admitted to her, hardly been outside of the castle in years. During his coronation festivities his 'keepers' had insisted he not stray from the top two tiers of the royal dais, even under guard. Crowds in the castle had usually meant something bad was about to happen – to others, if not to him – and Damien had spent most of his time alone or in the company of a few, trusted people.

The sound and energy, the sheer numbers of people in the marketplace, were beginning to make him feel anxious when Genevieve commented quietly. "It wasn't like this here two months ago."

He was dragged out of his own thoughts and emotions to answer intelligently, "Hunh?"

She was looking around them in a way that seemed casual, but he could feel her sharp focus – how could she pay attention to so many different things without going quite mad? "Two months ago – under your grandfather's reign – the people crept about to do their business. The streets were empty, except for those things that *had* to be done out of doors."

Damien looked about again, noticing now that the smiles looked relieved as much as happy, that the hawker's cries seemed perhaps slightly too energetic. The – "Where are the children?" he asked, noticing the lack he hadn't even thought about until this instance. Surely, in a city this size there should be some out and about.

"The people are beginning to trust you – but maybe they aren't quite ready to believe what their hearts and eyes are telling them yet."

Damien wondered if she was including herself in 'the people,' and his stomach cringed a bit. Not that he hadn't given her cause to distrust him these last two weeks... it looked like a toddler's tantrum to him now, but could she believe it wouldn't happen again? Did he trust *himself*? Could his *people* trust him if he was so fickle, even with the woman he had loved since he was a child?

The young king was deep in his thoughts and not paying attention to where they were going, unintentionally using his emotional confusion to block out some of the social confusion that was threatening to overwhelm him in an entirely different way. So, when Genevieve pulled him suddenly into a quiet alleyway Damien assumed she had pulled them out of sight of someone else. But she pushed his back up against a wall and peered sharply into his eyes.

"You *are* a good king, Damien," she told him fiercely. "This economic boom is all due to *you*. That flower seller could only obtain her exotic blooms since you took power and loosened trade restrictions – before that, anything special had to be sent up first to the castle, and then made available only to certain of the nobles. Anything left over – was to be *burned* rather than made available to mere commoners. It was the same with every other product and service.

"If anything, anything at all, should convince the other leaders of the Rebellion that you mean what you say, the way this market has rebounded in just the last month should do it."

He just looked at her, feeling like his eyes were slightly glazed, trying to take her words in and still wondering in some part of himself whether *she* was completely convinced.

He'd begun making the changes she described – small things, that Lord Prydeen and even most of his Royal Councilors and nobles *(as well as Adam and Ciriis and Jason)* – thought trivial and pointless… just as soon as he'd had the power to do anything at all. They'd all thought he was trying to assert himself without rocking any boats, though his own studies had suggested…

"Oh, hell," the Rebel Duchess growled. "It's the crowds and noise as much as anything isn't it? We need to get out of the city. But first," she kissed him, and his senses came alive again, all focused on the feel of her, the scent of her... He tried to put his arms around her, but there was something in one hand...

A passerby noticed them and snorted in tolerant amusement, and everything came back at once. Damien sagged...

"Oh, no you don't! Come on, we'll use the backstreets."

She pulled him away from the market, emerging from the side-alley into a back alley where they had to step around trash bins and over pools of stagnant water. Rats screeched at them as they went behind what must have been a prosperous inn, and Damien stared at them in shock. From inside the building, he could hear a cook berating some serving boy and a roar of laughter that must have come straight through from the public room. Genevieve pulled him aside suddenly in a dodge, as someone emptied a chamberpot from an upper window – a cynical laugh followed the splatter. There were almost no other people here, but the sounds and smells were sharper and overwhelming in their own ways.

At last, Genevieve led him out onto another, quieter, street, this one seeming to have only private residences, and he took a slightly deeper breath than he had dared in the alleys. "Thank you," he managed after a moment.

His beautiful redheaded love gave him what he hoped was a look of sympathy, and not condescension. "I've seen this before," she said. "Though it's always been when one of our mountain boys or girls decides to come down to Elaarwen to join the army. My capitol isn't anywhere near so big as yours, but those lads and lassies come from towns where a few dozen people show up for the Midsummer bonfires and they may not see anyone outside of their immediate families from first snow to last." She grinned at him. "I had no idea I'd be marrying such a *countryboy.*"

Damien had been trying to imagine a place so quiet and free of people – Adam's family home had been a bustling hive of activity, and that was his only point of reference for country living.

He completely missed that she was teasing him and answered absently, "Our numbers for Elaarwen's population density must be even more out of date than I had realized."

The Duchess of Elaarwen shook her head in mocking disapproval. "Not a countryboy after all, but an ivory tower elite." She let her tone grow more serious as they neared one of the gates through the city wall. "You probably saw aggregate numbers. The mountain-people are sparse, and most of the population lives in our city, with a scattering of farms in the lowlands. And... we've had a lot of losses these last fifteen years."

Since her father founded the Rebellion, she meant. Though it had been more of rebellion-in-name-alone until the Battle of Siovale nine years ago.

The young king shook his head, barely noticing as they made their way through the gate-tunnel. "Your province is like a natural fortress, but your resources are so limited. I can't see how my grandfather couldn't defeat you. He could simply have besieged Elaarwen and let you use yourselves up."

Genevieve gave him a shrewd look. "It wasn't all fairystories you spent your time on, was it?"

"The Royal Library is fairly complete," Damien admitted. "I made sure no one ever saw me looking at the other areas, though. And I did read a lot of fairystories and legends."

"Even Lady Theresa?"

He nodded. "Even her." It had been for her protection, though, as much as his. Although she might have suspected what use he made of her domain in the dark hours of the night, she could not let it slip to anyone else. Anyone else who might then try to extract more information from her about the king's only remaining grandchild.

Genevieve was regarding him rather oddly when they emerged back into what was now late morning sunshine.

"What?" he asked.

"Do Ciriis and Adam know how well-studied you are – outside of myth and legend?"

They were following the Royal Western Road that paralleled the Emerald River to their right, Damien noticed, just part of a stream of carts and people and livestock going in both directions. The city hardly so much as paused, beyond the wall. Some ancestor had decreed a spear's-throw be kept clear between the wall and any other structures, but it was obvious that the encroachment had begun long ago – perhaps with the passing of that very monarch who had decreed it.

"Damien?" she queried, when he did not respond.

It sent pleasant shivers up his spine when she said his name, even when her tone was interrogative, rather than sensual. "No," he admitted. "I've never told Ciriis and Adam how much I know. They – it would seem like *bragging,* wouldn't it?" He tried to ask for her understanding with his eyes. "Or – it would seem like I'm telling them I don't need them. They've spent so long and worked so hard to get me to the throne... taken such risks. And I couldn't do this without them, even now."

Genevieve pursed her lips, and looked ahead, guiding them to a northwesterly branch of the road. "Maybe not. Not yet. But you can't truly rule if they don't understand that you're ready to do it."

"I'm not *hiding* what I know," he protested. "I'm just not... showing it off. It's just that they don't–" he broke off, but Genevieve completed his thought.

"They don't listen. They hear your words, but they don't listen to the depth behind them." She shook her head. "This can't go on, love."

"It's been working," he muttered truculently. "After I say something a couple of times, they seem to think it was their own idea."

"A couple of times? Or a couple *dozen* times?"

He refused to look at her and concede the point. She was right, it wasn't an efficient approach, but *they* had been out in the world beyond the castle – beyond the capitol city – and what had he ever done? Read a few books?

What had they *let* him do, a traitorous piece of his mind whispered. How could he ever get past his protectors to gain the experience that would let him gain their respect?

Genevieve sighed. "I'm half-minded to kidnap you away to Elaarwen so you can get a feel for what it's like to be on your own." Her words echoed his thoughts.

The autumnal breeze suddenly seemed cooler as Damien realized he was out of the castle, out of the city, and no one knew where he was. His only companion was the infamous Rebel Duchess who had been trying to overthrow his throne, a redoubtable warrior who doubtless could do just what she had said. For a moment the fact that she was his soul-bonded mate and true love receded from his immediate consciousness and the noises of the carts and people around them became very loud. Would any of them believe him, with his basket of bread and flowers and a sword at his side, that he was being abducted against his will?

He didn't realize he had stopped moving until a carter cursed at them for blocking the road and Genevieve tugged him through a goose girl's flock and out of the roadway, while the goose girl cursed them quite as soundly, despite her tender years.

Genevieve was looking at him with worried eyes again. "I really need to get you out of this mess. Can you walk any faster? We're nearly to the real country roads, and then it's only a few more miles. Are you hungry? I was hoping to make it to the grotto first, but if you need to stop..."

His fearful fantasies melted away from the love in her eyes, and Damien felt ashamed for ever having entertained them... even as he admitted silently to himself that she could simply twitch her finger at him and he would follow wherever she led. If an abduction there was to be, it wouldn't be *against* his will at all.

"I can make it," he said. Truth to tell, he probably *was* hungry, but the plethora of smells and noise had completely subsumed his ability to tell.

She guided them a little faster, past the remaining bustle of the outer city, past homes that became cottages and gardens that became small farms. They moved onto progressively smaller roads, always in a southwesterly direction, until the spaces between farms were fair indeed, and copses of trees were being replaced by outcroppings of forest. Damien's sense of personal balance recovered as the venue became quieter, and by the time he realized it had been a quarter-hour since they had seen another human, he was almost entirely back to normal.

At last, Genevieve gave him a mischievous grin and led him off the road into one of those forest outcroppings along what was surely no more than a bridle path – perhaps even just a deer-track. It wound behind some unexpected rises of stony cliffs and down, always down, until they were surrounded by high stone walls and a peaceful little stream that cavorted off a rocky overhang, and then burbled with more enthusiasm than musicality on its watery way. The flattish bottom area was carpeted in moss and long grasses, overhung with trees just starting to show their autumnal splendor. Low bushes and wildflowers surrounded the clearing, but the thin layer of leaf mold covering the shelf of rock was too thin to let them invade the center.

"I rather suspect the Spring floods clear this area out every year," Genevieve mused as she set down her bow and quiver and leaned fondly against one of the smooth, sheer cliff walls. "I was expecting to find it completely overgrown when I rode in." She turned to Damien, her eyes sparkling as she loosened the bodice of her hunting vest. The tips of her nipples were proud against the thin fabric of her shirt in the cool air of the grotto. "Are you hungry?"

He was, but the basket of food didn't interest him at the moment. It fell to the ground without either of them noticing, as he nudged her back against the cliff and covered her mouth with his. It had been *hours* and *hours*... and perhaps the magick was not encaging them, but it surely still coursed through their veins, and Genevieve responded eagerly to his kiss, sending her tongue licking up around his lips until he could bear it no longer.

There was something wilder, more free about being out here in the forest. About pressing her up against the cliff wall. About knowing that there was likely no one else within *miles* to hear them...

When they were done, they stood in each other's embrace, panting and leaning on each other for several moments.

"*Now* I'm hungry," Genevieve said at last, and Damien laughed a little lightheadedly. He was somewhat past hungry.

He stepped back to give her room, then felt horrified as she winced a bit, stepping off the cliff and bending to pull her pants back up.

"Your back!" he exclaimed, trying to look at her injuries.

Genevieve shrugged, again with a slight wince. "Very worth it." Her smoldering gaze did much to ease his conscience. "The shirt may never be the same again, but I'll be fine. If you feel badly about it," she added, finishing with the drawstring of her pants, "you can give me a backrub later. You can do penance by making it *only* a backrub," she added with a laugh.

She started picking up the spilled food and flowers and he hastened to redo the buttons on his own trousers and join her. They settled down on the mossy shelf to share their spoils. The bouquet had come apart, and they began a game of tucking the sprigs of flowers into every possible location on each other, beginning with the hair and getting much more... creative.

At last, Genevieve stood up, dumping a load of flowers onto Damien and the ground, and offered him her hand. Gamely, he took it and stood up, wondering what her plan was now.

"I told you I was taking you hunting," she reminded him. "You're going to at least shoot a few arrows. And I want to see how good you are with *that* sword–" she looked pointedly at the blade he had discarded so quickly earlier in favor of having *her,* "for myself."

"Not as good as Jason," he began, blushing a bit at her *double entendre,* but she cut him off with a dismissive wave.

"No one is as good as Jason. But he's been your teacher. But first the bow."

Damien wanted to hem and haw, but gave it up as a lost cause. "I've never shot a bow."

Her eyebrows flew up and he wanted to crawl into a hole. Yet another thing she expected of him that he couldn't do. The holes in his experience seemed to widen every time they found a new topic. He was utterly surprised when her tone was speculative, almost purring. "Well... that opens up a lot of interesting possibilities. Let's start with the basic position, then."

He immediately saw what she meant. She ran her hands down his thighs to position his legs, and reached around him from behind to show him how to hold the bow. It was almost impossible to concentrate on anything she was telling him. Raising and pulling her longbow took more strength than he had expected, and he had a better understanding of why her torso was so well-muscled after giving it a try himself.

After a short time, she bade him set the bow down, however. He was afraid that she was going to insist on immediately trying some swordplay, and his arms were a little shaky after the archery session. Pulling a bow used an entirely different set of muscles than wielding a sword – or at least used them in an entirely different way. Instead, Genevieve gave him a thorough massage of his arms and back, using some sort of liniment that she must have picked up in their trek through the city.

Then she took him to explore the grotto, pointing out the tracks of rabbits and hares (he hadn't been aware there were differences between the *animals*, let alone their footprints), deer, raccoons... She squealed with delight when they discovered a pond a bit farther downstream, and a dam built by beavers. Even Damien had to admit that beaver tracks were entirely distinctive, with the trail left by their wide tails.

"I love beavers," Genevieve admitted as they headed back to where they'd left the basket and the remains of their meal. "They are so clever. Did you know that the only way to get into those lodges of theirs – that mound of sticks in the middle of the pond is where they live – is to swim underwater? They build their dams to make a moat, then fell trees to build their impregnable castles right in the middle!"

"Just like humans," Damien volunteered.

"Even better in some ways. Watching their babies play in the water is so funny!" She replied. Then paused and added, "I almost hate to say it, but they taste good, too, especially those tails."

He had no idea what to say to that, but found he didn't have to. They were back in the beginning of the grotto, and Genevieve was ready to try him at swordplay.

"Isn't it getting kind of late?" he temporized. It was true. The grotto was just beginning to darken, the cliff-walls blocking out some of the late afternoon sun. "Shouldn't we be heading back?"

"Or we could stay the night?" she suggested.

"Won't that be kind of cold?"

"So, we'll keep each other warm. I can build us a fire."

That definitely sounded good, but... "What about food?"

An arched eyebrow. "We came out here to hunt, remember?" He cringed internally... and possibly externally as well, because she softened. "There's food all around us, love. Early Fall is berry season. There's dandelions for greens and cattail roots..." She listed a few more things he could no more cook than identify and had, in all probability never eaten. Damien began to feel less like this was a romantic excursion than a rapid-fire test of his non-existent survival skills.

He became convinced of it when she unsheathed her sword and said "Ready?"

It was almost as bad as he had feared. Genevieve had all the marks of what Jason called a 'natural' with the sword, and Damien was only too aware of his own shortcomings. It didn't help that they were sparring with edged weapons. And no armor. Though he supposed they could hardly have raided the armory for practice swords, and carrying his own armor along would have been nearly impossible and hers was back in Elaarwen… it made him nervous about getting hurt. Or worse, injuring Genevieve. Unlikely as the latter might seem, he had to admit.

Their bout was short but intense. She never let up, and she seemed to have a second sense as to where his own guard was about to slip. She also never let her sword touch him, despite what he felt to be his vast clumsiness.

At last – after far too long for the young king's taste – the woman who was shortly to become his warrior-queen called a halt. They were both sweaty, warm even in the light Autumn chill.

"I would have preferred to do this with proper practice gear," Genevieve admitted as she sheathed her blade. "But I didn't think it would be a very political move."

"Because you could beat me to the ground without half trying," he answered, sheathing his own blade and sagging down to a kneeling position on the floor of their impromptu salle.

He hoped he didn't look quite as dejected as he felt. He knew he had come late to the blade – he had been seventeen before he'd ever so much as held the hilt of anything larger than an eating knife – but he had hoped to make a better showing than this. It didn't help at all that *she* looked almost as fresh as when they had begun.

Genevieve knelt down on one knee before him and lifted his chin. "You are recovering from two weeks of the equivalent of a serious illness; we walked out here – a longer distance than you've ever walked in your life, I'll wager; and I did my darnedest to wear you out in every other way." She waggled her eyebrows and he had to laugh a little despite his dejection. She kissed his nose and sat back a bit on her heels. "I wanted to see how strong you were – physically – and now I know."

"I'm pathetic," Damien muttered.

"Not at all," she surprised him by saying. "You have stamina to spare, or you will once you're fully recovered. You're reasonably impressive right *now*. Your swordplay is excellent, or it would be if you weren't holding back. I can't entirely tell if it's because you were fighting *me*, or if it's a habit you've developed... but you were just a bit too good at it, so I suspect the latter. Have you used an edged blade much?" She tucked an escaped curl behind her ear. Flyaway bits of her braided hair were the only real disarray to her appearance.

"Not... recently..." he admitted, still stunned that she said he was good at this. "Jason has had me back to working with wooden blades since my grandfather died. He's always after me to..." Damien stared at her. "To not hold back."

Genevieve grinned. "Exactly. Great minds think alike – or at least can see the same problem. The *other* problem is that you've been trained entirely by the best swordsman in the Realm."

Now he was confused. "How is that a problem?"

"Because you're not likely to have to defend yourself on the field of honor – or battle. You're much more likely to have to fight in close-quarters against an assassin than sword to sword," she told him bluntly. "Have you ever had one of the ladies of your Royal Guard instruct you in how to fight off someone who is stronger and takes you by surprise?"

Damien shook his head mutely. It had never occurred to him, and he could see why it might not have occurred to Jason, or perhaps even Adam... but Ciriis?

"Hey there." Genevieve lifted his chin again, and he realized he'd started shrinking into himself. "It's all fixable, love. You can't be brilliant at everything, that's why you have people. And that includes me, now. I'm a strategist, and that includes keeping alive my king – who happens to have an amazingly encyclopedic knowledge of the entire Realm *and* be able to recall every random fact at will and connect it to five others..." Her voice was frankly tinged with awe. "I can do that sort of thing when it comes to tactics, but battles are short-lived things. Trying to do that for just Elaarwen was giving me headaches. I can't imagine how you are doing that for the whole Realm."

"I'm not doing anything special," he tried to argue. He wasn't really. He had no real experience, just close to ten years alone in a library.

Now she reached out and shook him. "Yes. You are. I've been watching you in the Council meetings." She laughed with just the slightest remaining tinge of bitterness. "Gods! Watching you is all I've been *able* to do, or think about. You always know the fact that the others are grasping for, or where to find it. You see connections where others see disparate cases. That, my love, is what makes a truly good ruler, or," she added thoughtfully, "an extremely effective corrupt one. I'm sure Lord Prydeen has noticed, too," she said pointedly as he tried to object. "And it's probably why he'd rather suborn you than supplant you. You are *good* at this. You are better than good at this. The best I can ever do will be to support you... I could never replace what you give to this kingdom, and I haven't seen anyone else who could do it either."

Damien was dumb with shock. He'd thought he was simply doing a good job at playing along with the role. His friends had taught him that he could be who the Realm needed him to be, and that it was another way – perhaps his only way – to survive. Sometimes he had even started to feel like he really could be the confident prince – or king. Inevitably something would turn up to burst that bubble.

But Genevieve – Genevieve, who had been ruling her own duchy for nearly three years and been *trained* to do just that.

Genevieve thought he was doing it well.

"Which is not to say," she added, poking him in the chest gently. "That you don't have anything left to learn. We all do. And," she grinned. "At least you're a helpless fawn when it comes to surviving the woods. I don't think I could stand it if you were better than me at everything."

Abruptly she stood up. "Come on. Let's bathe and I'll show you how to find cattail roots before it gets dark. They're scrumptious roasted in the coals of a fire."

The water was... cold. Very cold. But Genevieve plunged right in and splashed him and teased until he followed her. 'Bracing,' *she* called it. Damien was just happy to get out again and let his bride-to-be teach him how to build a campfire while the air was still blue with dusk. His head was still a-whirl with everything she had told him.

At last, they were settled beside the fire, the cattail roots buried at the edge under hot coals. Genevieve had laid her head down on Damien's lap and was braiding the remaining flowers from the bouquet into a garland. Her hair was unbound now, the curls flowing across his lap and coiling on the ground. She had dressed again in her pants and his shirt, but he was bare-chested at her request. He was watching her, barely daring to breathe for fear of disturbing this perfect moment of peace. Surely a king and a queen-to-be were not allowed moments like this.

"I wish..." the words whispered out before he realized they were his and too late to call them back.

Genevieve turned her head to meet his eyes. "You wish?" When he didn't answer immediately, she grinned. "Or should I guess?" She rubbed her head from side to side, and his body responded as she'd planned.

"Wicked woman." He smiled down at her, but went serious again. "I wish this moment could last forever." The smile faded from her face as she took in how much this meant to him. "I wish we could live in a land where you and I could go off and be together and not be responsible for fixing, well, *everything.*"

"I know." Genevieve put her fingers over her mouth, kissed them, then reached up and pressed them to his lips. Damien kissed them back, capturing her hand and pulling it to his chest.

"So, this is where the two of you got to," said a voice out of the dark, and Damien nearly jumped out of his skin. All her talk of assassins had him more than slightly jumpy, underlying even a moment like this one. Genevieve, however, seemed completely unsurprised and completely unready to move, which kept him from moving as well.

"Hello, Jason," she replied calmly. "*Do* feel free to join us." Her tone was very flat. "Have a seat. I'm afraid we only have enough cattail roots for two, so I hope you brought your own dinner."

Jason Solway stepped closer in to the fire so that they could clearly see his disapproving expression as he looked around the dim grotto. "What were you thinking, Genny? Do you have any idea how vulnerable you are out here? You were recognized a dozen times before you reached the city wall."

"I was sure I would be," Genevieve replied. She was? She had? It was all news to Damien. "But isn't it interesting that the only one to find us, is you? And don't you think you should at least acknowledge your liege-lord, Lord Solway?"

"Damien." Jason nodded politely, if distractedly, his focus still on the erring duchess. "Genny, *you* may think it's all fine and dandy to abandon your province and the Rebellion to play children's games of spy, but if something happens to *him*, the country is going to fall into chaos. This was foolish."

Damien squirmed under that assessment, even though it wasn't directed at him. Jason had been his teacher, his *protector*, for so long. He owed Jason too much to ever repay, and it wasn't right to give him even a moment's worry. Though he had *thought* Jason had listened to him more than the others, had some better idea of who Damien really *was*. And some part of him was irritated that Jason just assumed their outing was entirely Genevieve's idea... even though it had been.

Genevieve looked up at him again. She squeezed the hand he still held, reassuringly. Then, with a sigh, she let go and sat up. "Really,

Jason? *That's* the best you can do? No wonder it's hard for the nobility to take *my lord king* seriously if even his nearest and dearest friends treat him so casually that they barely acknowledge him. I thought it was mostly Adam and Ciriis. I had thought better of *you.*"

"For the Gods' sake, Genny! It's not like we're surrounded by the full Court, and it's not like you keep such a level of formality out in rusticated Elaarwen!" Damien had never seen Jason get this irritated with anyone. It was kind of fascinating, in a weird way.

She shook her head as if she was disappointed in Jason, but setting it aside without conceding the point. "So how did you find out we were gone, anyways? I'm fairly sure *my* people wouldn't have reported to *you.*"

Her people? Rebel spies?

Jason's jaw set as if he understood all the unspoken subtext. "They went to the Countess of Zialest. Who went to Ciriis. Who came to me. They assumed that I would somehow know where you might go."

She smiled her charming smile up at him. "Which you did."

Damien had never seen Jason Solway succumb to a woman's smiles for anything more than politeness' sake. Seeing him sag and sink down cross-legged across the fire in response to Genevieve's made him feel... jealous. Calling it something else made it no more attractive.

As if she was aware of his prickling jealousy – which she might well be, down the bond – Genevieve leaned back against Damien's chest as if to demonstrate she was still his, and picked up her abandoned garland. It helped. Some.

"Genny..."

"Jason, I knew no one besides you would be able to find us here. My father spent *months* trying to find us that Summer. And can you honestly tell me that he's safer in that snake pit of a castle?"

"You'd been here with Genevieve before?" Damien felt like it cast a pall over the whole day. He had thought this was a special place that Genevieve had shared with just him, forgetting that her only opportunity to find it would have been the Summer that she had, by her own admission, spent most of in Jason's company.

Jason sighed. "I found this place the year before she came to Court. When Genevieve started climbing out of windows to go exploring the city, I thought it would be a safer place for her than some of the more... *questionable* parts of town."

"Jason's such an old stick in the mud. Just because our parents were friends, he thought he had to look out for me."

"Genny," he said with a pained look, "you were *twelve*. That's prime kidnapping age in those parts of town."

She laughed. "I knew what places to avoid, goose. It was just fun to convince you I would try." She looked at Damien again. "He brought me out here and started teaching me the sword. Or he thought he was." She snickered.

Jason sighed again. "Never play cards with this woman, Damien," he advised.

A history between them that he didn't share. It didn't matter, Damien told himself. Her future belonged with him alone. His arms snaked around her, and he felt a little better when he could feel her hum of pleasure in his touch.

The moment of silence stretched on.

"Genny. Damien. It's time to go." Jason informed them. If it had been Damien alone, it would have worked. He would have gotten up and moved without questioning Jason's reasoning. But... if it had been Damien alone, he would never have been out here. He would never have swum beside a beaver dam and tried to learn the difference between rabbit tracks and hare tracks, would never have dug up cattail roots and gotten stuck and sticky picking just slightly overripe raspberries.

None of these things would change his life, but doing them somehow had.

It wasn't Jason's grotto anymore, or Jason and Genevieve's grotto. It was Damien and Genevieve's grotto. The whole *Realm* was his, for that matter, as the Gods-anointed king.

"No," he surprised himself by saying, possibly even more than he surprised them. "Genevieve and I are going to stay here tonight and eat cattail roots. We'll come home in the morning. Or at least sometime tomorrow. Go back and tell everyone not to worry."

Jason's handsome face crinkled with an anxious frown. "Damien. I can't go back and leave you here unprotected."

"Then stay and guard us. But we're not leaving tonight."

"If you're staying, you'll want to setup your camp up the trail," Genevieve suggested. "Out of... earshot."

Damien had also never known Jason to blush unless it was at some whispered comment of Adam's. "Genny," he pleaded. "Talk some sense into him."

Damien could feel her eyebrows arch, even though he couldn't see her face. "Your liege-lord has given you an order, Lord Solway. As his Knight Champion as well as a lord of the Realm I would think you duty-bound to adhere to it."

Jason snarled in frustration, threw himself to his feet, and stalked off into the darkness. Moments later he was back, throwing blankets at their feet. "It'll get cold," he stated, then stalked back to where he had presumably left his horse.

Genevieve sat up, turned and put the garland around Damien's head. It was a little large and fell down over one ear, then slithered down around his neck. Then she reached around and pulled him to her for a long, passionate kiss.

"In some cultures, this would make us married," he gasped when they broke apart at last.

"Which?" she asked, breathily. "The kiss or the garland?" She began to dig the cattail roots out of the ashes and Damien spared a thought to hope that they actually tasted good after all this fuss.

"Either," he answered her. "Or sharing a meal and a fire... and a bed."

"No bed here," she grinned, handing him a root.

"You know what I mean. How do I eat this anyways?"

"Let it cool a bit, then just take a bite."

He eyed it dubiously. "But isn't it, well, ashy and such?"

"Trust me. I'd hardly dare feed my liege-lord substandard forest food." She paused. "Though I've always thought salted butter would go nicely with cattail roots."

"Mmmm... about that..." Damien began.

To his surprise, his confident beloved actually ducked her head as if she were blushing, though the flickering firelight made it impossible to tell. "I didn't mean to step in there."

He frowned. "What are you talking about? You backed me up."

She shook her head. "That's just it. Jason should have listened to you without me saying a word. I shouldn't have let him get away with it." She looked down again. "I'm sorry. It was so – so *sexy* to hear you exerting your authority like that. I wasn't paying attention to how it would sound... I was just thinking about, well, *you*... and how extremely... *nice* it would be if he left right then..." She *was* blushing. He could feel the warm thrum of it down their bond. So, she liked it when he gave orders?

"I seem to recall," he purred, "that I was supposed to give you a backrub later. Take that shirt off, woman, and tell me where you hid that liniment you used on me."

She gave him a startled look at the seeming change of subject. "It can wait till after we eat–"

"Where is that liniment, Your Grace?" Would the reminder of her status work? Oh. Oh, yes, it would.

"In the basket," she breathed, and Damien had to tear his eyes away as she pulled off her shirt – *his* shirt – to look through the remaining shreds of food to find the small bottle.

He spread out one of the blankets that Jason had tossed at them. "On your stomach," he instructed, and Genevieve lay down obediently. He sat beside her and poured a small amount of oil onto his hands, rubbing them together to warm it up. "What is this?" he asked at the unfamiliar scent. "I'm familiar with the usual horse liniment, but this is different."

"*Arnica montana* oil," she murmured, her head pillowed on her arms and turned to face him. The firelight sparkled in her eyes. "It's from a little flower that grows in my mountains and is absolutely the best for sore muscles. It also prevents bruising and promotes healing of bruises that one already has. The flower vendor said she had something that would be as effective on you as the jasmine flowers would be on me... I told her I didn't think we needed either one," Damien smiled at that, "but if she had some arnica oil it would be much appreciated. She didn't but she knew who did, a little farther down."

"And here I thought you were just idly shopping as part of our camouflage while leaving the city." He looked more closely at her back and hissed in surprised. "We should have put this on you right away. My poor love." He began caressing the oil onto her back.

"Mmmmn. But if we had, we'd never have gotten anything else done after," she replied.

"A-a-ah! This is *just* a backrub, remember? My penance for inflicting this on you?" He grinned, because he could see her reacting to his touch. He let his fingers slide farther down her sides, grazing the edges of her breasts, and she whimpered slightly.

"I think," she panted slightly. "Some of the bruising went a bit... lower. May I get up for a moment, my lord?"

The young king was confused for a moment before recalling he had ordered her to lie down, calling on his status as her liege-lord. "Certainly, Your Grace."

She stood, demonstrating how the formal title befit her so very well, then proceeded to peel off her pants and lie back down. "I do hope," she commented. "That not all of your nobles get this version of the 'royal treatment'."

Damien warmed up some more oil in his hands as he leaned forwards and whispered "Just you," in her ear, allowing his breath to stir the red-gold curls that she had kindly swept out of the way for his caresses. He started at the top again and worked down her spine. Lower, and lower... she hadn't merely been tempting him, there *was* a bruise coming up on her lower back. He anointed it carefully with what he hoped was as magickal an oil as she claimed, but he didn't stop there. Her long, lovely legs could surely use some attention as well, after all.

He made his way down the outsides of her thighs, her calves, massaged each foot in turn, down to the toes. Then made his way back up, this time concentrating on the muscles of her inner calves, her thighs...

She was moaning now, and he grinned again.

"Hmmmmn," he said. "This is supposed to be a penance for me, not you, so maybe I should stop..." she made whimpery negative noises as he lifted his hands, "or I can do something else... something *more...*"

He ran his hands up and down her torso again, this time not even pretending to avoid her breasts. She began to turn over and he pressed her back down onto her stomach with one hand spread wide on her back and almost no pressure at all.

"A-a-ah," he admonished again. "I said to lay on your stomach, milady." She relaxed into his touch, tensing up in entirely different and delightful ways as he leaned down to plant a string of kisses along her spine, his hands wandering down to her thighs.

He stretched out alongside her, caressing her...

Genevieve's eyes fluttered open, and she smiled at him until he leaned forwards and kissed her. She snuggled closer. Then closer. Then her nearer arm wrapped around him, to draw him in for another kiss, to which Damien yielded with smug satisfaction.

Moments later, he found himself on his back and Genevieve smiling down at him as she sat astride his... abdomen.

"I'm afraid I've always been a most *rebellious* subject, my lord king," she murmured, with suppressed laughter that made his breath catch in his throat.

"Is that so?" he managed.

"Indeed. I seem to have this – *insatiable* – belief that I know what's best for you. For example, I don't believe it's right for a subject to leave her king... unsatisfied in any way." She wriggled down his torso until she was sitting over his hips, her hands were trailing over his bare chest, and he was deeply regretting not having taken the time to undress. Although that had been part of his plan... somehow it no longer seemed to make sense, even in retrospect. Though part of that might have been the lack of air to his brain, because he seemed to be having trouble breathing.

"A bit high-handed to imagine yourself wiser than your king," he suggested, reaching up for her to emphasize 'high-handed.'

"I'm a hard taskmaster as well," she added, rocking her hips. "I made you walk all the way here, knowing full well that you aren't used to all this... and that you'll have to walk all the way back tomorrow." That cut through the delightful fog in Damien's brain. His feet hurt already, though he had tried not to let it show, and the return was going to be painful.

While he was still processing that through a brain gone thick as molasses, Genevieve somehow switched around and bestrode his lower legs, reaching for his feet. His feet! Damien tried, futilely to kick, remembering how effective she was at tickling him.

"Stop that," she said over her shoulder. "Hand me the bottle of oil. I'm going to give you a foot massage so you stand some chance of making it back tomorrow." Oh. That was... thoughtful instead of somewhere between delightful and terrifying. Wordlessly, he hunted around for the small bottle, stretching his hand to where he remembered it to be.

Handing it to her was another matter. Damien managed to sit up so he could place it into her questing hand. She worked out the stopper and began to massage first one foot, then the other. It made him aware of other aches all down his legs, and wish that she would do the same to those muscles... but that would involve removing his pants... He reached to gently, softly, caress her back and sides, enjoying her shivers of pleasure.

"Your feet aren't actually in very bad condition," she said in an attempt at a conversational tone as she worked on his feet and he... worked on her. "I guess that having a superior cobbler is a perk of being king."

"More like a perk of having clever friends who, between them, know everyone in the city," Damien murmured back, caressing her.

"Damien..." she murmured, setting the bottle safely down.

He lay back down. "Come back here, Your Grace,"

She turned to face him. "I really should do the rest of your legs... but... you'd need to take your pants off..."

He smiled. "And we both know that rubbing oil into my legs isn't what's happening then. Or rather *now*..."

His pants came off between urgent, eager kisses. They'd made love like this before on his soft mattress – they'd tried all sorts of things in the grip of the insatiable and unpausable *desire* impressed on them by the soul-bonding fires – but it was... different when it was unyielding earth beneath him.

Different and magickal in its own way – but altogether familiar as the building waves of passion carried them both away.

At last, the ultimate wave crested, and they lay together in a sweaty heap, not moving for awhile.

"I love you, Damien Alsterling," Genevieve murmured into his neck, and he was instantly ready for her again. Was the magick of the bonding taking them over again – or were those words simply so magickal to him that he reacted this way?

It didn't matter. This was a gift, and he would enjoy it thoroughly. And share...

This time there was less urgency, and they took their time until the very end.

Genevieve leaned in for a long, sweet kiss, still panting a little. "I'm almost afraid of saying anything now," she teased. Then she tensed and jerked slightly in his arms.

Damien held her close as she began shivering. "Are you okay? Is something wrong?"

She shook her head, not saying anything, and he waited as patiently as he could. At last, shakily, she said, "Something seemed to – *connect* – inside me. Here." She moved a hand to indicate her abdomen. "It was like a – pop." She raised her eyes to meet his. "Damien, I think... it's possible... I might have conceived." She was clearly trying to hold down any hope in her tone, but her eyes were shining. It must have been a distinct enough sensation that she was more confident than she wanted to admit.

Conceived. A child. *Their* child. Made here and now... if that wasn't the most arousing idea ever...

"Damien!" Her exclamation was startled, but not at all unhappy. It had to be the magick... he began to make love to his soul-bonded beloved all over again...

Later... *much* later, they rearranged their cloaks and the blankets Jason had given them. Genevieve insisted on two layers beneath them, claiming that the cool ground would steal heat faster than the chilly air. Damien worried aloud that Jason would be cold through the night.

"It'll help him stay awake, then," was the Rebel Duchess' unsympathetic reply. "*He* decided he would stay on guard. *You* told him to go back to the city." After a moment she unbent enough to add, "He'll have built a fire, and he'll have his horse. We're taught that, when we're on campaign, our horse can keep us warm enough even without a fire."

Yet another thing he didn't know, Damien sighed as he curled himself around Genevieve, making sure she was on the side where the banked fire barely glowed. *She* might think he had what it took to be a king, and a leader, but *he* was far from convinced. So long as he could continue to fake it...

Chapter TEN

Reality...

THE SMELL OF FRESH BAKED goods tantalized Genevieve out of sleep.

Damien's arm tightened around her, reflexively, then relaxed slightly as he came awake as well. He nuzzled her neck and she could tell that food was *not* the first thing on his mind. Or other parts. She smiled to herself and wriggled closer.

"Good morning, my lord. My lady," Jason's dry voice interrupted her plans.

Genevieve's eyes flew open to see the handsome, golden-haired knight sitting cross-legged across the fire from them, a basket of sweet-smelling pastries in his lap. Damien propped himself up on one elbow to look over her shoulder. "Good morning, Jason. Go away, Jason," he said pleasantly.

The older man rolled his eyes, but didn't argue this time.

Damien was nibbling on her shoulder before they were entirely alone, murmuring sweet nothings into her ear. Genevieve had never thought being compared to a doughnut would feel so alluring.

It was still early when Damien wandered up the trail to call Jason – and his enticing offering of baked goods – back, leaving Genevieve to dress in private. She took the time to dash to the stream and refresh herself in water that she would never admit to her young king that she found overly chilly. Her back was feeling much better, and she made sure to stretch out her muscles while she bathed and dressed. Swimming in the cold water the day before had helped, but warmth was what she had needed afterwards and Damien had done a good job of keeping her muscles from freezing up with cold while they slept.

The two men entered the bottom of the grotto just as she was pulling on her boots.

The crisp Autumn morning seemed designed to make Jason almost impossibly handsome. The sunlight brought out highlights in his golden hair, and the green-gold leaves of the not-quite-turned-color bushes and trees made a perfect backdrop. His skin glowed a light, golden tan, and he stepped silently through the light cover of fallen leaves, the mark of a man used to the outdoors. His powerful muscles were enhanced, rather than hidden, by his leather tunic and pants, and his slender hips were emphasized by the huge sword hung at his side – a silent reminder that he was the foremost swordsman in the Realm. His almost lambent image of perfect masculinity was hindered not at all by the large basket he carried.

Genevieve noticed all of it almost absently, her attention riveted by the younger man at his side.

Damien was slighter than Jason, shorter and less muscular both, and his skin was so pale it was almost white – all particularly noticeable because he hadn't bothered to put on a shirt despite the early morning chill in the air. His black hair looked shaggy, since he hadn't bothered to comb it yet this morning, and his beard was starting to sprout after several days of neglect. His musculature was clearly that of a swordsman, if not so overdeveloped as his friend's, the sword hanging at *his* side underscoring that point as well – and she was pleased to note that he hadn't been so trusting as to not strap on the blade first thing, especially when he went up the trail alone.

Damien was talking animatedly to Jason, probably not even noticing that he was looking to the older man for approval. She suspected that even a far less biased eye than hers would say her soul-bonded young king was incredibly handsome – no less so than his golden Knight Champion, though from a rather different aesthetic.

The Rebel Duchess finger-combed her curly tresses as they approached, waiting for the moment that Damien met her eyes again.

When he smiled at her it was an almost physical shock and she found herself drifting forwards to where she could stand in the circle of his arm.

She had also felt the moment when Jason's eyes first fastened on her, but it had been a minor distraction from her fascination with Damien.

Genevieve took a pastry from Jason's basket without much noticing and began nibbling it absently.

"Survival skills, Genny?" the knight asked, his eyes and tone both warm with amusement.

She glared at his expression. "Damien is a passing-fair swordsman, Jason, and doubtless could be excellent if he had the time to pursue it. But he's more likely to face an assassin in a corridor than another swordsman on the field of honor. When we get back, I'm going to make sure he starts training with Lena and the other women, but I want to make sure he has a solid start on it right now." She gave her old friend a smirk to combat the somewhat condescending expression he continued to favor her with. "He's already proved that with me he'll hold back, so *you* get to be his practice dummy."

Jason sighed and rotated his shoulders to limber them. "All right. If you insist." Genevieve took no real umbrage at his lack of enthusiasm. Most physically powerful men, she had found, were unimpressed with the risks of being accosted in unfavorable situations. Honorable men like Jason could barely conceive of such a concern.

She nodded firmly, then stepped reluctantly away from Damien's half-embrace and turned to regard him as dispassionately as she could. "We'll start with the assumption that you're more valuable to an assailant alive than dead."

This was mostly because she couldn't bear to think of the alternative right now. Or possibly ever. Genevieve had to shove aside the thought of losing Damien forever or she wouldn't be able to do this at all. She'd leave *those* lessons for someone more likely to stay levelheaded, like Aryllis.

"Let's start with what you need to do if someone comes up behind you and puts you in a full-nelson hold." She gestured Jason to set it up.

Still shaking his head, the knight stepped behind Damien and threaded his arms under the younger man's shoulders, lacing his fingers behind his neck but not yet exerting any pressure.

"A little pressure please, Jason," Genevieve instructed, fighting her instinct to step in and protect her soul-bonded mate.

A 'little' pressure was all it took to force Damien's head down towards his chest. The young king looked both startled and extremely uncomfortable. Genevieve gestured to Jason to release him.

"If your head gets forced down like that, you won't be able to breathe and you'll lose consciousness. So, preventing that is your first priority. Now," she said, as Damien shook himself slightly, "here's what you do if someone grabs you like that. Lace your own fingers together, and use the backs of your hands to press back against your forehead–" she demonstrated. "This prevents your head from being forced down. Try it."

Gamely, Jason put the young king back in the full-nelson and let him push back as she had directed. Genevieve narrowed her eyes at the knight. "Put some effort into it, Jason, you're doing him no good if he thinks that's all he needs to do." Jason shook his head again, but put some of his considerable strength into the task, and Damien's face went a bit white, fighting the pressure.

Genevieve quickly called a halt. "Good. But that's not enough. You have to break the hold and get away." She paused, trying to figure out how to explain the movement. "You need to side-step and hook your leg behind Jason's. Then your knee is poised to knock him off his balance. Most people will let go when they lose their balance," she added, "but even if your assailant doesn't let go, you'll fall down on top of him and knock his wind out – then you should be able to get away."

They set it up and tried again, but Damien couldn't quite understand what she was asking him to do. After a few minutes the two men stepped aside, Damien looking baffled and frustrated and Jason just looking bemused. "What's the point of this, Genny? If someone is trying to capture Damien – from behind, in some situation where no one else is likely to notice – why wouldn't they simply give him a rap on the head and be done with it?"

She gave him a grim look. "There's nothing I can teach him to prevent that situation, but there's something we can do about this one. And stealing someone's breath to make them faint lets you wake them up faster and is less likely to do permanent damage. If they're bothering to keep him alive, then they might need him alert as well."

Jason put up his hands in surrender. "Fine. But how are you going to show him what he needs to do?"

The three of them looked at each other, reminded of the awkward situation they found themselves in. Genevieve had promised Damien that no other man would touch her – especially not Jason. She was fairly sure that Jason didn't want to touch her and feel the temptation they were both apparently subject to. And now there might be another concern... her hand drifted to her abdomen.

No one had ever accused Jason Solway of being slow to notice things. "Genny... are you pregnant?" he asked.

She smiled slightly, her eyes seeking Damien's. "I might be. It's too early to be sure."

The knight's face lit up almost as much as his king's. "That's wonderful!" He paused. "Then you definitely don't want to be trying these sorts of moves. Let's go back to the city and make sure you're taken care of. Someone else can teach Damien to defend himself in the castle hallways."

Genevieve lifted her chin as she noticed the young king looking like he might be swayed by this argument. "You know what happens when one member of a soul-bonded pair is killed. I might be carrying the Heir to the throne and I might not – but I won't live to see her born if Damien doesn't."

It was blunt, and both men paled a little at her words, but they had no rebuttal.

She stepped in front of Damien. "Put the same hold on me that Jason did on you." There was a long pause, and she could see Jason giving him a dubious look – which she imagined Damien was returning with interest. "Would you rather we do it the other way around so that *you* land on *me* when I fall?" she asked dryly.

Nervously, Damien threaded his arms under hers, his hands laced behind her neck. Genevieve knew full well that there was no way her soul-bonded mate was going to put any pressure on her head, and his physical nearness was an instant distraction for her. And in reality, the instant a person realized she was being put into a dangerous hold was the instant she should react – hopefully *before* the assailant had a sure grip.

So, she wasted no time, putting her laced hands before her forehead, side-stepping, and using her left knee to knock his right out from under him in a modified foot-sweep. Jason leapt forward to catch them, but they landed relatively lightly, with Genevieve rolling to her feet and sprinting a few yards away, dodging the helpful hands of the knight.

Damien sat up slowly, blinking in surprise. He had let go of her as soon as he began to fall, but had not had the presence of mind to roll or otherwise lessen the impact. Something else he had to learn, she realized.

"Now, you try it on Jason," Genevieve instructed.

They set up again, Damien now frowning as he reconstructed the movements she had made and tried to translate them for his own body. Jason looked somewhat resigned. He knew his own strength and he knew his young king's – he had small belief that this would work.

A moment later he landed hard on the ground with Damien on top of his chest – Jason's instinct had been to hold on. His look of surprise was almost funny.

Damien's expression was a curious mixture of awe and delight.

Genevieve smiled.

"Ok, gentlemen," she said. "let's try that again."

By noon, Damien had learned how to break a half-dozen holds and how to break his fall, roll to his feet and sprint. He winced every time he moved, and his bare torso was slick with sweat. Jason was in only somewhat better shape, having had to 'play practice dummy' the entire time – he had probably been knocked over more times that day than during most of his early days as a squire.

Eventually it was Jason who insisted they end the session.

"We don't want Damien to be so exhausted that he's easy prey for the same assassins – excuse me, *kidnappers*–" he corrected himself at Genevieve's suddenly pale face, "–that you're trying to teach him to defend himself from. The lad hasn't had a workout like this in–"

He looked over at Damien for a timeframe.

"Ever," the younger man said, his tone morose with exhaustion.

Jason nodded firmly. "Enough then. Damien, you and I both need a wash in that pond you said the beavers have built. There should still be enough food in the basket for lunch, since Her Grace wouldn't let us take the time to eat any of it." He gave her a grin, then turned back to the young king. "You head down to the stream. I'll catch up in a moment."

It might have been his trust in them as his friends and teachers... or simply exhaustion, but Damien did as requested, his footfalls heavy as he trudged along the deer-track at the edge of the stream.

Jason reached for Genevieve's arm, but she stepped out of reach, still looking after Damien's departing form. She turned to face the knight and caught a glimmer of sadness in his eyes. The easy friendship they had enjoyed for so long would never come back, and she regretted it as much as he – and resented whatever Gods had decreed this awkward state of affairs.

"He's doing well, Genny," the man assured her. "And I've learned a few things myself."

"I know..." She shivered and hugged herself. "I just don't know if it will be enough. It's damned disturbing to know that my life is tied to someone else's – no matter how much I've come to love him. But there's more. I can't believe Lord Prydeen hasn't made more of a grab for power already."

Jason looked at her sharply. "Ciriis told me what was going on. You don't think casting enchantments to control Damien's thoughts is enough for him? He was satisfied to be the power behind the throne before."

"But he wasn't," Genevieve replied. "The old king – he had to have been the more powerful sorcerer of the pair of them. Some of the reports I've gotten mentioned that he called Prydeen his 'apprentice' occasionally. Yet the *old king* is dead and buried and it's the apprentice who is left and an inexperienced young man is on the throne. For now." For now indeed. Now that Damien had demonstrated that he *wasn't* a puppet to be controlled... "What has Lord Prydeen been doing since, um..."

"Since you and Damien disappeared after the reception to welcome the Countess of Zialest?" Jason gave her a wry look as she had trouble finishing the sentence. Then his eyes became thoughtful. "Not much, as far as I know. Ciriis said he wasn't even showing up for Council meetings." He paused, his open, honest face trying to compose itself into reassuring lines despite his active, intelligent mind clearly following along her own train of thought. "Surely if he had any other plans he'd be trying to take Damien's place on the Royal Council, not ignoring it entirely."

Unless Prydeen felt the Council didn't matter in his plans...

...or unless he knew the Council members to already be in his pockets.

Genevieve felt another shiver work its way up her spine. She turned away, still hugging herself. "You should go make sure our liege-lord doesn't drown himself out of exhaustion."

"Genny..." She could sense Jason's hand hover over her shoulder. But it didn't settle, and finally withdrew. "We'll make it turn out right." She listened to the faint sounds of his boots as he followed Damien, hoping and wishing that it could be true.

Chapter ELEVEN

Lost!

JASON, IT TURNED OUT, HAD brought extra horses. They were all tethered within the woods, but before the trail took its sharp downward twist between outcroppings of rock. Genevieve took one look at the tall, proud steeds and blanched. Damien wondered what the problem could be, given that she was reputed to be an excellent horsewoman. He himself was looking forward to not having to walk the whole way back.

"Damien..." She pulled him close and whispered in his ear. "I... don't think I can sit astride a horse." He looked at her in surprise, then began to grin as he realized just why she couldn't sit a horse just now. Her pallor turned into a deep blush.

"My lord and lady?" Jason asked, one eyebrow raised, from where he stood holding the reins of all three beasts.

Damien laughed aloud and swung himself up in one smooth movement. In addition to swordplay, Jason and Adam had made sure he was a competent rider, though he had only been able to practice in the riding court within the castle's walls.

"I find myself unwilling to deprive myself of your gentle presence for even the length of the ride back, Your Grace," he declared, making it a royal command by the use of her title. "Ride with me."

He reached a hand down to her in an imperious gesture. Genevieve gave him a wry look, but accepted his hand, placing one booted foot over his in the stirrup to leverage herself up – Jason was behind her immediately, giving her an extra boost into Damien's arms.

The knight stepped back with a bow as the young king settled her – side-saddle fashion – over his knees. Genevieve took the briefest bit of her attention from settling into as comfortable as possible a position to glare at the knight for his presumption, but he murmured "For the protection of the possible unborn Heir," and she had to subside.

Jason's ironic expression made it clear that he wasn't a bit fooled by their subterfuge, but Damien's heart was bursting with happiness and he simply wrapped his arms around his beloved and took up his reins. "Lead on, my lord Champion," he invited. "Let's go home."

The knight mounted up, and led the way up the trail, leading the remaining horse, with Damien riding along at the rear.

It was a beautiful mid-Autumn day, and perfect for riding. The roads were dry, and what dust they stirred up didn't make it past the horses' fetlocks. Jason dropped back to play rear-guard as they continued on their path, so all the young king had to do was follow the road and hold his Genevieve close.

Unfortunately, even the easy pace they were taking was still uncomfortable for her. She began to squirm, and much as he loved her, she was a well-muscled warrior near to his own height and no light load. The third time she re-adjusted her seat, he couldn't restrain a yelp.

"Damien?" Jason was instantly at their side. "Is something wrong?" He looked like he was about to offer to put Genevieve on his own saddle, but immediately re-thought the idea and held his tongue.

"I'm going to have to get down and walk," Genevieve said with resignation.

Damien doubted she would mind doing so – after all she'd had the two of them walk all the way out there – but he really didn't want to have to walk the rest of the way back himself. He wasn't about to let her walk while he rode, however. Which left Jason either mounted to protect them or walking also... and either way it would be an awkward picture with the several unmounted horses. He sighed. What must be done would be done.

"Jason..." Genevieve was peering into the distance. "Is that a hay wagon?"

The knight followed her gaze down the road. "I believe it is."

She looked at Damien and smiled. "That's the answer then. Catch up to that wagon and we'll catch a ride on top of the hay."

The wagon-driver was only too happy to give his king and the Rebel Duchess a soft ride into the city. He was actually bringing in his load in for a local livery service within the capitol, so the castle was barely out of his way. He actually refused the coin that Damien tried to offer him.

" 'Tis my privilege to give ye the ride, yer Honor," the old farmer insisted. "An' I'd do the same for any childbearin' woman, even if she weren't me future Queen. Horseback's no place for a lassie in her condition." That had stunned all three of the nobles for a moment. The old man's eyes nearly disappeared into his wrinkles as he grinned at them. "Ye've got the glow, lassie, same as me own sweet Marabell did with each of ouren, and each of our daughters, too. Not every woman has it," he confided to Damien, who still looked somewhat poleaxed, "but those that do, ye can tell almost immediate. Hup there now, the both of ye. It'll sway some now, but 'tis softer by far than any saddle I've ever seen."

The rest of the ride was, indeed, much more comfortable, although they swayed mightily, being perched at the top of more than ten feet of baled hay. The wagon creaked fearfully at every bend and dip in the road, but the old farmer whistled as he drove his team of mules so Damien assumed that this was the way it was supposed to be.

As they entered the city – a hay wagon with two people perched on top and guarded by the King's Champion, leading two fine horses – they made enough of a spectacle that Damien and Genevieve were soon obliged to wave in response to all the good wishes.

"Is that the king?

"And the Rebel Duchess? So, it's true they're to be wed?"

"They look a pretty sight, don't they?"

"Wonder where they've been all this time? I hear they haven't been seen in days!"

"I heard they were seen in the city, dressed plain as you or me – guess it was true!"

"The Princess Kandra, she what worked her way up in the army, he's her brother, isn't he? Guess some of her rubbed off on him."

"Think he's gotten her with child yet?"

"Hush now – have some respect!"

"Gods' blessing on you, Your Majesties!"

Damien found himself grinning as he held Genevieve close and waved to the people. *His people.* And they waved back. They seemed delighted to see their king and future queen dressed like themselves, seated on a hay wagon like any countryfolk on a trip to the city. It touched his heart that they still remembered his sister fondly. And it made him blush to hear some of their franker comments – but he didn't stop smiling and waving.

The young king resolved that he would not let himself get holed up in the castle again, no matter the fears of friends and protectors. Like his sister before him, he would see the city as one of its citizens, or as close as he could manage. Genevieve would help him, surely.

At last, the hay wagon creaked across the castle's drawbridge and into the central courtyard. "Down ye go, Yer Honors," the old farmer called up to them. "Just ye slide down the hay now, sir, then ye turn and catch yer lady."

Damien did as he was told, enjoying the wild sensation of sliding down the steep stack of hay, then turning to catch Genevieve. "Thank you," he turned to tell the old farmer, and got a twinkle and a wink in response. "Jest ye be sure and marry the lassie afore that babe pops out," he was advised.

"That's the plan," Damien replied happily, looking to Genevieve and expecting to see his own smile mirrored in hers. But she was looking over his shoulder with trepidation. He turned around, one arm sliding automatically around her waist, to see Lord Prydeen standing not ten feet away. A quick glance around assured him that the courtyard was filled with soldiers and not Lord Prydeen's bullyboys, but something was wrong...

"Your Majesty," the sorcerer said quietly and coldly. "I was told that you and her Grace were immured in your chambers."

Damien felt his smile falter a bit.

Genevieve, bless her brave soul, never paused. "Lord Prydeen," she said with an expression between happiness and embarrassment. "It's my fault, I'm afraid. I'm not used to being within walls for such long stretches of time, so I importuned the king to come with me for an outing." She blushed prettily, and Damien wondered how she could do it on command. "I didn't mean us to be gone long enough to concern anyone, but Lord Solway tracked us down..." She threw a glance at Jason, who had remained mounted, then stepped forwards to take the old sorcerer's hands. "I'm glad we took the time, though. I'd done you a great disservice in my thoughts, Lord Prydeen, but Damien – I mean, my lord-husband-to-be – has straightened me out and explained what a great friend you have been to him. He says your wise counsel has been truly indispensable since the old king passed away."

Lord Prydeen allowed her to take his hands in what would normally be a gesture of friendship. "Is that so? How fortunate."

"I really must get to know you better, my lord," Genevieve continued, turning and tucking her hand into the crook of his arm, turning the sorcerer to begin walking towards the main entrance to the castle. "Would you join us for dinner?" She smiled coquettishly back at Damien over her shoulder, though he knew she must be cringing inside at having to touch the evil old man. "Damien mustn't be allowed to have a monopoly on your advice, surely."

"Indeed not, Lady Genevieve," Lord Prydeen responded dryly, picking her hand off his arm as if it were a dead bug. "King Damien has been less interested in my 'wise counsel' than some other persons. This gentleman, for example."

He gestured ahead of them and a tall, broad-shouldered man stepped out from behind a row of particularly tall, broad-shouldered soldiers. Damien began to realize that the men – all the men around the courtyard – were wearing the wrong set of colors, though they were close enough to mislead at a casual glance.

The late afternoon sunlight tried and failed to bring out highlights from the newcomer's dark brown hair but sparkled on his fine, gold-threaded brocade doublet. His face might have been good-looking if not for how it was twisted up into a smirk of smugly superior vindication flavored with what must be a lifetime's worth of discontent. Which was rather a lot to get from one unpleasant expression – Damien had never seen a man who wore his thoughts so clearly upon his face.

From behind her, Damien could not see Genevieve's face. What he *could* see was that she stopped as still as if time had come to a halt.

"Harald?" she whispered.

He strode forward, coming to a halt directly in front of her. "So, you remember me, Wife," he sneered. "Even though you've hopped into bed with this pretender." He jerked his chin at Damien, who had come up beside her and taken her hand. She clutched it tightly, lacing her fingers with his.

The whole courtyard was filled with men in Siovale colors – dark green and black, instead of the black-trimmed dark-blue of the Castle Guard. Where were Damien's own men? What was going on?

"Crowned and anointed before the whole city," Damien said mildly, retreating to his usual non-threatening style while he tried to assess the situation. "And chosen as Heir by the old king himself. And Her Grace of Elaarwen is no longer your wife. You were declared dead and stricken from the royal archives nigh on three years agone, Harald of Siovale. Death severs all ties."

"Harald..." Genevieve barely seemed to have the breath to speak. "If you are here... *where is my father?*"

The tall man shrugged carelessly. "Oh, I brought him along at Lord Prydeen's request. Bring out the old man, boys."

Damien had not seen Duke Aldred of Elaarwen since he was eight years old, but he had followed his career for the last seven years since Ciriis began compiling reports for him. He had been past his prime three years ago, but powerful still, his hair gone ginger from the same intense red-gold his daughter sported. The old fellow the Siovale soldiers half-dragged forwards in chains was withered, hair thinning and fully grey, beard long but scraggly. He looked ill and poorly fed. He met the young king's eye with a shrewd glance quickly hidden.

Genevieve gave a low cry and would have rushed to him, but Damien wrapped his arms around her and braced himself to stop her. The old Duke had given him a warning in that single glance. He didn't dare risk the old man's safety by looking for more.

"What do you want, Harald?" the Rebel Duchess demanded.

"I?" the big man laughed cruelly. "Why only what is my due! Our old lord king planted me in my mother's womb, so I am his true son. I want my throne and my wife. And a tankard of fine ale wouldn't hurt either."

He looked around with a broad grin as if he'd made a great joke, and his soldiers chuckled dutifully.

"I'm not your wife, Harald," Genevieve retorted.

"You always were a little spitfire, Genny. Training you back to better manners will be a pleasure," he leered at her, *loomed* over them both.

Damien guessed Harald of Siovale was a good head taller than Jason and Adam, both of whom were very tall men. Genevieve's hand trembled in his own and flashes of repressed memories flashed across the bond between them, things Damien's spies could never have known to report. This man had done much worse to her than berate and humiliate her over her barren state...

Time to do something. Surely his own people were here *some*where. Adam, Ciriis, the irrepressible Sir Tim... *the hundred members of the Royal Army who formed the Castle Guard?*

Damien forced himself to chuckle easily.

Harald of Siovale stared at him. So did Genevieve.

"My dear Harald Elsevier," the young king said with amusement. "You cannot expect us all to believe that, simply because you *claim–*" he paused artistically for emphasis, "to be my grandfather's *bastard* son, that the people of this country are to simply acknowledge you over the king they saw crowned and anointed not a month gone? Even if your claim is valid, there are at least a double dozen others with the same lineage, ranging from the daughter of a dock-worker to the son of a merchant-baroness."

He ached to go on and challenge the man over his right to Genevieve... but he had to win this point first or he'd have no power to protect her from this man who had so nearly broken her before.

Lord Prydeen chose that moment to speak up. "Oh, his claim is quite accurate. I oversaw his conception myself. Duchess Lydia was... most accommodating when we explained that her son would have a chance at the throne. She was a woman of impeccable breeding." He looked down his nose at Damien. "As I recall, *your* mother was of common stock."

Damien forced himself to raise an amused eyebrow. "Hardly. But that is entirely beside the point. If Harald had presented himself anytime in – oh, the last thirty years – he might have convinced my lord grandfather to choose him as Heir. Any time before the last *month* he could have presented his case to the Council. It's simply too late.

"Too late for a chance at the throne, and too late for a chance to regain the hand of the Duchess Genevieve. Even had he not been declared dead, a soul-bonding frees the partners from any previous marriage contracts."

Harald of Siovale snarled at him and reached for Genevieve. "You rigged that, you smarmy bastard. Where've you been these last days? Swiving her in the gutters? She's mine until *she's* dead or *I* am."

"Are you challenging the king, Harald Elsevier of Siovale?"

The calm voice came from behind them, and it was Jason's. He was still mounted, and he looked every inch the conquering hero, the King's Champion, the most redoubtable swordsman in the Realm.

Damien wished he could tell Jason to shut up. There were *several dozen* Siovalese soldiers in the courtyard – even *Sir Jason Solway,* the King's Champion and the most redoubtable knight in the Realm, couldn't fight them all, and the young king much doubted that *they* would follow the rules of chivalry. Not under Harald of Siovale's direction – Adam had told him the story of his slain horse in his first real battle too many times to believe that. No, they'd mob him off his horse, and although he might take down a dozen of them, they'd still win in the end.

Where, where, *where* was Adam?

"Oh, I don't think *you'll* fight me, Sir Solway," Harald sneered, and waved a signal at his men.

Now it was Adam dragged forth in chains and forced to his knees, his face bruised and his clothes torn. And not just Adam.

Rosa.

Ciriis.

Timothy Ancellius.

The other members of his Royal Guards – the whole dozen of them. Thankfully, none of the ladies, other than Ciriis... and Rosa, of course.

"I hear some of these people mean something to you. Especially *this* one." He gestured to Adam, who snarled back from behind a gag. Harald's lip curled in disgust. "Unnatural 'men' that you are."

Jason's voice from behind Damien was a model of imperturbable calm. "I am His Majesty's Champion. If you challenge the king or seek to do him harm, Harald of Siovale, I will remove your head from your shoulders. On the field of honor if you so will. Or right here if you will not."

Not a hint in his tone or phrasing of what it must be taking for him to say that. Damien ached for his friend and teacher. If it were Genevieve at risk, could *he* do the right thing for his oaths to his country? How could he ever be worthy of such loyalty and voluntary sacrifice?

Harald sneered at the knight, then turned to his men. "Punch the yellow-haired one in the balls." He looked back at Jason. "Let's see how noble you are now, *Sir* Solway. Or perhaps I should call you 'Jason of Brindlewell'. It's no credit to you that *you* could earn *your* shield because your mother bent her knee to the tyrant."

Then surely it was no credit to Harald of Siovale that his mother had spread her legs for that same tyrant...

But before Damien could open his mouth to make that comment, one of the Siovalese men followed Harald's instruction.

Adam doubled over in pain, and it was Genevieve's turn to tighten her grip on Damien as he involuntarily lurched forward towards his other dearest friend and mentor.

"Stand down, *Sir* Solway," Harald demanded. "Or your *lover* gets another one in the nuts. How many of those can a man stand, do you know?"

"Enough of this, Harald." Another tall man came striding forward.

"Tomas!" Genevieve almost gasped with relief, and Damien was nearly ready to agree. The Duke of Siovale had always seemed brighter, less small-minded than his younger brother. Younger... *half*-brother?

"My lord Duke," Damien greeted Tomas Elsevier courteously, but with some tension. Surely if the man meant to put a stop to this he would not have been standing just out of sight, would not have lent his men to this – Damien admitted the word to himself – this *coup*.

"Damien," the man said neutrally, almost mechanically. Omitting Damien's title was telling but not a complete loss: he had officially joined the Rebellion with Harald's marriage to Genevieve over ten years earlier. He had yet to acknowledge Damien as his liege-lord, or swear the oaths that would bind Damien to protect Siovale in turn. Come to think of it, neither had Genevieve on behalf of Elaarwen.

The Duke turned to his brother. "You hold the trump card. Play it and end this farce."

Harald looked petulant, but capitulated. "You'll all surrender. Or I separate Duke Aldred's head from his shoulders right now."

Genevieve went stiff.

No. Hadn't Damien just told her – two days ago? three? – that there was almost nothing he wouldn't give up to bring his parents and sister back.>That he'd have given up their *soul-bond* if it would have spared her the pain of losing her father?

He looked at Harald of Siovale. A vain man, and foolish, self-centered. But a brave warrior from the counts he had heard, and a clever battlefield commander. A streak of cruelty, obviously. But if his brother – or even Lord Prydeen – could manage him, would he be so bad a king?

"Jason, stand down," he heard his own voice saying.

"Your Majesty?"

"I will not be responsible for the deaths of everyone here. Stand down."

Leather creaked as Jason Solway slowly dismounted from his horse. The sound of steel as he drew his sword and Harald, along with his men-at-arms, all tensed, though Duke Tomas, tellingly, did not... followed by the clatter of steel on stone as Jason discarded it, along with his knife. Damien closed his eyes briefly.

"Tomas, *why?*" Genevieve asked, her voice full of tears.

The Duke of Siovale turned to her, his voice and movements still mechanical. "I would rather be the brother of a king than the vassal of one." Something sparked in his eyes, briefly. "I'm sorry, Genny. Your father will be held safely as long as you cooperate."

She turned her gaze to Harald. "Such a big man you are, Harald. A pity you're not... proportional." There was a vicious tinge to her voice that Damien had never heard before. He barely registered the deadly insult she had given her former spouse.

Harald strode up and seized Genevieve by the arm, pulling her away from Damien, who didn't dare to resist. "Perhaps you've merely forgotten what a real man is like after hopping into bed with this puppy. I suppose I'll need another wife eventually, since you're barren, but I'll keep you on for a whore, if you've gotten any better in bed. If you're good enough, I might spare the lives of some of these people. Wasn't Jason Solway a friend of yours as a child?" He turned to his brother. "Put the pretender and his *friends* in the room he had my Genevieve in. It's dismal and secure enough for noble prisoners."

"All of them?" the Duke's voice didn't even rise in surprise.

"Why not? There's no escape."

"And Duke Aldred?"

"Whatever you like." Harald sneered at the shrunken old man. "I'm going to take this erring wife of mine up to the royal suite and remind her of her proper duties to her husband. We'll see how many of these others she manages to earn my mercy for."

"What about securing the castle and city?"

"Whatever you think best, brother," Harald waved dismissively. "I need to crush a little rebellion in the family."

"King Harald," Lord Prydeen stepped forward, a vial in his hand. "A cure for barrenness. Give the woman a taste of this."

Harald preened a little at the undeserved title, taking the vial and shaking it to see the blue liquid within slosh around. "You have the solutions to all my problems, Lord Prydeen."

Genevieve seemed sunk in despondence and didn't resist as he dragged her towards the stairs to the entry hall. She didn't even look up or back to catch Damien's eye. But he saw her free hand go to her flat abdomen, and it felt like a stab to his gut.

He looked away from her to see Lord Prydeen looking at him with an unpleasant smile and a speculative look in his eye.

Chapter TWELVE

Faith

"WHAT THE *HELL* DID YOU think you were doing?" Adam croaked as soon as the lot of them were sealed into what had been Genevieve's suite. The sitting room was too small for fourteen men and two women, and neither water nor food had been provided. They had helped Adam to the leather couch, and he lay now with his head in Jason's lap. He wasn't the only one looking reproachfully at the young king.

"Saving all of our lives," Damien replied mildly. "What happened here? Where are the other ladies and the Council members?" Lady Theresa, he wanted to ask, but didn't. She had survived his grandfather's reign; surely she could survive this.

It was Countess Rosa who answered. "They arrived last night, flying a flag of peace. Tomas of Siovale has been one of the Rebellion's greatest allies. I... have never had reason to question his motives before. I went out to meet him, to see why he had come. He said that the Rebel Council had decided Genevieve and I should have some backup – some military aid to help us get away in case negotiations went sour. He seemed to have about two dozen men and a similar number of servants and retainers I... vouched for them." Her tone was bitter. "No one saw Harald or Duke Aldred until just before you appeared."

Damien looked to Ciriis to take up the tale, but she wouldn't look at him.

After a moment, Tim continued explaining. "We think Lord Prydeen brought in his own people to do the dirty work. They contaminated the royal kitchens. Everyone who ate food prepared there is ill–"

"Some have *died.*" Ciriis' voice was harsh.

"–we do our own food preparation, of course, so we were all fine," Tim continued after a moment. He looked like he was in pain. His voice was... less energetic than usual. "Aryllis and the other ladies... were seeing to the sick. Lena found me to tell me that it couldn't have been just a bad lot of meat or something... just before we discovered that we had four dozen Siovalese soldiers – no servants at all – roaming the castle. They caught us by ones and twos."

He looked at Damien miserably, and Damien remembered that Tim was engaged to be married to Aryllis.

"I don't know what happened to Aryllis and the other women. Lena..." He stopped abruptly, and Damien was afraid he knew too well what had happened to golden, laughing Lena. Tim was holding a hand delicately to his side and breathing somewhat shallowly. All of the other men were limping or holding an arm or a gash in a leg, though none of them looked *quite* as torn up as Adam.

"We should have supplies to bind up your wounds in the desk," Damien suggested. He looked around. "Most of your wounds, anyways. I hope."

Rosa went over to the desk and began rummaging around.

"So now we're trapped in here," Adam said bitterly. "You could have made a break for it, Damien. You and Genevieve. Now what hope have we." He didn't even make it a question.

Jason leaned over and kissed his lover's brow. "Where there's life there's hope, Adam. I don't think I could have cleared enough of a path to get either one of them out, let alone both." He sighed. "And as Genny reminded me this morning, it's both or neither with them. A soul-bond doesn't give much leeway on that."

Adam snorted painfully. "Well, since I doubt Harald of Siovale is planning to let Damien live long, he'll be in for a surprise when Genevieve keels over, too." Almost everyone glared at him over that, but it was Jason's expression of pain that made Adam look mildly remorseful.

Damien simply turned and walked into Genevieve's bedchamber.

It looked the same as it had the day before, which seemed almost unfair when everything else had changed. He could even see the dents in the smooth sheets where he had lain down to wait while she dressed.

He narrowed his eyes. Harald's people clearly hadn't taken the time to thoroughly search the room. Would Genevieve have any sort of weapon hidden away here? She had taken her sword, her bow, and her knife on their excursion – those had all been taken away from her by now, just as Damien and the others had been disarmed before they were sealed into these airless rooms. Aryllis and... Lena... had been her closest companions these last two weeks – they might know where the Rebel Duchess had secreted a small blade or two. If only they were here. If only... for so many, many reasons.

"How can you *stand* there so calmly?" Ciriis demanded from behind him. "Don't you *know* what is almost certainly happening to Genevieve *right now?*"

Damien looked at the richly carpeted floor and forced his hands not to clench into fists. "I know exactly what is happening to her. She's keeping her end of the bond open. I asked her not to close me out." Harald seemed to be turned on by the prospect of humiliating her more than anything.

"Then how can you–?"

"Cirii." Countess Rosa's calm voice. He turned to see her wrap an arm around Ciriis' trembling shoulders. The familial resemblance between the two women was evident in their dark hair, their short stature, and their fine features – but all the sharp corners seemed to have been rounded out in Rosa's face, and she radiated an unshakable inner calm. By contrast, Ciriis seemed more like a thunderstorm about to happen, her frail form a container for deadly energies.

The young king met the countess' eyes. "Do you have a plan, Your Majesty?" she asked quietly.

He nodded. "When she tells me the time is right, I'm going to go get Genevieve and then we'll all leave."

"Just like *that?*" Ciriis demanded.

"Pretty much."

She barked a bitter laugh, tears rolling down her face, the stoicism with which she had faced the soldiers in the courtyard a long-ago memory. "You're going to waltz past all the Siovale men, and snatch her away from a man nearly twice your size? *You*, Damien? You barely know which side to butter your toast on without Adam or me to show you."

In stress comes truth. Damien looked sadly at the woman who had been his first lover. Genevieve had been right – Ciriis did not take him seriously at all. Adam's recent words confirmed that he felt the same. Damien thought – *hoped* – he might have won over Jason a bit.

"And then we'll all *just walk out of here?* Again, past all these guards? What are you thinking? Or *are* you even–"

"Cirii. Hush." Rosa said again. "Somehow he and Genevieve got past all of you."

Ciriis gave another bitter laugh. "You don't see it, Rosie. When he says we'll *all* leave, he doesn't mean Aryllis or Terellie or... Lena..." She glared at him through her tears. "You know what will happen to them here."

Damien didn't look away. "No. Nor will we have Lady Theresa or Duke Aldred with us. I can get the rest of you away to safety and have a chance of getting them back. Or we can all stay here and die, Ciriis."

"I promised these women that they'd never have to go through this again, Damien! But *you'll* leave them to suffer," she said viciously, "just as you're leaving Genevieve to suffer now. You say you can get her out of there, but all *I* see is you standing here. You're not the *man* I thought you were. And you're not much of a *king."*

"Ciriis Celavell!" Rosa exclaimed.

"No, milady, let her speak her mind," Damien said, his tone still mild, though he said it through clenched teeth. "I may not be much of a king – *or* of a man – but I'm all we have right now. And I would not be the kind of king who would stop his subjects' mouths."

As his grandfather had been. As Harald of Siovale surely would be. The thought that he was leaving his people, his *country* in the hands of that man for even a short time was quite nearly as painful as what was coming across his bond with Genevieve. At least this fight was a distraction, keeping him from responding too soon.

"You're just *leaving* her, when you say you can get her *out*–"

His short, blunt fingernails were starting to cut into the skin of his palms. Damien forced himself to relax his hands, leaned back against one of the posts of the four-poster bed, and folded his arms casually. The appearance of nonchalance had been his armor against Lord Prydeen. It would do for Ciriis Celavell.

"What would you have me do, Ciriis? Harald of Siovale stands a head taller than even Jason or Adam, and at last report he had a reputation as a champion wrestler. Jason may be the finest swordsman in the Realm, but we haven't so much as an eating knife between us, and there's not a man in that room who could back him up in a fight just now."

"Harald of Siovale is a pig," Adam croaked. Ciriis spun around to see Jason supporting him into the room. The rest hastily made way for the pair to seat Adam on the bed. He did so, and nodded his thanks to Jason. "He fights dirty, even on the battlefield, where he claims the right to fight as if he'd actually won his shield," Adam went on. "Jason would be a fool to face him on his own terms. And Damien twice so."

Jason's face was set. "I'm not leaving Genny to him."

"Jase–" Adam's expression was fearful – not for himself, but for Jason. It was a look Damien hadn't seen in seven years, and had hoped never to see again. Not since Oskar...

Jason turned to his king. "I'm coming with you. And we're not waiting any longer."

"Jason–" Adam's pleading gaze transferred to Damien as his lover refused to meet his eyes. *Not again,* his eyes said. *Don't let Jason sacrifice himself again.*

Damien stared his Champion down. "Nothing has changed, Lord Solway. You still have no weapon and Harald of Siovale can still wipe the floor with both of us and–" he stumbled over the words slightly, despite his efforts to stay calm, "–have his way with Genevieve without breaking a sweat. My Queen says we wait until he's asleep or leaves the room. She's the strategist. We wait." His arms were still folded, but he stood erect now, his stance set as if prepared for battle.

Ciriis had taught him the power of body language.

But it was his *grandfather* who had shown him, by example, how to project *power*.

It was something Damien had never tried with his friends and mentors before, and rarely with anyone else, since his safety had seemed to reside in not being taken seriously. With these three – Adam, Ciriis, and Jason – especially, he had felt he owed them too much to ever command them as if they were any other subject. It had taken Genevieve to show him that he would have to at some point.

Jason glared back at him, then, finally, lowered his eyes and turned away. His powerful muscles flexed beneath his tunic as if he was restraining himself from some more violent reaction by sheer force of will. Adam gave his king an openly grateful look – the first such Damien had ever seen on the cynical man's face – before reaching out to tug at his lover's sleeve and pull him into a sympathetic embrace.

Ciriis, outside the axis of the power struggle, had missed the intensity because it was so focused. She threw up her hands. "So, you're just going to leave her to be raped by that, that *man?*" she cried. "If this is the devotion of a soul-bonding, Gods spare me!"

It said worlds, some part of Damien reflected, that 'man' was the worst word she could think of to describe Harald.

The young king swallowed hard. "She says... It's not in words, you have to understand," he closed his eyes. "She says that this is nothing she didn't know for the eight years of their marriage. That it's nothing compared to what Rosa – and Lena, and so many of the others – have suffered. That if it keeps the rest of us safe... she... can manage..." Damien's shoulders slumped and he put his hands up to scrub at his face, running his fingers into his hair. Her image of Lena had been so clear... That, on top of all the rest...

A sympathetic arm draped over his shoulders. Rosa, of course.

He tried not to think about it. He had promised Genevieve never to let another woman touch him again, just as she had promised him the reverse. And here they both were... he didn't think she would mind Rosa offering him the sort of comfort his sister might have done.

If only he could say the same about Genevieve's situation – it was all he could do to restrain himself from dashing for those hidden stairs. To protect his beloved soul-bonded mate... and because of the bonfire of jealousy that he would *not* let control him.

He would do the *right* thing. The *safe* thing. The thing that would get them all out of here *alive*. His Champion, the men of his Guard, Rosa, Ciriis... and Genevieve.

So long as she said '*wait*', he would follow her direction.

And wait.

And wait.

Rosa's fingers were surprisingly strong as she pried his hands away from his head. He hadn't even noticed that he was digging the nails into his scalp. Or that he had sunk to a squat, back braced against the tall bed, his elbows braced on his knees.

Ciriis made a disgusted noise and stormed back into the sitting room, slamming the intervening door behind her.

"She'll come around," Rosa said softly, but her eyes were troubled as she looked at – or rather past – the closed door.

Lena, Aryllis, Felena, Terellie, Sasha, Elsa, Emerie, Thielda, Nalda, Kamauri, Licia, Mirabelle. *Lena*. Their names were a litany in Damien's mind, pounding against what he was all too aware was happening in the room right above his head.

He couldn't see a way to rescue them. Or the old Duke, Lady Theresa... or any of the others, servants and nobles alike, who might have inadvertently been trapped in the castle when the Siovalese forces made their move. Though he suspected that most of the nobles would simply shrug and hitch their fortunes to Harald's wagon, as they had done with his grandfather and attempted to do with himself. They would doubtless be disappointed that Genevieve was still set up to be queen...

...if he failed to get her out of here safely.

So far, he was getting more *anger* down the bond than any other emotion. Humiliation wasn't something Harald could force on Genevieve. And, as she had told him, this wasn't anything he hadn't done with – *to* – her during their marriage. If that hadn't been a humiliation, she could choose for this not to be either. He could tell that she almost pitied Harald's obsession with her – though not his attempt to usurp the throne or his imprisonment of her father.

One last night with him. It was already too many as far as both she and Damien were concerned, but she could cope... Damien told himself again that if she could, he could.

A large shape settled in front of him, and Damien blinked to come out of himself and focus. Jason. Kneeling on one knee, his head bent. He had never done that before, even when he had sworn fealty to the confused young prince in the middle of the Royal Library nearly ten years earlier.

Rosa had politely stepped away to give them privacy, and Adam appeared to have fallen into what Damien sincerely hoped was a healing sleep on the bed.

So there was no one else to hear Jason's low-voiced request.

"Take me with you to retrieve Genevieve, I beg you, Your Majesty."

It was... heartbreaking... to hear his friend and teacher speak so formally, so accepting that the final decision would be his king's and not his own. Jason's eyes stayed fixed on the floor, as if hoping that meekness would win him what boldness had not.

"Jason – Sir Solway..." the moment seemed to call for the more formal title, but Damien had little idea what to say.

"I'll wait until you give the word," the blonde knight promised, then gave a quiet laugh that held no mirth. "Not that there's another choice, since I have no idea how you intend to get to her. But you can't expect me, as your Champion, to let you go into harm's way without me at your side."

"Your role is to take my place on the field of honor–"

"My place is to protect you." He had always done that, and to his own great harm. "My place is to protect your chosen queen." Jason Solway looked up at last, and Damien could see tears standing in his eyes. "Damien. Please. I can no more leave her behind than you can."

The admission cost him; it was obvious. His voice was even quieter than it had been. His eyes flickered to Adam's sleeping form, then to Damien's face, then back to the carpet.

"I'm sorry," he added, just as quietly. "She is my dear friend, but I didn't want this."

A long moment passed where Damien's thoughts were frozen.

He almost couldn't feel Genevieve down the bond, he felt so utterly still.

"I know," he said at last, releasing the last bits of resentment around the strange attraction his beloved and his Champion had for each other and accepting that this truly was not a situation of their making. And that nothing would come of it except that Genevieve had acquired a second powerful protector... one who had already demonstrated his willingness to sacrifice himself for Damien.

"I know," he said again and cleared his throat to say more, when a stab of sharp pain eclipsed anything else down the bond, and he shot to his feet without thinking.

He was on the hidden staircase and heading up, knowing only that Genevieve had been hurt – deeply and unexpectedly – and she needed him. He emerged into the upper chamber – his own bedchamber – and automatically reached for one of the heavy candelabras that his Royal Guards ensured were always stocked with candles. A weapon, though he had never thought of it so before.

The waves of pain from Genevieve were still blanking out conscious thought. He could see her, bent forward over the foot of the bed, hear her crying out in pain as Harald plunged heedlessly at her bare bottom, a malicious grin on his face, his ham-sized hands encircling her waist.

Someone restrained Damien, plucked the candelabrum from his hand and proceeded to knock the villainous fool unconscious with a sharp rap at the base of the skull, far more effectively than Damien would have known how to do. The giant man collapsed slowly, and Genevieve gave one last, anguished cry as he withdrew all unintentionally.

Damien gathered her up in his arms, holding her carefully. She wouldn't open her eyes, but went limp in his embrace, mute now by force of her will, tears of pain still leaking down to soak Damien's shirt.

The rest of the world gradually came back into Damien's perceptions, and he realized it was Jason who had followed him up a set of stairs the other man could not have seen. He must have had a grip on Damien to be able to even touch them, though the younger man had no memory of it.

Jason had dragged the unconscious Harald out of the way, and was now cautiously checking the next room for soldiers. He turned back to give Damien a wry smile. He didn't say anything, but ducked into the next room.

"It'll be ok, love," Damien murmured to Genevieve. He carried her into the bathing room and carefully cleaned her up. She was all but fully dressed, Harald not having bothered to do more than pull her pants partway down and wad her plain, full skirt up over her back, but she was bleeding... and she was completely limp and unresponsive. He could only tell that she was awake because of the small whimpering sounds she made every now and then... and because she clutched at him if he stepped the slightest bit away.

"I'm sorry," Genevieve whispered at last, as Damien prepared to carry her back into the bedchamber. "I'm sorry." Her eyes stayed closed.

He was confused. "Whatever for?"

She buried her face in his shoulder, new tears adding to the sodden shirt. "I was supposed to distract him. I was supposed to be strong enough to take anything he could do to me."

Damien smoothed her hair. "You were. I'm the one who didn't react the way we planned." He didn't mention that her pain had eradicated his abilities for rational thought.

She simply shook her head and clung to him.

Jason tentatively knocked on the door, then peeked around it. "Is she–?" Damien shook his head, and the knight's face went grim. "We need to get going. I gave Harald another rap on the head to be sure he stays out, but we shouldn't stay here longer than it takes to get out."

Damien nodded and brought Genevieve out of the bathing room.

"The good news," Jason said, "if I can call it that, is that Harald simply dumped their weapons in the sitting room – his as well as hers. We'll be armed with more than candelabras as we make our escape."

Damien stared at the two sword belts, the knives, and even Genevieve's bow and quiver that filled his Champion's arms. His jaw worked, and the half-formed thought became a full one from one breath to the next. "Take her," he demanded, pushing his limp betrothed at the knight. "And give me her sword."

Jason tried to juggle the hardware and not drop Genevieve as Damien released her and she whimpered. "Damien – my lord–" he said warily, "what are you planning to do?"

"I'm going to kill that monster over there." It was all crystal clear. Revenge on Harald for Genevieve's harms. Reclaim his throne by eliminating the usurper.

"No..." Genevieve struggled to reach him. "Damien, you mustn't kill Harald."

He looked at her in disbelief. "You can't tell me you harbor some fond feeling for him."

She shook her head weakly, giving up on reaching for him and leaning heavily on Jason. "No, most certainly not." She shuddered. "But he's not the whole problem. He couldn't avoid boasting to me. Lord Prydeen has been behind it all. He planned the 'hunting accident' with Harald in order to abduct my father. He provisioned an old keep in Siovale for them – and did something to Tomas. If you slay Harald, *Tomas* is still under Lord Prydeen's control and the castle is full of his soldiers." She took a deep breath. "And Harald will be a stone around the sorcerer's neck. He's a fool. He'll require constant management."

"And if you kill Harald without a trial," Jason added, "Duke Tomas can call blood-feud on you. Reasonable or not."

"And under Lord Prydeen's influence, he most certainly will," Genevieve shivered. "Harald will make it easier to defeat the sorcerer. He's too clearly a usurper, too stupid, too willful. Tomas... could be a different matter. You need to name him – both of them, and Tomas as well – Traitors to the Realm in a public trial. And deal with them as such traitors are dealt with. *Publicly*. So that the people know that the threat from the sorcerer is ended – and to discourage others who might think to try the same thing."

That meant sending out heralds to post the charges and sentence... and nailing the traitors up on the outside of the castle wall until they rotted. That it would have been Genevieve's fate as well – had she ever been caught before the soul-bonding, or at least before Damien's coronation – didn't need to be stated. The young king was all too aware that it could have been *his* fate, and that of his dearest friends, as well if his grandfather had chosen to view the preparations Adam and Jason and Ciriis had been making on his behalf as a threat, rather than appropriate care for his only remaining legitimate Heir – it had happened to at least two score of his close kin when they wore the Heir's Ring, after all.

He'd already faced several challenges from some of his grandfather's *other* bastard children, though obviously none so well-organized and well-supported as Harald. But he'd found more subtle ways to handle them. Ways that didn't involve gruesome executions and public shaming...

Were Tomas Siovale's wife and children even aware of his perfidy? Would Damien have to name a new family to rule Siovale... and would the Siovalese accept such interlopers? The province was the one closest to Emeralsee, saving only Reyensweir, and was large and prosperous – a fifth of the Realm in area before the county of Farivera had seceded nearly a half-century ago. Half their source of grain, and the training grounds for the greatest mounted warriors in Ilseador.

When Siovale had joined the Rebellion – with Harald's marriage to Genevieve ten years earlier – it had nearly been a victorious blow for Duke Aldred's Rebels all at once. Only the loyalty of Reyensweir (the other 'breadbasket' of the Realm) and that of Embervest (with its warriors trained up against their incessant bandit problems) had sustained the supremacy of Emeralsee and the monarchy.

Reyensweir, Embervest... And his grandfather's tight hold on Emeralsee, which had the Realm's only decent port and was thereby the ultimate source of all financial capitol.

Damien's succession was still too new and, demonstrably, too unstable. He needed to make an example of Harald Elsevier – and of Duke Tomas and Lord Prydeen. A brutal, unquestionable example that went against everything he believed in and against everything he meant to be as a ruler... or he would only face challenge after challenge after challenge to his authority and there would be neither time nor energy to fix all the things that his grandfather and Lord Prydeen – and the nobles who had followed their example – had broken. The state of the Realm would continue to deteriorate – perhaps Ilseador would even break up into separate pieces, as the Lost Provinces had already done – and the state of the land and the people themselves would deteriorate as well.

Perhaps the Realm *could* be ruled by the common sense and intelligence of a well-chosen committee... once the situation was settled. Damien could work towards that end.

But right now, there was no path forwards towards that goal but a public – a *very* public – trial and execution for Harald and Tomas Elsevier. And Lord Prydeen, if they could somehow capture and contain a sorcerer.

Even if the idea sickened him. And even if it meant – right now – leaving Harald of Siovale here, alive, if not exactly unharmed.

Damien glowered. Their words made too much sense.

"Damien..." Genevieve reached for him again, and he quickly handed her sword back to Jason to take her in his arms again. He scooped her up, and started towards the stairs. How he had the strength and energy to do this, he had no idea, but he'd use it while it lasted.

"Wait a moment," Jason called out. Damien turned to see the knight holding out the vial of blue liquid that Lord Prydeen had given Harald. "Genny, he didn't make you take any of this, did he?"

She shook her head.

"Good," he replied. "I have a feeling that Prydeen's idea of a 'cure for barrenness' could include a simple poison. You've been a thorn in his side for too long, my friend."

She sighed, and laid her head on Damien's shoulder. "Maybe Lena will be able to tell. That's her specialty, she told me." The two men exchanged a glance. Jason shook his head minutely, and Damien nodded agreement.

Damien started down the hidden stairs, the risers more invisible than usual, with the bulk of Genevieve's body blocking him from seeing his feet. They seemed wider and deeper than on his previous excursions, almost as if they knew he needed more space to carry her.

"Damien!" He looked back to see Jason looking frustrated as he tried to step down the – to him – entirely invisible staircase and finding only solid stone flooring.

The young king turned carefully, and climbed back up to the floor.

"I was holding onto you on the way up," Jason told him. "This must be some enchantment keyed directly to you."

"To me and to Genevieve," Damien told him. The same idea occurred to both of them – that it would make sense to have Jason carry Genevieve and Damien carry the weapons – and they both discarded it instantly.

"Just go slow enough that I can keep a hand on you," Jason said. "We can make this work."

They made it down to the lower chamber to find their imprisoned companions in an uproar. The entire lot of them had relocated to the bedchamber, where they were diligently searching for secret passageways. To them, it had looked like their very unmagickal king – a young man many of them had helped raise – and Jason had run up the wall on thin air and vanished through the ceiling. After some explanations, the men settled down and began to plan while Rosa and Ciriis surrounded Genevieve and carried her off to the sitting room for some privacy.

Damien's back was beginning to feel the night's exertions, and it was clear that only he or Genevieve could get people through the hidden passageways. And that the Rebel Duchess was in no shape to make the full trek herself. So, loathe as he was to let anyone else take care of her, it was agreed that Jason would carry Genevieve when she could not walk, and Damien would ferry back and forth to bring everyone through to where the passageway became truly open.

It was easier said than done. The magickal passageways were interspersed with sections of solid stone.

Damien had never noticed those solid sections on his own; nor had Genevieve on her single pass through. To them, it had all seemed clear and open after initially entering, but to the others it was distinctly obvious – which was probably a good thing, since they were able to tell Damien before he let them go. Being entombed in solid rock wasn't a terribly good alternative to staying and facing Harald and Lord Prydeen.

The 'open' sections were often short, walled-off stretches that could fit no more than a handful of people, and those only if they were very friendly with each other. A chain of one person holding another's hand who was holding onto Damien could pass through the stone, and that worked if he was in the middle of the chain as well. But since only he could see where a new section of magickal passage began, it didn't work terribly well.

Damien couldn't breathe easily until he had managed to get every last one of his Guards and friends out of Genevieve's suite. But that merely meant that he had them stashed in a variety of sub-pockets along the way. Jason, carrying Genevieve, and somehow effectively trailing Adam and both of the other women had made it the farthest, but eventually even he had to stop for a break.

It was a very long night.

At long last, they were all in the very real tunnel passageway on the far side of the moat. It was as dark as it can only be deep underground, and dank with the nearness of the water. They were all hungry and thirsty, and all of them but Damien, Jason, Rosa, and Ciriis were in pain from some sort of injury or other. The only good part of the situation was that Damien could finally hold onto Genevieve, and Jason could embrace Adam.

"Only one more magickal section and we're free and clear," Damien told the barely perceptible figures seated around him. The same magick that let him walk through certain sections of solid stone seemed to also allow him to see as if there was a pale glow everywhere. He had never consciously noted it before, having never shared the route with anyone other than Genevieve, for whom the same magick also worked. The complaints of his people about the darkness had actually startled him.

His announcement, which had been meant to reassure, garnered a somewhat different response than he had expected. The air suddenly hummed with apprehension.

"Then we need to plan," Rosa said calmly into the tense silence. "Where exactly are we coming out, Your Majesty?" He had suggested that she call him by name, given the circumstances, and she had replied that she would not because he needed to maintain his authority, in these circumstances most especially.

"In an alley," Damien replied. He paused, trying to think how else to describe the location.

"We'll be a mile from the closest gate through the city wall," Genevieve volunteered unexpectedly. She had been uncharacteristically silent during their transport, and it felt to Damien like she had wrapped herself in a cloak of morose guilt. "That would be the west gate. It's another mile from there to get all the way out of the city proper by foot."

Someone huffed in the dark. "It could be worse," Sir Tim suggested from somewhere else in the dark. "If we were heading south, we'd be looking at a good five miles to the gate and then another ten before we were free of the city."

"Unless we want a ship," someone else – Sir Randolph? – replied. "The docks are east."

"We want to go west," Damien told them. "We're going to Elaarwen and the Rebellion. It's the safest place for us." He hugged Genevieve, and she squeezed his hand back, though a bit tentatively.

A third someone barked out a laugh – Damien had never realized how hard it was to identify people by voice alone, but he didn't want to look around for faces and disturb Genevieve, who was resting in his arms. "Well, if that isn't turning things around on their head."

"True, though." That was Tim again.

"Oh, aye, not arguing. Just noticing."

"It'll be daylight soon," Rosa guessed. "We'll need to make our way through the city in daylight. And we have to assume that our absence has been noted and there are troops out looking for us."

"He only has four dozen soldiers," Tim objected. "And he has to hold the castle. How many could he possibly send out to look for us?"

"If *he's* even recovered his wits enough to be doing any of the planning after those raps on the head Jason gave him," Sir Otto chuckled. By silent agreement they had all decided to refer to Harald of Siovale simply as *he*.

"That's assuming *he* had enough wits in the first place for anyone to tell the difference," Tim quipped. The young knight's voice was weak and raspy and worried, but he was clearly trying to hold himself together and give the rest heart as Second-in-Command of the Royal Guard despite his injuries.

"You're forgetting Lord Prydeen's bullyboys," Adam put in sourly.

"And spies," Ciriis added in a subdued voice. The spymistress was very much out of her depth in this adventure.

"I have another complication to add," Damien told them and waited until the chorus of groans ended. "I want to warn as many of the common folk as we can. *He*... is not going to be a kindly ruler, and I swore an oath to protect them. If all I can do is warn them what's coming, it's... something."

"We'll return with an army at our backs to free the city!" Adam declared, and the rest murmured agreement.

"I can tell you that will be welcome news," Rosa said dryly, "but the average shopkeeper or street-vendor still isn't going to be thrilled at the prospect of more turmoil to come. King Damien is absolutely right. We need to get the word out to as many people as possible – then if they want to get themselves and their families out of the city before... *he*... makes their lives miserable, they can do it."

"You can say his name," Genevieve said, slightly waspishly. "Harald won't become any more appealing by refusing to speak his name."

There was a moment of awkward silence in the darkness.

"I think we're just trying to spare each other's feelings," Rosa tried, diplomatically. "All of us here have been injured by Harald of Siovale in some way. It's too soon to know how we are all coping with that."

Genevieve started to huff, so Damien kissed her, hoping to settle her before she threw the small kindness back in everyone's face. He understood that she needed to sound strong and he knew, down the bond, that she was feeling anything but. On the other hand, the other members of their party had also been through a hellish experience,and repudiating their attempted kindness would do no one any good. And... he'd been longing to kiss her for this whole long hellish night. Her simple presence centered him, and having her draped across his lap, so she could rest more comfortably during this break had made him begin to feel real hope.

In what was utter blackness to all but the two of them, it was as private a moment as might be found.

Her reaction to his kiss took him entirely by surprise however. She froze stiff, and a wave of fear down the bond cut off his ability to sense her subtler emotions. He stopped immediately, of course. Genevieve did not pull away from him, but she stayed tense and closed off.

The young man knew this must have to do with... what had happened earlier. *Face it,* he told himself. *Harald raped her. I was wrong to let her sacrifice herself... her emotions were too involved for her to be the brilliant strategist she usually is.*

He had watched the ladies of his Royal Guard slowly recover from the abuses they had been subjected to. More, he had eventually realized that Ciriis had given him to each of them as a final step in *their* healing process – he had been so non-threatening, so overawed by them, and more than half in love with each of them, that they had been able to go past their traumas.

When Tim Ancellius had begun to court Aryllis there had been a period of awkwardness between the knight and his prince... but just after they announced their engagement, Tim had come to him and thanked him. No further explanation. He had been the first, but there had been several others since then as the men and women of his Royal Guards naturally found like minds amongst each other.

Damien knew this would take time. All he could hope for was that the soul-bond between them would help her recovery go more easily... and that it might in somewise make up for his failure to protect her in the first place.

It occurred to him, though it felt a betrayal even to think it, that her strategy had actually worked out perfectly, since they had all made it out this far. Though whether it was a betrayal of Genevieve or of Lena, Lady Theresa, and the others left behind, Damien wasn't sure.

The conversation taking place around them had moved on, discussing how to move a group of seventeen people through the streets of the city without notice, a subject to which Damien could not contribute much. It gave him the chance to ignore everyone and whisper fiercely into her ear. "I am not Harald. I am Damien. I love you and I will never touch you without your consent in any way... other than to save your life or someone else's. I am *not Harald.*" The qualifier seemed like it might be more than she needed to hear right now, but he would not lie to her. He hadn't asked explicit permission to carry her away from Harald's unconscious form, after all.

A miniscule nod. A slight lessening of tension in her body. It was clearly a conscious decision, the force of her powerful will fighting to defeat her instinctive reaction.

The young king forced himself to relax as well, leaning his head back against the stony tunnel wall. He left his arms around her, but let his muscles go limp, hoping that would keep her from feeling entrapped. A little bit more tension went out of Genevieve.

For now, it was enough.

Chapter THIRTEEN

The Once and the Future Queens

"I FOUND A FRIEND," JASON reported.

Ciriis had taken the lead on getting everyone out of Emeralsee City. As soon as Damien and Genevieve had started leading the party up into the alleyway, she had started sending the Royal Guards off by ones and twos to contact her spies scattered throughout the city. Rosa and Otto, she had sent off to shop for more inconspicuous garments. Ironically, Damien and Genevieve were the least obvious members of the party, besides her red hair, since the men were all wearing uniforms as Royal Guards and the other two women were in their fine Court gowns.

"That's singularly uninformative," Genevieve commented dryly.

He grinned at her. "It's our friendly hay farmer. He managed to make it out of the castle with his load and dropped it off to his customer without a hitch."

"That's a relief," she replied. It was. The old man's kindness would have been poorly repaid if he'd gotten mired in the Siovalese coup.

"Better than that, he's done the shopping for his homestead. His womenfolk wanted a number of bolts of fabric. Apparently, they make a new set of clothes for each family member and farmhand for Midwinter gifting. He showed me the fabric. It's quite nice."

The Rebel Duchess gave the blonde knight a baffled look. "I'm happy for him?"

Jason actually laughed. At the unexpected sound, Ciriis broke away from where she was giving instructions to another one of the young men to find out what was going on with them.

The Champion filled her in quickly, then added, "It's a very *large* homestead, ladies. And a lot of fabric. He doesn't actually need to sell his hay in the city, but it gives him an excuse to bring the hay wagon in to collect what they need – spices for the Winter, some special seed, and a *lot* of fabric."

Genevieve suddenly realized what he meant. "He's willing to smuggle some of us out under his load!"

"Exactly!" Jason beamed at her. "So as soon as Damien finishes bringing out the rest of our merry band–"

"I'm here," the young king was looking a bit worn. "Everyone's out. What's going on?

"How many do you think your farmer friend can fit in his wagon, Jason?" Ciriis asked before the knight could explain.

"Two. Three would be a squeeze. And we'll have to re-stack the fabric carefully to create a cavity that will let them breathe and still look like it's not there."

Ciriis looked at Damien, then at Genevieve, and took a deep breath. "We *were* going to have to split you up to get you both out of the city. Together you're just too recognizable. Especially that hair – red hair doesn't take dye easily and we don't have the resources to do anything more than a quick job of it. It would be obvious to even a brief glance."

The young king lifted his chin. "Then have Genevieve go in the wagon. Who will you send with her?" Genevieve gave him a pensive look. The logic was sound, but if he didn't make it out, the point was moot for her.

"Adam." Ciriis said firmly, and they all looked at her in surprise. "And Tim, if we can fit him. They're both hurting more than they'll admit," she explained. "A wagon-ride won't do them much good, but it'll be better than walking several miles." She hadn't sent either of them out on any errands, and a quick glance gave evidence of her words. The fact that neither of them would be of much aid to Genevieve in case of trouble went unremarked – anyone unburying them from under all that fabric would have them at an extreme disadvantage anyways. "What is our rendezvous, incidentally?"

Genevieve exchanged a glance with the king and his Champion. They all knew where it would have to be. She explained the grotto's location to Ciriis. "Jason and I can each find it–"

"I think I can, too," Damien volunteered.

"–so, it would make sense to have each of us head up a party."

Ciriis clicked her tongue. "We need to split into at least five groups, not three."

"Adam could probably find it, too," Jason offered, blushing as Genevieve gave him a raised eyebrow.

"Hmmmn." Ciriis said thoughtfully. "Well, if we can only fit one person in with Genevieve, I suppose it'll have to be Tim, then. Presumably they can all follow directions, though – and whomever reaches the trailhead first can leave a small cairn to mark it."

"Where are we meeting our friend?" Damien asked Jason.

"By Queen Marian's Well," the other man replied. "It's quiet at this time of day. The old king discouraged people from using it, and habits are slow to change."

Ciriis nodded sharply. "Jason, take them and get it done. Damien–"

"I'm seeing them off. Jason will need help to build a safe space under the fabric." His tone brooked no argument, and the gaze he gave his spymistress was a level one.

She threw up her hands and walked away. She didn't need to say just what a foolish risk this was, and Genevieve agreed with her. But the Rebel Duchess saw it as a small victory for Damien and she didn't try to dissuade him. There was a longer game here as well, after all.

It was a short walk to the little-used well. The party of five stuck to backstreets and alleys, even though they had hidden Genevieve's distinctive red-gold curls under a plain shawl and the men all had shabby caps which they had grabbed in passing as Rosa and Sir Otto returned from their shopping mission. A short walk, but a nervous one and a slow one, with the two injured knights.

The farmer was already there, watering his team of mules in the attached trough. Queen Marian – Damien and Genevieve's shared ancestress – had been an eminently practical woman and had insisted on putting in a well in one of the less affluent areas of town, rather than the more flashy but less useful fountain with which many of her predecessors had chosen to memorialize themselves. Her grandson – Damien's grandfather, the now-nameless king – had never quite dared to destroy the piece of public works, or his grandmother's statue that overlooked it, but he had managed to have it kept off-limits and 'under construction' for 'repairs' during most of his eighty-three-year reign.

Both the young king and the Rebel Duchess paused to look at the statue of the late queen. The statue showed a woman of determination, rather than beauty, memorializing her in her late middle years. In her right arm she held a small child – perhaps representing the Princess Alexandria, her 'Autumn child' conceived late in her life as a last-ditch effort to produce a worthy heir... Genevieve's own great-grandmother. The child's presence as part of the statue might alone have been the reason the old king – her grandson – had hated this well.

In her left hand was a sword, the point held low as if she were threatening anyone who might damage the well. It was of a different stone than the rest of the statue – a shimmery limestone rather than the golden marble that depicted queen and child. Eighty-some years of neglect had not been kind to the soft, water-soluble limestone: the sword looked saggy and half-melted.

"Rather intimidatin' to get water here," the old farmer had come up beside them. He gestured at Queen Marian. "But there's niver a line, and the water has always been good, no matter what the signs said. Niver understood why they put that sword in 'er hand. The Queen was known as a warrior, but without it, 'er hand would look like it's invitin' people to the well. And that there sculptor did a piss-poor job of carving it to stand the test o' time. It don't even look like it was part o' the original statue but added on later." He shook his head at the foibles of artists, then looked at Genevieve. "I hear you're comin' with me, milady. I'm right glad to be able to get ye outta this madhouse of a city – a woman in yer condition, her men should be takin' care o' her. 'Tis too easy to lose a babe this early on, and that's what we men are *for* after all."

From where they were trying to help Jason re-pack the hay wagon, Adam and Tim exchanged an alarmed look at that offhanded comment. The uninjured knight was head-and-shoulders deep in the wagon bed, only a hand emerging to wave off their attempts, and completely oblivious.

Something else had caught Genevieve's attention in the old man's words. She looked at Damien and realized he'd had the same idea – was, in fact, already acting upon it.

The young king was walking around the watering trough, heading for... Genevieve frowned at him and headed the other way, for the statue's swordhand. Why was Damien heading for the arm in which Queen Marian held the *child?*

Genevieve laid her hand over the hand of the stone queen, and the melted-looking limestone sword began to glow. She watched in fascination as the glow seemed to peel something away. As if the sword knew they needed to keep a low profile, the glow never got terribly bright, and in the bright Autumn sunshine might not even be noticed by a casual passerby, and certainly not by anyone merely glancing down one of the rundown streets that led to this small square.

Then the glow began fading, and a real, metal sword remained. It was of good steel – the wavy ribbon of pattern down the blade from the many layers folded into it during its forging attested to that. The hilt and guard were plain to the point of insignificance. It was also, Genevieve noted, to her frustration, still firmly held in the stone queen's hand, and no amount of tugging seemed likely to budge it from those frozen fingers.

She looked over to where Damien stood, also frozen in fascination with the weapon's transformation. He seemed to shake himself out of a fog, met her eyes, then turned to the statue.

"Great-great-grandmother," he said almost too quietly for Genevieve to hear, "Genevieve is from the line of this daughter of yours who never had the chance to hold the throne." His hand rested gently on the back of the child-statue. "I may be descended from the line of your unworthy grandson, but I will strive to protect my people and restore this Realm, together with her. Please let us have the Monarch's Blade." He looked into the unseeing eyes of the ancient queen as if waiting for an answer.

Genevieve rolled her eyes at his little speech to the hunk of stone and tried to take the sword again. It was frustrating. Her touch had caused the blade to reveal itself. Why wouldn't it come free? The irreverent thought that they could *break* it free of the statue's hold occurred to her, but she had no stone-carving tools... and she wasn't sure if it could be done without damaging the sword... or if violence done to Queen Marian's statue would somehow void the magick even if there was no apparent harm to the weapon. This was going to be a nine-day wonder once the citizens of the capitol saw what had happened. It was small comfort that no one else was likely to be able to extract it either.

She looked up as Damien crossed in front of the statue and laid his own hand on the sword hilt.

And the queen's stone fingers released it into his hand.

"Thank you, Your Majesty." Damien bowed to the statue – *did Genevieve catch a glimmer of humor in those unseeing marble eyes? how could she?* – then turned to Genevieve and smiled dreamily at her. She had been caught unexpectedly by glimpses of him – occasionally accompanied by gentle touches of his hand – throughout the morning, quick reminders of how very handsome he was... and how much she was in love with him despite all her efforts to retain a certain sensible distance. This time, though... something about Damien had changed...

Jason strode up and eyed the magickal sword in his young king's hand. "Well, that's handy," he commented. "Now we have three swords. Genny, what's this I hear about you being pregnant?" His eyes twinkled as he pretended it was all news to him.

Chapter FOURTEEN

The Sword from the Stone

DAMIEN WAS STILL HALF IN a dream when he made it out of the city. The sword – the Monarch's Blade – was stashed in a rolled-up carpet along with Harald's long broadsword. He and Jason were carrying the roll of carpet. Sir Otto held up the middle so it wouldn't sag – a task far more necessary with the weight of the swords hidden inside and Damien's odd grip on his end.

Exactly why this disguise would work, he was still vague on the details. Damien had been under the impression that large, expensive carpets were a luxury that the nobility kept within their townhomes, and even if they were to have a carpet delivered to a country estate, they surely would have it delivered by cart.

He didn't worry it. Ciriis had clucked and complained, but had figured out how to make it work. Her hasty plans had been thrown into disarray when he and Jason had returned carrying the Blade. And when they had discovered that he couldn't let go of it. It was like the soul-bonding all over again, although completely different in its way.

The city looked different. The young king saw sparkles where there surely shouldn't be sparkles. Every person they passed glowed with a depth of spirit that he had trouble prying his eyes from. As did the plants – flowerboxes and even weeds making their brave way up from cracks in the cobbled pavement. And then there were the *animals* – oxen and horses and stray dogs and feral dogs and even rats and honeybees and *mosquitoes...*

He stumbled a lot.

Ciriis had thrown up her hands again and decided Jason had to escort him... as Jason had been quietly campaigning to do anyways, in his capacity as King's Champion. He was the only one of the party who could wield Harald's giant broadsword, and with Damien in this odd state, the rest agreed that the young king needed a proper guard with him.

This, however, meant that, instead of three or four guides to the hidden grotto, they had just two, since Genevieve and Adam were both gone with the hayfarmer.

Rosa fluttered around the three of them like a fussy housewife, admonishing them to be careful with her carpet. Ciriis followed at a discreet distance with a market basket filled with food. The remaining nine Royal Guardsmen variously ranged about them, pretending to errands and disappearing down side-streets before reappearing some distance farther along the same path.

Going through the gate-tunnel of the city wall nearly undid Damien. The wall was laced with the sparkles that he was beginning to guess meant long-ago spells. Rosa unobtrusively caught his arm to scold him for carelessness, and shot Jason a worried look. Damien wished he could find the words to explain to them what was happening to him... but communicating was rather beyond him just now.

When they eventually made it past the outer-limits of the city beyond the walls and he could see the countryside of his Realm, it was like starting the process all over again. The young king had thought he was beginning to be used to this new level of seeing or understanding or knowing or... whatever it was. But when he could see past manmade structures and roads he was stunned and froze briefly in the very center of the road.

His Realm was so very, very *beautiful*. The magick seemed to explode from every roadside stand of goldenrod, pool up in every slight depression, trickle into streams that ran down mown hillsides of corn that had never seemed so vibrant when they were green with Summer. It almost blinded him.

At last, they made it down into the grotto.

Genevieve was waiting there, with Tim and Adam. The rest trickled in after Damien's group, and Damien had not the slightest idea of what logistical skills it had taken for seventeen people to traverse the empty, open country roads without being noticed as odd. He barely even registered the presence of his soul-bonded: the magick pooling up on the fern fronds – each of which was more exquisite than the last – so fascinated him. The grotto fair blinded him with the magick it had collected, and it no longer surprised him that Genevieve and Jason had managed to keep this place a secret. A soft voice seemed to whisper "Shhh, shhh," deep inside his head and he guessed that this special place called to it only those who... needed it, maybe?

"Are you *sure* he didn't get hit in the head?" Sir Otto was asking when Damien was able to rouse himself from his fugue... possibly because after staring long enough at the sparkles in the gathering darkness it finally did begin to seem 'normal.'

"Nope," Tim answered. He was leaning back against a rock that had been padded with blankets and cloaks... and a certain large and ridiculously expensive carpet. His cracked ribs were the worst injury they had, with Sir Leverett Childress' broken arm coming in second. Adam was still in difficulty, but it looked like a good night's sleep would have him mostly to rights.

"I saw the whole thing myself," Sir Tim went on. "Milady touched the sword and it went from rotten limestone to – that," he gestured at the blade: still naked steel in Damien's grasp. "But the sword wouldn't come free. Then Damien said something I couldn't hear to the statue of Queen Marian, went over, and plucked it right out of her hand. The statue's, I mean. No head knocking at all."

"So, it's a *magickal* sword?" Otto still seemed skeptical. "Good magick or bad? It seems to be doing something to his brain."

"It's the Monarch's Blade." Genevieve's voice came out of the darkness beyond their campfire. She had been standing there, outside the circle, watching everyone for some hours, mostly in silence. Watching *him*, Damien realized. "My grandmother told me that Queen Marian – her grandmother – had hidden it where only her worthy descendants could find it."

Damien cleared his throat and everyone's gaze riveted to him. "That's why it would reveal itself to Genevieve, but not release itself to her hand, of course."

That was followed by an uncomfortable silence that suggested not everyone else saw it the way he did.

"She wears the Heir's Ring," he explained. "She's not the Monarch." He finally realized that there was a problem with Genevieve officially being his Heir – if the soul-bond would not let her outlive him, it would do the Realm no good at all. It wasn't wise not to have a clearer chain of succession, not that he had any choices just now.

Genevieve turned away.

"Back in the land of the living, are you?" Adam queried. "You'd better eat something while the food lasts. It's going to be thin rations the next few days, but we'll need a good start."

Jason brought him some bread and cheese with a thick slice of soft Summer sausage. Damien fumbled to eat with his right hand. The Sword still wouldn't release his left. He remembered that the statue had also held it in her left hand.

"So, what's our situation?" he asked before he took a bite. He was famished, it turned out, and the plain, good food tasted better than any feast.

Jason sighed.

"We all made it out without being noticed," Ciriis reported. "It should take us a week or so to make it to Elaarwen."

Adam snorted, painfully. "That'd be if we had horses and supplies. We'll be lucky to make it in triple that. We've injured, we'll have to stop well before dark to make camp, and we'll have to keep stopping to hunt and gather food."

Sir Leverett looked up at that. "Can't we just stop and buy food at farmer's crofts? Or sleep in their haybarns and buy their horses, for that matter?"

"You'd know all about the haybarns," Sir Otto muttered, and got a dark look in return. "All right. Not since you began courting...

Terellie." He dropped his head. By consensus they had been avoiding mentioning the names of the others who should have been with them... and whom they had no surety of seeing safe again.

Jason spoke into the awkward silence. "We put any crofter who helps us at risk, Lev. Siovale is in control of the capitol, like it or not. He can bring his troops up from his own city to complete the occupation at his leisure. For now, we live off the land."

Genevieve snorted from the darkness. "Survival skills, Jason?"

An echo of – was it really only the previous morning?

"What do we have in the way of supplies?" Damien asked, more to be saying something than because it would do him much good to know. Genevieve was the strategist and any of the other men had more experience with making camps and hunting than he did. The idea of killing an animal still turned his stomach, but the sausage in his hand didn't bother him, oddly enough. "Will we be roasting cattail roots?" he asked, lightly. He and Genevieve had never actually gotten around to eating the ones they had prepared... here, night before last. Had anyone come across them?

Rosa answered this time. "We have food for at least two days. Cloaks, hats, blankets. Fire-making kits. A handful of knives, some better than others. A large carpet." She smiled a little wryly at that last, and Sir Otto rolled his shoulders ostentatiously.

"Thank goodness those goons didn't strip us of our ornaments," Ciriis commented flatly. "A few bracelets and necklaces and we've financed this expedition." The young king wondered which jewels she had had to sell. Ciriis was not taking any of this well, for all that they had relied on her expertise to get them this far.

"And three swords – Genevieve's, this one," Jason indicated the huge broadsword that had belonged to Harald of Siovale, "and... yours. And Genevieve's bow and quiver."

"Are we planning to move on towards Elaarwen in the morning, or let everyone heal up a bit first?" Damien asked.

There was another uncomfortable silence.

"It... hadn't been decided yet," Rosa explained, her tone diplomatic. "We thought perhaps we should wait for you, Your Majesty." In other words, he translated to himself, they had spent the last few hours arguing. He could probably guess who was on which side.

"We shouldn't stay so close to the city," Adam stated, as if it were incontrovertible. "We need to get you both – all," he waved to include Rosa, "back to the Rebel powerbase so that we can begin planning to re-take the capitol."

Damien caught the glance that Rosa sent Genevieve. She didn't look convinced, and he revised his guesses about who was arguing to do what. The rebels, he remembered, were governed by a Council. Would they even recognize him as king, or would they simply see him and his people as beggars, hats in hand, to be helped or turned out as they saw fit? He swallowed his last bite of bread, and discovered his mouth was dry in a way that had nothing to do with the food.

"You need some rest, Adam," Jason said quietly. "You, Tim, Lev. Everyone, but especially you three."

Adam drew breath to reply, and Damien abruptly stood up. If he let them, they would simply re-hash for him all of the arguments he had managed to miss in his absorption with the Sword. In detail. Possibly verbatim.

"We'll reassess the situation in the morning," the young king stated firmly. "Right now, it is utterly clear that everyone needs a real night of sleep." Adam looked surly about it, but subsided when Jason settled down and put an arm around him. "Adam," Damien asked the knight-commander of his Guard, "Do you have a roster for who will stand guard tonight? No one is going to find us here, but since we're all exhausted, we're going to sleep fairly heavily. I think we'll all feel better if we have a guard set. Not you, Tim, or Lev," he added.

"Not you or Genevieve either," Adam retorted. "We're all here to make sure the two of you make it back to Elaarwen."

"Very well," Damien agreed. "See to it, if you please." It was a small enough task, but it was Adam's to do. If he felt useful and needed, perhaps he would let himself relax enough to rest.

The young king took a step away from the fire, and Rosa jumped up to come after him.

"I purchased these, also, after you came back with...that..." the Rebel Countess told him. In her hands were a sword-belt and a plain scabbard that looked like it would fit the Monarch's Blade.

She helped him fasten the sword-belt on and he sheathed the Sword. It meant his left hand was held across his body, but at least he wasn't waving naked steel around. It was also a spouse's place to assist one with arming... but perhaps it didn't count if it was just an empty scabbard. It still felt like a betrayal of Genevieve to allow Rosa to buckle on the sword-belt and nevermind that he could neither do it one-handed, nor was Genevieve handy to be asked for her help.

"Thank you."

"You're welcome." Rosa's dark eyes seemed to want to say something else, so he let her shepherd him into the darkness outside the circle of fire-light. "It's Genevieve and Ciriis," she began in a low voice.

"Countess... Rosa..." Damien paused. "I know what happened to Genevieve. Did Siovale or his men... *'lay hands'* on you or Ciriis?"

She shook her head. "No, they didn't rape us. Or even particularly handle us."

He ran his free hand through his hair. "Then why–?"

She sighed softly. "Ciriis... has always had trouble coping with change. And with not being in control. She originally volunteered to spy in Emeralsee as a lady-in-waiting to the last two queens because it kept her from feeling entirely helpless in the vicissitudes of the old king's reign. Right now, she's also coming to terms with the realization that everything she knows will be useless to us until we make it to Elaarwen. And possibly not even then, until she can re-establish contact with her network of spies."

Damien nodded. "And you?"

Rosa smiled a little. "I'm fine. I'm not a woodswoman like Genevieve, but I'm not a complete babe in the woods either. I have a few ideas to speed up our trip, but I need to work out the details first. That's not it."

"Then what is?"

She looked troubled. "Sir Childress can walk, and I believe Sir Loveress will be in better shape tomorrow. I'm concerned about the risk of infection for a few of the others' gashes, but we've bandaged them. It's Sir Tim. Lord Solway says Tim's ribs are just cracked – but the way he moves... and breathes... I'm worried that they're actually broken. He shouldn't be walking anywhere tomorrow. He probably shouldn't be walking anywhere for the next *week*. When we got here, he'd been off the hay wagon and sitting down still for a good two hours and he was still white as a sheet. Joking around, of course, but that's–"

"–just Tim." Damien chorused with her. They both smiled slightly, then Damien awkwardly scrubbed his right hand through his hair again. Another thing to sort out in the morning. If – *when* – they were able to retrieve the ladies of his Royal Guard, Damien did not want to have to tell Aryllis he'd somehow let her betrothed die after getting him out from the city.

"And then there's Genevieve...." Rosa sighed. "She's not herself–"

He winced. "Gods' *Teeth*, milady," he interrupted. "She was just raped yesterday."

The Countess' eyes seemed much older, and he remembered what she herself had been through – and past – to win forth to the serene demeanor she had now. "It's not that. Or not all that, anyways. Trust me, her marriage was far worse than anything he could have done to her in an hour or two." She closed those too-old eyes. "Genevieve went to her marriage-bed a virgin, and Lord Harald definitely did not. The things she told me – that she accepted as 'normal' or even simply 'acceptable' at his word–" She shook her head and looked at him again. "She... needed a lot of time to re-think things when I met her."

For the first time, Damien really understood why Tim and the others had given him their heartfelt thanks: Rosa had helped Genevieve heal. Without her, his beautiful soul-bonded might never have been able to love him.

"She was shocked to see him alive again, and he definitely hurt her physically, but she's stronger than that. The secret to surviving," Rosa told the young king, "is not to let them get inside your head and make you think something is wrong with *you*. And that takes more time than Harald had." She didn't say that he couldn't have done it *eventually,* Damien noted.

"Then... what's wrong?" he asked, trying not to think of all the ways others had gotten into his own head. His grandfather, Lord Prydeen, Prince Oskar... in some ways even his own dear friends who treated him like a child still. Perhaps he deserved that... he hadn't actually done very much as a king... and now he didn't even have his throne...

"I'm not sure," Rosa admitted. "At first, I thought it was because we had to leave her father behind. Now... I'm not sure. You need to talk to her."

"I'd planned to." Had actually been on his way to do just that when the Rebel Countess pulled him aside. "Rosa... milady Countess... was she advocating for pressing on immediately to Elaarwen or for staying here to rest awhile?" Genevieve had been the one of the group whose position, perhaps ironically, he had not been able to guess.

Her grin was a flash of teeth in the darkness that had seemed to fall heavily, like a cloak, even as they spoke. "Neither. *Genevieve* wants to go back and re-take the castle."

The darkness wasn't so very dark to Damien, with the sparkles of magick illuminating every leaf and branch and eddying in the swirling rush of the small stream. It was the work of a few moments to find Genevieve, despite her having stalked away from the rest of the group and the campfire.

"Oh, it's you," she said without enthusiasm as he came up quietly beside her. She must have sensed his approach through the bond – unless his footsteps were much louder to her hunter-trained ears than he realized. Did even city-born Ciriis have a quieter step than he? His spymistress was quieter *indoors* than any human had a right to be...

"Yes," he said simply. And added, "Did your wagon-ride go well?" when it became clear she wasn't going to say anymore.

She snorted. "Stuck under a suffocating weight of fabric in a creaking, bumpy wagon between two aching, groaning men – both of whom seem to think *I* need to be treated like spun glass? It was delightful." There wasn't much reply he could make to that. After a moment she added, "At least once we were off the wagon, they were in too much pain to do anything but what I told them." She snorted again. "So, I got those two sitting down and being sensible and then the rest of you showed up, and they told *everyone* that I'm pregnant, and now they're *all* acting like I'm made of spun glass."

Part of Damien thought that was a brilliant plan – taking care of Genevieve and their unborn child was high on his list of priorities. But there *were* also other priorities.

"That sounds annoying," he offered quietly.

She sighed. "You have *no idea.*"

The sigh seemed to take some of her frustration away with it.

"Walk with me," the young king suggested.

"In the dark? We'll trip over something and drown in the stream."

He smiled, knowing she couldn't see it. "It's not that dark for me. Take my hand. I think I can share this with you."

Damien reached out with his left hand, noticing only belatedly that it was no longer attached to the sword-hilt, and caught Genevieve's blindly reaching hand.

"Now what – oh!" He knew the moment she shared his vision, and he could feel her wonder. Genevieve began turning around, trying to see it all, and inadvertently pulled her hand out of his. "Oh!" she said again, this time in disappointment.

He recaptured her hand, and tugged her down the streamside trail.

They walked in silence, hand-in-hand for several moments.

"It's beautiful... like stars or fireflies and yet nothing like," she murmured.

"Romantic," he murmured back.

She pulled her hand from his and started at the sudden return of total darkness, blinking her eyes rapidly as if in disbelief, even rubbing them. "I can almost still see it all," she said.

"Maybe a little longer and it will stay with you," Damien suggested.

She glared blindly towards where she knew he was. "Why did *you* get this? Why did *you* get the Sword? Am *I* not worthy enough for dear Queen Marian?"

She sounded both hurt and offended.

Damien sighed. "I told you – it's because I'm the monarch and you're the Heir and it's the *Monarch's* Blade."

He hesitated. There was more, but should he tell her? Would she even believe him? No, no secrets between them.

"Queen Marian's spirit is tied to that statue. She spoke – answered me when I spoke to her. I'm not sure why I did it, but I think that's part of why she gave the Sword to me also. She liked that I addressed her directly." He paused again. "I had the impression that if you'd done that, she might have given you the Sword anyways... she seemed happier with you being a descendant of Princess Alexandria than with me being a descendant of Prince Anthony.... and she liked that you're a woman. She said something about the Realm going to hell in a handbasket when men are in charge."

Genevieve snorted. "Well, I suppose you'll have to disprove that, but recent history does seem to agree with her."

"Queen Marian also said if she handed the Sword straight to you, it would make you the monarch, instead of me." He paused again.

Apparently, he paused a little too long.

"You didn't actually consider that!" Genevieve exclaimed, trying to peer at him and finally going up and reaching again for the hand which he readily gave her. "You did. Damien, you idiot, didn't you pay attention to a thing I told you when we had this damned – blessed – grotto to ourselves?" The swearword slipped out, but she corrected herself so fast that the young king knew she had sensed how special this place was, too, and not just to them.

"Um, yes?" he said uncertainly.

"I don't *want* to be Queen, Damien, except at your side. I've studied all my life to be able to rule Elaarwen because I was – I am – my father's only Heir." She stopped. "This is so confused. *Am* I still Duchess of Elaarwen?" She laughed a little hysterically, and Damien could see tears rolling down her cheeks. "If it comes down to it, *Father* was the one who was confirmed in his title by the king. I haven't been. So, *I'm* nothing but an usurper. Much as Harald is."

"Hardly that," he began, trying to sound soothing.

"It could all be moot by now anyways," she went on, not listening. "Tomas said Father would be safe as long as I cooperated... and I am definitely *not* cooperating. Am I a duchess? A wife? A daughter? Who knows? By all the Gods, Damien, his children are my *nieces* and *nephews.*"

She was shaking as she fought the urge to sob, and Damien stepped forwards and wrapped his arms around her. She tried to push him away, but not very hard, and he could tell down the bond that she appreciated his presence, so he kept holding her.

"*I* know who you are," Damien said softly into her hair, and she looked up at him, her eyes glistening with tears by the light of the magick that only they two could see. He kissed away the tears. "You are Genevieve Stellarine, the infamous Rebel Duchess of Elaarwen and the most brilliant strategist of our generation – except maybe for my sister Kandra, but since we can't compare you directly..."

She glared up at him, not quite sure how to respond since she'd never yet heard him refer to his sister so casually before. He grinned. "Except when you're pretending to be 'Erawan the Kind Robber' and sneaking into enemy cities without backup – then your strategic brilliance might be a little questio– hey!"

Genevieve had made up her mind and kicked his legs out from under him, falling with him, just as they had done in the practice session with Jason... was it really just a very long day and a half ago? This time, though, Damien had been anticipating something like this, and he didn't let her go out of surprise. He had even made sure that there was nothing particularly pokey or prickly where he'd be most likely to land. And since he was ready, he was able to keep from having all his breath knocked out.

They came to rest with Genevieve still in his arms.

"You are my soul-bonded mate," he murmured into her hair. "And my own true love. And my future Queen."

"And mother of your children?" Her tone was dry, with just a tinge of bitter irritation.

Damien shrugged. "Gods willing. We have a few other things to take care of first." He made to sit up, and she squirmed off of him so he could. "One thing, we take care of right now." He took both her hands in his. "Genevieve Stellarine, wilt thou guide and guard my fair province of Elaarwen as its Duchess, placing the needs of thy people before thy own and caring always for their prosperity and well-being?"

She went very still. Then bowed her head. "I so swear."

"And wilt thou take me as thy liege-lord, accepting the rule of my fair province of Elaarwen in my name? Wilt thou further swear to be a loyal and faithful subject of this Realm and to raise arms only in the defense of thy people of Elaarwen or of this Realm?"

She looked up sharply, then bent her head once more. "I so swear."

"Then accept my fair province from my hands unto thine and rise. From the Power granted me by the Gods as King of this fair Realm, I create thee Genevieve Stellarine, Duchess of Elaarwen."

She paused, then rose as he bid her. A sense of lightness seemed to envelope her as the full meaning of the ancient words – even with Damien's minor modifications – sank in. And more... he had never realized that the oath of fealty was a spell, and perhaps it had not been before he touched the Sword. But it was actual sparkles of magickal light that flowed from his hands to hers.

Damien beamed up at her, knowing that now Genevieve was connected to the Land as he was, could see it as he did, even without touching his hands. He wondered faintly if this was the result purely of the oath, or some side-effect of their soul-bonding.

"Your oath to the present king supersedes your father's to the last one," he commented quietly.

"Notwithstanding that he was an oathbreaker and traitor for raising arms against his king," Genevieve answered dryly. "You changed the words."

Damien shrugged up at her. "It seemed appropriate. You might be receiving your grant of land from the crown, but your fealty should be to the people. It's an older form," he admitted. "But completely legally valid. You are now Duchess of Elaarwen, no matter what else comes to pass."

"Even if Harald manages to get himself crowned?"

"Even then. We hold the Heir's Ring and the Monarch's Blade. We *could* offer to let him see if the Sword speaks for him." Damien chuckled. "He might be stupid enough to agree." He saw her quizzical look. "It's been so long since anyone tried that, it's only in the oldest stories. The Sword will make clear who should be the next Heir... exactly *how,* I never could determine. If, however, an usurper tries to *take* the Blade from the crowned and anointed monarch, it will sever his head immediately. Even if the usurper managed to have himself crowned and anointed."

"Oh." He couldn't miss her wicked grin. "We should definitely give that a try."

"We still have a few things to take care of first," he reminded her, and Genevieve deflated.

"Things like this," he added. He boosted himself up into a proper half-kneeling position, reclaimed her hands, and looked up into her eyes. They were still shining with the magick that had flowed into her with the oathswearing. She looked like a goddess of the night, the Huntress bedecked in stars. "Genevieve Stellarine, you are the most beautiful woman who has ever walked the earth. Your wisdom and strength astound me at every turn, and I cannot imagine my life without you. You have been the dream of my heart and the bond of my soul since I was eight years old. Will you marry me and rule this Realm beside me as the Queen of my heart and of my hand?"

She sucked in her breath.

"I never did ask you before," Damien explained, a little worriedly, as the silence stretched out. "I supposed that you should have a proper proposal, and... the chance to say 'no'..." he finished in a very small voice, dropping his eyes to her booted feet. His fingers went lax and slipped from holding her hands. The moment had seemed right, and magickal and... he really was an idiot. The last two days, not to mention the last several minutes, had been too physically and emotionally taxing to throw something like this at her.

And what did he have to offer her anyways? Genevieve was a warrior-queen, a beautiful goddess-incarnate. He was a king without a crown, a weak, bookish, dreamer. He was basically a liability to the brave knights in the clearing behind them who would risk – and even sacrifice – their lives to see him to safety. They had already given up so much for his unworthy self...

Slowly, she knelt down before him. Lifted up his chin. Looked into his eyes with her starry ones.

"Yes." She whispered it softly. Then kissed him as purely and delicately as if she had never done this before with anyone.

Damien didn't dare move, except to let his mouth respond to her kiss.

At last, she sat back on her heels and regarded him with a wondering look.

Damien's fingers rose of their own volition to touch his lips, where hers had so lately been. Then he reached out and touched her lips, and she smiled and kissed his fingertips.

"I didn't expect that," she said softly. "I didn't expect you to propose formally. And I didn't expect to feel so – so–" Words failed her. "After all we've done together..." He knew she was blushing, "I thought it was just a formality. One we didn't really need." Her eyes were shining still. "But I'm so glad you did."

"*I'm* so glad you said 'yes'." He *meant* for his tone to be light, easy. It was anything but.

"Well," Genevieve said, also trying for a lighter note, also failing. "If it took me twenty-eight years and one failed marriage to finally get a wedding proposal, I should accept it, shouldn't I? Especially when it's from the man I love with all my heart. And soul."

He felt warmed by her words, but–

"Harald never proposed?"

"No. Well, Tomas did. To my father. I suppose." She sighed. "Father tried to talk me out of it, but I knew we needed the alliance. I didn't meet Harald until the day before the wedding, though they did send a portrait a few weeks earlier. And we reciprocated with one of me. His was... rather artistically rendered, let's say." Portrait artists didn't necessarily earn their keep by being entirely truthful. She paused. "Father tried to talk me out of it the night before the wedding, even."

Damien winced. "He was that obviously awful?"

Genevieve shook her head and stared down at the ground between them. "Not to me... not then. And after the wedding... do you remember how you felt the first time you slept with someone?"

He did. Vividly. He also knew better than to remind Genevieve that Ciriis was a few hundred feet away. In any case, he understood what she meant. The warm glow, the impossibility of believing anything ill of the other person, the slight unreality of the whole world.

"He was... sweet... at first. In his way. He only became horrible after he was sure I wasn't going to divorce him. He was... careful never to leave marks on me where Father might see them. Physical marks anyways. The ones he left on my soul... I'm not sure if those were visible or not."

Damien stayed quiet, leaving the bond open between them, though it cost him to do it. Not sending anything, but listening. It wasn't as if he could *do* anything to help the long-ago Genevieve anyways. And he could hardly do worse to Harald than he planned to already, condemned as a traitor to the Realm. And right now... she just needed Damien to listen.

Genevieve looked up with something close to shame on her face, and her voice was very flat. "When he decided he wanted us to move into one of the towers, on the opposite side of the castle from my father's rooms, I thought he simply wanted us to have some privacy. The wind whistled down from the mountains on that side, and there was a splendid view of our waterfall. Our very noisy waterfall. He said... he wanted me to squeal when he made love to me, but he didn't want anyone else to hear me. He... made it sound romantic. Somehow. At the time."

Damien knew where this must be going. He'd grown up knowing where to avoid the sounds coming from the dungeons, after all. And from his grandfather's and Lord Prydeen's suites as well. He wanted to take her in his arms and kiss away the memories, but he had the feeling this was something she needed to say out loud... or something, perhaps, that she needed him to *hear*.

Genevieve swallowed hard. "I was such a fool. A starry-eyed fool too full of my own pride to admit when things had gone too far. He wanted us in that tower so that no one could hear me *scream*. After the first night... after the *first* night... I was too proud to admit what was happening. I thought the novelty would wear off after a while. We'd moved to the tower rooms because he'd gotten bored with me, after all."

"How long–" Damien had to clear his throat before he could get the words out.

"How long after you were married did he make you move?"

She frowned up into the trees. "Two years? Two and a half? Something like that."

And they had been married for nearly *eight* before Harald – and her father – disappeared.

She looked at Damien with pleading eyes. "I didn't dare have him thrown out by then, or let Father know. Siovale's forces, their political support, had become too important a linchpin for the Rebellion, just as I had known they would be. And at even the slightest hint that I might, Harald would – hurt me – and then threaten to tell his brother I had humiliated him and have Siovale withdraw from the alliance."

"I wish I could go bash his head again," Damien muttered. "Or better yet, go back and do it *then.*" He wanted to tell her it wasn't her fault... but he sensed that she had already come to terms with that, for all that it half-sounded as if she was asking his forgiveness for not being strong enough to protect herself.

Thank you, Rosa.

But perhaps even Rosa hadn't heard all of this.

"Again?" She tried for a half-smile, but it didn't really work. "I thought it was our brave Champion with his trusty candelabrum."

The young king shrugged apologetically. "I'll choose holding you over bashing Harald any day, though it's good that got done, too." He reached for her hands again. "I wish you hadn't felt trapped. For so long. At all."

She looked away again. "He did get bored. That's when he started buying whole new sets of clothes as an excuse to seduce the clothier's apprentices and demonstrate his manhood."

Damien snorted. "Any drunk in the street can sire a child. Manhood is about raising that child to be a good person and taking care of its mother." He said it matter of factly, not noticing how Genevieve's eyes glowed at the simple words.

Time to pivot the conversation – he could tell down the bond that she had said enough for now. "Do you have any idea when he made contact with Lord Prydeen? I had the impression from that bit of gloating in the courtyard that the 'hunting incident' was pre-planned on Harald's part."

She looked startled. "That... would make sense. I haven't been thinking about this very well, I'm afraid. It would explain why he picked that particular fight with me on that particular day. Father's way was always to try to mend things by taking someone out for a long ride." She smiled sadly. "Except I don't think he meant to try to mend things with Harald that day. I think he was going to tell him to get out of Elaarwen."

Damien raised an eyebrow. "Brave man, your father. *I* wouldn't go alone into the woods with a man Harald's size and disposition in order to tell him I was throwing him out." He smiled sweetly at her. "We'll have to ask him if that was his plan after all. Tomorrow?"

Her eyes went wide. "Rosa told you I want to go back."

He nodded.

"Not just for my father," she said quickly. "I think we can liberate the castle if we act quickly, now that we have the Sword."

The young king lifted her hand to his lips. "And the Ring. They work best together. I think you're absolutely right. And I think our dear, wounded friends and protectors are going to knock us both over the head if we try any such thing."

She deflated slightly, then caught his small smile and gave him a sharp look. "You're planning something as reckless as I would, aren't you?"

Damien blinked innocently. "Me? I am betrothed to the most brilliant strategist of our generation – probably – and she's sitting right in front of me. Would I dare to fabricate a plan when she most certainly has a better one? I've always wanted to play 'Erawan the Kind Robber,' with someone else," he teased. "My pretend games always had to be on my own."

She gave him a sideways look instead of the look of abashedly amused outrage he had been hoping for, and the young king realized he had given her another unintentional window into his childhood. Best to keep it to that bare glance. He remembered the look of pity she had given him when he told her about taming the mice in the library.

"I don't know what the Sword can actually do," she temporized.

"Our grandmother gave me a few pointers."

"'Grandmother'?" Genevieve's brows shot up, and Damien shrugged a bit self-consciously.

He didn't mention that the dead queen's spirit was already a better grandmother to him than the dispirited and discarded queen who had borne his father, or the minor noblewoman who had borne his mother – and disavowed his desperate plea to flee to her. He didn't want to judge those women, and he knew the reality of the fear they had felt... but his parents had been braver somehow, and he had expected, hoped, *needed* more from the women who must somehow have taught them that bravery. Another subject to evoke pity and thereby to be avoided.

"That's what Queen Marian said I – we – should call her. She claimed 'great-great-grandmother' made her feel old, and I forbore to mention she's a spirit bound to a statue next to a public well and has been dead for eighty-three years. It seemed impolite, and *Grandmother* doesn't seem like the type to appreciate 'backtalk'." The young king gave his bride another impish grin. "She said the Sword will shield both of us from magick, and 'whatever else it needs to do.' I got the impression that opening locks and finding hidden things were some of the simplest things."

"You do know that not one of *them* thought this was a good idea." Genevieve jerked her chin back in the direction of the camp. There was life and light in her eyes again, and strength in the way she tilted her head. It would almost be worth doing this just to have pulled her out of that black depression.

But there was a real, true mission at stake.

"I figured as much," Damien admitted. "But we can't take them with us, so it doesn't really matter what they think about it."

Genevieve pursed her lips and gave a low whistle. "You're getting ruthless in your old age, Your Majesty." She paused. "I assume we're going back in the same way we came out. So, we *could* actually take a few of them with us."

He shook his head. "Jason and Ciriis are the only ones who would be useful, and not only would those two be the hardest to convince, they're going to be needed here, to look after the rest."

She nodded slowly. "Once we're gone, they don't need to hurry on to Elaarwen. They can even find that old farmer with the hay-wagon and purchase food for a day or two more. He might even have a Healer on his farmstead... he looked as worried over Tim as I was when we disembarked."

"Good. Should we find a way to leave them a note and suggest that?" Damien asked.

Genevieve shook her head. "No. They know how to do their own jobs. And," she added wryly, "they know *us*. Once they realize that we've disappeared–"

"And argued themselves out about what to do about it."

She nodded to yield the point. "They'll realize we have too much of a head start to try to stop us, and make the right decisions to take care of the rest of the group."

Damien gave her a skeptical look. "You realize that they have a completely valid chain-of-command sitting there. They might actually just mobilize to hunt us down, instead of arguing about it first, and drag us back to their version of common sense. Technically, Adam can order that all on his lonesome."

"Then we have to make sure we have a good enough – and obvious enough – lead. Though they'll still have to figure out what to do with Tim. And Rosa's sense of personal responsibility should require her to get back to the Rebellion as quickly as she can." Genevieve sighed. "This is going to be impossible on as little rest as we've had the last couple days. I think we'll have to convince everyone to stay put tomorrow and then sneak off after it gets dark."

Damien tilted his head slightly with a slight smile. "'Convince' them?"

She frowned. "You were really bonding to that Sword and missed the entire argument, didn't you? Should I be jealous?"

"Never," he breathed, momentarily losing track of the conversation. She smiled, and he almost stopped breathing entirely.

Genevieve's eyebrows flew up. "Damien!"

He took a breath, and suddenly realized that he had actually stopped breathing for a moment.

Genevieve shook her head with a bemused smile. "Tim was very sure you didn't get hit in the head... does this mean that you do this sort of thing *all* the time?"

Damien felt himself blushing and hoped that the strange, magickal light didn't reveal it.

She shook her head in bemusement again. "You were saying something about convincing everyone to stay and rest here tomorrow?"

His flush receded as he focused again on the problem at hand. "We don't need to convince them, Genevieve. You told me yourself – how many times now? – that I can, that I *need*, to make command decisions. No one raised a single objection when I told them we'd make a plan in the morning instead of deciding tonight–"

"True, but none of them were actually arguing to move on *tonight.*" She gave him a slightly pitying look. "They didn't have anything to really lose, and they each feel they can get their way in the morning. They're too used to – erm," she hesitated, but he could practically hear the remaining words down the bond. *They're too used to walking all over you. To your needing them to fix things for you. To barely noticing when you speak.*

"Your Grace. You wouldn't tolerate a debate on the battlefield once you had made your decision. Neither will I."

"This isn't a battlefield, Damien." Politely, she didn't weigh in on whether he would 'blink' when it came down to it.

"Isn't it?" he challenged. "We're not sleeping out in the woods by choice *this* time. Would *you* argue with me if I stated that the party was going to stay another day to rest as the command of your king?"

"Well, not in public..." she admitted.

Damien nodded. "Neither will they."

Chapter FIFTEEN

Once More Unto the Breach...

DAMIEN HAD BEEN RIGHT, GENEVIEVE had to admit.

It had made for a very long day indeed, since every ambulatory member of the party – which meant everyone other than Sir Tim at this point – had to find a private moment of the young king's time and argue his or her viewpoint. He had handled it with a level of patience that she had to burrow very deep to find within herself, and he definitely let them explain themselves – each – for far longer than she had ever put up with.

She stayed in the background, practicing her marksmanship or sharpening her sword, close enough to overhear in case he needed a rescue. He never did, and her opinion of Damien's skills in dealing with his people rose by several notches. Perhaps what she had been interpreting as them not taking him seriously had been a difference in command-style... though she still felt her critiques were valid in how he would be perceived by those beyond this inner circle... and she *did* notice Ciriis and Adam looking slightly discommoded as Damien simply took charge without a fuss or a challenge.

Genevieve had been amazed that most of their arguments had been about the next step, however, besides some general complaints about the situation. Of course, Damien had cut the feet off of their argument that leaving immediately was a matter of safety by announcing – to her surprise as well – that the Sword had granted him the ability to protect the grotto from any potential spies, even more thoroughly. As he explained to her in a private moment, Queen Marian had appeared in his dreams to give him instructions – and as disgruntled as he'd looked, she'd had to believe him. Given that they had slept snuggled together, she had some idea of what sort of dreams the old woman had invaded... and perhaps commented on.

The protections had involved Damien pointing the Sword at the sky, and then sketching out a brief X to the four cardinal directions. He'd also explained privately that it was this simple only because the grotto was itself a protected space and needed only some direction about *who* needed to be protected from *what*.

"This is odd," the young king said. He was just ahead of her in the not-dark-to-them secret passageways within the castle. Not-dark was now a euphemism. With the acquisition of the Monarch's Blade, the passageways fairly *shone*.

"Hmmn?" Genevieve asked, pulling her mind back from how easily they had snuck away and whether the others were still safe. But she had asked Damien about those magickal protections a half dozen times since they'd left. He had humored her request every time by pausing to send his mind to search – somehow. She could feel him doing it down the bond, but hadn't been able to do it herself.

Every time he had said the protections on the grotto were solid. She appreciated that he took her as seriously the sixth time as the first, but had sworn to set the question aside so as not to distract him while they were in the castle.

Damien seemed connected to every part of the land now. This had some downsides, chief among them being extreme distractibility. She hoped he would learn to cope with it as time went on, but they didn't have time for him to do that now, and it worried her.

For herself, she had felt a vague pull towards the south and west – towards Elaarwen – since he had formally granted her title. A powerful pull, but one that felt almost smug and satisfied, as if the province had merely been waiting for this last bit of claiming her as its own... and vague, as if it knew she would come back but it was at peace with where she was and what she was doing right now. A fine bit of a fancy, she tried to laugh it off to herself.

"The passage," Damien pointed. "I've been down here a dozen times in the last few years, and I've only ever seen one route. But now this seems to bifurcate." She could see what he meant. Walking this route without the others meant that they didn't even notice when the passages were open or solid rock; Genevieve wasn't actually certain whether the path they now saw was leading off of one of the open galleries where Damien had stashed their party on the route out.

"We don't really need to go back up to your rooms," Damien was going on. "That doesn't really help us, it's simply where we knew we would come out. I think we should see where this goes."

Genevieve considered the options. They had roughly sketched out a strategy, but as he had mentioned, it was based on having to come out in that one specific location and hoping that the empty room was neither occupied nor guarded. There had really been nothing to recommend it as a location to begin re-taking the castle.

On the other hand, they had no idea where this new passage might take them.

In for a lamb, in for an ewe... "Let's do it," Genevieve agreed.

Damien nodded and started down the new – or at least new to them – passageway. The Rebel Duchess followed, alert now for other possible directions. Could Lord Prydeen access these byways?

They had to find out what had happened to the ladies of the secret Royal Guard and Damien's army regulars. Two alone could not re-take a castle against the four dozen men Duke Tomas had brought and whatever bullyboys Lord Prydeen employed. They had tried to pick Ciriis' brain about the latter throughout the day – since Genevieve had made no secret of her desire to go back right away, before Siovale could bring up more troops, she had had the perfect excuse. Ciriis' descriptions had included just enough details – more than twenty, the scum of the streets with neither conscience nor consideration, but well-trained nonetheless – to let her look genuinely disheartened. Damien had stood quietly listening as well, then sympathetically rubbed her shoulders, kissed her hair, and wandered off as if he assumed she had given the idea up.

No, two could not retake a castle alone against so many.

But there were a hundred soldiers who were housed within the castle itself, to provide four watches-worth of sentries stationed throughout. Another hundred were bivouacked outside the castle-proper and presumably had no more access to the interior just now than General Direlien and the army division at their headquarters complex just outside the city.

Neither Damien nor his advisors had suggested they flee to the Royal Army's commanding general... her weeks sitting in on the Royal Council had given Genevieve to understand that most of the generals were cautiously supporting Damien but were not yet solidly in his camp. That Lord Prydeen and Harald and Duke Tomas had dared this coup suggested that they had some reason to believe that General Direlien would not show up on their new doorstep with his thousand soldiers in residence as soon as he had the word...

A weak king was no one's favorite to rule.

Many of the servants also came up daily from the city, but at least as many lived in the castle itself. And if they could find the ladies...

Damien had confessed to her that they had no idea if any of them had survived, or in what state they might be... and that they suspected Lena was dead. Tim had seen her go down, and had not been allowed to check her prostrate form.

Genevieve forced her jaw to relax. They were doing everything they could.

And her fiancé was muttering to himself as he led the way down the new passageway.

No, not muttering to *himself*. He was talking to someone else. Arguing about strategy.

"Unless you can give me a reason to go to the throne-room first, we're not doing it, Grandmother." "Our best estimate is about seventy." "No, I will *not* summarily execute Duke Tomas. He seems to be controlled by the sorcerer in some way, so does that even make him a traitor at all?" "Yes, I know, he's been part of the Rebellion. So has Genevieve. Arguably *they* were the ones on the side of the angels." "*No*, Grandmother, *I* don't know any angels personally." "Oh, yes, *he* will see no tender mercies."

The last was said in a tone of grim anticipation that Genevieve would never have attributed to the young king if she hadn't heard it herself. She shivered. She had no doubt he – they? – were discussing Harald.

Damien turned back to her and ran a frustrated hand through his hair. "Queen Marian wants us to go to the throne-room first for some reason. She's being very mysterious about it – just says we'll understand when we get there."

"Don't we have to just go wherever this passageway takes us?" Genevieve asked, trying for a reasonable tone while discussing advice from a ghost while traversing a passageway of solid stone.

"Apparently not. Her Maje– well, *excuse* me then, I was *trying* to be polite." He glared at what looked like empty air to Genevieve... though it might as easily be rock, she thought nervously. "*Milady* Grandmother says that now that we have *her Sword*, the passages will take us wherever we want to go in the castle."

The red-headed duchess considered that. "Impressive," she said at last. "Though it's *your* Sword now. Tell Queen Marian that if she wanted any say in it, she should have made sure Princess Alexandria ended up on the throne."

Damien winced. "She says she can hear you just fine, and – oh, *I'm* supposed to call my affianced bride and the leader of the Rebellion an 'impertinent young lady'? I think *not*, madam!"

Genevieve had to bite her lip on a giggle. It was just too impossible to watch him arguing with thin air.

"Oh... Oh... Well, that expl– ... Oh." Damien turned back to her. "Apparently the Sword didn't speak for Princess Alexandria either."

"Oh." Genevieve had always imagined that the princess had been cheated out of her inheritance by her much-older nephew, and that she would have been a splendid ruler. But if the Sword would not speak for her, would not declare her a worthy heir when the only other option was... the now-nameless king... how awful must she have been?

"It's not like that," Damien rushed to reassure her. "There was nothing wrong with Princess Alexandria – and she doubtless would have made a better ruler than my grandfather did. But whatever the Sword is looking for, she didn't have it and neither did he. Queen Ma– *Grandmother* says she was planning to give Alexandria the Heir's Ring at the upcoming Midwinter holiday, but she died first."

"Oh." Genevieve looked down. "Bad timing."

"No," he contradicted. "She says she was assassinated. Yes, Grandmother, murdered sounds more dramatic, but you know very well that the proper legal term–" He sighed and scrubbed through his hair yet again. "My grandfather had been the last one to wear the Ring, although she'd taken it back, so he used the excuse that the princess was barely seventeen and he was a man of thirty." A pause. "She says you remind her of her daughter. The princess was also an excellent strategist, hunter, and was due to earn her shield."

"She never did," Genevieve murmured. "She came to Elaarwen and found my great-grandfather before her mother's ashes were cold." That was the story that had come down, and it had always felt somewhat shocking to her. The old king had not shown any signs of becoming a tyrant for some years... though if he had been involved in his grandmother-the-queen's death, disposing of one inconvenient underage aunt could hardly have troubled him.

"Grandmother says she told Princess Alexandria to do just that," Damien confirmed her guesses. "She says that only Elaarwen was both powerful enough and remote enough to protect her daughter. She doesn't know what happened after that, as Alexandria never came back to the capitol." He gave Genevieve an odd look. "The Royal Archives don't say who Princess Alexandria married, but they show her daughter, Grand Duchess Alicia marrying the heir to the Duke of Elaarwen."

Genevieve smiled wryly. "The family story goes that Princess Alexandria didn't trust the Duke to protect her from his liege-lord. She hid out in the forests and mountains, fighting the beginnings of the old king's tyranny in her own ways – raiding royal tax collectors and quietly redistributing their collections to the poor. She tried to keep her daughter from getting involved, but Nana – Grandmother Alicia – was as headstrong as *her* mother and took matters into her own hands. This would be about the same time that Duke Emmeren had to respond to threats from the old king about the tax payments not making it out of Elaarwen, and he sent his son and Heir to protect the next installment."

"Oh, no!" Damien laughed. "I can see where this is going."

She nodded. "Great-grandmother had decided to let that one pass, having heard that the ducal Heir was involved. Nana only knew her mother wasn't trying for it and took her own group of headstrong young people and captured the whole thing. Including Duke Emmeren's Heir. Upon finding out who he was, she decided to hold him for leverage, which her mother did *not* approve of–"

"Milady Grandmother wants you to know that *she* wouldn't have approved either," Damien put in. "But she's sort of impressed that Alexandria had finally figured that out."

Genevieve chuckled. "Nana told me she kidnapped him again – this time from her mother's stronghold, and hid him away in a cabin she had built deep in the mountains. Where they got trapped by the early snows of Autumn, and ended up spending all Winter together. My father said *his* father told him that he didn't try that hard to escape before they were snowed in, thinking that he was doing his job by keeping the notorious robber queen away from the tax collectors... and also starting to fall for her. No one ever claimed that Nana wasn't beautiful, and of course there was the whole tragic story of being a princess of the Realm driven to robbery... And all Winter long, Great-grandmother Alexandria was trying to find the missing pair and ended up making common cause with Duke Emmeren. By the time the snows melted enough, the pair were half-starved, but completely smitten with each other. Their exasperated parents had to accept it, since Grandmother was already pregnant with my father. Duke Emmeren had to do some fancy footwork to get the marriage recorded in the Royal Archives... Great-grandmother Alexandria insisted she'd been properly wed, but refused to give the name of Nana's father. Of course, since there was no question that Nana was her daughter, it didn't matter."

"Queen – *Grandmother* says thank you," Damien told her, then narrowed his eyes. "Wait. Robbed the tax collectors in Elaarwen to give money to the poor... *Princess Alexandria* was 'Erawan the Kind Robber'?"

Genevieve nodded.

"Hunh," he muttered. "That explains a lot." He glanced to his side again. "Milady Grandmother says that she gave the Monarch's Blade to Alexandria."

The Rebel Duchess' eyebrows flew up. "I never heard anything about that. Nana mentioned her mother had once held the Sword... I guess that could have meant more than just had it in her hand once."

"Then how did it end up in the statue's hand?" Damien wondered.

Genevieve frowned. "Father told me that his grandmother – Princess Alexandria – went away on a journey that she said was incredibly important, and never came back. His mother – Grand

Duchess Alicia – had been making noises about overthrowing the old king; that her right to the throne was better than his. But after her mother disappeared, Father said she never spoke of it again. Could it be that she knew about the Sword?" she asked with some excitement. "Could the Sword have spoken for *her?*"

Damien looked down. "If so, wouldn't Princess Alexandria have supported her in rebelling against the crown?"

Genevieve began to pace in the confines of the passageway. "Not necessarily. Grandfather – Duke Siegfrid – had built his whole life around protecting his wife and mother-in-law, since they seemed the most likely challengers to the crown. Elaarwen was planning a defensive strategy, not an offensive one. Perhaps Princess Alexandria merely knew that they weren't ready."

He sighed. "It sounds like that might not have been an answer the Grand Duchess was willing to hear. Didn't you tell me she was a redoubtable jouster? There's a lot of stories about jousters becoming more reckless after a few knocks on the head."

"Old people's tales," Genevieve retorted, but she didn't exactly disagree.

"There's another thing, Genevieve," Damien's clear grey eyes met hers. "Milady Grandmother tells me that the Sword will not speak for someone who will rule heedlessly or heartlessly. And although my grandfather could never have wielded it, if it hadn't spoken for her as the true and worthy Heir, the Sword might well have seen her as an usurper against the duly anointed and crowned king."

"So, Princess Alexandria might have brought it here to the city to take away the temptation?" Genevieve sighed.

Her memories of her grandmother were wonderful ones, but she had to admit self-restraint hadn't been the old lady's strongest suit. "None of this is getting us out of these passageways any faster. Queen Marian really won't tell you why we should go to the throne-room before finding your soldiers or the ladies?" *Or my father...*

The young king shook his head. "No, but she says it will be important." He paused. "She seems kind of frustrated that she can't tell us more." He looked into her eyes again with that serious, trusting look that made her breath catch if she wasn't paying attention. "You're the strategist, love. What should we do?"

In for a lamb, in for an ewe... if they had decided to re-take the castle on the strength of the Sword and the Ring, shouldn't they listen to the ghost of the ancient Queen as well?

"The throne-room," she decided. "But there better be something worthwhile enough to delay the rest of the mission if you expect us to keep listening to you," she told the air at Damien's side.

He gave her a wry smile, and led the way.

This was the throne-room that Genevieve remembered from her childhood Summer at Court.

Not the warm, well-lit, low-ceilinged room that Damien had used – this was an immense cavern of grey stone. The same sort of clerestory windows that provided so little light to Damien's tower allowed beams of sunlight to illuminate pillars of dust-motes over single patches of floor. Ancient war-banners draped from high on the walls, and the only carpet softening the floor was a long red strip that would unroll to the main entrance but was currently neatly coiled at the foot of the dais to prevent any lesser foot than a monarch's from touching it.

It was stark and empty – not even benches to seat the nobles that might gather here at their king's beck and call. They would not have dared to sit in the old king's presence even if seating had been available. Odd stains on the grouting between the smooth flagstones attested to the fate of those who might have considered even such small forms of rebellion while in this hall.

"I hate this place," Damien muttered, shivering. "I just... hate it."

Genevieve put an arm around him, and he leaned gratefully into her warmth. Had he actually seen his parents killed here? She wondered, but did not dare ask.

"All right, all right," Damien mumbled and pulled away to focus on the intimidating shape of the massive throne at the end of the hall. It looked like it had been carved out of a single, unimaginably large rock – though surely that was impossible, for such a thing could never have been transported here from the nearest quarries, three days away. And those quarries produced marble and limestone, not basalt.

The young king squared his shoulders and marched straight towards the dais. Genevieve glanced around, but the room was still deserted, as it had been when they had cautiously crept out of the... wall. The iron-bound doors were clearly thick enough to muffle any sound of mere footsteps. She could wish for some more light, but supposed it was just as well that the torches were burned to nubbins, with not even ash marking the floor below.

Damien skirted the rolled-up carpeting and climbed the dais – five simple stairs up the center, with three levels of wide wings for advisors and sycophants to display their power by proximity.

He stood, at last, facing the throne. An odd sight, since he bore the Monarch's Blade unsheathed in his left hand. It looked like he was ready to fight the throne.

"I've sat in it before, you know," he muttered to the ghost at his side. Genevieve could almost imagine the ancient queen's response. Something would be different this time. Different because he had bonded to the Sword... and to the Realm beyond it. She shivered, thinking about that connection. It had bothered her to be bound similarly to Damien himself, and she was not ready to consider her own new connection to Elaarwen – in some sense that connection had always been there, and she was used to it, though she sometimes felt strangled by her responsibilities. How could Damien, who had never dared to believe he would survive to adulthood, let alone be king, bear these bindings without bending beneath them?

This is why I did not give the Sword into **your** *hand, granddaughter.* A whisper in her head – no, not even so much as that, but she knew her ancestress was speaking to her as much as she could. Yes, she was unworthy. Even as the Princess Alexandria, and the Grand Duchess Alicia had been unworthy. She felt and did not feel an impatient clout on her ear. *Not unworthy, not unable, but* **unwilling.** *The Sword would have spoken for you, as it tells me it has spoken for one other since my passing. But* **you** *would not have accepted the* **Sword.** *You're too rooted in the things of this world, my girl.*

Genevieve blinked. Was it her imagination that she could hear the queen herself now?

Tell the boy to sit on the damned Throne, the irascible old woman's voice went on inside Genevieve's head. *You've other things to do today. It's not going to bite him.*

What **will** *it do?* Genevieve found herself asking.

I can't be sure. The old queen's not-quite-voice admitted. *If it does for him as it did for me, plenty but not enough. He's a dreamer, and that may be enough to unlock what else it can offer him. He can already do more with that Sword than I ever could. But it's that imagination of his that's stopping him. That and his memories. He seems to think he'll turn into Reggie if he sits on it. Kindly remind him that was* **my** *seat for over fifty years before young Reggie caused this land such havoc.*

Why not tell him yourself? Genevieve queried distractedly as she watched Damien dither and shift from foot to foot, staring at the throne with what she could only call a mixture of fear and loathing and... *longing?*

He's shut me out! The voice was suddenly indignant. Could she actually *see* a swirl of color in the air beside Damien? Golden hair and piercing grey eyes over a swirl of royal crimson?

"Damien?" At the sound of Genevieve's voice, he turned to look at her, his eyes begging her not to make him do this.

Does he need to do this alone? Genevieve demanded of the presence she still couldn't quite believe in. *Can I help?*

A thoughtful pause. *You're soul-bonded, so you're practically the same person for all magickal intents and purposes. I don't see why not.*

Good enough. Genevieve trotted over to the dais and climbed up beside her... affianced husband. She had barely let herself think those words before. The word 'husband' still triggered too many mixed emotions. It was easier to think of Damien as lover, soul-bonded... even liege-lord, though his often-diffident demeanor made that last a trial as well. But... husband he would be. By his request and her promise.

She wrapped her left arm around him – her right was holding her own unsheathed blade – and she had a moment to be grateful that their dominant hands were opposite. His own sword-free arm went around her own waist as if without conscious thought.

"There's no one else here, my love," she whispered into his ear, making sure he could feel her warm breath. "And while everything else in this room is unforgiving stone, the Throne itself has been well-padded and seems to have plenty of room..."

Was that a spluttering she heard inside her head from a certain non-existent old lady? Genevieve suppressed a smirk.

Damien made a strangled sound that took her a moment to recognize as a cross between terror and a choked off laugh. "In the middle of a mission, Genevieve? And with Queen Marian looking on?" He paused. Then, "Would we have time?"

She laughed, knowing she had him. "Let's find out." She put some air between them so that she could safely sheathe her blade, then pulled him into a long kiss. When he was gasping for breath, she twirled away, laughing. "No more until you've sat down on that Throne!"

"Only if you come with me," he breathed.

Genevieve looked into his warm, grey eyes and let herself truly believe.

"Always," she answered, and didn't resist as he pulled them both onto the Throne and claimed the kiss she had promised.

Their soul-bonding had been vividly, publicly spectacular. Their recovery of the Monarch's Blade and Damien's bond to it had been gradual and much less flashy.

This... didn't need flash to be impressive.

Through their soul-bond, through the kiss, Genevieve could *feel* what was happening.

The Throne, the very Castle itself seemed to be coming awake. Empty spots in the web of connections the Sword had woven between Damien and the Realm were being filled in. Places that had worn thin were being re-knitted – like the connection to her own Elaarwen. There were holes as well, some with a feel of burned away edges, and some with a feel of having been nibbled by moths – and those holes were being mended as well. The whole was a fabric of immense strength and flexibility, somehow more tangible than the room around them.

It was a fabric, the Realm, but it also seemed alive and aware – and voracious for the attention and care it had been denied for so long. Denied? No, worse, *punished* for seeking, ripped and torn and used up in bits to weave things that were anathema to it. It needed... it *needed* so badly... but it had not the intelligence – now? ever? – to realize that its voracious *need* could destroy the very thing that was letting it heal and mend.

Genevieve could feel Damien being pulled into the warp and weft of it, and set herself to hold him to this reality. The Realm might need him, but it needed him here, as King, not merely as some ephemeral mote of magick.

She needed him, though she sensed that if he vanished into the fabric of the Realm's magick he would not be dead – she might not be able to touch his hands, but he would be wrapped around her and the Sword would speak for her and she would rule... and it would speak for their unborn child...

No, dammit, she needed *him*, not just some vague sense of his spirit supporting her. And this Realm needed a king who might not have seen much of it with his eyes or walked it with his booted feet – but who could quote every precedent and trade-treaty from memory, who could listen patiently to every side for as long as it took and then make his own decision... Who could be as shyly interested in the life and work of a flower-vendor or a farmer as in the doings of his nobles.

Too rooted in reality, am I? the Rebel Duchess thought a bit grimly. But *reality* was that Damien had been born for this and she neither could nor wished to fill his shoes. Not really knowing how she was doing it – not really caring – Genevieve Stellarine wrapped her soul around him and wrestled the Realm to win back the only man she had ever loved.

She fought at first with images and feelings. The instant of their soul-bonding. The intimacies they had shared, both physical and from their wounded hearts. The grotto, when it had been just the two of them. The blaze of pride she had felt when he casually told Jason to leave them alone the next morning. The strange feeling when she had conceived – and the moment when the old farmer had confirmed it... through whatever mysterious sixth sense of his own. The way her fear had melted into security when he rescued her from Harald. The miracle of the spell that confirmed her title to Elaarwen... and the even greater miracle, in its own way, of his proposal.

Damien responded to those images and feelings, but wistfully, as though he was saying goodbye. She felt herself being pushed gently back along their soul-bond... as if he was making sure she wouldn't be pulled in, too. *You'll be okay,* he seemed to be saying. *You and the baby.*

Frantically, she threw back at him, *I don't want the damned baby, I want YOU!*

A soothing, wistful touch that soothed her not at all.

Maybe that was the answer – it had been their answer before...

It was all Genevieve had left to try.

She retreated into a sense of her body... a sense of *his* body. She ripped at his clothes, trying to touch him, rouse his body and – hopefully – bring him back to himself. She stripped off her own tunic and blouse and rubbed her breasts against his face – it had been long enough since he'd been able to shave that his cheeks were going from scratchy to silky.

She wriggled out of her pants and sat astride his lap, trying to undo his belt while kissing him, desperately, passionately. Damien had felt too inhibited by the near presence of all their friends and protectors – and they had both been too emotionally and physically taxed by the escape and its antecedents – to make love in the grotto after his proposal. Then they had used the following night to make their escape from their friends and protectors. Three nights they had shared no more than a kiss or a touch – surely, surely, his *body* at least would respond.

She got his sword-belt free and growled in frustration, as that just left the belt for his pants as the next barrier – and a tighter one, in this position. Genevieve kissed him again, tears running freely down her face, as her fingers fought this next challenge. She could no longer feel him down the soul-bond, not even so much as when he had tried to block her out for those two terrible weeks.

It wasn't *working* and she had nothing left to try... She squeezed her eyes shut, trying to force herself not to give up. Someone less *rooted in reality* might have another idea, another option... but she had nothing, nothing.

Her fingers were pushed gently aside. Larger ones with softer sword-calluses finished the job. She opened her eyes to look into his and thought she saw a flicker in those clear grey depths.

His fingers completed their work and his hard, hot shaft burst forth from its confinement.

Hoping, praying to every God she'd ever heard of that this would not be the very last time they made love – and Damien not even really there – she lifted herself up and slid down onto him. Slowly at first, to make sure everything was in the right place. Was that just a reaction of his body when she sank all the way down?

The high walls of the Throne gave no purchase for leverage. Genevieve braced herself against his shoulders and raised herself up again, though not quite as far. She held tightly to her awareness, afraid that if she let go to just feel, she would miss the moment when she lost him entirely. But her determination disappeared as his hands came up and went around her waist, then began to move along her body, squeeze her buttocks. Surely, surely that was a good sign.

She felt him reach his climax at the same moment she crested her own wave. His face was buried between her breasts, and she kissed the top of his head not daring to hope. She slid down again and felt him tense and relax as she melted into his shoulder, his chest. His arms were wrapped tight around her.

When Genevieve dared to look, his eyes were open and Damien was looking out.

"And here I thought you were just teasing when you suggested this," he murmured. A tired smile was all the indication he gave of the battle that had just been fought.

She curled into his shoulder again. "Promise me you'll never do that again," she whispered.

"That's what every man hopes to hear after making love with his fiancée," Damien said lightly.

She shook her head. "I'm not joking. You are the best man – the best *person* – to wear the crown of this Realm. No one else knows as much about the Realm, its history, its laws, even its economy. And I was wrong. You don't have a problem with commanding. You just have a different style – it might not work as well on a battlefield, but it's incredibly effective the rest of the time."

Genevieve looked up at him, her eyes shining with tears. "If you can't believe how perfect you are for this yourself, believe in *me* and in *my* judgment."

He smoothed the tears away with a gentle thumb. "I came back because of *you.*"

"No," she disagreed. "You came back because your *body* responded to mine and pulled you back."

She wrenched herself away from him and began picking up her clothes. "You've said it over and over – that you don't think you're fit to be king. That you don't think we – I – the Realm – need you. Despite the Sword choosing you, the Realm itself choosing you. Adam and Ciriis and Jason – *all* your Royal Guards – choosing you. *Me* choosing you, above and *beyond* the soul-bond."

She jerked her shirt back on over her head with sharp, aggressive motions. "If all *that* can't make you feel worthy and needed, Damien Alsterling... I don't know what else I can–"

"I saw them killed, Genevieve." Damien's eyes were shadowed. "In this room. Right there." He pointed. A spot on the floor that she realized he had avoided on his march to the Throne. "He called them up in front of him, and then had them beheaded.

"Right there, in front of everyone.

"No charges. He didn't bother with such things by that point. I was in the crowd and I didn't do anything. I didn't scream or faint or even run away when I saw my parents lying in a pool of their own blood and the courtiers went back to their petty gossip. I waited until I could leave the room without it being obvious, and then I hid in the library for the next five *years* and wet my pants if I was summoned to a meal with *him*.

"Lady Theresa had to *tame* me, like I tamed those mice I told you about. If not for the books – I was barely human.

"And don't tell me I was only ten years old. I know that. I know there was nothing I could have done. It doesn't *matter.*" He looked at her directly. "I clung to the idea of *you,* because that was the only good thing left in my life. But would you have had anything to do with me without the soul-bond? Would Adam and Ciriis and Jason – any of the rest – had anything to do with me if I weren't the last scion of the Alsterling name? Would the Sword or the Throne?"

Her heart ached for him, but she couldn't keep going through this fear as he tried to give himself up over and over.

"Do you think it would it be better – easier – if you'd made your own mistakes rather than simply trying to survive the consequences of other people's actions?" she asked sharply. "I *chose* to marry Harald and went through eight years of living hell with him. And *I* didn't do anything about it either. Not a day goes by that I don't regret that time – but I'd do it all over again because we needed Siovale.

"We don't always get good choices in our lives. Sometimes we don't get *any* choices. I only escaped the prison of my marriage because – it turns out – Harald colluded with an evil sorcerer behind your grandfather's back in order to make a play for the throne."

She laughed abruptly, and knew there was a faintly hysterical edge to it. "If only he'd actually bothered to read or listen to any of the family history – he'd a better claim to the crown through *me* than as the sorcerer's goat."

Genevieve stuffed her feet back into her boots and strapped her sword-belt on and glared at her king and her love. "You grew up, Damien. You grew up, you learned what you needed to, and you became the king we all need right now. Get dressed. We have work to do."

And she strode away down the dais, looking for something to pretend to do.

Good, came the firm thought from outside her head. *Now go rescue my great-grandson and the rest of your people. And give over that Ring as soon as you are able, child. It's unwise to put all the Realm's eggs in one basket and then carry the basket into a burning house.*

Chapter SIXTEEN

Dear Friends

IT WAS, PERHAPS, NOT THE wisest idea to be skulking through the walls of a castle filled with an occupying force while simmering with resentment.

They had agreed on finding the soldiers first and solving whatever situation kept them contained. As best they could, anyways. If they were still suffering from the effects of food-poisoning, Damien wasn't sure what he and Genevieve could do about it... Something stirred in his new other awareness – the Realm wanted all its denizens to be healthy. Perhaps there *was* something he could do after all.

All Damien had to do was think about his soldiers and he knew which way to go to reach them. He couldn't place them in his mind on a map of the castle, but he could *feel* where they were in relation to himself. It made navigating the walls a new challenge, since if he just went directly to them, he and Genevieve wouldn't stay within the safe confines of the walls. She had to keep grabbing him and pulling him back into the walls as he started to emerge into a room or a corridor that he hadn't noticed. And then she'd hiss at him – *again* – to be more careful.

Which didn't help his temper any.

Why had she pulled him back, anyways? He could do so much more for the Realm from inside the web of magick that underlay it all. The untended parts nagged at him, and the parts his grandfather and Lord Prydeen had damaged *itched* like the seam of a poorly made tunic. Anyone could serve as king or queen, but fixing *this* was something that only he might be able to do.

Genevieve pulled him back into the wall yet again. Damien shook her off angrily, denying the fear he could feel from her down the bond. Fear – not for their situation, but at how close she had come to losing him.

Not because she would have died of it – she knew he would have been alive enough to prevent that – but because he wouldn't have been with her. Because she had given him her heart. He didn't want to feel her fear and love; he didn't want to feel guilty for having tried to do what he felt was best for the Realm... or easiest for *him*.

He pushed all of that away and tried to match his sense of direction to the walls that he had to keep them within.

Likewise, the young king ignored the increasingly shrill voice of Queen Marian, striding (or floating?) along beside him with more and more advice. Would the woman – *both* women – never let up? He wanted to cover his ears like a child, but he couldn't entirely block the bond, and he was afraid he'd simply learn that it wasn't his *ears* that conveyed the ancient queen's voice into his head.

Surely someone who was truly meant to be a sovereign would listen to the brilliant strategist and seasoned duchess. Surely, they would appreciate the words of wisdom from the last monarch who was acknowledged to have ruled wisely and true. (Though, a piece of him whispered, not a one of her children or grandchildren would the Sword speak for, so perhaps *she* wasn't perfect either.)

At last! Queen Marian's voice made it past his ignoring. *Yes, I was a passable Queen – it all grows more appreciated by comparison to Reggie. But I was a terrible mother. And grandmother. And one* **not insignificant part** *of a monarch's job is to ensure the succession goes to a worthy Heir. I failed at that utterly.* She paused. *You and your Genevieve, I think, will not. But that's if you're together. On her own, she's going to do the same damn thing I did and throw herself into governing because she feels she hasn't a choice, and neglect the baby.*

On **your** *own, you'd get caught up in your children and begin leaving the ruling to those friends of yours. Which might get the job done, but leaves out the heart and soul that only the monarch knows about. That web you tried to jump into – I couldn't see it like you can, but I could feel it enough to use it to guide me to what really needed doing.*

If you care about the Realm's future, it's going to take you both.

There was a pause.

Something's not right about that child she's carrying. It's early to tell, but I'm not sure she can carry it to term. And then where would you leave her?

Damien stopped abruptly and whirled to face Genevieve.

"Are you all right?" he demanded. "Do you feel okay?"

She gave him a baffled look. "Why? What are you planning?"

"You said you could feel when you conceived. Does everything feel all right?"

Genevieve shrugged. "It was one moment. I really haven't felt any different from normal other than that moment." She frowned. "What's wrong?"

Damien tightened his lips. "Grandmother says there's a likelihood you won't carry this baby to term."

Lovely, the old queen's voice echoed in his head. *Now you'll have to tell her it's something wrong with the child, not her. Foolish boy! Why do you think I spoke to you, and not to her?*

Genevieve went absolutely white, her dusting of freckles standing out against skin that no longer had the warm glow of Summer. She swallowed hard, then set her chin. "And I suppose she knows this because of some mystical abilities she's picked up in that afterworld that she doesn't seem too inclined to join?"

Tell her it's the damned Sword. You'll be able to see it yourself once you get some practice in.

The young king said nothing, just glowered at his duchess. His soul-bonded. His betrothed.

Genevieve's head dropped. "I told you..." Her voice trailed off, and her head came back up. He pretended not to see the trails of tears. Fresh ones, still glistening, not the salt-tracks that he had awakened on the Throne to find. "We don't need to deal with this now. We need to liberate your castle. How close are we to your soldiers?"

"About a hundred paces forwards." He felt like he should say something now, but the moment seemed to have passed. *'Your'* castle she had called it; it had been *'the'* castle since they began planning this mission, and once or twice even *'our'* castle. Ever since he'd bound her as his vassal and she'd accepted his proposal of marriage...

...promises which should bind him as well, after all...

"Then let's go." She brushed past him to take the lead, then spoke to him over her shoulder as she pushed ahead, "I won't object when you pick some pretty young thing to warm your bed and produce the heirs you'll need."

Moments are what you make of them, grandson...

He caught at her hand, feeling like the biggest idiot in the Realm. "Genevieve..."

She pulled free. "I'll stay up in Elaarwen as much as I can. The bond will pull me back, of course, but now that you've confirmed my title, Elaarwen is pulling at me, too. I can use that to balance."

"Genevieve." Damien caught up to her in a couple of quick strides and put his free hand around her waist. She resisted, then gave up and sank back against him, leaning her head back on his shoulder. "There will *never* again be any woman but you in my bed. *Or* in my heart."

"You'll still need an Heir..."

"We'll find a way." He tightened his arm, wishing that he didn't have to carry the stupid Sword unsheathed to use its magick. He would have liked to put both arms around her. "But that way won't involve me sleeping with any other woman ever again."

His red-headed betrothed turned in his embrace, and put her arms around him. She hadn't had to carry *her* sword unsheathed while they traversed the walls. "I'm sorry, I was too harsh. I was just so terrified I'd lost you."

"You were right," Damien whispered into her hair. "I don't know if I'll ever feel worthy. In my heart, I'm always still the child who..." He couldn't finish. Couldn't talk about it again.

Genevieve cupped his face in her hands. "The child who *wasn't at fault."* His eyes slid away from hers, and she called him back with a kiss. "None of it was your fault, my Damien. None of it. No more was it my fault that Harald hurt me. The fault is in those who did the hurting. And it doesn't make us any the less worthy for having been hurt."

"Mmmmn," he said, non-committally. It sounded right when she said it, but it didn't match with how he felt.

"Jason didn't tell you this? Ciriis and Adam?"

He thought back. "Jason... told me it wasn't my fault, what Prince Oskar did to him. Ciriis and Adam told me it was up to me to make his sacrifice worthwhile. I... never talked to anyone about my parents. Except you. Back there."

Genevieve sighed. "And your Lady Theresa? Who tamed you like a pet mouse?"

He winced. "She... may have said something. Once."

He hadn't confided in Lady Theresa. And it hadn't been her choice to look after him. She'd simply taken on the task when she realized she couldn't root him out of her precious Library, and that if she made sure he was clean and fed and more or less dressed as befit a prince and arrived at the meals his grandfather summoned him to, that he was less likely to be the source of a disruption.

It wasn't that she didn't have some personal warmth and caring for him, but he had been too dangerous to rest too many sympathies on, he knew. She hadn't been the maternal presence in his life that Genevieve seemed to imagine.

"Oh, Damien," his beautiful soul-bonded held him closer, perhaps picking up some of his thoughts and memories through the soul-bond. "Rosa had to pound it into my head for over a year... but she was remarkably believable, given what had just happened to *her.*" She hesitated, and he sensed there was still more to the story than he had been told.

"I love you," the young king whispered. "I'm trying to believe."

Or at least trying to accept that *she* believed in him, in his worthiness to be king.

"I love *you,*" she replied. After a moment, she went on, "Now let's go get your crown back. Your lead, my liege."

The men of the Royal Guard were confined in the root cellars next to the kitchen, rather than in a dungeon. It made Genevieve wonder if Duke Tomas had some hope of turning them to his service, or at least some sense that what was being done was wrong. She'd always rather liked Tomas and she hoped that this was a sign that, underneath the control the sorcerer had over him, there was still a wise and capable Duke fighting back.

Or perhaps Lord Prydeen didn't want to share his dungeons.

The soldiers were duly surprised when she stepped out of a solid wall, followed by their liege-lord. Duly surprised, but surprisingly unfazed, and ready to follow orders.

There were twenty men in the first root cellar, stuffed in among more carrots and onions than Genevieve had ever seen in her life. There was a dim light from the ill-fitting door, enough to make out a bit more than shapes. It was almost standing room only – they seemed to be taking it in shifts to lie down. Most of them looked pretty sick, and a couple had already died.

Damien's appearance didn't faze them, but his unsheathed blade caused a commotion, largely because they were so closely packed together that the Sword was a menace. He sheathed it immediately, but the glazed look in his eyes as he gravitated to the sickest men also unnerved these solid soldiers somewhat. It also unnerved Genevieve, too, but she forced herself to act as if his behavior was completely to be expected. When Damien's touch served to Heal, all further doubts and questions were set aside.

"You want us to stay in here, milady?" the young lieutenant who was the highest-ranking officer in the root cellar clarified as Damien moved carefully amongst them.

Genevieve nodded. "Just until we've made sure where everyone is, and His Majesty has had a chance to Heal them as well. We'll be back for you immediately we have that taken care of."

"We haven't any weapons, Your Grace," the lieutenant pointed out. "And you said there are *how* many enemy troops we need to handle?"

"Our best guess is about seventy," she answered. "Some four dozen from Siovale, and they should be in Siovale colors. The rest are the sorcerer's bullyboys."

"We can recognize *them,*" someone said grimly from the back. "My brother's on the City Watch. They've been warned not to interfere with them. No matter what they did. And they've *done* plenty."

Genevieve gave him a grim smile. "That's over with. We're taking this place back. We're taking the city back. We're taking the bloody *Realm* back." She looked at the lieutenant. "I don't know what I can promise you for weapons. We're right beside the kitchens, though, so that's a start. There can't be enough knives and pokers to arm you all, surely–"

Someone else guffawed. "My sister's a knife-sharpener and works full-time in the castle kitchens. I wouldn't be so sure of that, milady!"

"Well, that's good news." She gave them a wry look. "We'll see when we get you out of here. Right now, I don't yet know how well guarded these root cellars are, nor the dispersal of those enemy troops. But remember, they're trying to do the job you trained and practiced, but with fewer men and *no* practice. They also have to guard a number of prisoners, so there's a good chance they're bunched up here and there."

"Who're they holding?" someone asked, at the same time as someone else wanted to know if Genevieve and Damien planned to bring them all through the stone walls.

"We can't," she admitted. "We can each take two to three people through at a time, but that would be too long for assembling a fighting force. We'll be opening the doors – for you and for the *rest* of the Castle Guard." She hesitated. "We're not sure who all is being held. Lady Theresa Anvliyar, some of the other Royal Councilors. Not just nobles. The maids and other castle servants are just as much hostage to our actions, for all that they aren't locked up. There are maybe a dozen young ladies–"

"The King's Ladies," the fellow with the brother in the City Guard commented. "They'd be under guard. Would have put up a fight, they would have. And it's known they were... special... to His Majesty."

There was an uncomfortable shuffling around as they remembered who they were talking to and why the ladies had been special. It would almost have been comical in other circumstances, but Genevieve didn't have time to explain the complicated beginnings of a friendship she had developed with many of the secret Royal Guardswomen.

"There's one more hostage," Damien made his way to Genevieve's side. "Duke Aldred of Elaarwen was brought here by the Siovalese. They've been holding him prisoner for the last three years."

That started an angry rumble. Several of the men had apparently known – or known of – Duke Aldred. He'd had a reputation for fairness, and the soldiers in the Royal Army who had served as the Castle Guard would know better than most people how hard that had been under the old king.

Genevieve realized that Adam must have also gone through the ranks of the Castle Guard to winnow for men of good character. When he would have been able to do so, she could not guess, but he had clearly done a thorough job.

"Your father, milady?" the lieutenant confirmed.

"Yes..." She wished her voice were steadier, but she did her best as she went on. "But he cannot be our first objective. While the king and I are here, your words and ours are shielded from the ears of the sorcerer. But once we have left, anything you say may find its way to Lord Prydeen's ears." Gods, yes. Prydeen's enchanted mice must surely have plenty of ways in and out of these root cellars.

"And he's not exactly known for sorting the innocent from the guilty," Damien said with dry grimness.

"*Your* first objective must be to capture the usurper and Duke Tomas of Siovale," Genevieve went on. "Make no plans that can be overheard. We'll be back shortly – by the door."

Damien drew the Sword again, took her hand, and stepped into the stone wall.

They repeated the exercise for another twenty men squished between sacks of potatoes and yams. And then for nearly forty men in very bad shape between kegs of wine.

On leaving that group, the young king slumped against the inside of a stone wall that somehow stayed solid for him.

"A moment, Genevieve," he said quietly. He looked quite grey with... not exactly fatigue. He didn't even exactly sound *tired*. Drained, perhaps.

She stepped close. "Is there anything I can do? What do you need?"

He gave her a sad smile. "A week without worry? Nevermind. You bring the light back just by being you."

The Rebel Duchess frowned past a smile she couldn't suppress. "What are you talking about? What's wrong?"

Damien shook himself and stood straight. "Nothing. It's... nothing. Let's go on."

She gave him a skeptical look, but judged him able to make his own decisions. "Last set," Genevieve noted. "Then we'll have accounted for all your Castle Guard."

"All who survived," he answered soberly.

The last storeroom was filled with apples – the kind that are near hard as rocks when harvested and only ripen fully after some six months of storage. Cider-making apples, not eating apples. And only eighteen men. The Captain of the Castle Guard had not been in any of the storerooms, dead or alive.

This time, after Damien Healed the ill and Genevieve made her speech and laid out her plan, they stepped through the walls and out into the kitchen.

It was a risk, but a necessary one. The storerooms full of soldiers had to be opened from the kitchen, and it was the kitchen that would provide them some semblance of arms – and armor, with pots and lids put to new uses.

They didn't step out into the bustling center of meal preparation, however, but into a pantry off to the side from which they could peer out. The teenage girl already hiding in there was clever enough not to scream when she saw them. And clever enough to recognize her king and his bride-to-be.

"There's ten of them out there," the young kitchen-worker whispered without encouragement. "Most are milord Duke's men, but it's the lord sorcerer's men who are in charge. The one with the green small-cape has the keys on his belt. I tried to soften him up with some wine, to get to the keys, but he and the other bullyboys had other plans for me." Genevieve looked her up and down, but the girl looked determined, not traumatized. "Siovale's men just stand there like blocks of wood."

"How did you get away?" Damien asked sympathetically.

"Cook setup a huge row – nonsense about the pastry chef not doing his job. Even the bullyboys had to duck when they started flinging ladles at each other." She grinned. "The both of them have deadly aim. No one gets out of line down here... normally." The grin faded. "I'm Maree. I'm the kitchen's knife-sharpener. My brother's in one of those storerooms."

Genevieve nodded. "With the carrots. He mentioned you."

"How are you going to get them out, milady?" The Rebel Duchess noted wryly that the girl didn't have any doubts what they were about. Nor did she seem to think it was incredible that her king and queen-to-be had just walked through walls of solid stone. Clever enough to figure it out or too dull to be surprised?

"Will the kitchen staff stand with us?" Damien asked quietly.

Maree looked at him, and Genevieve knew the moment she met his eyes... that here was yet another one who would do anything for him. And he'd never notice and go on thinking himself unworthy and replaceable. It was enough to drive a woman mad.

Although it explained why the girl was so accepting of their impossible arrival and plan. Clearly she believed that Damien could do *anything*.

"We will, Your Majesty," Maree answered. She bit her lip. "But we're not warriors."

Damien looked the question at Genevieve.

She peered out of the pantry to observe the setup. Like most communal kitchens, this one was a huge open space with neatly aligned tables. Little seating, though a pair of old grannies sat chopping steadily at vegetables while younger folk bustled around. Even in the midst of a coup, dinner needed making. Huge ovens deep-set into the far wall radiated a powerful heat. Knives everywhere, but none more than a couple hand-spans in length.

Lord Prydeen's bullyboys lazed against the abandoned end of a table far from the hot ovens. Siovale's men stood in ones and twos, stiff and still, each in front of the entrances to the storerooms. The bullyboys had tankards of ale.

She noted the one in the green mantle eyeing the kitchen workers. Whenever one came too close, they got a pinch on breast or buttock. The man looked like a cook testing out the quality of the vegetables at the greengrocer's stall in the marketplace by checking for firmness. The other two were no better; they kept their hands to themselves...

but only until they saw that their leader had rejected a given lad or lass.

Genevieve withdrew into the closet shaking her head. "There's too many. And it's too open. Tomas trains his men well, and they grow them large in Siovale. And the bullyboys will fight dirty. In a fair fight I might take out a couple of them, and you could probably do the same if you're as good in a fight as you are in practice," she told Damien. "But there's *ten* of them out there, and no way to sneak up."

"What if *we* could distract them?" Maree asked eagerly. "The kitchen workers, I mean."

"That would be dangerous," Damien began.

"Begging Your Majesty's pardon, but we'd all just begun to believe that maybe life *wouldn't* be dangerous from here on," Maree interrupted him boldly. "We're used to danger. I'd rather take the risk to put you back on your throne than go back to wondering if I'm the next one to vanish in the night." She gave him a starry-eyed look, and added, "Cook says you're our true king and will make everything right, if only you get the chance."

Damien looked startled, and Genevieve thought with a grim humor that if there were any chance at all, it might be worth it just to hammer it into his head that his *people* believed in him. But as it was...

"No," she answered the girl's question. "You might be able to get enough of the bullyboys' attention that we only have to deal with the Siovalese guards, but that's still four or five too many."

She was confident of her skills, though she knew herself a more effective warrior when mounted, but she knew how good the Siovalese could be. She'd sparred with Harald's guards until he'd become annoyed and forced her to stop – and then sent them home to Siovale.

And... she had no idea whether Damien would be able to carry through in a real fight. And more to the point, neither did he.

The girl ignored her and actually reached out to clasp Damien's free hand. "You can do it, Your Majesty. I know you can." There was something beyond blind-faith in her eyes... normally a girl who sharpened knives in the castle kitchen would never have a chance to approach her exceedingly handsome young king and her girlish infatuation would never come to light. But surely even an infatuated child should have better manners than to throw herself at the king with his betrothed standing right beside him...

Genevieve raised an eyebrow, but the young king was looking at the girl with an odd mix of emotions on his face. He raised his eyes to meet Genevieve's. "Queen Marian is telling me... that maybe there *is* something I can do."

She wasn't ready to discount anything at this point. A Sword that could let them walk through walls, his own touch Healing the sick soldiers... the terrible fabric of the Realm that had nearly devoured him and that she could still sense vaguely beyond her bond to the young king. Genevieve Stellarine's wildest dreams had involved liberating her country and riding off to explore the world, not fairy stories of magick and miracle. And yet here she was...

...liberating her country with magick and miracle.

The riding off to explore the world would probably never happen, but she hadn't really had much hope of that even as the only Heir to Elaarwen. Let alone as Queen of Ilseador.

"What?" she asked, ready to add to her strategy whatever new ability was about to be revealed.

Damien shook his head. "I'm not sure. Grandmother says that the Sword will know what to do." He gave her a wry look. "The problem is that I don't actually think it's the Sword this time that's ready to do something. I think it's me. And before you ask, I'm not sure what *I* can do either. Just that I can do *something.*"

Genevieve fought down the urge to say caustically that if he couldn't tell her what he could do then it wasn't wise – or even possible – to plan a strategy around it. It went against her instincts and her training, but there really wasn't any other option. She shut away the part of herself that was counting the minutes since she had last seen her father alive... and the thought of what might be happening to her friends.

She gave a short, sharp nod. "Do it. Whatever it is. I'll back you up."

Damien gave her a relieved smile, then turned to Maree. "Go set up that distraction. Try to get the kitchen workers on the opposite side of the room. Whatever happens, it isn't going to be pretty, and I don't know how well I'll be able to control it."

Maree's eyes had grown huge at the mention of Queen Marian and mysterious powers that even Damien didn't know what to do with. She didn't move.

Damien pulled his hand away, turned her around and prodded her towards the kitchen... with a pat on her rear. She gave him a last heart-in-the-eyes look over her shoulder, and trotted out to wreak some havoc.

He sighed, shook his head, and turned to meet Genevieve's disapproving look. "What?" he asked.

"That child thinks she's in love with you," she told him bluntly. "And you just gave her hope that you might be interested."

"What are you talking about?" Damien sounded genuinely baffled. "Interested in what?"

"In taking her to bed. Don't give me that look. You're nowhere near that innocent."

It was hard to tell in the dim lighting, but she thought he might be blushing. "That's ridiculous. She's just a child. Do we really have time for this right now?"

She sighed. "No. Go do whatever you need to do, love. I'll be guarding your back." *And more,* she thought.

The battle between kitchen workers and bullyboys had begun – possibly even before Maree made it back out there. One of the scullery lads was weeping into the bosom of one of the vegetable-chopping grannies, and the floor was getting slippery with food spilled and flung. The bullyboys were definitely distracted, though they still seemed to think it was a fun game. Siovale's men stared straight ahead as if they didn't even notice.

Damien stepped out of the closet and stepped into the kitchen. Abruptly, he knelt on one knee, balancing the naked steel of the Sword on the palms of his hands, his head bent as if in offering. On impulse, and with no real idea why she did it, Genevieve sheathed her own blade, and stepped up to place her hands on his shoulders.

The Sword began to glow... *Of course* it did.

Siovale's men all turned slowly, as if through molasses, to look at the young king. Genevieve was hard put to maintain her place, as there seemed no personality behind those stares. The eyes were focused, aware, but...

They took a step, almost in unison, towards the kneeling king and his bride. The pikes they held were lowered in a deadly array of glittering steel points. Genevieve wanted nothing more than to draw her sword and pull Damien back into the safety of the stone wall, but something told her she didn't dare let go of him even to do that.

The Siovalese soldiers took a step. Then another, slower one. A third step seemed beyond them, though some trembled. The glitter of their eyes said that they were still awake, still aware... and *still* no one was at home behind those eyes.

Another heartbeat, and Damien rose, hefting his Sword in a more useful grip. At approximately the same moment, the bullyboys realized that something was wrong and began to leave off their efforts to prey upon the kitchen workers. Their swords were already out, and they seemed only slightly discommoded by the living statues of Duke Tomas' soldiers as they advanced on Genevieve and Damien.

"Remember," she muttered as she drew her own sword again. "They'll fight dirty. Don't try to be honorable about it. Just kill them and have done."

Her fiancé nodded, and she couldn't help but recall his distaste for the idea of hunting... and his tendency to hold back. Genevieve could only hope that he would keep them busy enough that *she* could dispatch them.

She stepped to the fore and engaged one of the bullyboys first. He wasn't expecting much out of her, apparently having been taken in by the old king and his pet sorcerer's disdain for female fighters... or perhaps he had been one of those in the courtyard who had seen her give up without a fight a couple days earlier. Her blade slipped past his guard almost before even she realized it, and she skewered him in a clean shot through the heart.

The green-mantled fellow had been holding himself to the rear of the kitchen, away from the affray, but now he began to edge away towards the door. Genevieve spared a glance for Damien, who was fighting the third fellow. Her heart wanted to go to his aid, but he really wasn't doing poorly, responding with a feint of his own when the fellow tried to cut at his feet. She still wasn't convinced he could actually end it, but she had to trust him to keep the fellow busy. Green-mantle had the keys... and the ability to rouse the rest of the enemy.

She lunged across the kitchen, mindful of the slippery footing, and got in the first cut as Green-Mantle had turned his back on her to reach the door. A flesh-wound only, low on his thigh, as if she had overreached herself in trying to tag him. Genevieve wasn't above a bit of subterfuge herself, and besides it would still hurt and slow him down. She was perfectly balanced still, of course, but Genevieve overacted the moment to pretend her lunge had been a little too far and left her wobbling to reset her feet. The truth was that she knew his type and that he wouldn't doubt she was fool enough to do that – instead of choosing the slighter, but painful and distracting, cut rather than risking losing her footing to take a chance at killing him in one blow.

He turned back to face her with a look of smug superiority. She knew that look too well. It was a shallow echo of the one Harald had worn every night of their marriage when he would finally let her cry herself to sleep. The same expression her former husband had worn when she surrendered to him in the courtyard to try to save her father's and Damien's lives.

A cold satisfaction took her in the thought of wiping that expression off of someone's face. Even if it wasn't – *yet* – Harald's.

Green-mantle flipped his short-cape over his head and tried to use it to foul her sword, using the same motion to draw a wicked-looking dagger. She side-stepped the cape, letting it fall fluttering to the ground. Her sword-point never wavered from its aim at his heart.

He'd meant to step close and stab her while her blade was fouled, and had followed through on his intention, even though the ploy had failed. He still outweighed her after all, and had the advantage of having no notions of honorable fighting to hamper him.

Under normal circumstances, Genevieve would have had no troubles with scum like this. She sparred regularly with men who outweighed and outreached her, and employed street-fighters as her opponents in order to practice the counters for any dirty trick they could invent. She had fought in numerous battles against the old king's army and would not shy from awarding a killing stroke. The Rebel Duchess was more than prepared to handle an oversized opponent who knew to try to close with her.

However, these were not normal circumstances. She'd had less than a week of recovering from two weeks of near self-starvation, and was barely two days away from Harald's battering of her body and soul. Her potentially problematic pregnancy – and the need to therefore shield her abdomen from blunt-force blows – and her instinctual awareness of Damien distracted her focus just slightly... but 'just slightly' was too much on top of the slack in her physical condition.

The bullyboy bound up her sword with his, stepping close enough to overpower her. But he didn't stab with his wicked dagger, instead using it to bind her own daggerhand. And *there* was her advantage.

"King Harald might have a reward for bringing *you* in," he smirked, "And when *he's* done with you, and milord's done with you, then I think *we'll* have some *other* plans. In the meantime, the Pretender over there should surrender now I've got hands on you."

He wanted to take her alive.

Genevieve let herself go slightly limp, let something like fear enter her eyes. He smirked again, forcing her to drop her weapons and sheathing his own, shifting her into a grip very similar to the full-nelson hold she had taught Damien to escape from. He wasn't expecting the shift of her hips, the sweep of her leg. The fall was more chancy with her sword and dagger on the floor beneath him, but she made sure to fall heavily on him, knocking the wind from his chest, and to scramble up.

She stabbed him in the gut with his own dagger, it being closest to hand, and turned to see what Damien had wrought, there being no sound of clashing steel coming from that direction.

Her love and liege gave her a wry smile, his opponent on the ground before him. And pretty little Maree was holding a cast iron frying pan of immense proportions and looking immensely pleased with herself. Genevieve gave him another raised eyebrow, and bent to locate the ring of keys.

The cook came forwards to take the keys once she stood straight again, and led her over to the storerooms. It was just as well, since Genevieve was somewhat disoriented by the fight and having traveled within the walls rather than between them. Identifying where the soldiers were might have taken several tries – and several attempts with the keys – but the cook knew his domain and released the men without drama or fumbling.

The lieutenant from the carrot room was the highest-ranking officer, it turned out. Genevieve left him to sort out and arm his troops, borrowing liberally from the kitchens and Duke Tomas' seven 'en-statued' men-at-arms. Maree and the other kitchen workers were doing their best to help, and to ensure that their kin among the soldiers were safe. A handful of soldiers had died, despite Damien's best efforts, and those were laid out on the food preparation tables with a grim sorrow. Tablecloths made serviceable shrouds.

The young king was staring at the fallen body of his opponent. He'd sheathed the Monarch's Blade.

"We'd best tie him up," Genevieve commented as she came up to him.

Damien gave her a dubious look. "Wouldn't it be better to run him through and get it over with? He'll have to be executed anyways."

She raised an eyebrow at him again. "Are you going to tell me that you have it in you to do that while he's unconscious?" It wasn't so much of a question.

The young king sighed. "Perhaps not. It would have been a cleaner end – I just about had him..."

"When your little helper came along," Genevieve finished. "Well, you can't fault her bravery. And you might want to be a bit careful with that one. If she sharpens knives, she probably knows something about how to use them, and she clearly has some muscles..." She tamped down her expression, trying to look serious. "And now she's a Hero of the Realm for 'saving your life.' What *will* you do when she asks for her reward?"

"Genevieve!" Damien captured her around the waist and drew her close. "If that's what she has in mind, she'll just have to choose something else," he whispered, and pulled her in even closer. She laid her head on his shoulder, briefly. Too briefly, but they had a castle to re-take now that they had the men to do it.

The lieutenant had his men organized. Only ten swords were available for the ninety-some soldiers who were left, but the kitchen had outfitted nearly half the rest with knives and pokers, pots and lids.

"Where to first, Your Majesty?" The lieutenant asked Damien.

He deferred to Genevieve. "Her Grace is the strategist of the family."

He probably didn't realize quite how much his heart was in his eyes as he looked at her, the Rebel Duchess mused. Maree wilted slightly in the background.

Genevieve nodded sharply. "Can you sense where the others are being held, milord? Or where the enemy is located? It's how we found *you,*" she told the lieutenant.

Damien frowned in concentration. "Yes... and no. *I* could find them, but I'm not sure I could tell you where they are, or lead you to them."

"What if you had a map, Your Majesty?" a senior maid servant asked.

He looked at her curiously. "That might work."

The woman smiled triumphantly. "We have maps of the entire castle here, Your Majesty. It's how we plan the cleaning schedules and teach the new staff." She clapped her hands, and one of her juniors sped off. "We also know the castle fairly well, Sire. If you can give us a direction, we might be able to identify the location."

Several soldiers nodded as well. They, too, needed to know the layout of the castle for their work.

Damien looked impressed. "That I can do. Direction, and probably distance."

The next half-hour was spent with the young king pointing in one direction or another and muttering out distances. The maids and soldiers worked together to plot out the locations he was giving them on the maps of each floor of the castle. Unfortunately, he was much less specific about *who* and *how many* were in each location.

"I'm sorry," he said in frustration. "You men," he nodded to the soldiers, "Were easy to find. There were so many of you, and you were so sick. Healthy people don't pull so much at the fabric of the Realm." They gave him blank looks; except for Genevieve, they had no clue what he meant. But they murmured reassurances that it was workable nonetheless.

"You haven't pointed out the dungeons," Genevieve asked him quietly, as the maps were discussed and organized. "There must be sickness and suffering there."

The young king's grey eyes were shadowed. "Much too much. First things first."

She put a hand on his shoulder in empathy. “How are we going to deal with Lord Prydeen? We can’t go on like we were before this, letting him do as he pleases.”

Damien gave her a grateful glance for saying ‘we’ when she had been given no choice in the matter at all. He hadn’t felt like *he* had a choice in the matter either, of course, she knew...

“I’ll have to face him. That’s why we wanted to find the Sword in the first place.”

He tried to hide how hard he had to swallow after saying that, but Genevieve could feel his trembling under her hand as well as the almost incoherent fear he was keeping so heavily tamped down when the sorcerer was mentioned. Lord Prydeen – even after she had met the man and felt the sense of menace he exuded – was still a somewhat abstract threat to her with regards to his magick. His name had been a sort of ‘boogey-man’ used to frighten children into behaving up in Elaarwen, but never quite real.

Damien, by contrast, had grown up expecting to have those foul spells worked upon him someday and seeing the very real results of said spells cast upon other people, including some that he had known and cared for. Like his sister.

“Not alone,” she promised, and he looked at her gratefully again.

She squeezed his shoulder and strode over to the tables where the maps were spread out. It was time to be the Rebel Duchess and strategize how to take over the king’s castle, she thought ironically.

Damien trailed after her, sneaking his hand into hers for reassurance.

The whole group weighed the likelihood of this group or that being here or there. The maids had one set of ideas about appropriate quarters for the various hostages, and the soldiers different ones. The maids, however, won most of the disagreements, because they had knowledge from the past few days of having been summoned thither and yon to deliver food and empty chamberpots for rooms without indoor plumbing. They hadn’t been allowed in to see any of the prisoners, but they could make guesses based on how much food and how many chamberpots. They had all been put off by the thoughtlessness of stashing people for days in rooms without modern sanitation.

"I doubt Harald – or even Tomas – would think of such things," Genevieve said dryly. "Siovale is a very *traditional* sort of place, and Elaarwen hasn't had the wealth or safety to add such amenities."

"And Lord Prydeen wouldn't care," someone else muttered.

They had ninety men of the Castle Guard, but only half were armed. The kitchen workers and maids numbered another fifty, but included pot boys barely big enough to see over the tables and the two old grannies who had been chopping sitting down. And Damien and Genevieve.

Their estimate of the enemy forces was down to thurty-eight men-at-arms, with the elimination of the ten in the kitchens, and perhaps just under twenty remaining bullyboys. Along with Harald, Duke Tomas, and... Lord Prydeen.

Damien had identified several sets of unhappy people. One set was spread out over several corridors in the wing of the castle where the Royal Councilors had kept rooms, so it made sense that those worthies were being confined to their rooms until they would swear allegiance to the usurper. The maids confirmed that meals sent to those rooms were sumptuous and singular, one to a room.

The second set was confined to the solarium where Genevieve had once practiced at arms, and that involved food prepared in a batch for perhaps a dozen people... likely the ladies of the Royal Guard.

Two others were near the usurper's rooms – Damien's tower that Harald had claimed for himself. Those two were each accorded a singular meal of good quality, but nothing fancy. They guessed that one of those was Duke Aldred, but could not guess whom the other one was for.

The maids claimed that they had seen some of the Councilors moving about the castle – under guard, but otherwise freely. Damien and Genevieve had exchanged a grim nod; it wasn't exactly unexpected. After the old king's rule, loyalty was too easily bought in this Court and those who looked to the main chance for their own survival were all too willing to sell it. Damien asked which Councilors, but the women all exchanged uncomfortable looks and equivocated. They, too, knew that this was less a matter of loyalty and treason than of personal survival.

Lord Prydeen, of course, was seen wherever and whenever he chose.

The servants had confirmed that a token force of Siovalese men-at-arms and bullyboys held the gates, and that there were between two and four guards at each of their target locations, as well as around Harald, and that about half of the invading force was off-duty at any given time. The soldiers growled to hear that their barracks rooms had been taken over as sleeping quarters by the Siovalese.

Genevieve stepped away from the tables to think before telling them the strategy they would follow. Their necessary plan seemed obvious to her. As always, it amazed her that the others couldn't see it... but in this case she anticipated plenty of disagreement, at least from Damien. It wasn't what he was going to want to do, nor was it what pulled at her heart. But it was what needed to be done.

The senior maid approached her as she stood aside, watching her love going over the locations again with the lieutenant and the cook and a handful of the other men and maids. Maree was staying close, clearly trying to get his attention again.

"Your Grace," the senior maid began, "About those Councilors who are walking free..."

Genevieve focused instantly. "Yes?"

The woman wrung her hands, in a gesture that didn't fit with her otherwise grimly serene demeanor. "We didn't want to tell the young king... 'twill break his heart." She gave Genevieve a direct look. "It's not just the nobles like Sir Loveress and Sir Solway and Lady Celavell have been watching over him, milady. We had little power to help him, but anyone with eyes to see could tell he was the best hope this Realm had. The best hope *we* had. Have."

The Queen-to-be nodded.

"There's three Councilors, milady," the woman said sadly. "The Ministers of Trade and Public Works... and the Chatelaine, the Dowager Baroness."

Genevieve's eyes widened. "Lady Anvliyar of Cedarwen?"

The woman nodded. "The same. We know she has a special place in His Majesty's regard..." She sighed. "But we know her well, especially since she's taken her new role. And, milady?" She put a tentative hand on Genevieve's arm. "I can't vouch for this myself, but word is that *she* was never locked up in the first place."

The Rebel Duchess knew what that must mean. Her heart also shrank from the task of telling Damien, but someone had to. "What is your name?" she asked.

"Elista, milady," the woman answered. "I began my service in the castle the same day as Prince Eric and Lady Miria were put to death." Damien's parents. "I followed the prince to where he was hiding in the library and left him food and such as best I could." So, it had been her, and not... "After some weeks, milady Anvliyar caught me and was going to have me disciplined for it. I thought she'd turn me out, and then there'd be no one to feed the young prince, so I told her about him. I don't know how she hadn't noticed him there before that." Elista looked down. "Perhaps if I hadn't told her... but she made a pet of him after that. Brought him clean clothes and made him bathe when the old king wanted to see him. And she made sure food was delivered for him. I thought... maybe it was a good thing. 'Twas more than I could do for him."

Genevieve was wracking her brain. There was something she'd heard long ago about Cedarwen, and the Baroness... something to do with Damien's parents? Or maybe his sister? The Dowager Baroness had been so warm when she'd met Genevieve, it hadn't even crossed her mind. After all, it wasn't hard to imagine feeling sympathy for the orphaned child hiding in the library; Ciriis and Adam had done the same after all.

Ciriis and Adam had *used* Damien, the more skeptical side of her insisted. They might have grown to care for him over time, but they had been hunting for a vulnerable, manipulable Heir that *they* could control.

She didn't exactly blame them, since they'd done an excellent job of keeping him safe and had helped build him from a frightened child into a man who was the best possible king in her opinion. On the other hand, she wasn't sure she wanted to know what would have happened without Jason's mitigating influence. Ciriis, she feared, would have been happy to control Damien through sex and debauchery, and possibly Adam to let her... all in the name of providing a better government than his grandfather had done. Though perhaps she was doing them a disservice to think such things.

Had Lady Theresa done much the same? Letting him hide in the library for five years seemed, now that she thought on it, rather less than a caring person should have done. By his own accounts, the only times he had left it had been when he was required to clean himself up and appear at a dinner with the old king. And surely there was no one besides the Dowager Baroness – or, apparently, the servants – who had known where to find him to make that happen. And Damien seemed convinced that Lady Theresa had no idea how well he had educated himself beyond the fairy stories and legends... had she paid him no more attention than a pet cat? Or, worse yet, someone *else's* pet cat...

But what was Lady Theresa's long game, then?

Ciriis had yielded to Genevieve's 'interference' in her plans for the Realm with fairly poor grace; Genevieve had accused her of malfeasance but had become convinced that the dark-haired woman had not actually realized how dangerous it was to mess with a soul-bonding. Seven long years of taking care of Damien in every conceivable way had not led her – or Adam – to particularly *respect* their young king, but they seemed genuinely fond of him. And they had taken him – *wooed him* – away from Lady Theresa. Ciriis had said that Lady Theresa was Genevieve's 'adherent' and was planning the wedding enthusiastically...

Was that because Ciriis' influence was thereby diminished?

"Thank you, Elista," Genevieve pulled her mind back into the present. "You saved him then, and you may have saved him now."

Elista ducked her head and dipped a micro-curtsy. "Anything we can do, milady. We're all right furious that our men in the Castle Guard were hurt because of food we prepared and served. Cook is too upset to talk to you himself, but we'd all swear – we've been over it a dozen times – that no one touched the Guards' mess save us."

Genevieve gave her an understanding look. "We're dealing with a sorcerer, Elista, who can control the very mice and birds. You've fought for Damien today, when you know how much it could cost you."

The senior maid gave her a worried smile. "The Captain of the Castle Guard isn't here, milady. We don't know where he is, but we've no call to think he was... was slain. I'd hoped His Majesty could find Robert..." Worry was giving way to heartfelt fear, and her eyes were bright with suppressed tears.

"Your – sweetheart?" Genevieve guessed.

"My husband," Elista replied. "We've three children down in the city, with my mother."

"A blessing..." Genevieve murmured, thinking of her own unborn child. Perhaps never-to-be-born if Queen Marian was right. Was something wrong with her? "We'll watch for him, Elista. Perhaps it's him in that other room."

The woman gave her a nod that didn't allow for much hope. They all knew that Lord Prydeen and his bullyboys were past masters at making bodies vanish. Their only cause for hope here was that there was no reason they would have bothered; the bodies of the other Guards they'd slain had been left out for the servants to deal with.

Elista took a calming breath and resurrected the sense of grim serenity that had marked her out from among all the rest. "It's nigh on breakfast time, milady. They'll think it odd up there if we don't get to serving."

Genevieve looked out over the kitchen with concern. "Is there food to be served? We've made a right mess of things..."

"Oh, that was luncheon preparations, milady. The breakfast things are set aside." She gave the younger woman a knowing look. "You've been trained only in the ruling, haven't you, milady? You'll be needing a true Chatelaine for running the castle when this is done."

Genevieve gave her a wry smile. "And I should choose more wisely than poor Damien did? Truer words never – no!" She gasped. "Does Lady Theresa come down to the kitchens at all?"

"At least once a day, yes," Elista answered. "She has her consult with Cook, then with me, then with the chief butler... oh. I take your meaning. No one would have batted an eye if it were her ladyship checking on the soldiers' mess. She's usually seen such details as beneath her dignity, but she looks over the various foods in preparation often enough that no one would have thought it odd." She looked even grimmer. "If that's so, someone will recall it. And then there'll be those of us with more to task her for, personally, than a high and mighty manner." She looked significantly at the bodies laid out on the tables, mercifully covered with good linen sheets now.

The Queen-to-be regarded the determined senior maid. "The disposition of traitors to the crown will be His Majesty's duty and privilege, Elista."

The woman waved this off with a twitch of her pristine apron. "Wouldn't dirty our hands with the likes of her, milady. Or whomever it was did it. I'll ask around, but I'll reserve judgment until we have some evidence. May we get started with serving breakfast?"

"Certainly," Genevieve approved. "Let's not alert the enemy to the fact that anything has happened."

Elista nodded again, bobbed another small curtsy, and headed back to work.

The Rebel Duchess sighed and headed back to her own work.

Chapter SEVENTEEN

Dear Enemies

A TRIO OF MAIDS CARRYING breakfast trays came down the corridor, just as they did every day. Two, each of whose load looked heavier than that of the third, turned to the left and headed up the spiraling stone stairs towards the king's apartment. The third approached the door on the same level as the corridor.

One of the two tall men in Siovale's colors who stood ready at the door accepted the tray from the third maid. The other looked suspiciously at her. "What happened to the usual girl?" he demanded.

"She's sick," the woman answered, beginning to turn away. Suspicions mollified; the guard knocked on the door to signal someone inside to open it.

"Wait," said the guard with the tray. "I know you. You're–"

He stopped speaking as Genevieve whirled around and placed a knife at his throat. Her eyes widened. "Douglas. Don't make me use this." It was one of the men she had once sparred with... ten years agone. One of a handful of men who had stayed on after her wedding to bolster Harald's status. She had wondered, since, whether Tomas had sent them along to keep an eye on his reckless younger brother.

Harald had sent them all home to Siovale shortly before he had insisted on moving her to the more private apartment...

"Milady," the startled Douglas said automatically.

The stout oaken door was too thick to call through, and it was already opening in answer to the knock. The second guard – a man she didn't know – was cursing as he tried to stop the door from being opened, and the tray dropped from Douglas' nerveless fingers as he felt his blood pulse against the sharp edge of her blade. The ring of the metal tray against stone and the sound of breaking crockery was loud in the silent hallways and Genevieve cursed – silently – though the invaders were really spread too thin for anyone else to be likely to hear it.

"I wouldn't, if I were you." Damien's calm voice sounded beside her. He had insisted he be as close behind her as the subterfuge allowed... meaning just past the nearest turn of the corridor. The Monarch's Blade now had its tip hovering very close to the second guard's vulnerable throat. He walked the guard back, inch by inch, and gestured the men behind him to rush the door as it opened.

The plan worked flawlessly, and they were inside the rooms that had been Genevieve's without shedding blood. Douglas and his mate were marched inside, and two of Damien's Castle Guard in Siovale colors – their uniforms stolen from a raid on the barracks – were stationed at the door.

Two of Lord Prydeen's bullyboys had gone down in the sitting room under the fast movements of the Castle Guardsmen. One's throat was cut; the other had a contusion on the side of his head that suggested he might not wake up. Unlike the two Siovalese men-at-arms, no pains had been taken to ensure the safety of these jumped-up scum of the darkest streets.

Genevieve opened the door to the bedroom, her heart in her mouth. Could it be?

Duke Tomas looked at her from the bed she had once slept in, and raised his eyebrows. "Genevieve?"

She stepped back, blushing furiously, and Damien gave her a curious look.

"It's Tomas," she explained. "He's... still in bed." And apparently had the habit of sleeping in the nude. And must have had a restless night.

"Hmmmn." Damien nudged her out of the doorway and stepped through without hesitation.

Feeling obliged to guard his back, she stepped in after him, trying to look anywhere but at her former brother-in-law.

"It's good to see you, my lord Duke," Damien began as casually as if they were meeting in his audience chamber, and he didn't have his unsheathed Sword leveled at the naked nobleman.

"Likewise, Your Majesty," Duke Tomas said just as calmly. "I haven't been feeling quite myself lately." Genevieve gave him a sharp look as he used Damien's title easily.

"Indeed," the young king replied. "How so, Your Grace?"

"I seem to be missing some of my memories," the duke explained. "I have no idea how I ended up *here*, for example. I've been here for a few days, and I've been informed I may not leave. My brother Harald has come by and informed me that I am supporting his bid for the throne, on the strength of him apparently being an illegitimate son of the 'old' king. Which, I suppose, means that your grandfather cuckolded my father. And I have been made party to all of this by giving shelter to Harald and imprisoning Duke Aldred for the last two years."

His eyes flickered to Genevieve, then returned to Damien. "Somehow, I know that King Reginald has died and that *you* are our new monarch. I don't quite know why or how I have that information. I would swear I'd never seen you before in my life. Harald also informs me that my three sons are hostage to my support of him – and I only remember having *two* sons." A blaze of anger in those dark eyes now.

A shock ran through Genevieve at hearing the old king's name. How did *Tomas* know it? And how had *she* forgotten?

"Ah." The young king inclined his head. "Am I given to understand, my lord Duke, that you would see these things righted if you could?"

"Damn straight, I would."

"Even if it meant your brother's life? There... is not much that can be done for an usurper."

Duke Tomas sat up slowly, mindful of the Sword held rather negligently in Damien's hand. "Harald has been nothing but a pain in the arse since he was a boy," the duke growled. "Our – *my* –

father asked me to look after him, or I'd have thrown him out on his ear. He's stolen my memories of my *son.*" He looked at Genevieve. "When you offered to marry him to bring Siovale into the Rebellion, Genevieve, I feared he would cause trouble, but there seemed no other pledge to make that both sides would trust. I could never have imagined *this.*"

Damien looked at Tomas thoughtfully. "Will you swear yourself my vassal then, Duke Tomas? I can protect your mind from further incursions once you are sworn to me."

He could?

Tomas poured himself out of the bed, to kneel on the floor. He bent his head and offered up his hands. "I will."

Damien sheathed the Monarch's Blade and took the kneeling man's hands in his.

"Tomas Elsevier, wilt thou guide and guard my fair province of Siovale as its Duke, placing the needs of thy people before thy own and caring always for their prosperity and well-being?"

"I so swear."

"And wilt thou take me as thy liege-lord, accepting the rule of my fair province of Siovale in my name? Wilt thou further swear to be a loyal and faithful subject of this Realm and to raise arms only in the defense of thy people of Siovale or of this Realm?"

"I so swear." He gave Damien nearly a twin of the look Genevieve must have worn on her own face when she had taken the oath at his hands.

"Then accept my fair province from my hands unto thine and rise. From the Power granted me by the Gods as King of this fair Realm, I create thee Tomas Elsevier, Duke of Siovale."

This time Genevieve could see the sparkles of magick that flowed from Damien's hands to Tomas'. Could *feel*, through her bond to Damien, how Tomas was being linked into the web of the Realm. His stunned expression told her that he had not expected any of this. And he had sworn to the old king, to *King Reginald*, so *he* should have known what to expect. The Vassal's Oath given to Damien was truly a different beast.

He stood up slowly, blinking as if all the world were new. Then shook himself, and gave Damien a fierce grin that held nothing of humor. "Let's get that bastard brother of mine off your throne."

The young king inclined his head. "We have a plan in motion, Your Grace. Genevieve, my love, perhaps we should step out to allow Duke Tomas to put on some clothes."

Damien led Tomas and Douglas up the magickal stair, with Genevieve leading the other Siovalese man-at-arms – who had been relieved to see his Duke well and more than willing to follow new directives – and one of his own Castle Guard. Another group was making a frontal assault on the normal stairs, as a distraction.

The young king only wished that he could have left Genevieve back on this mission, but he needed her to bring more fighters up. He would have spared her this if he could.

Actually, *she* had tried to send *him* to rescue the ladies of his Royal Guard instead, quite reasonably suggesting that some of them might be hurt and need his Healing touch.

And *he* had wanted to send *her* to find her father. Or to take back the castle gates. Or anywhere other than having her confront Harald again. His instinct to protect her from all harms to body and spirit was something he was going to have to set aside, he realized wryly; she would be his warrior-Queen, and if anyone did the protecting, it would likely be her.

At least the minor delay while Tomas Elsevier got dressed had given Genevieve the time to change back into her own hunting leathers. She'd looked fetching in a castle maid's uniform, but being dressed in more fighting-capable clothing would likely make it easier for her to deal with Harald. Although… most of those were the garments she'd worn when she'd been Harald's captive…

They emerged into the upper chamber in the usual space, and had the distinct lack of pleasure to interrupt the illegitimate king hard at work attempting to produce yet more illegitimate heirs. For a horrible moment, Damien thought that the girl in Harald's bed was one of the maids who had brought up his breakfast; that he had himself sent her into this situation.

An even more horrible moment later he realized it was the beautiful and fragile-seeming Lady Aryllis Ieldore who was suffering the usurper's attentions. Damien's one-time lover. Sir Tim's fiancée.

Fury swelled, and what he would have done, he didn't know... it was important that Harald be captured alive, but...

A slender sword-tip appeared inches from the big man's chest. It wasn't his.

"Get off of her, you oaf," Genevieve hissed as Harald suddenly froze in shock. "Move!"

"Genny...?" the big man mumbled in sex-fogged bafflement.

"Off!" She emphasized it by drawing a few drops of blood.

Harald scrambled backwards.

"Ryll, are you okay?" Genevieve's sword-point followed the big man back, but her tone was all solicitude. *Damien* hadn't had any notion that Aryllis had a nickname.

"I will be," the other woman replied grimly. "Is... Tim all right?"

"Safe and secure. Broken ribs. Damien's picked up a few new tricks. Once we get him back to Tim, he can fix your lad right up." Genevieve waved at the other men. "Go clear out the sitting room."

Duke Tomas grinned that fierce grin again. "You heard the Queen-to-be." On his way past, he slapped his erstwhile brother on the shoulder. "I told you not to underestimate this one. Pity for *you* that you didn't listen."

"Tom...?" Harald mumbled in confusion.

Duke Tomas snorted.

"There's four men in the sitting room," Aryllis volunteered. "Two Siovalese, two of Lord Prydeen's."

Duke Tomas bowed to her. "Then we should have more help than we dared count on, milady. Your Majesty," he turned to Damien, "do you stay back from danger while we clear out the rabble."

The young king inclined his head graciously. His small experiences of fighting thusfar had cured him of any romantic notions. Far better to allow those who were good at it to do the fighting. And he was disinclined to leave Genevieve and Aryllis alone with Harald.

"Aryllis?" he asked, putting a world of question into his tone.

"I volunteered to be here, Damien," she replied. "Better me than Kamauri or Terellie. Or Lena..."

"She's alive?" he exclaimed, his heart leaping.

"If you can call it that. She seems fine, but her mind is as a child's. Not that this great oaf cared, since her body is all *he* wanted." Aryllis glared at Harald, pushing her fine white-gold hair out of her face. "I couldn't let her go through this. Not while she's... like that."

Damien tried to wrap his head around the idea of golden, laughing Lena alive... but with the mind of a child.

"You haven't the brains the Gods gave little green apples, do you, Harald? Or the conscience of a thief?" Genevieve commented.

"A thief like your precious 'Erawan'?" he sneered, at last recovering his wits enough to say something. "Aren't you a little old to be idol-worshiping fairy stories, Genny? I heard what you were doing when you arrived in the city."

The Rebel Duchess laughed at him. "Better fairy stories than delusions of grandeur. You never bothered to listen to anything about the Stellarine family, did you, Harald? Erawan the Kind Robber was my great-grandmother, the Princess Alexandria Alsterling. *My* claim to the throne is as good as Damien's, and far better than that of a cuckoo's bastard chick."

Harald gaped again, as his half-brother stuck his head back through the door. "King Damien? It's all clear out here, Your Majesty."

"Tomas!" Harald roared.

The Duke of Siovale regarded his bastard brother coolly. "You sought to *compel* my support, Harald. Don't be surprised that I make a different choice when the compulsion is broken." There was... something wrong about all of that... but the man had pledged his oath to Damien and was magickally bound. Not to mention that his ire at having been so deceived, at having lost a precious piece of his youngest child's life, was certainly not feigned.

Harald fumbled at a pendant on a thick chain about his neck, muttering. He looked expectantly at Tomas. The Duke winced a bit, but stared him down regardless. "His Majesty has warded me against your foul spells. As is a *true* king's duty to his sworn vassals." He narrowed his eyes. "Was that meant to be a chain about your neck or a chain about my soul, Harald?"

"Let's move this into the next room," Damien suggested mildly.

Genevieve began to prod Harald with the tip of her sword until he moved, not hesitating to draw blood as she did so. Tomas had his own sword unsheathed and looked willing to use it as well.

Damien started to follow, then turned to Aryllis. "Do you need anything, dearheart?"

She gave him a wavery smile. "I'll just clean myself up and get dressed, Damien. Go be king." Her expression grew fierce. "And take *all* the bastards down."

He bowed respectfully. "That is my plan, milady Ieldore," and he strolled into the sitting room that had been his since his elevation to Heir.

Damien was well aware that it wasn't merely what he did, but how he did it that was important. Tomas and Genevieve were both sworn to him now, but he had left them an out in their oaths intentionally, and was even more glad of it after realizing that he was actually binding them magickally. While his grandfather's binding had not been magickal, so far as he knew, the oaths sworn by men and women of good conscience could harm them as surely as any magickal consequence, were they forced to break their word.

Thus, he would bind them to the Realm and to the people, but not to himself.

An older version of the Vassal's Oath, he had told Genevieve. And it was. This was the Oath as it had first been given, by kings and queens who claimed their power by the acclaim of the people – and lost it if the people's confidence was lost. Which was as it should be.

Damien knew he wasn't worthy of his people's confidence. But he was beginning to realize that no one ever really was. He was a caretaker for a Realm that was broken by his grandfather's long reign. It was his task to restore the Realm, to rebuild the noble class to live up to their name, to end the Rebellion that had taken so many lives, to reclaim the Lost Provinces. And, yes, to provide an Heir who could carry on the work and, perhaps, be a more worthy recipient of the people's faith than he, himself.

And **now** *you* **are** *ready, grandson,* Queen Marian's voice echoed in his ears.

And then, perhaps, he could let himself dissolve into the fabric of the Realm...

He could 'hear' her tongue clicking in disapproval. *And then you backslide. Welladay. It will be years before that day might come. Your Genevieve might change your mind by then.*

Damien let a mild smile form on his face, and moved to sit in his usual, favorite chair, stretching his legs out to rest his heels on the low table, ankles crossed, as he leaned back and tented his hands casually, elbows on the arms of the chair. A pair of Lord Prydeen's bullyboys were held by two of the Siovalese men-at-arms that he didn't recognize – presumably the ones who had been placed here to guard Harald but had defected from that duty when so instructed by their sworn lord. Genevieve prodded the usurper into place to face Damien, and Tomas stood alertly to his brother's other side, sword drawn. The remaining men kept a close eye on the three prisoners.

"A kingly breakfast," he commented, looking over the heaps of rich and expensive foods – pastries covered in chocolate and sugar, fat-trimmed steak, pheasant dripping with gravy and decorated with its own colorful feathers. He picked up a donut and began to nibble on it, less out of hunger than to establish that all things meant for the king were *his*.

"You won't get away with this," Harald said threateningly. "Prydeen wants *me* on the throne, not you."

Damien raised his eyebrows. "Really. Somehow, I think he could be persuaded to change his plans if you were no longer... available."

"You think my *wife* or my *brother* is going to kill me, little man?" Harald sneered. For a naked man with swords pointed at him, the big fellow actually did a fair job of keeping his cool. Damien almost had to admire him for his gall. Unless it was simply such a lack of intelligence and imagination that he literally could not accept that the tables had turned. "Or these men from Siovale who've known me since I was a boy?"

"I ceased being your *wife* when you kidnapped my father and faked your deaths," Genevieve snarled.

"And knowing you from childhood may not be a point in your favor," Tomas added dryly. "As for being my brother – you can hardly imagine I take pride in knowing my mother cuckolded my father to produce *you.*"

Damien waved them to silence. "It's all beside the point now. Harald, you made a play for the throne, and you failed. The traditional punishment for such treachery is to be nailed above the castle gates. Alive, I might add. At least at first." Sardonically, he noted that this last finally made the big man pale. "It's supposed to be a fairly effective discouragement to others with the same idea. And you are hardly unique in claiming to be an illegitimate offspring of my grandfather."

"You wouldn't..." Harald looked faintly greenish now. He grasped for his bluster and sneer. "You're not man enough. Admit it, Damien. You're a virgin when it comes to killing. You're not going to string me up when you can hardly stand the sight of blood."

He had a point...

It's not like you'd be doing it entirely yourself, Queen Marian commented caustically. *Or that you need to go look at him once he's up there. I had to execute a few people that way – including my poor cousin Larissa. And Gods only know how many people Reggie put up there.*

"It's not the way I'd prefer to begin my reign," Damien admitted easily. "My poor people have been through enough, and I hardly think seeing your rotting corpse covered with flies is going to do much to reassure them that things have changed." His eyes flickered to the bullyboys. "Now seeing *Lord Prydeen* up there might have an entirely salutary effect..."

One of them had a rather dazed expression, but the other one sneered rather more effectively than Harald and seemed amused at the thought that Damien might take down the sorcerer. "Little boy like you's gonna try to take down milord? He won't even bother."

Damien smiled, and he thought he saw Genevieve blink at his expression. He felt a bit predatory, and hadn't bothered to conceal it. Several ideas were beginning to gel in his mind, and he found himself almost looking forward to confronting the sorcerer who had been the architect of so much of his people's – and his personal – misery.

"Normally, I'd agree with you, sirrah. But he's gone to all the trouble to crown Harald and present him to the city as king. I believe I have *bait*..."

Chapter EIGHTEEN

Truths That Cut

THE DOORS TO THE GREAT audience chamber burst open – literally burst, exploding into splinters as Lord Prydeen stalked in, his cape swirling around him. A handful of his bullyboys spread out behind him.

"Do you think to stand against me, *boy?*" he demanded.

"My dear Lord Prydeen," Damien responded lightly, ignoring the flamboyant display – and waste – of magick as if it were inconsequential... as indeed it was. "Surely you didn't mean to place *this* buffoon on Our throne?"

He gestured idly to Harald, still naked, kneeling on the floor with Duke Tomas' sword to his throat. The room was lined with Siovalese men-at-arms and Castle Guardsmen – all of them clearly answering to the young king. The ladies of the Royal Guard added touches of floral brilliance to the dark green and black that were Siovale's colors and the black-trimmed dark blue of the Castle Guard.

Damien was sprawled over the great basalt Throne where he had nearly given up his life to the Realm the previous night. The Monarch's Blade lay unsheathed and shining across his lap, but his posture was calculatedly, insultingly relaxed. He had taken the time to dress as befit a king, in the royal colors of gold and turquoise, his once-stolen crown firmly upon his head, his scarlet and miniver robe draped behind him. Genevieve sat at his feet, be-gowned and bejeweled, with the coronet of the Heir shining on her loosened red-gold locks, and looking rather more alert than he did. She hadn't particularly liked having to set aside her sword and leathers, but had agreed that the portrait they presented was part of their power. Her left hand resided in his right, almost negligently, as if they were any other young betrothed couple.

The tableau they presented was intended to be one of utter ease and power. They'd had to scramble to assemble all of this before the sorcerer had gotten wind of what they were doing. Their people had managed to free Damien's ladies, and the other mystery room had proved to hold his much-abused Captain of the Guard Guard – to the delight and joy of the helpful maid, Elista.

There hadn't been time to hunt for Duke Aldred or secure the Royal Council members.

Damien suspected that there had only been time to do this much because Lord Prydeen had withdrawn to amuse himself in the dungeons... and he feared that Genevieve's father had been stashed there alongside the other unfortunates. At least he'd taken a number of his bullyboys with him to whatever dark entertainments, leaving fewer to subdue or sound the alarm.

After this was over they could rescue the remaining captives.

Those who still survived.

The sorcerer's eyes narrowed at her. "Apparently, I should have taken the time to properly deal with *you*, Lady Genevieve. You've managed to make a fool of *three* kings now."

She bristled, but stayed silent.

"Harald hardly needs help with that," Damien commented. "And Our grandfather – *King Reginald,*" he emphasized the name and thought he saw the sorcerer's eyes widen slightly, "Was many things, but never a fool. For love or anything else. As to whether *We* are a fool..." He waved negligently. "Your game is up, Lord Prydeen. Your power is broken and you are no longer welcome in Our Realm."

"Bold words," the sorcerer returned. "Do you think you'll keep that throne long, Damien? Your grandfather needed me, and so will you. And if you think not... there are other fools than that one, or perhaps this time I shall not bother with a puppet at all."

Genevieve laughed. "I rather doubt King Reginald was *your* puppet, sorcerer. You were *his*, were you not? His lackey – in more ways than one? The apprentice he carefully kept his secrets from, who ran his errands and did his dirty work." She leaned forward. "Are you a regicide as well, *'Lord'* Prydeen? Did you steal King Reginald's powers by stealing his name? Why then, you have surely lost them again."

He glowered at her briefly, but denied nothing, then turned his attention back to Damien. "I am the most powerful sorcerer in this Realm *now*, and with the resources I can now command, unfettered, my reign shall last a thousand years. I have no interest in administering the Realm. I would have permitted you to keep your crown and throne, your pretty girls, even *that* one," he indicated Genevieve, "but you have proven too troublesome."

Damien inclined his head ironically. "Coming from you, my lord, a compliment. But let us cease with these unnecessary preliminaries. You are no longer welcome in Our Realm, nor shall We inflict your presence upon Our neighbors. You will yield yourself immediately or suffer the consequences."

Lord Prydeen actually blinked, as if he hadn't believed that the young king would dare issue him an ultimatum. Unfortunately, he recovered himself quickly. "I think not, young fool. Bring him in," he called over his shoulder.

Genevieve's hand tightened on Damien's.

They had not been able to locate Duke Aldred. There was little doubt that *he* was the bargaining chip being brought in. Queen Marian wasn't very happy about this either, but they had all prepared for this tactic as best they could.

What Damien was *not* prepared for was that the person escorting Duke Aldred in – and holding the knife to his throat – was Lady Theresa Anvliyar. Genevieve's hand tightened further on his, and a feeling of sad apology drifted across the bond from her. She had known, apparently, though there was a sense that she had not known for terribly long and that she simply hadn't had time to warn him.

The young king forced his expression to stay mild, and his tone neutral. He had small doubt that he succeeded; he had, after all, spent his entire life dissembling to this man in particular. "I see you're still resorting to compulsion spells."

"Not at all," Lord Prydeen's spotty, withered face contorted in a cruel smile. "This is your chance, my dear. Tell the young *king* what you think of him – of all the Alsterlings, for that matter." He gestured to his bullyboys to take Lady Theresa's place holding Duke Aldred.

"No."

Damien looked at Genevieve in surprise as she rose, still clasping his fingers tightly.

"Dowager Baroness, your plaint will be heard in its own fair time. You will have your day in Court, even to reprimanding the entire Alsterling line, should you choose it. But unless it is Cedarwen Vale that challenges the King, you will stand down."

"Bold words from a girl without a title of her own," Lady Theresa sneered.

"I am the Duchess of Elaarwen, confirmed and sworn and Bound to the land. I am Heir to the Throne, as designated by the duly crowned King." Genevieve told her calmly. "Bold words from a woman whose own title is only by courtesy. Stand down, Lady, or you place Cedarwen in rebellion against the Crown, with all the consequence that may befall therefrom."

"No more than you and your father have done with Elaarwen! What consequence to that?" the woman retorted.

Damien couldn't see his betrothed's face to be sure, but he knew she must have met her father's eyes by the small nod Duke Aldred gave her. "I – and my father before me – have known we might lay down our lives for the Rebellion."

"But instead, *you* merely lie down," Lady Theresa sneered. "Such a brave warrior you are to vanquish such a dissolute young man in the bedroom."

Damien was ready to respond to that, but Genevieve wasn't done. "So I have done before for the greater good of the Realm." She didn't have to look at Harald. "But not this time." She tightened her grip on Damien's hand and he could feel down the bond that she had just fitted some things together in her strategist's mind. "Tell me, Lady Theresa, when you betrayed Cedarwen – and Princess Kandra – were you prepared to lay down *your* life? Does your son, Raphael, who now rules there, know how you gave over his father and his true love to King Reginald and Lord Prydeen?"

Kandy... Damien had to truly struggle for composure this time. His sister had been twelve years older than him. He'd adored her and followed her around until she called him a pest and drove him off, always coming by later to ruffle his hair and give him a hug and listen to the stories he played out with his toys... but she hadn't confided in him. He'd overheard his parents talking to her about a marriage, but hadn't paid much attention to whom... his nine-year-old focus had been on the fact that she would be going away, much as she had when she joined the army when he was six. Had she been planning to marry the Heir to Cedarwen? Lady Theresa's son, Raphael?

"She would have destroyed Cedarwen," Lady Theresa hissed. "She and my foolish husband were planning to bring us over to your Rebellion. It took everything I had to make sure my Raphael stayed clean of it, and still the king kept me here as *Librarian* – to ensure his loyalty." She laughed slightly hysterically. "As if Raphael has wanted anything to do with me since then."

Duke Aldred cleared his throat. "We'd been in communication with Prince Eric and Lady Miria through Princess Kandra, Lord Raphael, and Baron Seldrig for some months."

The young king's mind was leaping. His parents – and Kandy. A royal prince joining the Rebellion... No wonder his grandfather had them executed. And he... he himself might have grown up in Elaarwen, in peace and love instead of fear and desperate loneliness. Beside Genevieve. She might never have married Harald...

"A *Librarian*... Useless, powerless position." Lady Theresa was still fuming. "After all I gave up, such an insult. And then the king ordered me to look after his *grandson* after I discovered him lurking in my library a month later – the *brother* of that chit who broke my family."

Ordered... So, it had all been an act. A month... Someone had left food for him before that. Who? A picture came over the bond from Genevieve's mind: a maid from the kitchens, the one who had offered maps of the castle. A kind face, and a familiar one, though he didn't know her name. The wife of the Captain of his Castle Guard, he realized.

But... the one person who seemed to know and care about him even a little had been ordered to do so. By the same king who had executed his parents in front of him.

And giving her prominence as his Secretary and Chatelaine, having Ciriis – his true second-in-command – report to her, none of it compensated for the insult she felt she'd been dealt. After she had betrayed his sister. And his parents. To their deaths.

He could not – *could not* – think about this right now.

Damien focused on Lord Prydeen, who was gloating. This was going according to *his* plan, it seemed, despite the young king's careful preparations and Genevieve's attempt to intervene. If she'd had the power to have Lady Theresa carried off without beginning a brawl... they had enough guardsmen to overwhelm Lord Prydeen's bullyboys, but the young king and his advisors didn't want to see how Lord Prydeen's power might be turned against the others. He knew, *bone-deep*, that with the Sword and the Throne and Genevieve wearing the Ring he could *stand* against Lord Prydeen... but he was less sure he could *defeat* him... or *protect* the innocent bystanders whose presence had been necessary to lure the sorcerer here and to demonstrate how much control he had lost to Damien.

The young king's instinct told him that the sorcerer must be enticed to strike first.

But he must be ready to respond instantly, and now his attention was scattered by 'what-ifs' and 'might-have-beens'.

"Lord *Prydeen* understood," Lady Theresa was sniffling. "*He* knew what I had given up. *He* understood what I'd prevented – King Reginald's own son and Heir going over to the Rebellion!" His father had worn the Heir's Ring? Damien's attempt to pull his scattered wits together dissipated again. "Why, the Rebels would have had a claim on the throne itself!"

"We already did," Genevieve said dryly. "My father's claim is as good as Prince Eric's."

"Pishposh," the older woman replied. "The son of Princess Alexandria's *bastard* daughter? Compared to the *trueborn* son of King Reginald. Hardly." Even Harald raised his head to glare at her over that one.

"This isn't getting us anywhere," Damien interjected, making sure his tone was slightly bored. "Stories of what happened fourteen or fifteen years ago aren't going to change what needs to happen right now."

Lord Prydeen gave him a sly look. "'*Fourteen or fifteen years ago*'. As if you don't remember." He gestured, and his bullyboys pulled Duke Aldred forwards. To a particular set of flagstones stained a dark shade...

Oh, Gods. Fourteen years to the *day*.

How could he possibly have put it out of his head so thoroughly that he had lost track...?

And he was about to see Genevieve's father slaughtered on the same exact spot.

Damien could feel himself going pale. He could fake his demeanor, his tone... but not this.

Duke Aldred looked serene. His eyes met his daughter's, and her hand in Damien's began to tremble. Then he looked at the young king. He wasn't resigned to this fate. He still had hope. But the old duke's hope, his optimism, was not focused on himself. It was focused on his daughter, on his province, on the Realm that he had been born to rule and never would.

Abruptly Damien remembered that Queen Marian had said that the Sword had spoken for one other after her besides himself. And he knew who that other had been.

And why Princess Alexandria, in her not-so-old age, had sacrificed her life to get the Sword out of Elaarwen before her hotheaded daughter could attempt an unprepared and unsuccessful coup in the name of her young son.

Duke Aldred would lay down his life for the Realm, just as he, Damien, had been willing to do mere hours ago. Because it was his birthright. Because the Realm was more important than either of them. Because it would let Damien and Genevieve have a chance to defeat Lord Prydeen.

If so much might be conveyed in a single glance, how much more might Damien learn if he could only save Duke Aldred's life?

Genevieve's hand crept to her abdomen... a last gift, to tell her father that a grandchild would come. The old man's eyes lit. She sat down at Damien's feet again, slowly and with all the grace of a warrior born and trained... but the young king knew it was because she could not trust her knees to hold her any longer.

Unfortunately, her small gesture had been noted by others as well.

"A child already?" Lord Prydeen crowed. "They say soul-bonds are fruitful. What a pity that–"

"You lied to me!" Harald roared over the sorcerer's words, surging to his feet and batting his brother's sword out of the way before the duke could react. Damien had asked Tomas not to actually kill him – it was grimly necessary to publicly execute the usurper – so Harald got several feet closer to Genevieve than he should have before a handful of Siovalese men restrained him. "You *bitch!* You swore you were trying to conceive! Eight wasted years! But you're with *him* for less than a *month* and he knocks you up! You wouldn't even let me *touch* you until we were married!"

Damien felt Genevieve recoiling slightly from the big man's fury. He wondered uneasily how many bruises she had suffered over this specific complaint.

"It's the soul-bond," Lady Theresa informed the irate man, somehow managing to look down her nose despite his far greater height. "It makes even the infertile conceive. It can't be the *boy* – else every one of those so-called *ladies* over there would have borne his whelps." She dismissed the Royal Guardswomen with a sniff that turned the word 'ladies' into a deadly insult.

And from the ladies in question... "Have you never heard of contraceptives, old doomcrow?" Aryllis asked scornfully. The others were – thankfully – chuckling. At least some of them were. Damien dared not spare a glance and simply prayed that the blood that had drained from his face moments earlier had not returned full force.

Harald was still roaring. Tomas came up and gave him a ringing slap to the head, shutting him up at least momentarily.

Could this go any further from his plan to force the sorcerer's hand? The young king would have put his face in his hands if he could. He should have kept the room empty except for himself and Genevieve, needed bait or not.

"A child..." Lord Prydeen was staring at Genevieve. "They say men – and women – will fight harder for a child of their own getting than for any other cause. It was certainly true for our lovely Lady Theresa." He smiled at the woman, who nodded back regally, not seeming to notice the nasty quirk to his lips. "No one would have been good enough for her Raphael. Certainly not a princess who would lower herself to enlist as a common foot soldier. Not even if that was what won his heart... or would give him a chance at the throne."

"The throne or the executioner's block," Lady Theresa sniffed.

"Indeed. What a choice." His eyes glittered. "A child can compel such complete rejection of reasoned risk. One expects to lose one's parents. Eventually." The vile old man's eyes flickered to Duke Aldred. "But a child is supposed to outlive its parents. And of course, the *loss* of a child–"

Beware! Queen Marian's voice snapped. *Ward the child!*

Damien was on his feet, the Sword up, and Genevieve thrust behind him in a heartbeat.

It wasn't fast enough.

He felt the wave of magick, heard her cry out.

Duke Aldred surged forwards in automatic response to her cry. The bullyboys holding him did... something... and he collapsed. Damien wasn't sure what had happened. His attention was divided between Genevieve and Lord Prydeen and he had none to spare even for that wise old man.

The Sword, however, had its own ideas.

Damien had known he had to face Lord Prydeen in this room without knowing exactly why. The Throne was here, of course, and the Sword had helped him *connect* to it, and thence to the Realm. But the *connection* had remained: still dazzlingly powerful when he stood up and stepped away from it now, if not as seductive as last night immediately after that *connection* nearly pulled him down into itself.

He had thought the Throne merely a lock, and the Sword the key; once the door had been opened, the lock was largely pointless.

It was more than a fancy chair. It was more than a lock opened for him. This entire throne-room was more than just a royal audience chamber filled with moldering banners and unspeakable memories.

Now he knew. *Now* he understood his instinct. This was the Center of the monarch's Power. Magickal, temporal... moral. Had his grandfather chosen to rule from a different seat, the rot would not have spread so far.

The Throne called up the Realm, and the Sword focused it.

The Ring... it should have protected Genevieve, and by extension, the child barely three days conceived. He would have to trust. He felt anger and vengefulness, but no pain down the bond.

The Sword – wanted him to protect Duke Aldred.

And Lord Prydeen had made the first strike.

It had been... *weaker* than he had expected, actually.

The old sorcerer continued to throw Power at him – at them. Genevieve's hand remained clasped in Damien's. She was his link to a reality beyond a Realm that recognized Lord Prydeen as a source of its pain and sought its own revenge. The young king was less trying to defeat the sorcerer than to restrain the Realm from wholly obliterating him – and anything in its way, such as himself, the room, the people, the Castle... the *City*...

But not Duke Aldred.

Almost absently, Damien blocked spells that seemed like blobs of unfocused magick rather than planned attacks. When Lord Prydeen sent one off towards the other inhabitants of the room, Damien blocked that almost absently also. The Sword was focused on Duke Aldred, and his own attention was, perforce, as well.

Barely noticing, the young king was descending from his dais, the Sword having decided he did not need the physical connection to the Throne any longer. It was taking him to Duke Aldred.

His offhanded approach to a serious mage-battle was enraging Lord Prydeen.

"It is *I* who am Reginald's true Heir!" he shrieked. "*I* who should have inherited his Power. None other served him so well or so long!"

Damien tried to pay attention. "But not so well, actually," he said conversationally. "Or he shouldn't have aged. With that much Power at his disposal, surely he should have been able to keep himself young and healthy. Isn't that what evil sorcerers *do?*"

"It was the Realm," Lord Prydeen returned spitefully. "It ate him away, despite all we could do. No matter how much Power he took in. No matter how he obtained that Power. As it will eat you, too, *boy*. In the end I had to sever his connection to the Realm to bind what Power he had left before it devoured him entirely and there was nothing left for me to claim."

Damien looked at him curiously, still in some other space where things were... not so urgent. The Sword's perspective perhaps? The

Realm's itself? His sense of time and space seemed very... different than he was used to.

He was still fending off the attacks – even as they dimmed in intensity – as if brushing off a persistent fly. "But you can't sever a King from his Realm – he didn't have all the proper Bindings without the Sword, but he'd sat on that Throne so long that he'd been Bound to it in his own way." Light dawned. "*That's* why you're losing your Power. My own completed Binding to the Realm broke the lesser one you tried with his name. *That's* why we can remember his name now." He blinked. "But *you* didn't feel that break. You didn't *know.*"

"Perhaps I should have taken you as *my* apprentice, boy," Lord Prydeen said grudgingly. "If Reginald had only let me." He shook his head. "More like he would have forsaken me for an apprentice of his own bloodline. The very last – and the only one with such potential. What irony." He laughed – painfully. The effort of pounding at Damien was using up his stores of energy, and he was a very, very old man after all. Some of that energy had gone to maintaining his life.

"Irony?" Damien asked.

"*You* won't even care that the Realm will devour you, because you'll die of natural causes long before you even notice. Oh, you'll be old by normal standards." The evil old man had sunk to his hands and knees, and was panting, though he still raised a hand to shoot off yet another blast at increasingly infrequent intervals. "The Gift that drew me to Reginald's attention was prophecy, young king. Foresight. The things that are most our own are what we are left with at the end. So, mark my words. You'll have no firstborn to rule after you. *She* will never conceive your firstborn – at least not first."

"Are you literally cursing us with your dying breath?"

"Not a curse... a vision. And your youngest will be *my* true Heir." The sorcerer smirked. "What a *champion* of a problem for you, young king."

And with no more ado, the second-most evil sorcerer in the Realm collapsed and breathed no more. His body looked more sunken and dilapidated with every second, and Damien wondered if there would be enough of him *left* to nail to the castle walls.

The Sword – which he now knew was really the Realm, manifest and focused – and Genevieve, both tugged him down to Duke Aldred's side.

The bullyboys had cut his wrists and he was almost bled out.

"Love... you... child..." the old man gasped as his daughter pulled his head onto her lap, weeping. "Bless... you... both..." He smiled. "All."

"Damien!" Genevieve cried, but he was already moving to lay his hands on the duke, the Sword clattering to the floor in all contravention of everything Jason had taught him. He hadn't needed it to Heal the soldiers – or his ladies, when they had found and liberated them. It made sense actually, for a sword seemed a poor tool for healing. This seemed to be his own personal Gift, given by the Realm or awoken by his contact with it, he did not know.

He stopped the bleeding. Closed and sealed Duke Aldred's wounds. Mended a dozen smaller cuts and bruises.

But the Duke was nearly sixty, and he had been abused and half-starved for the last three years. Damien could not replace nutrients that his body did not possess.

And he had lost a lot of blood. Damien could encourage his body to make more, but not, it seemed, fast *enough*.

He met Duke Aldred's eyes and shook his head.

"Well... no pain at least," the duke whispered. "You're a good lad. She deserves good."

Queen Marian's ethereal spirit appeared, kneeling on his other side, and Duke Aldred's eyes widened. "Mother?" he said falteringly.

No, the ancient Queen told him, then looked at Damien. *Give him the Sword, boy. It was meant to be his.*

"Grandmother, if it still speaks for him–" Not that Damien wanted the throne, but it was his responsibility... even if Duke Aldred would be the better king, he could not so simply give over his duties, he realized. And if the Sword chose to see Duke Aldred as a potential usurper instead...

There's no time for this. ***Get the Sword,*** she commanded.

Damien gritted his teeth – it would be like ripping his own arm off to have the Realm unroot itself from his soul, but if it would save Genevieve's father... He could heal. And he could serve the Realm in some other way.

It Chose you, boy, she added more calmly as he stretched to pick it up from where he'd dropped it. *It's not going to* ***un****Choose you.*

The Sword glowed when Damien carefully wrapped Duke Aldred's bloodless fingers around the hilt. Genevieve gasped as the glow grew to surround her father and Damien both. A fainter glow trailed around her... and dissipated off into the air where only the young king and the old duke could see their ancestress.

Color came back into the old man's cheeks – just a pale flush of rose, but enough to suggest that he might not be dying. He breathed more steadily. Damien felt the rush of a pulse as blood flowed back into the fingers he still clasped around the Sword's hilt.

The pulse of the Realm's Power seemed to beat in the hilt itself. In Damien's own veins.

He didn't realize when he stood up.

The Sword stayed in Duke Aldred's hands, still glowing, though not so brightly as he himself was – or so they would tell him later.

There were... pools of darkness. A sense of not-rightness. Pain. A cloudiness of spirit.

Later they told him that he walked through the throne-room, and his light pushed away fears and darkness of soul. Lord Prydeen's bullyboys fell down weeping. Lady Theresa covered her face with her hands. The Siovalese men-at-arms, the castle guardsmen... they came up to him trembling to touch his sleeve, some shuddering away as if burnt, some staring at their fingertips as if they had picked up some of the glow. Harald fainted dead away. Duke Tomas bowed and received a hand on his head that left an afterglow.

Damien knew only that when he knew where he was again, Lena was in front of him. Golden, laughing Lena with her clever tongue and sharp mind, who had emerged from her own tale of horrors to help lead the other ladies out one by one.

Who had told him once, laughing, that if he ever gave up his mad quest for some girl he remembered meeting once she *might* consider marrying him. Or maybe not, she had added. A joke, because as the daughter of a mere squire she was fairly far down on the list of whom he dared grace with the title of Queen-Consort. She had been the only one of 'his' ladies that he had told about Genevieve.

The one who had warded not just him, but all of his Royal Guard by watching over food preparation for them all – and who had truly saved all their lives these last few days because of it.

Lena, with her mischievous humor – he remembered the suggestive meals she'd prepared for him and Genevieve – and her unceasing thoughtfulness. The only one of the secret Royal Guardswomen – other than Ciriis – who had remained unpaired with one of the young knights officially assigned to his Guard.

He could see the huge swelling on her left temple.

The innocent, trusting eyes that looked up at him from the familiar face with the unfamiliar expressions... Lena would not have wanted to live like this.

The Power he pulsed with could kill or heal. If he touched her, he didn't know which way it would go.

He offered her his hands.

She took them trustingly, and held on with a grip of steel as the glow crossed their linked hands and surrounded her.

And, suddenly, she collapsed.

Damien staggered back, utterly drained.

The other ladies had pulled back and barely caught her before her head hit the floor.

"Is she...?" He couldn't bear to ask the question, was vaguely aware that Duke Tomas had come up and was holding him up from collapsing himself.

"She's..." Aryllis' words were swallowed up in a clatter of hooves.

Hooves?

Inside the Castle?

Damien tried to turn quickly and nearly fainted with dizziness.

He had to blink several times to make sense of what he saw, because horses did not belong in his throne-room. Especially – *especially?* – big, sturdy, shaggy drafthorses better suited to pulling wagons than the riders they now bore.

Jason Solway looked down from bestride a horse the height of which even he usually forbore to ride. Following him were most of the men of the Royal Guard, Adam at his side as always.

Damien's Champion surveyed the wreckage of splintered doors beneath his horse's hooves, the weeping bullyboys, dead sorcerer. Genevieve holding her father's head, the old Duke holding the Monarch's Blade. Duke Tomas supporting Damien. The ladies, the castle guard and Siovalese men-at-arms.

"Well," he said, in the understatement of the year, "It seems you were right about re-taking the castle, Genny."

Chapter NINETEEN

Aftermaths...

LATER – *MUCH* LATER – they gathered over dinner in the apartment that was once again Damien's. The castle maids had cleaned and aired it thoroughly while the remaining confusions were sorted out, and the Royal Guard had checked it after them. No trace of Harald's brief occupancy remained to plague them.

Damien, Genevieve, Jason, Adam. Ciriis and Rosa had come in behind, by cart, with the heavily bandaged and sedated Sir Tim, and were present as well. Damien had recovered enough by then to Heal Tim, to Aryllis' relief.

The injured were sleeping, rebuilding strength.

The traitors – Lady Theresa and the Ministers of Trade and Public Works, Lord Prydeen's bullyboys – were in holding cells. *Not* the dungeons, which Damien had left to deal with on the morrow.

Harald... had been nailed to the castle's outer curtain wall beside Lord Prydeen's nearly unrecognizable remains. Facing the city on the spikes that some bloody-minded ancestor had placed there for the purpose. He was, at last survey, still alive. Whether he would be so, come morning, was in doubt.

There was no other way to deal with usurpers and regicides by the codes of the Realm.

Damien swore to find a better answer.

He, of course, had to attend the execution. Had forced himself to set the first nail. Genevieve had set the next. Duke Tomas had set the third, of his own choice; neither King nor Queen-to-be had asked for such a morbid display of loyalty, but it had settled tongues already beginning to wag.

Damien had stayed, watching, until the deed was completed, his arm around Genevieve.

The young king had stayed, watching, while the herald cried out the punishment in accord with the law.

He had stayed, watching, while the hastily written Royal Proclamation was posted for all to read of the treachery of Harald Elsevier – self-claimed bastard of Reginald Alsterling – and how the sorcerer had compelled the obedience of Duke Tomas. And how the Duke had absolved himself and been sworn to the king and Bound to his province. And the second Royal Proclamation stating that Lord Prydeen had declared himself a regicide and the instigator of Harald's treachery.

Damien had stayed when the crowds dispersed. Stayed when even Genevieve went back inside the Castle to see to her father.

Stayed until Duke Tomas finally turned away, stumbling as if blind. He'd taken the Duke's arm and guided him to his quarters – for now, still the rooms Genevieve had once used – and shut the door in the face of Jason and Adam and the other Royal Guards who had kept watch over their silent king and his vassal and then trailed them back.

And then Damien had stayed while Tomas drank himself drunk, and listened while the older man mourned his brother. The brother he mourned seemed to bear little relation to the Harald Damien had come to know, so thankfully briefly, and seemed more a creation of wishful thinking than anything. Though even in his cups, it seemed that Tomas could not entirely forget the irreconcilable dichotomy between wishes and memories. A little boy who followed his older brother around – and kicked a puppy to death. A youth who could outfight every other would-be squire – and ruined every horse he rode.

The duke went round and round, tying himself into knots, trying to avoid thinking and talking about what Harald had done to Genevieve... and her father... and to himself. The son he could not remember having. The years his older children had grown through that he had no memories from.

At last, Damien had guided the drunken duke to bed, helping him with his boots.

"Thank you," Tomas muttered, on the edge of sleep. "You're a good lad. Hope my sons turn out like you... not..."

Damien had stepped back out into the sitting room and taken a moment to lean his forehead against the cool, smooth stone wall. There was no one else who could – or would – listen to the Duke of Siovale. For anyone else, even listening might be considered as treason.

And... as much as Tomas was Bound to Siovale by his Vassal's Oath to Damien, so much so was Damien Bound to him. It was the young king's duty to bring what peace he could to the duke.

He had taken one last deep breath and gone up to seek his friends.

And now he sat, not in his usual chair, but on the couch, with Genevieve – once more in her comfortable leathers – curled up against his side. His choice of seating had caused everyone else to rearrange as well. Jason had taken Damien's chair, and Adam perched on the arm. Ciriis had Jason's old chair, and Rosa was across from the couch, filling the chair where Genevieve had been wont to settle.

"We'll need more chairs, I can see," Ciriis commented dryly.

"More than that," Jason smiled. "Perhaps you should consider taking other quarters, Damien. Your grandfather's rooms should be possible to secure – though it seems like that should be less of an issue now. And you'll need space for a nursery..."

The young king and his bride-to-be exchanged a look. "I hope..." he said softly, before he realized what he was putting out for general discussion.

Now you've done it, Queen Marian said dryly, from where she sat on the same chair as Ciriis. He rolled his eyes at her, and Ciriis gave him an irritated look.

"I hadn't said anything yet," she complained.

"Your face said everything," Genevieve covered for him. She could still hear the dead queen, though she couldn't usually see her.

Damien felt that was uncommonly lucky of her and simply hoped that their ancestress' helpful vigilance would end at their bedchamber door.

Of course, it will, the old queen huffed.

"What do you mean 'you hope'?" Rosa asked carefully. "Gen, love, is something wrong?"

Genevieve shrugged. "Nothing that I can tell. But," she exchanged another look with Damien, wondering how much to share. He half-shrugged. In for a lamb... "We – and my father – can see and hear Queen Marian's spirit. And *she* says there's something wrong."

Adam pinched the bridge of his nose. "Just when this day couldn't get any stranger..."

"Is she as wise as they say?" Ciriis asked eagerly, then caught herself. "What I mean is..."

Rosa laughed. "Cirii has always idolized the late Queen," she told them all.

A woman of excellent taste, Queen Marian applauded, leaning to one side of the chair to look at the living woman occupying the same seat. *A bit on the short side, though.*

Genevieve covered a smile. "Mostly she's sharp-tongued, but she does seem to know a lot."

Well, I never!

"She showed us how to use the Sword," Damien said placatingly in her direction. "And what I needed to do to complete my Bond to the Realm."

"Nearly got you killed," Genevieve muttered as Ciriis twisted around and asked "Is she here now? Near me?"

"Saved all our skins," Damien corrected Genevieve. "Since that's what broke the spell giving Lord Prydeen his Power. And told us how to Heal your father." Her eyes softened at the mention of her father again.

"I heard the ladies saying something about a – a prophecy that the sorcerer made right before he died?" Rosa asked.

Damien winced. "I was hoping I was the only one who heard that."

She shook her head. "You had over fifty people in that room. There will be variations of it all over town before morning. What was it actually?"

The young king just shook his head, but Genevieve spoke, softly. "He said that Damien will have no firstborn to rule after him. That I will never conceive Damien's firstborn or 'at least not first.' And that our youngest will be Lord Prydeen's true Heir."

There was a thoughtful silence.

"The first part isn't too bad," Ciriis suggested. "The Sword will choose your Heir, so it needn't be your eldest child. It will be the one most suited to the throne."

"At the moment," Genevieve said dryly, "just managing to have *one* child seems like a challenge. Harald wasn't wrong. We were married for eight years and I never so much as conceived."

"You were waiting for *me,*" Damien asserted, pulling her close. The others looked away politely for a moment.

"There's no reason to believe *anything* the man said," Jason asserted. His eyes met Genevieve's and they both looked quickly apart. Damien felt her settle a little closer to him, as if giving – or needing – reassurance.

Adam snorted. "There's other things to sort out anyways. The little matters of negotiating a settlement with the *rest* of the Rebellion." He lifted his glass to Rosa and Genevieve.

"Reclaiming the Lost Provinces," Ciriis added.

"Taking the Vassal's Oath of *all* the Realm's remaining nobles..." Genevieve tagged on. As a host of surprised looks met her, she explained, "When Damien does it it's a spell Binding us to the land. I couldn't cause harm to Elaarwen or its people if I tried, now. And if anything happens there that I need to know about, the information will come to me and sooner than later. But I don't know if I can Bind my own minor nobles. And after eighty-three years of King Reginald and Lord Prydeen, there are a lot of nobles who *should* be Bound – or cast out as unworthy to hold their lands and people."

I didn't exactly spend as much attention on such things as I should have either, Queen Marian admitted. *Finding – or producing – an Heir was too much of an obsession those last seventeen years. I wanted to make sure I didn't make the mistakes with Alexandria that I did with Anthony.* She snorted. *Well, that worked. I made different ones, including not guarding my back until she was old enough.*

"More like a hundred years, Grandmother says," Damien commented. "And you couldn't have 'held on' until Duke Aldred was old enough, milady. Princess Alexandria might have been a better ruler than my grandfather, but he'd have been working to undermine her and overthrow her all through her reign."

Ciriis started looking around again.

"She's sitting in the same chair as you," Damien told her, and Ciriis leapt up in dismay.

Hmmph, Queen Marian said. *Silly chit. I'm doing her no harm. There were others whom the Sword might have spoken for, given opportunity. Collateral lines. Your father, young man, though he was close in age to Aldred.*

"All of this is beside the point," Jason broke in. "There's something far more important to discuss." They all looked at him expectantly, and with some trepidation. He leaned forward, with a serious expression on his face, focused on the king. "Damien, what's this I hear about you *dropping a blade on the floor?"*

Damien flushed, the rest laughed, and the conversation moved on. But the worry over their child weighed on the young king's heart.

They made love tenderly, with none of the terrible urgency of the night before.

"You were beautiful today," Damien murmured into Genevieve's hair as she snuggled into his shoulder... *after.*

"In that dress? I suppose..."

"In the dress. In your leathers." He grinned. "*Now*, most especially." And he laughed when she twatted him on the nose. "I'm marrying a warrior-princess, my love. I love all the aspects of you."

She twisted to look up at him. "You sound... happier than I've heard you." Which was saying rather a lot, given how happy he generally was in her presence.

"I... suppose I am. There's a great shadow that's gone. One that's hung over me my entire life."

Damien sighed, but it was a very relaxed sigh. "I was born here, you know. In the Castle. Father said that grandfather had decided to keep his remaining children closer, and required them to live here. I think they lived with my mother's family when Kandy was small.

We lived with them for a few years when *I* was small, too. After Kandy ran away to join the Army, I suppose. Grandfather made us come back when I was eight." He'd never been able to talk about his parents before, even to her. "Father used to carry me around on his shoulders, up to the battlements, and Mama would scold him. And he would look into her eyes and tell her that neither he nor the Castle would ever let me fall. And then he would lean down and kiss her while I grabbed his hair and ears to keep from falling."

"You must have been very young to ride on his shoulders," Genevieve commented a little too casually. "I'm surprised you remember."

Damien waggled his head instead of shrugging, since her head was on his shoulder. "Not that young. Five years old, maybe? I was small for my age. And... I didn't have that many memories of them after to befog that." It still hurt, but he smiled. "They were very, very good parents."

"Good *people,*" she commented. "Queen Marian said that the Sword might have spoken for Prince Eric."

"She did, didn't she?" he marveled.

"It sounds like he knew *you* were something special, too," she prodded. "You said he told your mother that the *Castle* wouldn't let you fall."

Damien laughed again. "You'll pick up on any little thing to try to convince me, won't you?" He kissed her head. "Well, we'll never know. But you can stop worrying. I realized yesterday that I *can't* give this up – even to your father, though with all of his experience and wisdom, he'd probably be a better king. No, stop," he touched her lips gently. "I have a lot to learn. I know that. *You* know that. At this moment, if he were in good health, he *would* be a better king. But I'll grow into it. *We'll* grow into it."

He paused. "And while the Realm loves your father – and you – it's me that it wants on the Throne. I can do it," he added, "with you by my side, and Duke Aldred as my advisor."

Genevieve smiled. "Good." Then *she* sighed, and it was rather more pensively. "And what about Elaarwen? I'm Bound there, and I have no Heir... there's a collateral line, but..."

"When we crown you Queen, you'll be Bound to the whole Realm," the young king told her, "But there's no reason why you can't divide your time between here and Elaarwen."

"A certain soul-bond?" she reminded him.

"I didn't say I wouldn't go with you." He smiled as she gave him a pleased, if startled, look. "I want to see your home for myself. And the bond... should stretch more once we've settled into it. And more still as we have children."

"Children..." The smile fell off her face, and she laid a hand on her flat abdomen. "Damien, you didn't tell them the sorcerer's last words."

He looked into her beautiful, troubled, blue-green eyes. "Should I have done? In front of Rosa and Ciriis?" She looked down, but he lifted her chin to meet his gaze once more. "If the time comes, we'll face it then. We have only Lord Prydeen's word that he was a true seer, and in all the years I knew him I never trusted his word on anything, even the time dinner would be served. If that day *does* come, it will be a private conversation. You. Me. Jason. Adam. No one else."

Tears glistened in her eyes, and he kissed them away. "A soul-bond... it shouldn't be this hard, Damien. The one thing a soul-bond is supposed to provide is *children.*"

"It may not be. Don't count the mice when the grain is still sealed." He pulled her close. "And even if he is right... even if it takes our Champion to sire our firstborn... he also said we would have others. Enough that we *will* have a 'youngest' to worry over. There will be an Heir for the Realm, an Heir for Elaarwen. And children for us both – for us *all* – to cherish. Children with so many adults to love and care for them that they never feel lost or lonely or abandoned." His own eyes prickled with tears. *His* children would never have to hide in a library for years on end.

"Besides," he added, after a moment. "Think what a gift it will be to two we love so well. How likely are they to have a child else?"

"A child they can never acknowledge," Genevieve said sadly.

"Love doesn't always need words," Damien told her. "We'll make it work. Somehow."

Alsterling Family Tree

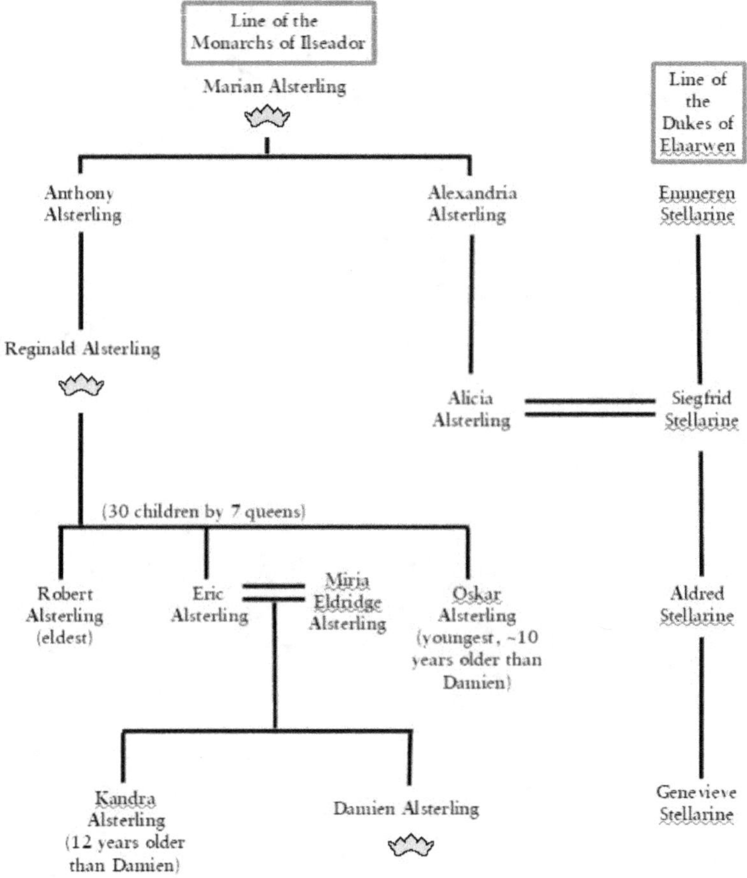

Index of Characters

Adam Loveress, Knight and Captain of the Royal Guard; mentor and support of King Damien; love of Jason Solway

Aldred Stellarine, former Duke of Elaarwen; father of Genevieve Stellarine; son of Duke Siegfrid Stellarine and Grand Duchess Alicia Alsterling

Alexa Solway, Countess of Brindlewell; mother of Jason Solway

Alexandria Alsterling, Princess of the Realm; daughter and youngest child of Queen Marian Alsterling; youngest sibling of Anthony Alsterling; mother of Alicia Alsterling

Alicia Alsterling, Grand Duchess of the Realm; daughter of Alexandria Alsterling; wife of Duke Siegfrid Stellarine; mother of Duke Aldred Stellarine

Alric Alsterling, Grand Duke of the Realm; clever poet; slipped on stairs and died of a broken neck

Anthony Alsterling, Prince of the Realm; eldest son of Queen Marian Alsterling; father of Reginald Alsterling; elder brother of Alexandria Alsterling

Aryllis Ieldore, Lady-in-Waiting and member of the Secret Cadre; engaged to Sir Timothy Ancellius; former lover of King Damien

Ciriis Celavell, Mistress of Protocol and Spymistress; mentor and support of King Damien; former lover of King Damien; niece of General Celavell

Celavell, General; Second-in-Command of the Army; Ciriis Celavell's uncle

Damien Alsterling, King of Ilseador, son of Prince Eric Alsterling and his wife, Lady Miria; twelve-years-younger brother of Princess Kandra Alsterling

Direlien, General; Commander of the Army; stationed just outside Emeralsee

Douglas, a man-at-arms from Siovale

Elista, Chief Maid in the castle; wife of Captain Robert

Elsa, Lady-in-Waiting and member of the Secret Cadre; former lover of King Damien

Emerie, Lady-in-Waiting and member of the Secret Cadre; former lover of King Damien

Emmeren Stellarine, former Duke of Elaarwen; father of Duke Siegfrid Stellarine

Erawan the Kind Robber, a real-life 'Robin Hood' figure who stole the king's taxes in Elaarwen and redistributed them to the people

Eric Alsterling, Prince of the Realm; second-youngest son of the old king; husband of Lady Miria; father of Kandra and Damien Alsterling

Felena, Lady-in-Waiting and member of the Secret Cadre; former lover of King Damien

Gavin Teraseel, younger brother of Rosa Teraseel

Genevieve Stellarine, Duchess of Elaarwen (the Rebel Duchess); daughter and only child of Duke Aldred Stellarine; former wife of Harald Elsevier; former lover of Rosa Teraseel

Harald Elsevier Stellarine (a.k.a, Harald of Siovale), former husband of Genevieve; younger brother of Duke Tomas Elsevier of Siovale

Jason Solway, Knight of the Realm and King's Champion; younger son of Countess Alexa Solway; mentor and support of King Damien; love of Adam Loveress; former bodyguard and Heir's Champion to Prince Oskar Alsterling

Kamauri, Lady-in-Waiting and member of the Secret Cadre; former lover of King Damien

Kandra Alsterling, Princess of the Realm and field-officer in the Army; daughter of Prince Eric Alsterling and Lady Miria; twelve-years-older sister to King Damien

Lena Devergnon, Lady-in-Waiting and member of the Secret Cadre; poisoner; former lover of King Damien

Leverett Childress (a.k.a., Lev), Knight of the Realm and member of the Royal Guard; engaged to Terellie

Licia, Lady-in-Waiting and member of the Secret Cadre; former lover of King Damien

Marabell, wife of the old farmer with the haywagon

Maree, a knife-sharpener in the kitchens

Marian Alsterling, former Queen of Ilseador; mother of Prince Anthony and Princess Alexandria; great-great-grandmother of King Damien Alsterling and Duchess Genevieve Stellarine

Mirabelle, Lady-in-Waiting and member of the Secret Cadre; former lover of King Damien

Miria, Lady-consort of Prince Eric Alsterling; mother of Kandra and Damien Alsterling

Nalda, Lady-in-Waiting and member of the Secret Cadre; former lover of King Damien

Oskar Alsterling, Prince of the Realm; youngest child of the old king

Otto, Knight of the Realm and member of the Royal Guard

Prydeen, Lord, 'Apprentice' sorcerer to the old king

Randolph, Knight of the Realm and member of the Royal Guard

Raphael Anvliyar, Baron of Cedarwen; son of Baron Seldrig Anvliyar and Lady Theresa

Robert Alsterling, Prince of the Realm; eldest son of the old king; slain by bandits after conducting a successful treaty negotiation

Robert, Captain of the Castle Guard; husband of Elista

Rosa Teraseel, Countess of Zialest (the Rebel Countess); elder sister of Gavin; former lover of Genevieve Stellarine; engaged to Zachary Miramar

Salleen Alsterling, Grand Duke of the Realm; too good at negotiating with merchants (poisoned)

Sasha, Lady-in-Waiting and member of the Secret Cadre; former lover of King Damien

Selda Alsterling, Princess of the Realm; died of an infection the Healers couldn't cure

Seldrig Anvliyar, former Baron of Cedarwen; husband of Lady Theresa; father of Duke Raphael Anvliyar

Siegfrid Stellarine, former Duke of Elaarwen; son of Duke Emmeren; husband of Grand Duchess Alicia Alsterling; father of Duke Aldred Alsterling

Terellie, Lady-in-Waiting and member of the Secret Cadre; engaged to Sir Leverett

Theresa Anvliyar, Dowager Baroness of Cedarwen; mother of Baron Raphael; widow of Baron Seldrig; Royal Librarian to the old king; Royal Secretary and Chatelaine to King Damien

Thielda, Lady-in-Waiting and member of the Secret Cadre; former lover of King Damien

Timothy Ancellius (a.k.a., Tim), Knight of the Realm and Second-in-Command of the Royal Guard; engaged to Lady Aryllis Ieldore

Tomas Elsevier, Duke of Siovale; older brother of Harald; former brother-in-law of Genevieve Stellarine; field-marshal for the Rebellion

Zachary Miramar, Count of Dalizell; engaged to Countess Rosa Teraseel

Glossary of Semi-Useful Information

SELECTED REGIONS of ILSEADOR

Emeralsee
- capitol: Emeralsee city
- Alsterling family
- King Damien Alsterling

Elaarwen (in Rebellion)
- capitol: Elaarwen town
- Stellarine family
- Duchess Genevieve Stellarine

Siovale (in Rebellion)
- capitol: Siovale town
- Elsevier family
- Duke Tomas Elsevier

Reyensweir
- capitol: Mirion town(secondary capitol at Reyensweir city)
- Mirion family
- Duchess Mirion

Embervest
- capitol: Embervest town
- Eledor family
- Duke Istvan Eledor

Brindlewell
- capitol: Brindlewell town
- Solway family
- Countess Alexa Solway

Zialest (in Rebellion)
- capitol: Rose Lake town
- Teraseel family

- Countess Rosa Teraseel

Dalizell (in Rebellion)

- capitol: Dalizell town
- Miramar family
- Count Zachary Miramar

Cedarwen

- capitol: Cedarwen town
- Anvliyar family
- Baron Raphael Anvliyar

The Five Lost Provinces (beginning with the most recently lost)

- Alpinsward Duchy
- Minglemere Barony
- Elendria County
- Everfields County
- Farivera County

SWORDS and ARMOR and CLOTHING

Armor parts

Helm. Helmet for the head. Unvisored, except for jousting helms

Chest- or breastplate, backplate. Can be light armor going over a chainmail shirt OR heavy plate for jousting

Epaulets. Shoulder armor

Gorget. Throat armor

Vambraces. Forearm armor

Greaves. Shin armor.

Cuisses. Thigh armor

Chainmail. Usually worn as a long, sleeveless shirt.

Gambeson. A padded jacket or jerkin made of leather and padded with cotton or silk, used to protect the wearer from their chain or plate armor. More heavily padded versions serve as practice armor for use with blunted weapons.

Swords (as distinct from Earth-based swords, where the definitions overlap)

- **Longsword:**
  - » slender (1-3")
  - » light (1-2 pounds)

» double-edged
» may be cross- or basket-hilted
» 32-40" in length
» intended for one-handed grip
» similar to a rapier (but wider and less flexible)
» typical weapon of a knight of Dawil
» often paired with a poniard or a shield
» can be used afoot or mounted

- **Broadsword:**

» wider than a longsword (3-5")
» heavier (3-5pounds)
» double-edged
» cross- or basket-hilted
» 40-50" in length
» 'hand-and-a-half' grip (one OR two handed, 2-handed grip is more common when in use) with a hilt length to accommodate
» rarely used mounted due to the risk of decapitating the horse
» usually considered more of a bludgeon than a fencing weapon, but certain exceptionally tall and strong people can wield it like a longsword and fence with it

Clothing (because these terms always confuse me and I hate having to keep looking them up)

- **Tunic.** A long shirt. In Dawil, rarely longer than mid-thigh, and usually sleeveless. Closed on the sides. A shirt is usually worn under it, and the tunic may be removed during heavier or sweatier work to keep it clean.
- **Tabard.** A sleeveless garment slipped over the head and open at the sides. A formal garment, such as the scarlet-and-silver tabards worn by the squires when on duty.

TIMEKEEPING

- Ilseador is SOUTH of the Equator. They are the only country around the Merutian Sea that counts years as starting from their own Vernal Equinox rather than the one celebrated in Wave (in Dawil).
- YEARS are dated by the reign of the sovereign

- Taridawil was destroyed (referred to in A Not-So-Sacrificial Maiden: Book One of the Knightess of the Realm) in the 7th Year of the Reign of His Majesty, King Theolore Tindilaar the Third, AKA the 38th year of the reign of King Damien Alsterling.
- same length year as Earth. Intercalary (leap) day is added before or after so that the Equinox stays on the correct date.
- NEW YEAR starts on the Vernal Equinox
- SEASONS of thirteen weeks
- three months per season: two 4-week months followed by a 5-week month
- weeks of seven days named 'First-Day', 'Second-day', etc. Seventh-Day is traditionally a rest-day or market-day
- Each season starts with a First-Day following Midsummer's Day, Autumnal Equinox Day, Midwinter's Day, Vernal Equinox Day
- Equinoxes and Solstices (Vernal, Autumnal, Midsummer, Midwinter) celebrated as the Four Corners of the Year

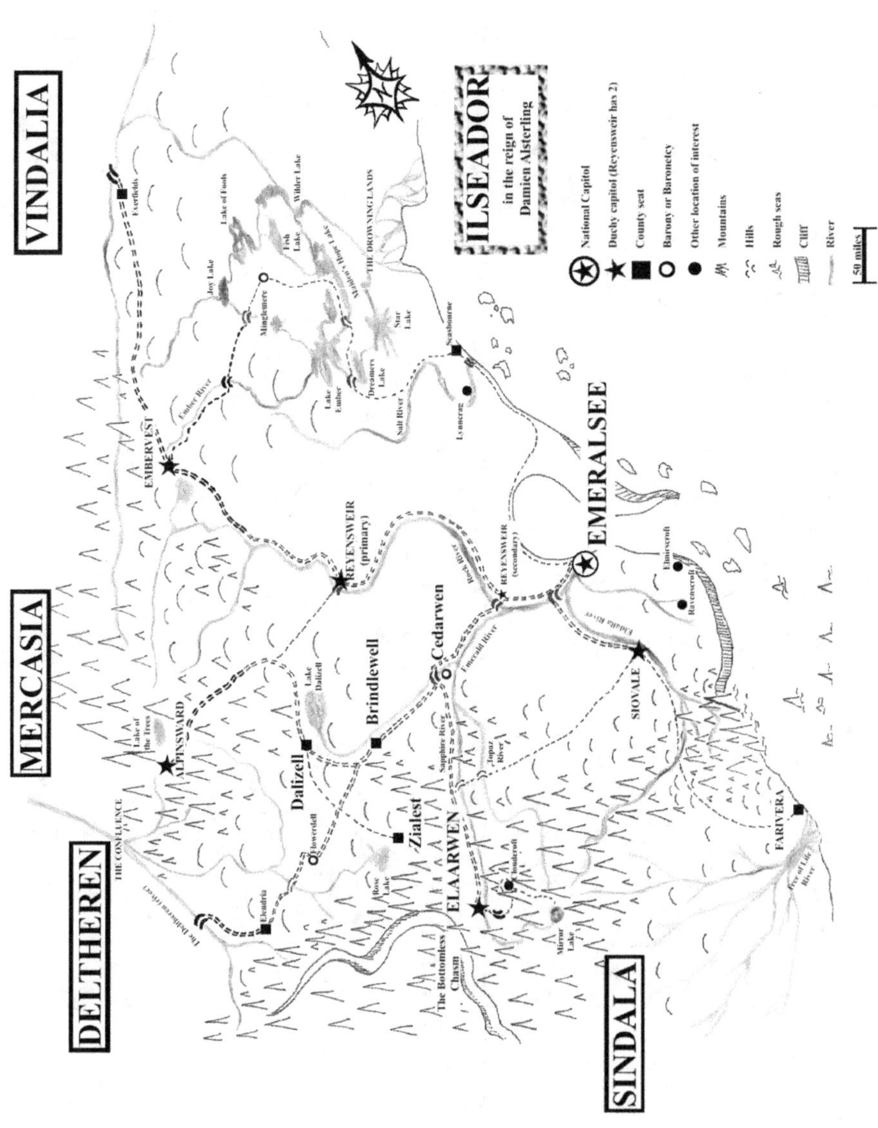
VINDALIA
MERCASIA
DELTHEREN
SINDALA
EMERALSEE
ILSEADOR
in the reign of
Damien Alsterling
National Capitol
Duchy capitol (Reyensweir has 2)
County seat
Barony or Baronetcy
Other location of interest
Mountains
Hills
Rough seas
Cliff
River
50 miles
EMBERVEST
REYENSWEIR
(primary)
REYENSWEIR
(secondary)
ALPINSWARD
Dalizell
Brindlewell
Cedarwen
Zialest
ELAARWEN
SIOVALE
FARIVERA
THE CONFLUENCE
THE DROWNING LANDS
The Bottomless
Chasm

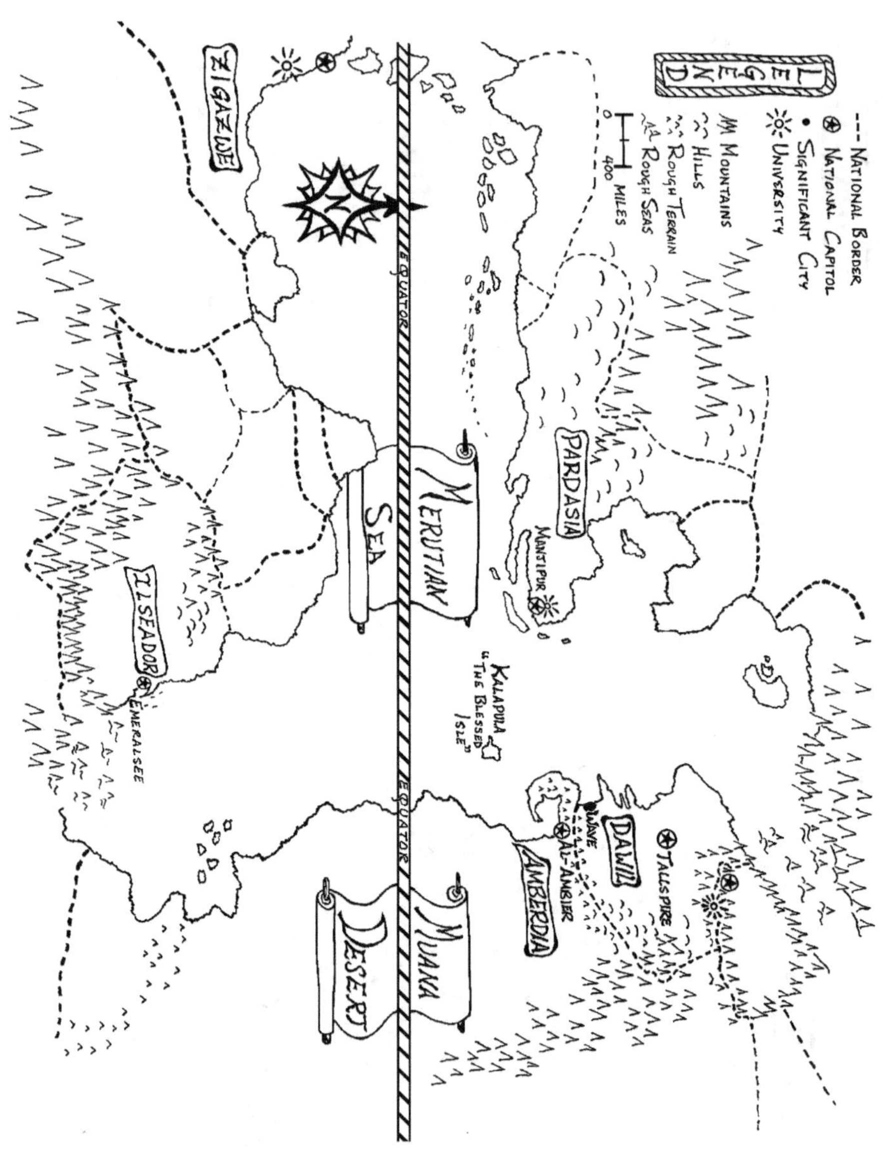
LEGEND
NATIONAL BORDER
NATIONAL CAPITOL
SIGNIFICANT CITY
UNIVERSITY
MOUNTAINS
HILLS
ROUGH TERRAIN
ROUGH SEAS
0 400 MILES
ZIGAZWE
EQUATOR
MERUTIAN SEA
PARDASIA
MONTIPUR
ILSEADOR
EMERALSEE
KALAPURA
"THE BLESSED ISLE"
DAWIL
WAVE
AL-AMBIER
AMBERDIA
TALLSPIRE
EQUATOR
MUANA DESERT

Author's Note

It seems like a cliché, but *The Rebel Duchess* really *did* come to me in a dream. A *recurring* dream, to be specific. The first chapter was utterly crystal clear that it needed to happen that way.

I actually spent a great deal of time second-guessing myself on this book. I hadn't intended to wander into the realms of adult romance... I thought of myself as solidly a fantasy writer and that the spicier parts of romance novels weren't necessary in my writing. Damien and Genevieve had other ideas.

I also wasn't planning to write from a male perspective. Damien's voice was just so *clear*, however, that again, I had no choice. He's become one of my favorite characters – Book 3 of the Chronicles *(The Captive King)* is all from his perspective, as well as most of Book 2 *(The King's Champion...* which also features Jason Solway, as you may guess).

And... this story ended up weaving together a variety of other stories – in some cases locating them in time and space to make a more cohesive whole. The Knightess of the Realm series (with Karana, Kefen, and Ivan) for example, takes place some forty-five years later. I also spent an inordinate amount of time (and math) on sorting out the map of Ilseador (and of the lands around the Merutian Sea). I wanted to get the distances right – I love maps but I'm the sort who pores over them and, while I don't hold anyone else to this particular standard of obsession, the goal for me was to create maps that were consistent with the stories.

One tidbit I'm enjoying in writing about Ilseador is that, since it lies reasonably far south of the equator, a number of small details need re-thinking, such as which direction sunlight comes from in the middle of the day.

I hope you enjoyed reading this book as much as I enjoyed writing it... and are psyched to see what happens next!

Also by Kerridwen Mangala McNamara

Fiction

- ***A Not-So-Simple Mission:*** *Book Two of the Knightess of the Realm*

YA Fiction:

- ***A Not-So-Sacrificial Maiden:*** *Book One of the Knightess of the Realm* (YA)
- ***Out of the Woods... Hopefully:*** *A Knightess of the Realm Prequel* (YA)

- ***Thony and the Much-Anticipated Adventure:*** *Book One of The Prankster Prince* (YA)
- ***Thony Goes Astray! (in the Deep, Dark, and Dangerous Fairy Wood):*** *Book Two of the Prankster Prince* (YA)

Coming soon...

- ***The King's Champion:*** *Book Two of the Chronicles of Ilseador* (November 2023)
- ***An All-Too Unexpected Revelation:*** *Book Three of the Knightess of the Realm* (December 2023)

- ***So You Want to Be a Hero?*** *Book Three of The Prankster Prince* (YA) (2024)

Non-fiction:

- ***The Homeschooling Parent:*** *Self-care and Feeding of the Person Who Makes It All Happen*
- ***The Homeschooling Parent Teaches MATH!*** *Bringing Math to the Math-averse (parents and kids both!)*

About the Author

KERRIDWEN MANGALA MCNAMARA IS AN Indian-American with a Masters degree in Bacterial Genetics who lives in Flyover Country (the far northern end of the US South) with her husband, The Professor, four of her six children, three goats and a very old Great Pyr-Coonhound mix dog. The goats eat, the dog sleeps, The Professor plays chess, and the children largely unschool while Mangala writes. (The remaining children are in college – you can blame the oldest for the excessive amounts of math showing up in Mangala's fantasy novels... and the second one for better attention to staging of scenes.) Mangala is a former professional bellydance instructor, currently coaches FIRST Lego League teams, runs homeschool parent support groups, and used to enjoy knitting, crotchet and embroidering Temari balls but now is much more boring as she rarely does anything but write, argue economic theory with her 17 and 14 year olds, and wonder loudly if her 11 and 9 year olds do anything other than watch Minecraft videos. She owes her love of books and reading to her mother, who was a professional folklorist and could recite – from memory – stories from every nation in the United Nations.

(The picture was taken at one of her favorite local bookstores: The Rosewater in Louisville, KY.)

Learn about Mangala's upcoming projects (fiction and nonfiction both) and sign up for email updates at https://www.RisingDragonBooks.com

www.ingramcontent.com/pod-product-compliance
Lightning Source LLC
Chambersburg PA
CBHW071412200726
48294CB00002B/371